RACHEL L. SCHADE

MANOR OF WIND AND NIGHTMARES

A FAE OF BRYTWILDE NOVEL

Cover by Get Covers

Map and interior designed with Canva

ISBN: 979-8-987-60597-4

www.rachelschadeauthor.com

RACHEL L. SCHADE

MANOR OF WIND AND NIGHTMARES

A FAE OF BRYTWILDE NOVEL

Dragon Shadow
PUBLISHING

ALSO BY RACHEL L. SCHADE

Silent Kingdom Series

Silent Kingdom
Forsaken Kingdom
Broken Kingdom

Cursed Empire Series

Empire of Dragons
Empire of Traitors
Empire of Monsters
Empire of Ruins

Fae of Brytwilde Series

Castle of Dusk and Shadows
Fortress of Blood and Power
Queen of Stars and Spirits (Novella)

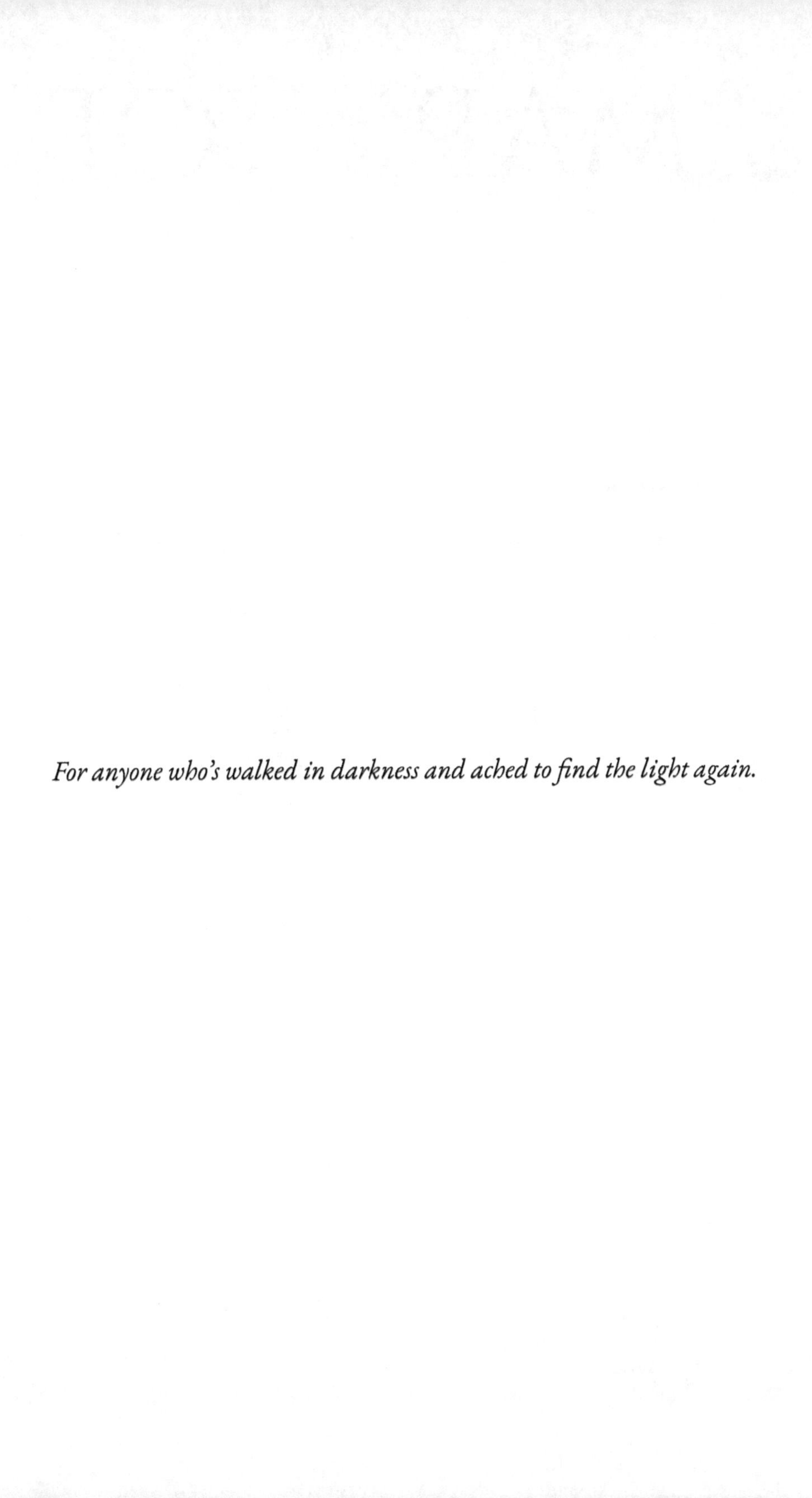

For anyone who's walked in darkness and ached to find the light again.

MAP OF
WILLOWBARK
ASHWOOD

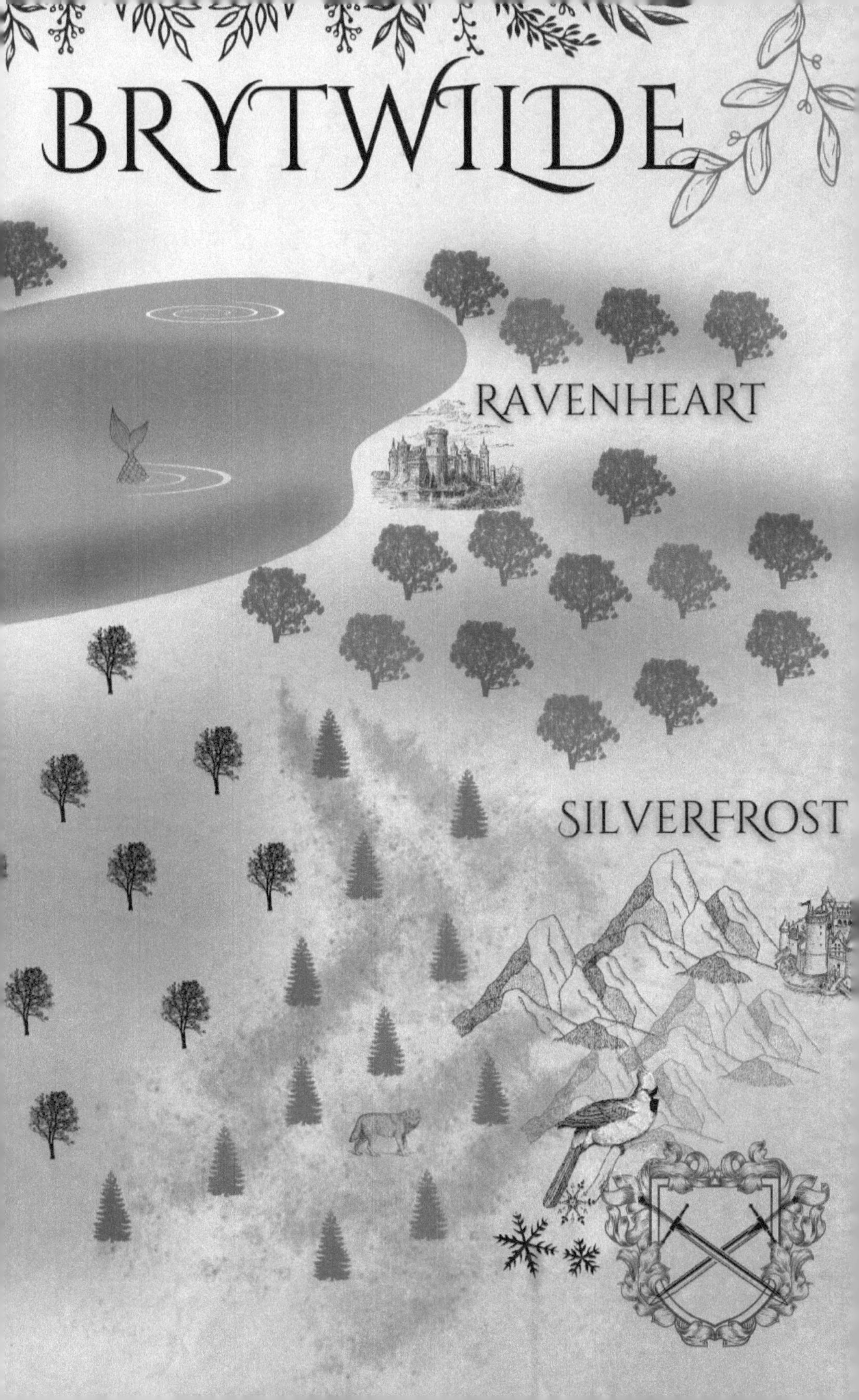

BRYTWILDE
RAVENHEART
SILVERFROST

CHAPTER ONE
THEN

O nce every decade, the fae across the Bittertide Ocean visited the citizens of Greybrooke. Supposedly, their kingdom, Emberglade, wasn't near any mortal towns, and so they made the voyage as part of a long-held agreement. For one week, anyone in Greybrooke could strike a bargain with the royalty of Emberglade. It was an opportunity to taste magic, for people to make their greatest dreams come true—or their worst nightmares.

After all, we were all warned from childhood of the dangers of the fae and their bargains. Immortals were tricksters, delighting in tormenting and taking advantage of us for their own desires or entertainment.

I'd never planned to make a bargain. When Mother was alive, I'd always vowed to her that nothing would persuade me to take such a risk.

But that was before.

Recently, I had become desperate. Callista and Lavinia and Father groaned about the ways I'd forced them to cut back on extravagances when funds grew tight, not realizing that that lifestyle we'd used to enjoy was in the distant past. Father had never been a good manager of his income, and without Mother, he'd only grown worse. I'd pored over the estate's books, spent countless hours calculating how we could cut costs, and yet it had always resulted in the same conclusion: unless Father and my sisters could see reason, we would lose our home.

Worse still, my family often spurned my concerns, thinking it ridiculous that I was so worried. But the truth stared me in the face, night after night, in awful numbers that didn't add up: I was going to lose my childhood home, full of memories of Mother and happier times. I wouldn't be able to sit by the fireplace where she'd once brushed my hair and told me stories before bed. Wouldn't be able to imagine her humming and walking through our gardens. Wouldn't be able to keep the staff we'd known all our lives, who'd tended the home so lovingly and provided endless comfort during the dark days after Mother had passed.

And, on a more practical note, I feared we wouldn't be able to survive for long after we sold the estate. Not when my father and sisters were so set in their opulent lifestyle. Lately, I had begun mending clothes that were growing a little too worn for proper society and helping our cook plan simpler, smaller meals than we'd once indulged in. Sometimes, I feared my family would rather starve than allow themselves to be debased in society.

These fears were what finally drove me to meet with the Emberglade fae on the last day of their visit. As was customary, they had taken up residence at Greybrooke Inn for the entire week, filling every room with their entourage. The innkeeper and his family had frantically prepared for a month, anxious to be accommodating. Though the agreement Greybrooke had with Emberglade stated the fae could not harm, glamour, or trick their hosts, I understood their concern.

Now, standing in the main room of the inn, I waited nervously in the doorway as a servant told me that my meeting with Wystan, King of Emberglade, would be next.

He was the first immortal I'd ever seen, and his beauty took my breath away. With perfectly symmetrical features, a sharp jawline, gleaming dark eyes, and silky, rich brown hair, I could not find a single flaw. It was unnerving. That, along with his pointed ears, made it difficult for me not to forget all etiquette and stare.

All too soon, Lottie Finch, a young lady close to my age, exited a room on the far side of the inn, closing the door carefully behind her. Her expression was oddly blank, so that I couldn't tell if she was happy or not with the results of her meeting.

"You may proceed," the servant said, gesturing toward that closed door as Lottie slipped out of the inn wordlessly.

No one else waited in the room with me—apparently, I'd been the last to arrive. The only other fae were guards posted throughout the space, lounging carelessly at tables or before the low-burning fire. The innkeeper and his family were nowhere to be seen.

Heart hammering in my ears, I crossed the room, trying to keep myself quiet and small as I passed the guards sharply assessing me. At the door, I knocked. Inwardly, I went over exactly what I wanted and how I should ask, running through the words all over again despite having prepared them for days. I wanted to ensure there was nothing I'd overlooked, no way the fae could avoid granting my wish or trick me into sacrificing something more than I was willing to give.

The trouble was, there wasn't much I *wasn't* willing to give to secure my family's future, but I wasn't sure what the fae would want.

"Enter," said a gruff voice.

The room appeared to be a small study. At a desk across from me sat a finely dressed man—if one could even call him that. Gooseflesh rose over my arms as my gaze met his burnt orange one, his eyes depthless and unreadable. This male was monstrous. Numerous twisting horns, spiraling like branches, rose from his cheeks and his hairless skull, which was the sickly grey sheen of a corpse.

"Bow to King Wystan of Emberglade," one of the guards stationed within commanded.

Concealing my fear and revulsion as best as I could, I gathered my skirts and dipped into a curtsey.

"You may rise," the king intoned. "What is your name?"

"Aurelia Sinclair, Your Majesty."

He leaned forward, his eyes boring into me. "And what is it you desire?"

"I would like to keep possession of my family estate and to live there as long as I wish, with a sufficient income to manage it and keep my family fed and happy."

King Wystan's lips twisted into a none-too-kind smile. Sweat beaded on my brow. "Wealth, food, a home, happiness. I imagine you know that my magic cannot guarantee mortal happiness. Neither can I prevent starvation or death." He chuckled. "But as a king, I am wealthy. So you came here asking for gold."

Heat suffused my cheeks. "I came here because my family's debts are so great we are at great risk of losing my childhood home. As a woman, I have few opportunities of finding an occupation of my own."

"Sentimental." He tilted his head. "Desperate." He chucked lowly. "And afraid, though you disguise it well. You self-sacrifice often, watching your sisters and Father purchase frivolities while you wear those rags."

My heart leapt into my throat, my mind racing as I tried to understand how this king knew things he shouldn't. Had he inquired about every member of town before arriving? Or did his magic allow him to simply...know things?

"Yes," King Wystan said. "I can read your thoughts."

I drew a deep breath.

"She is more promising than the others we've seen, I suppose." The female voice startled me, and I turned, noticing the young woman leaning against a bookshelf for the first time. She'd been half-hidden behind some of the gathered guards. Unlike the king, she was as stunning as the other fae, with wavy auburn hair and piercing eyes. Her dress was extravagant, fairly dripping with gemstones.

King Wystan waved her away. "Yes, she can learn. I agree that she has potential." He turned back to me. "I can guarantee wealth and security for your family for the rest of your days, with plenty of gold for your little home. In return, you must vow to serve me."

My mouth went dry.

He smirked. "No, you won't live in Emberglade forever. You will keep your home, and, as long as you do not fail, you will return to live here as happily or as miserably as you choose."

Heart hammering in my ears, I considered my options. Fae could not lie, which meant if I bound him to specific rules, I could ensure the bargain would secure my happiness without forcing me into an awful promise. "How would you want me to serve you?"

"You will return to Emberglade with us and live in the palace as we train you. You will complete a mission to my satisfaction; one that, if you do well, will keep you from Greybrooke no longer than one year." He smiled, as if the offer was purely benevolent. "Several months for a lifetime in your little town of squalor."

My thoughts whirled as I considered possibilities. "I will not harm anyone. Nor will I give my body to be used." My mouth soured at the very idea. "I also expect you to give your word that I will not be glamoured by you or any of the fae during this time. And you must vow that I shall be fed, clothed, and sheltered—and that when my service has ended, I will be provided safe transportation home."

The king smiled slowly, the look eerie on his nightmarish face. "Wise. Cautious. Very good." He repeated my conditions back to me, vowing to fulfill them all.

Nerves twisting in my stomach, I pledged my service to King Wystan of Emberglade.

As soon as I'd finished, he rose. "We depart today."

The world seemed to sway, and I realized I'd been breathing shallowly. *Today.* I shouldn't have been surprised, as I'd known this was their last day in Greybrooke, but I hadn't expected my bargain to take me with them.

"Pack what you need to; say your goodbyes. Return within two hours with your luggage. Don't be late." The threat was clear. "Oh, and take your first payment to leave with your family—my first step in fulfilling my vow as you make yours to leave your home." As if he'd already had bags of coins waiting—it was probably an embarrassingly common request from mortals—he plucked one from somewhere behind the desk and tossed it at me.

I nearly dropped it, my cheeks pinking as I fumbled. Numbly, I dipped into a curtsey.

I'd never left the confines of Greybrooke, yet now I was about to board a ship and cross the sea to live among the fae. I could scarcely fathom it.

"This is beneath your station. An abominable insult!" Father sniffed from his position in my bedroom doorway, watching our servant, Anne, finish laying the last of my clothes in my trunk.

With a sigh, I pulled on my best traveling gloves, noting I'd almost worn a hole at the tip of my right index finger. I'd have to mend it soon, if I had time in Emberglade. I swallowed thickly, not wanting to wonder too much about what my life there would be like.

"The fae view us as lesser, Father," I murmured. "I cannot convince them that my being a gentleman's daughter means I shouldn't serve them. Besides, no one need know why I'm away. You could tell our neighbors I'm staying with my old schoolfriend in Sonnville. It would be far more shameful if we fall into poverty and lose the estate."

Father pressed his lips into a thin line, clearly seeing my point and feeling displeased about it.

"Auri, who will help me prepare my bonnet for the Season?" Callista asked, pressing through the doorway and throwing her arms around me. "Who will be my chaperone if any gentlemen come to call?"

Tears burned the backs of my eyes. What if I *didn't* make it back home and never saw my sister again?

"I can help you," Lavinia intervened, leaning against the wall out in the hallway and rolling her eyes. "Don't be so dramatic, Callista. She'll be home in a year, and I can be your chaperone on outings. Besides, the money she will earn us will provide you with plenty of new ballgowns."

Callista pulled back, eyes wide as she looked up at me. "Truly?"

"Do not spend *too* much on gowns and frivolities."

Her expression crumpled. She was used to being spoiled by Father, who'd always let her have anything she wanted, a fact that had contributed to our current predicament.

I hesitated, hating to see the pain on her face even if I thought Father had doted on her to the point of nearly ruining her character. Brushing a hand over her hair and tucking a loose strand behind her ear, I softened my look into a smile. "That doesn't mean you cannot buy *any* gowns. Enjoy yourself." Straightening, I strolled toward my vanity and lifted the bag of coins I'd set there, the one I'd smuggled in like I'd been ashamed. Perhaps I had been. "This is for all living expenses while I am gone, so you must make it last until the next payment."

Callista and Lavinia rushed forward, tugging the bag from me to gasp over the bag of gold coins. Their conversation gushed over the things they could buy. Misgiving seized me—even Father's eyes had lit up with eagerness. I couldn't even count on him to be sensible with money, but there was nothing I could do about that now but caution them. I had to leave them to their own devices and pray they could last until the king's next payment.

Giving each of my family members one final hug, I bid them goodbye and prayed I'd see them again.

After the Emberglade servants—all fae rather than glamoured humans, I'd noted to my relief—took my luggage and the ship set sail, King Wystan and the female who'd spoken during our first meeting summoned me into the captains' quarters. It was clear the king would be staying here, from the elegance of the space compared to the cramped room with the tiny cot and scratchy linens the servants had shown me to earlier.

In the sunlight streaming through the window, the woman's beauty was on full display. Her face was flawless, her eyes bright and cunning. With full lips, long lashes, and flowing auburn hair, she looked more like a portrait than a living being. It was disconcerting, the way fae beauty took one's breath away.

It was almost as frightening as King Wystan's unusually nightmarish appearance.

Dipping into a curtsey, I tried to ignore the way my chest tightened with unease.

"This is my daughter, Princess Briar," King Wystan said. "You will learn how to mimic her grace and elegance to the best of your human abilities, along with the rest of your training."

I frowned. "I don't understand, Your Majesty. How would learning the ways of a princess help me as a servant?"

"Servant," Princess Briar scoffed. "No, you are to train to become our weapon."

My stomach jolted, my gaze cutting to King Wystan. "You promised. Our bargain stipulated that you would not have me harm anyone."

His smile was chilling. "And you assumed I am an ordinary fae, unable to lie and bound to my word. An unfortunate error for you, as I'm not fully fae. My daughter takes after her mother and is therefore cursed with the inability to lie and appears as lovely as other fae do, but I possess troll blood...and trolls can lie."

Chills erupted along my arms. I took an unsteady step backward, as if I could flee when I was trapped on a ship. "Does that mean our bargain is void?"

"Oh no, I am a king, not a vagabond." He laughed. "As long as you serve me as promised, you will keep your estate and have your wealth. But if you don't...I left some of my soldiers in Greybrooke. If you fail, I'll send word, and they will kill your family."

I bit my cheek to force my expression into neutrality. Though King Wystan could read my thoughts, I didn't particularly want him to see my terror.

"You see," the king said, leaning forward and steepling his fingers, "we've had long-standing animosity between our people and Willowbark, the Brytwilde kingdom closest to your little mortal town."

Princess Briar's eyes flared with hatred, and her voice filled with venom. "Their king slew my mother."

"There was war between us, back when Briar was quite young. My wife was powerful in magic, as well as a talented warrior. She encountered King Edwin in battle, and he stabbed her in the back. A coward's kill." He sneered. "Now, he lies on his deathbed, slowly wasting away." He shared a secret look with his daughter. "But our revenge is not complete."

"We want the king to suffer more," Princess Briar said, smiling prettily, as if she were sitting at tea and gossiping with friends rather than plotting death and vengeance.

"I've tried many times to assassinate the crown prince," King Wystan continued, "but he has survived every attempt, and now his father keeps him secure within the palace. No typical hired assassin will be able to get near to him now. And so...we have formed an alliance with Willowbark, but it is a farce."

"A marriage alliance," the princess added. "The best way to help lower their defenses against us."

"You see, Crown Prince Kaede has air magic, a rare gift among the fae. He can command deadly windstorms, suck the air from a soldier's lungs, and walk through the air itself. His magic could wield a gale against a fleet of ships to churn up waves so great they would sink them all. There are infinite ways he could use his element to win a war. He strengthens Willowbark unfairly, and of course, as King Edwin's heir, he is dear to him."

I swallowed thickly, understanding dawning. "So...I will serve as your weapon?"

The king dipped his horned head. "Briar is meant to travel to Willowbark as the prince's bride. You will go in her stead, disguised to look like her. With their defenses lowered after the wedding, you will be able to get near enough to assassinate Prince Kaede."

CHAPTER TWO

NOW

The front door banged shut as Callista darted into our townhouse from her shopping trip. "The fae are here! They're here!" she cried breathlessly as she raced up the stairs.

I jolted in my chair where I'd been working on my embroidery, pricking my finger with my needle. Breathing through my nose, I slowly exhaled until I pushed the fear down, clearing my mind. "What do they want?" I asked carefully as my younger sister burst into the room.

"Willowbark fae!" she panted, her fingers tangling in the ribbons of her bonnet as she struggled to undo it in her excitement.

At the fireplace, Father grunted and shook the paper. "Child, do compose yourself. I hope you didn't make a scene running through the streets like this."

Callista's cheeks were rosy, her eyes bright. If she was happy, I hoped it was good news.

But what if they found out who you are? What if they know you are here?

Ever since my family had moved to Riverside, a fashionable city close to Willowbark's border, I'd lived in anxiety. It seemed like taunting fate. And I'd already lost against fate once.

If Willowbark discovered my identity, their vengeance would extend beyond myself and to my family. I was certain of it. I could not expect mercy from anyone, nor did I deserve it. But for my family...

"No, Father," Callista said, tearing off her bonnet and tossing it onto the nearest vacant chair. "Of course I did not." Her gaze darted to our eldest sister, Lavinia, who read in a seat near the window, and then to me. "Willowbark sent their advisor to make an announcement. They are inviting eligible unmarried women to visit their kingdom for a chance to become their next princess!"

I frowned, my mind trying to make sense of it all. The fae rarely visited, keeping happily to themselves, so I had heard no news of what had become of Willowbark after I'd left it behind forever.

Callista clasped her hands. "They're choosing the one who will marry their crown prince!"

Lavinia gasped, setting aside her book. Even Father lowered his paper in interest.

"Crown prince?" A ringing had begun in my ears. Did I dare hope? But then…what did that mean for me? For my family?

"Yes," Callista swooned, twirling in place. "They are permitting unmarried women below the age of thirty from Riverside the opportunity to be chosen as the bride of Prince Kaede!"

"Thirty?" Lavinia, who was nearing her thirty-first birthday and had thus far refused all her suitors, huffed and sat back down. "Do immortals think we begin to turn to dust by that age?"

I scarcely heard her over the ringing in my ears, which had only grown louder. Hope, guilt, and fear were a storm within me, each so intense I could hardly tell which was strongest.

He's alive.

Tears burned my eyes, and I had to blink and glance down at my embroidery hoop to conceal them from my family. They didn't know what had happened during the year I'd been in the fae world, and they'd never asked for details, just as I'd never volunteered them. They only knew that I had been a servant to Emberglade's king, a fact that had granted them money to squander while I was away.

How *is he alive?*

But even as hope blossomed, mixed with the stabbing sorrow of grief, I knew he must hate me for what I'd done to him. I'd betrayed him in the worst of ways. There was no forgiving that, no returning to what we once had been.

"Imagine if I were chosen!" Callista cried. "You must help me pack, Aurelia, for they said they are only here for one day! Their carriages are waiting for the contestants and our luggage!"

I froze. "Callista, you can't go. The fae are not kind—who knows how they would treat their human guests…" I tried to finish my sentence, to explain they would want to watch the mortal entrants suffer, but my voice trailed off, vanishing into nothingness.

Typical glamour could not continue to influence a person outside of the fae's general vicinity, but King Wystan had used an especially powerful spell, something dark and sinister and awful, that made it impossible for me to speak about my time among the fae or what I'd truly been tasked to do.

And so, I forgot what I'd been trying to say, as if King Wystan's spell had wiped my mind clean of all thought.

I shook my head in frustration as Callista laughed like I was silly, as if I didn't have months of painful experience to back up my fear.

Even if Prince Kaede *was* somehow, impossibly alive, if he hadn't been crowned king yet, it meant that his father was still the ultimate authority of their kingdom. And I could not trust that any events or parties he held would be truly hospitable toward mortals.

"They're looking for their next *princess*. They'll want someone beautiful and graceful, someone who knows how to entertain guests with conversation and musical talent." She fluttered her lashes. She already knew she was stunning, the most beautiful of three sisters who'd been told all their lives how lovely they were. It was our father's great pride, how we had inherited so many of his fine features. He claimed we looked like nobility, and perhaps that was part of his justification for his extravagant style of living and self-centered nature.

She hurried from the room before I could say more, calling out for Anne to ready her belongings. My heart sank.

"This is a good thing for our family," Father said gruffly when I stood, setting aside my embroidery hoop and needle. "Don't dissuade Callista from something that would bring her happiness, status, and wealth for the rest of her days. It would benefit us all. It is not as if they want a servant, as you were. She will show the prince her talents at hosting parties, carrying on conversation, and playing the pianoforte. Even the fae would surely be entranced by her beauty and charm."

My throat ached. "She would be ..." My tongue grew leaden, refusing to let me finish my statement. "They value different things," I managed. But that was hardly the warning I wanted it to be.

Father's gaze was piercing, unyielding. "If she wants to make this choice, it is not up to you to stop her."

I gaped. "I'm her older sister, and you are her father. If anyone is going to stop her, it would be us."

Lavinia tsked from her spot by the window. "She is a woman fully grown and able to make up her own mind."

"She has no idea what they are like—" My voice cracked.

"Oh, don't go on about that again. So they made you polish a few floors and do their laundry. It may have been beneath you, but that's hardly worth fussing about."

My cheeks burned, but I didn't correct her. I couldn't.

Tongue heavy, I was forced to leave the room and attempt to intervene another way.

I moved to exit the room just as the butler paused in the doorway, clearing his throat. "Mr. Sinclair." His gaze shifted to me and he dipped his head. "Miss Aurelia."

"Excuse me," I said, hastening around him as he began sharing the same news Callista had just brought to us.

My stomach churned. How many other women were as eager as Callista, casting aside the nightmarish tales of our upbringing as nothing more than children's stories to convince themselves that it was worth the risk to visit Willowbark for the prince's hand? After all, few fae had come to Riverside, and those that had in recent memory had been harmless. No one had been stolen away or tricked into awful bargains—except for me. No one knew that the old stories were true.

I hurried down the hall, following the sounds of frantic packing as I approached Callista's room. Anne paused in her work of folding some of my sister's underthings when she noticed me hovering in the doorway.

"Where's my sister?"

"She went out the back way, miss. Said she didn't want to argue with you." Anne looked slightly guilty.

I swallowed thickly. Of course she'd left straightaway. Once Callista set her mind on something, she would not be refused.

Without wasting another instant, I dashed through the hall and down the back stairs, bolting through our garden, out the gate, and into the street. Neighbors gawked as I raced toward the town center. A few of the ladies whispered to one another, likely taking note of my lack of a bonnet.

The city center was bustling, a sizable crowd already gathered and murmuring amongst one another. Parked outside the main inn was a row of familiar green and gold carriages.

Was Prince Kaede among them?

I didn't see him, and I wasn't sure if disappointment or relief was my stronger emotion at his absence.

I swallowed thickly and averted my gaze when I noticed that I recognized several of the guards posted nearby, including Lavender, who scanned the crowd impassively.

They don't know your human form, I reminded myself, and though my mind understood this to be true, I still did my best to remain discreet as I wove through the men, women, and children all pointing and talking.

At the front of the gathering was Ji, Willowbark's chief advisor, and a lengthening line of women. Some held trunks or bags or had servants at their sides with their luggage. Others had nothing, as if they'd decided they did not care to take the time to pack before volunteering.

I gritted my teeth when I spotted Callista among the ladies. Apparently, she'd abandoned Anne to a futile mission, or had ordered the poor maid to race out with her luggage as soon as she finished packing.

The line was already moving, Ji either shaking his head and waving dejected women away, or nodding and signaling for some of the waiting guards to usher each into one of the carriages.

"Remember," Ji announced, "only thirty women will be brought as our guests. Any may volunteer, but we can refuse you, and we will not linger once we reach the limit. We return to Willowbark today!"

Urgency spurred me forward. Even if Prince Kaede or the guards *could* recognize my human appearance, I hoped the prince would have mercy on my family.

I forced myself into the line. "Pardon me, I'm so sorry," I said.

One of the ladies cast me a deathly glare. Being fairly new to the city, I did not recognize her. "Wait your turn," she snapped.

"I'm only trying to speak with my sister, up there."

Before I could hear her mumbled reply, I walked onward. "Callista," I whispered. The line was already moving closer to Ji, near enough I could hear what he said now each time a woman approached him.

"Too...round," he sneered, his critical gaze sweeping over Eva Thompson's fuller figure. Apparently feminine curves were offensive to a male fae who stood so tall and straight, his own figure reminding me more of a stick than that of a living being. "Why would we want to look upon such a plump form? We want shapeliness, not a princess who would be offensive to the eyes."

He waved away Miss Thompson as if she were a plague in his presence, and though I ached for the shame and sadness on her features, I was relieved to see our sweet neighbor spared from the competition.

"Callista." I clasped my sister's hand as she started forward.

"Don't you dare stop me." Her eyes burned. "Are you jealous, because you know that if you competed against me for his hand, I would win?"

Struck mute by her scathing comment, I lost my grasp on her as she pulled away. Only two women stood between her and Ji now.

For a moment, Ji assessed them silently as the pair curtsied together.

"I'm not envious. I don't want to return to their world," I whispered, hoping Ji was too distracted to overhear me with his keen fae senses. "You must understand that the stories are true—"

"Next!" Ji called. "Don't make me wait, or you will be disqualified." His dark eyes seared into Callista and me.

Callista stepped forward, dipping into a curtsey. "Forgive me, my sister had me distracted."

"Name and age?"

"Callista Sinclair, twenty-three."

He nodded, gesturing toward one of the carriages behind him.

I stared in horror. Anne met Callista at the door to the carriage with an overstuffed bag she handed to one of the nearby guards.

"Please, you can't accept her," I told Ji, desperation clawing up my throat. I scrambled for an excuse, something that would persuade even an unfeeling fae.

Straightening to his full, formidable height, Ji glared down his nose at me. Though his perpetual frown made him unattractive to me, his features were flawless, with smooth, pale skin that seemed chiseled from marble. He, like most other fae, seemed surreal—a living work of art. And his tall, lithe form only added to his intimidating aura. "Don't interfere further, or I'll turn you away. Give me your name and age."

I inhaled a shaky breath. I could have refused, could have told him that I had no interest in trying for the prince's hand. After all, if Kaede ever discovered who I was, he would want nothing to do with me. Surely even he couldn't find it within himself to forgive his murderer.

But I couldn't abandon my little sister, the one Mother had always pled with me to protect. The one who looked so much like her, with her shimmering dark hair and mischievous smile, it was as if Mother had left a piece of herself behind.

Resolve hardened within me. It felt reckless without time to solidify a plan, but I didn't have the luxury of time, and this felt...inevitable.

If I couldn't keep Callista from entering the fae world, I would go with her.

"Aurelia Sinclair." I forced a smile. "Twenty-five."

CHAPTER THREE
THEN

The churning, steel-grey clouds and rumble of distant thunder matched my tangled emotions. As I peered through the window to scan the Bittertide's rough waves, I prayed to gods I wasn't sure existed that the smudge of approaching land on the horizon would somehow never grow closer. Or better yet, that I could turn back time by eleven months and undo the moment I'd first met King Wystan.

When I'd made this cursed bargain.

When I'd doomed myself to months of grueling training spent among the cruel fae of Emberglade. And now, to the bloody mission I would have to carry out in Willowbark, or lose my entire family to King Wystan's threats. The worst part was, I couldn't even trust that he would keep his word even if I fulfilled my vow and slew Prince Kaede. Since he wasn't fully fae and could lie, anything was possible. But I knew testing fate any further and angering the king by refusing him was unthinkable. I had to cling to the shred of hope that I did have, that he would fulfill his vow if I kept mine.

Gods forgive me.

If they cared enough about the affairs of those on earth to pay me any heed now, the gods would condemn me for this.

By the time our ship reached the docks and its passengers descended, the storm had unleashed its full fury. Rain battered against the window, obscuring my vision of the outside world. A sharp knock drew me from my quarters, and King Wystan's personal guard escorted me, along with him and his daughter, off the ship, through the storm, and into a nearby pub.

Welcome warmth enveloped us instantly. I kept the hood of my cloak firmly in place to conceal my curved ears as I stepped inside, rainwater dripping from my clothes and leaving a slick trail along the worn floorboards. I took in the cozy fire flickering in the hearth and the smattering of fae eating and drinking. Most were sailors and dock workers waiting out the storm.

I had grown accustomed to living among fae, but Willowbark was unfamiliar. Here, the people were a little rough around the edges, reminding me of hard-working mortals. Men with large, calloused hands laughed over their meals, and a waitress in a homespun dress and apron chatted with some of the patrons at the bar.

My chest tightened with guilt. They didn't know I was there to start a war.

We settled around a table, a few guards leaving us to order food and drink on our behalf while the rest settled themselves at nearby tables, ever vigilant and dutiful when it came to their royal family's safety. King Wystan settled into the seat across the table from me. His own hood was drawn so low that I could barely make out the dusky glow of his inhuman orange eyes.

My heart skipped a beat. Rumors abounded within his own kingdom. He was greatly feared, his own people even claiming he was the offspring of a dark god and a fae. Others whispered of a terrible bargain he'd made with a demon of the underworld to gain the ability to read the minds of both mortals and immortals. A few shared King Wystan's own story of being half-troll, but that didn't explain his intrusive magic. I'd quickly learned that even among the fae, his ability was rare. He hadn't been born to the royal family, either—rather, he'd used his magic to rise to power. When he could discern exactly what his opponents' and allies' greatest fears and wishes were with a single glance, how could he not be fearsome and mighty?

I dropped my eyes, hating that I'd given him another glimpse at my anxious thoughts.

Beside me, Princess Briar Emberglade tossed back her hood with a careless wave of her red locks, flicking a shower of droplets toward my face. She wielded her beauty like a weapon, effortlessly influencing fellow fae, who seemed to find her especially stunning even compared to their perfect standards, to do her bidding.

"Your escort will arrive tomorrow," King Wystan explained.

Already, a flurry of harried staff members, along with the innkeeper himself, were rushing out from back rooms, likely notified by the guards that the king and princess of Emberglade had arrived. They couldn't have expected such illustrious guests to stay the night at their humble establishment.

"Your Majesty," the innkeeper said, his cheeks rosy from running. He bowed toward the king before turning and bowing to Princess Briar. "Your Highness. I am honored you have chosen to visit me, and my staff and I will be happy to provide you with anything you need during your stay."

King Wystan waved a lazy hand. "No need for extravagance. We would actually prefer that our presence remain quiet." There was an unspoken threat in his words. His eyes darted about the room toward the other patrons, who had gone quiet, staring in awe—and perhaps a bit of worry. The alliance between Emberglade and Willowbark was still new and tenuous, after all.

For being so powerful, King Wystan also seemed exceptionally paranoid about possible assassination.

Then again, if he was so preoccupied with killing his enemies, it was logical he would assume they spent an inordinate amount of time plotting his demise in turn.

"Of course," the innkeeper said, trying to conceal his fear with a smile. "I'll spread the word to all my guests and ensure the silence of my staff."

We ate in silence, heaviness settling over me with each bite I forced myself to take. I'd need my strength for all that was to come.

At last, Princess Briar turned to me. "Come with me. You will pretend to be one of my maids."

King Wystan gave a wave of dismissal. Silently, I stood and followed Briar through the dining room and toward the stairs, where several guards and her maids waited. Servants were already carting up the trunks that I would be using as I posed as Briar.

"We'll settle you in with a nice bath," said Daisy, one of Briar's personal maids, while we climbed to the second floor. On the right of the plain hallway, an open door revealed the princess's—*my* room—with an attached washroom and a steaming bath already drawn. The trio of maids instantly set to work unpacking a nightgown and assorted toiletries from some of the already-waiting trunks.

Briar sniffed at the sparseness of the room. "I'm glad I'll only be spending one night in this place," she muttered. "I can only imagine where they settled *me* when I'm pretending not to be royalty." She turned to another of her maids—Sage—as the last servant brought in a final trunk. "Close the door."

As soon as the door clicked shut, the princess whirled on me. "Tonight you begin your charade, and therefore, you must behave with the elegance and confidence expected of a fae princess. One of my maids will serve you your potion. Remember to take it faithfully each day from now on, or it will begin to wear off and reveal your human form."

I nodded. None of this was new information, as she, her father, and their trainers had drilled it into me many times, but Princess Briar enjoyed ordering others about and needed to feel as if she had control over this situation. It was clear that it irked her vanity to imagine that a human might behave ill while pretending to be her. Even if the one I had to fool the most was the one I had to kill. If I sullied her reputation, it wasn't as if anyone in Willowbark would care once I made her out to be a murderer.

"Most of all, you must be charming." Briar's gaze was intense. "The crown prince may be tied to this arranged marriage, but he is still royalty. As soon as you arrive, if they allow you to meet him before the ceremony, beguile him. Enchant him. Whatever powers you have as a mere human, use them. Take advantage of wearing my beauty. He might wheedle his way out of the agreement if you are too odious, or his parents may even undo it. Or he could go through with the wedding but avoid you afterward and reduce your opportunities to strike." She seized my arm, her grasp unrelenting. "Make him *want* a wedding night with you. Don't let my good looks go to waste."

"Of course," I said evenly. Inside, I was disgusted, but this wasn't the first time discussions of wedding nights and manipulation had been thrown my way. I no longer burned with shame at the mere mention of them.

"Don't let your human modesty destroy our plans." Briar frowned. "If he wants to kiss you or embrace you—or even more—before *or* after the wedding, don't act like a fool. Be assertive and don't pretend to be ignorant in the ways of love." She sighed. "If nothing else, pretend to be coy. Cover your shyness and naivety by behaving as if you're trying to pique his interest with delayed gratification. Beauty is power. Beauty is control. Use it."

Not knowing what else to say, I nodded furiously, all the while hoping I could assassinate the prince long before he ever pressed his lips to mine or attempted anything more. It was awful enough to know I was about to kill someone, but imagining kissing him and then killing him? It sounded particularly abominable.

"Don't fail," Briar finished, her words heavy and ominous, as if she would hunt me down and murder me herself if I did.

As she flounced out of the room, I was left to stare at all the stunning silk, lace, diamonds, rubies, and pearls spilling from multiple trunks. It all seemed so frivolous when I'd be traveling. But Princess Briar deeply valued her appearance. She'd commissioned each article of clothing from her personal seamstress and ensured they were all perfectly fit to my measurements.

"Time for your bath to wash the human stench off you." Daisy scrunched her nose, studying me with disdain. I knew she hated being forced to treat a mere mortal like I was her princess, but all three were loyal to their princess and king, and had vowed to help me maintain my disguise. "You need to make an impression, even on the guards and servants escorting you to the palace tomorrow."

Daisy, Sage, and Ellery insisted on helping me bathe, scrubbing me so hard I had to bite back my yelps. While Ellery helped me into a nightgown and Daisy combed through my wet hair, Sage fetched the first vial of potion from a hidden compartment in one of my trunks.

Sweet with a slightly sour aftertaste, the potion burned my throat as it went down. Warmth spread throughout my body.

"It takes time for the change to first take effect," Sage explained. "The other doses will all be to maintain it, but this first one may be a bit unpleasant. Then again, if you go to bed now, it's possible you'll sleep through it."

With that, they left me alone. The room felt eerily still and quiet in their absence. Nothing kept me company but trunks full of someone else's style of clothes, hidden instruments for killing, and the vials of potion meant to help me in that task.

I repressed a shudder, reaching for the hilt of the dagger secured beneath my pillow. It was the one comforting habit I'd begun since my training. Even though I knew I was mostly powerless in this world, surrounded by magical fae who could glamour and manipulate me against my will, the cold bite of steel grounded me. Reminded me that, win or lose, I *could* at least fight back.

Daisy's harsh voice pulled me from the first restful sleep I'd finally dipped into early this morning, after tossing and turning for hours. "Wake, mortal. The Willowbark escort has arrived, and it won't do to keep them waiting."

Sitting up, I blinked blearily at her, my fingers slipping up for the hundredth time to feel the tip of one of my newly pointed ears.

Daisy's eyes widened. "You *do* look just like her."

I ran my fingers through my hair, draping the now-red locks over my shoulders. It was an odd sensation, like, despite still possessing my own body and mind, I had become someone else entirely, but I shoved the notion aside. *Temporary magic,* I reminded myself.

There was no mirror in my room, which was probably for the best, as I had no time to gawk at my reflection.

"Come," Daisy urged, setting a tray on the bedside table. Ellery brought over a dress from one of the trunks. The cloth was a pale shade of lavender, its skirt embroidered with delicate vines and flowers. Its collar was adorned with tiny jewels in varying shades of violet, catching the light with every movement. I stifled a groan, wondering if Princess Briar had insisted on such an impractical outfit, or if the maids had picked it out just to spite me.

As I nibbled at my bread and eggs and sipped some tea, the maids finished their preparations for our journey, ensuring all my vials of potion were carefully packed and hidden away. Once I'd finished my breakfast, Sage urged me into the washroom. I cleaned my teeth and emerged in time to find all three maids waiting with toiletry items and my dress. Once they'd helped me into my outfit, Sage wove a complicated braid around my head like a crown. I fastened my traveling cloak around my neck and pulled on my boots. Withdrawing my dagger from beneath my pillow, I slipped it into the hidden pocket sewn within my cloak.

"You're ready," Daisy announced, giving me a none-too-gentle shove toward the door. "Now behave like a princess. We will escort you down, and your servants will load the carriage. Don't pay too much interest to the guards and servants Willowbark sent. They're beneath you."

Her scolding went in one ear and out the other as I trailed her out of my room, along the hall, and back down the steps toward the dining room. Smoke from the low-burning fire mingled with the scents of bacon, eggs, and toast hovering thickly in the air. Based on the slant of the sunshine trickling through the windows, the hour was early, but many of the tables were already full of sailors and dockworkers eager to return to work now that the weather had improved.

Commotion at the door drew my attention. Emberglade servants were filing out with my trunks while King Wystan looked on, his orange eyes blazing. The real Princess Briar was nowhere to be seen, either cleverly concealed as one of the king's guards or still upstairs in bed, dozing through the early hour.

As Daisy guided me toward the door, I noticed one of the Willowbark guards standing in the entryway with King Wystan, dipping his head low in deference as he spoke. His green and gold uniform was pristine, each button on his jacket gleaming and his dark leather boots polished to a shimmer despite the miles he and his companions had traveled. "Your Majesty," he was saying, "it is our honor to escort your daughter through our kingdom. Know we will defend her with our lives."

The young man lifted his head, revealing his face. My gaze swept over his sharp jawline, which was dotted with stubble, his high cheekbones, and his piercing gaze. His short black hair was swept neatly back but for a single stubborn strand that hung over one eye. As I watched, he stiffened and brushed it away. It was impossible to guess a fae's true age, since they were nearly ageless, but he appeared young, not much older than I was.

As if sensing my stare, the man's eyes flicked toward me. Heat seared my cheeks, and I glanced down at the floor before inwardly reprimanding myself. A fae princess wouldn't be caught eyeing a lowly guard, and if she were, she certainly wouldn't be shy about it. Here I needed to be the opposite of what was expected of me at home: I needed to take up space, use my voice loudly, and be unabashedly proud and bold.

Lifting my chin, I found that the guard was still studying me, so I flashed him a smile. Briar would likely be mortified that I'd given the man notice at all, but now that I was playing her role, I had the freedom to choose who I'd be. I could be a more gracious princess than she, one who took the time to be kind to those who were protecting and serving her.

The guard's answering grin revealed his dimples and made something in my stomach flutter. I told myself to pay those silly feelings no heed. "Your Highness," he said as I approached, his voice deep enough to reverberate in my bones and smooth enough to send a chill through me. "The stories of your beauty fall short. You're exquisite in person."

King Wystan huffed. "Your flattery is needless, bodyguard. Your duty is to keep her alive, not woo her for your prince."

"Indeed." The guard straightened, pressing a hand to his heart. "My name is Nam Junseo, Captain of the Guard. I've been assigned by His Royal Highness himself to personally attend to you as your bodyguard. You'll be safe with my guards and me, princess." Junseo turned to King Wystan with a final dip of his head. "Your Majesty."

Junseo offered his arm, so I looped mine through it and allowed him to lead me from the inn and out into the cool morning air. The cobblestones were slick beneath my boots as we approached a small caravan of gold and green carriages. Fine white steeds stomped impatient hooves. As the Emberglade servants finished loading my trunks into the nearest one, countless Willowbark guards settled into the carriages.

My maids were directed toward the second carriage with their own traveling bags, but Junseo led me to the first. "You'll ride with me," he said in his smooth voice.

My heart fluttered. I'd hoped to be placed in a carriage with my maids, where even if I had to tolerate their dislike, I would be safe from scrutiny.

If the prince's assigned bodyguard was tasked with keeping me near, I'd have to be extra careful to keep up my ruse.

CHAPTER FOUR

Now

"**D**o you think we'll attend a feast or a ball?" Callista asked, clasping her hands as the carriage jerked forward. "Or will the prince want to meet and spend time with each of us individually?"

Both of the young women across from us, each with pale blonde hair, bright blue eyes, and nearly identical features, exchanged a glance. The one with her ivory bonnet settled askew on her head giggled. "I assume it might be a little more dangerous," she said, her eyes sparkling with excitement.

Hands in my lap, I fiddled with my fingers, wishing King Wystan's spell didn't prevent me, even now, from sharing just how dangerous time with the fae could become. I'd seen plenty of horrors occur during his celebrations, ones they freely committed against one another. If there had been more humans there, I could only imagine how much worse they'd have been treated. And then there were other creatures, even more monstrous than the fae, that lived in their world.

Callista gave each girl an appraising look before turning away again.

"I don't believe we've met—we are newer to Riverside," I explained. "My name is Aurelia Sinclair and this is my sister Callista."

"I'm Laura Everett," the lady who had spoken first said, "and this is my twin sister Hattie." She nudged the girl beside her playfully, and it was then I realized how young the pair were. Neither of them could have been older than twenty. No wonder this seemed like a grand adventure to them. They were at an age when one still felt invincible.

"You can tell us apart by the scar above her eyebrow," Hattie explained with a giggle, gesturing toward Laura's face, where, sure enough, there was a delicate pink line gracing her brow.

Laura grinned mischievously. "I couldn't resist galloping on Father's prized mare, but I took a tumble. That was years ago, but Mother still likes to fret about my desire for adventure."

"Sometimes it makes you reckless," Hattie muttered, shaking her head, but her smile belied her scolding words.

Beside me, Callista sighed and leaned against the window, mumbling about a headache. "I forgot to ask Anne to pack my fan and I'm feeling a bit faint."

Using my hand to waft some air toward my sister, I studied the twins.

"What do you think the prince will be like?" Hattie asked me, leaning forward eagerly.

Laura raised her eyebrows. "We've heard he commands the wind itself and is quite powerful."

"I heard he was brought back from the dead," her sister added, awe in her voice. "I overheard some guards speaking of it, how he'd been assassinated and magic from their allies in Ashwood brought him back. They said he's changed, whatever that means." She shrugged, uncertainty clouding her features. "I wonder if one can still see the mark from whatever weapon killed him?"

Laura's eyes rounded. "You didn't tell me you overheard that! Fascinating." Then she smirked. "I heard that he's *unspeakably* handsome. Whatever happened to him must not have scarred his features too much."

Hattie fluttered her lashes. "One of the female guards spoke of deep, dark eyes."

"They were swooning about chiseled features."

"A dimpled grin."

"A muscled figure—"

"Laura! How scandalous!"

Their words erupted into more giggles and squeals.

"Oh, but we aren't going to be in the human world anymore, are we? And if *I* get to marry him, I can ogle him all I want!"

"And what if he is to be *my* husband? You will have to be proper then!"

I tried to laugh their comments off and pretend they didn't pain me with memories. "You would think the two of you had seen him yourself," I said, forcing lightness into my tone and trying not to dwell on their talk of Kaede being brought back to life. Of being *changed*. Had the experience altered his character? I shuddered to consider it. "Perhaps the rumors exaggerate his good looks."

But I already knew they did not. My thoughts wandered to places I hadn't let myself remember for a while. The scent of cherry blossoms. Strong arms encompassing me. His earnest smile.

The pain and betrayal on his face when I'd stabbed him.

I squeezed my eyes shut and tried to block it all out.

"Aurelia," Callista whined, and my eyes flew open as I realized I'd stopped fanning her.

I sat up as the carriage slowed on a winding gravel path. At some point on our journey, even the twins had grown quiet and I had fallen asleep.

Now I peered out at the moonlit-dappled grass on either side of us, my gaze snagging on familiar rows of cherry trees and weeping willows leading toward the sparkling river and the immaculate Willowbark palace grounds.

Squeezing the windowsill, I tried to steady my breathing. Every second I expected to see Kaede watching the approach of the carriages. Had he learned who I was? Or had he narrowed down my age and the city I was living in? What if this was all a scheme to find his assassin? What would happen to Callista then?

I tried to dispel my fears, but logically, it made sense. They didn't know me by name or appearance, but that didn't mean they hadn't been given other hints.

If he did discover my identity, would he immediately sentence me to death? Would he kill me himself? Or would he be as full of sorrow and regret as I was?

"Oh," Hattie gasped, and I was drawn from my musings to focus on the stunning palace grounds once more.

Even in the moonlight, everything was spectacular: the manicured grass, the sparkling ponds, the endless flowers and shrubbery, the distant rolling hills and orchards. But most imposing and breathtaking of all were the palace buildings. They were wonders in architecture, the likes of which we didn't see in our modest mortal towns. From intricate wrought iron balconies to carved bannisters to endless paintings of nature winding over the spotless white stonework, every building was a sight to behold. There were countless towers and arched windows, multiple courtyards fragrant with flowers, window boxes overflowing with greenery, and small trees growing from pots dotting the rooftops and balconies.

Within walking distance of the main palace buildings was Willow Manor, a sprawling estate that boasted its own full-time staff and housed frequent guests, from favored families and nobility within Willowbark to the rare visitors from other Brytwilde kingdoms or even from off the continent. It was toward the manor that our line of carriages turned, and this time, Hattie, Laura, and Callista all gasped with glee.

"How beautiful! Are we really staying so near to the palace?" Laura cooed.

"We will be waited upon like royalty," Callista sighed.

I remained quiet as my companions gushed about a fine supper and cozy beds for the night. When I stared at the manor's windows, glowing with the inviting warmth of candlelight, I couldn't banish the sense that I was being watched, and a chill consumed me. A bat fluttered through the twilight, darting across the sky.

Callista nudged me impatiently, and I realized we'd drawn to a stop in the gravel drive. A line of servants was already waiting, helping women out of the carriages before us, and more were approaching our own. When a man swung open the door and stepped back, offering his arm, Laura stood and hopped out fearlessly, a smile upon her pink lips. Her twin followed, and then Callista.

Trepidation swelled in my chest as I stepped into the manor's shadow and studied it once more. My first visit to the palace had never brought me here, so this was the first time I'd been able to look at it closely. Unlike the pristine beauty of the palace, Willow Manor had a more imposing appearance. Gargoyles adorned the corners of its rooftop, scowling at us with gruesome faces.

The servants themselves were not dressed in Willowbark green and gold, but in solemn shades of black and grey. When the man closest to us—with curving ram's horns protruding from his shaggy brown hair and piercing grey eyes—gestured toward the manor, Callista visibly shuddered. I'd nearly forgotten how unnerving it was to first encounter fae with such unusual features. It was a stark reminder that they weren't human.

"This way," he said gruffly, and I could tell by his tone that he must have been instructed to treat the mortal guests well and he begrudged the fact. I wondered vaguely if the servants were allowed to glamour us.

I strolled forward with feigned nonchalance. Unlike my last time here, I was weaponless, with nothing but experience and caution to guide me. My old habit of keeping a dagger on my person at all times had been discarded when I'd abandoned my Emberglade weapon, too disgusted by what I'd done with it to ever look at it again.

We passed rows of waiting servants who assessed us with sharp, hungry eyes, and then up the steps and through the open double doors. Joining women already gathered in the foyer, who were still oohing and ahhing over its grandeur, we were greeted by a new servant who offered to take our traveling cloaks and coats. Enveloped in a warm glow emanating from shimmering chandeliers, I found the welcoming atmosphere disconcerting. A plush rug sank beneath my steps and stunning tapestries graced the otherwise stark stone walls. Boughs of cherry blossoms freshly gathered from the grounds were strung overhead in eye-catching arrangements.

A maid stepped forward and gestured down the hall. "Follow me to your room, and we will prepare you for dinner."

"My sister Callista will be staying with me," I said, reaching back to seize her hand. She gave me a disgruntled look but didn't protest.

The maid nodded, signaling to another to join us. "Very well."

While other servants took the remaining ladies in different directions, the pair guiding Callista and me started up a wide, shadowy staircase. Though the paintings and tapestries we passed were lovely and grand, full of colorful depictions of nature or portraits of past royals, there was a cold austerity to the manor. I had the strangest feeling that it did not welcome us. As if it had emotions and thoughts of its own and felt closed-off and hostile.

Don't be silly, I chided myself. I didn't lack an imagination, but I had never let mine carry me away.

When movement out of the corner of my eye made me pause, I glanced toward the nearest painting of a stern-looking male. A cold sweat broke out over my skin, even though I knew it was impossible. It had been a trick of the lighting and shadows, surely. I had *not* seen his eyes tracking my movements.

Shaking off my unfounded worries, I focused on my more pressing one. With my sister also keeping a slower pace, unused to exerting herself back home, we had fallen behind enough that I figured whispered words could go unheard by even fae ears. "Callista," I murmured. "Please be careful about letting others know I spent time in the fae world."

Her brow scrunched in confusion, so I hurried on.

"I cannot give details, but Prince Kaede cannot know who I am. If he finds out...we could both be in danger."

Her confused look left me fearful she'd ignore my warning, but before either of us could say more, the maids turned, noticing the growing distance between us.

"Don't dawdle; we haven't much time," one of the maids snapped, and I hastened to follow her.

Overhead, something darted through the air, making my breath catch. But when I searched the darkness, unable to see the ceiling because it was so high above us, I found nothing. The shadows must have been playing tricks on me.

The servants showed Callista and me to a long hallway several stories up, where doors painted in colorful representations of nature lined both walls. Along regular intervals, stoic-faced guards stood at their posts, each heavily armed with an array of weapons, from bows to swords to wickedly curved daggers. My fingers twitched uneasily at my sides as I studied them, wondering if they were there to protect us from something—or to keep us within the manor.

"Hurry!" a maid snapped again, and I picked up my pace.

The maids took us to a door adorned with a winding river decorated with cherry blossoms floating along its surface.

Within, the vast quarters held an expansive four-poster bed that would easily fit Callista and me with room to spare, along with an adjoined washroom. Everything was dark and elegant, with deep purple drapes framing the huge arched windows, rich gold accents in the bed linens and rug, and carved mahogany furniture. The candles in the wall sconces already burned, and a warm fire danced in the hearth.

The maids wasted no time preparing washbasins full of steaming water to scrub our faces, necks, and arms.

One, whose skin had the appearance of tree bark and eyes were the color of moss, crinkled her nose as she worked. "If only we had time to give you each a proper bath."

The other, who looked more human than the bark-skinned woman, snickered at her companion's words. "Oh, Wisteria! Mortals do have a peculiar scent, don't they?"

Callista looked affronted, but she had the presence of mind not to say anything.

Ignoring her insult, I allowed Wisteria to help me out of my simple day dress. She turned and snapped her fingers before the wardrobe. "Gown, please."

At my curious look, Wisteria smiled, though it wasn't a kind look. "The manor is magical. It will provide us with dresses in your sizes for tonight's feast, for it serves Willowbark, and this event is for our kingdom. If you do anything that will harm our land, the manor will not take kindly to you."

My stomach curdled as I remembered the sensation I'd felt, that the manor didn't welcome us. Or, perhaps more specifically, didn't welcome *me*. I'd never heard of a building with a will or magic like a living being, but the fae world was a strange place I was only beginning to fathom.

Could Willow Manor sense who I was? What I'd done?

Wisteria opened the wardrobe, revealing the most beautiful dress I'd ever seen. Frothed in black lace that climbed up the full skirt and bodice, it was a style one would never have seen in the human world. The sleeves were long and made of sheer lace. In stunning contrast to the dark piece, bright pink cherry blossoms adorned the skirt, like the fabric had been laid out beneath one of the trees to catch a shower of flowers and petals.

Wisteria removed it so the other maid could close the doors and request another dress for Callista.

When Wisteria finished buttoning me into the gown and started working on my hair, I realized the dress was a perfect fit. Just as she had said.

Nearby, Callista gasped in delight as her maid assisted her into a bridal-white gown with shimmering gold and pink beads. They caught in the candlelight as she twirled until the fae sighed in annoyance and demanded she hold still so she could tend to her hair.

Wisteria brushed a glittering powder over my eyelids and some sort of rouge over my lips. As I stood waiting for Callisa's maid to finish, I stared out the window at the deepening night. A shape darted across the moon, and I looked up to find a bat fluttering through the sky. The prickling feeling of being watched struck me again. I glanced about the room, wondering if it was the manor itself, once again reminding me that I was not wanted here.

In the distance, a bell sounded.

"Time to go," Wisteria said sharply, ushering Callista and me toward the door. Both maids guided us back down the stairs to join other women in elegant ballgowns, all streaming into a great hall. Strains of sweet music and toasty warmth greeted us, along with the mingling aromas of assorted foods.

Within, we found musicians playing in one corner, flames dancing merrily in the fireplaces along the walls and in the chandeliers and sconces decorating the room, and more arrangements of cherry blossoms and greenery above an enormous table laden with the most exquisite spread of food I'd ever laid eyes on. My mouth watered from the tempting scents of roasted poultry and beef, an array of seafood, tureens of soups and stews, and overflowing bowls of fresh fruits and steaming vegetables. On the far end, decadent sugar-dusted pastries, chocolates, and frosted cakes were heaped generously.

Ji and a group of other well-dressed fae men and women chatted together, already seated at one side of the table. To my relief, Prince Kaede was not among them. Guards, along with a few servants, stood vigilantly along the walls, studying the scene with impassive expressions. Meanwhile, servants filed in through a separate door that I assumed led to the kitchens, all bearing trays with more food and drinks.

"Oh!" Laura breathed from where she stood just in front of Callista and me. She clasped her hands in rapture. "I'm famished. What a welcome sight!"

"It's beautiful," Hattie agreed, her eyes wide as she scanned the table.

The servants who'd been waiting by the walls stepped forward to pull out chairs.

Ji waved a servant carrying a tray of wineglasses over, seizing one and raising it toward the ceiling in a toast before everyone else had even had the opportunity to take their seats.

"Welcome, mortal guests, to Willow Manor, where you will stay for the duration of your time here," Ji announced as we all settled in our chairs. "We will explain our rules for winning the prince's hand momentarily, but first, a toast to our fine Prince Kaede, who will join us shortly. Rest and eat your fill. Later, we will dance and celebrate the fact that soon, we shall find a bride for our prince and a future queen for our kingdom. Enjoy the hospitality of the fae."

Prince Kaede, who will join us later. The words echoed in my head and my blood roared in my ears, but I tamped down my desire to panic. Fear would get me nowhere. I had to keep a level head—to prepare for the worst while pretending as if I were innocent.

As servants deposited glasses in front of us so we could toast with Ji, I leaned toward my sister's ear. "Callista," I whispered. "We have to be discerning. Mortals can't consume fae food or wine without consequences. Make sure whatever you eat you recognize."

She frowned. "What do you mean? Surely they wouldn't feed us anything that would harm us when one of us is to become their queen."

I seized her arm. "Listen to me. You can never trust their intentions. Be careful."

Biting her lip, Callista said nothing as she reached for the glass of ruby red wine a servant offered her. She swirled the liquid slowly, studying it as if mesmerized before glancing toward me. I nodded. Red wine was safe—it was the gold I knew to be wary of.

Together, we raised our glasses and sipped our wine.

The musicians in the corner started playing a new melody, one that somehow evoked both beautiful and eerie feelings all at once. I focused on the way the wine's warmth spread through my chest with each sip. Servants began to offer us food, which thankfully was all recognizable and edible.

Though it felt like there was a rock in my stomach stifling my appetite, I forced myself to eat with the others.

Glancing about the room to ensure none of the fae were looking at me, I grasped the knife at my place setting and slipped it into my boot. It was the sort of lesson King Wystan and his trainers had drilled into my head. Always search for a weapon. Even if the thought of wielding one made bile slither over my tongue.

While Ji and the other fae who'd seated themselves near him—ones I hadn't seen accompanying us on our journey from Riverside—began their own conversations, we mortals began talking amongst ourselves.

"Do you think we will be permitted to speak with the prince tonight?" a dark-haired woman across from us asked eagerly.

A woman with blonde ringlets arranged around her shoulders shrugged elegantly. "One would have to make quite the first impression to stand out from among nine-and-twenty other ladies." She scanned the table shrewdly.

"Perhaps we should introduce ourselves?" a petite, grey-eyed woman asked softly.

The blonde shrugged again. "As if we will remember all these names." Her eyes turned sharp. "Are we not in competition against one another, after all?"

The grey-eyed woman pressed her lips together and shifted uncomfortably in her seat.

"Well," Laura piped up bravely as she set down her fork, "I think it's a grand idea." She gave her name to the room and then gestured to her sister and introduced her.

Hattie turned to me, indicating it was my turn. Clearing my throat, I offered my name and then Callista's, and so we went around the entire table in that manner.

"Molly Baker," the petite woman who'd suggested we share our names offered, smiling shyly. I shot her an encouraging grin back.

"Charlotte Hart," said the blonde beside her with a devious smirk.

The dark-haired woman who'd first spoken gave her name as Emily Winters. She picked nervously at her food, her plate looking mostly untouched.

Others around the table offered their names as well until they began to blur together in my mind. Verity Earnshaw, Audrey Hyland, Mary Beresford, Caroline Layton, Edith Williamson...

As we finished eating and servants cleared away our empty plates, Ji and the other fae stood. The music came to an abrupt halt. Without warning, the servants also halted, dipping into bows and curtsies. Heart thundering in my ears, I shoved my chair back and stood, urging Callista to follow my lead. The other women did as well.

A tall, lithe form stepped through the open double doors, clothed in rich black embroidered with subtle silver designs. The light caught his sharp jaw and cheekbones, making his face look severe, mysterious, and heartbreakingly handsome. His dark eyes were fathomless as he scanned the crowd.

After a full year, I stared into the face that had haunted both my wildest dreams and my darkest nightmares.

My churning emotions were almost unbearable, and as I dipped into a curtsey, I lowered my gaze to conceal the tears burning in my eyes. I doubted he would see them from his position across the room, but I didn't want anyone else to notice and become suspicious.

"Ladies," Ji announced after a long, heavy silence. "Please welcome Prince Kaede. Over your time here, however long it takes, the thirty of you will be competing for his hand to prove who will be the best future queen. He is forbidden to interfere, but he can spend time getting to know you and observing the proceedings. Tonight, he will dance with each of you so you may become acquainted."

I inhaled deeply to soothe my mounting worry. Kaede might not recognize my appearance, but what if he knew me when we danced? What if my voice or mannerisms were familiar?

I'd already been involved in a dangerous game with King Wystan—and lost horribly. I hadn't thought my heart could break any worse, that I could ever lose more than I already had. Now I knew I'd been wrong.

Tonight, I'd begin playing my most dangerous game yet.

CHAPTER FIVE

THEN

J unseo jested with the driver and some of the other guards as we approached the carriage we were to share.

When he turned to me, offering me a gloved hand and a warm smile, I
forced myself to take it, grinning shyly before hurriedly averting my eyes
and settling myself on one of the cushioned seats. *He will see through your
disguise in an instant if you don't remember yourself,* I thought scathingly.
*A fae princess wouldn't be bashful over the attention of a mere guard. She
would be used to the handsomeness of her own people, and she would be proud
of her own beauty.* Hoping to hide how flustered I was, I busied myself with
rearranging the skirts of my dress and folding my hands primly in my lap.

Thankfully, Junseo didn't speak once he settled into the seat opposite
me, instead gazing contemplatively out the window as the wheels creaked
and the horses trotted forward. He seemed sociable enough, but perhaps
even he understood that princesses did not expect to make idle chat with
their bodyguards.

I turned to stare out the opposite window, running through the things
I'd been taught: the palace layout, as King Wystan's spies had described
it, the little they knew of the royal family and their daily habits, the best
places to stab or cut someone when striking to kill, the surest methods
to cut off someone's air supply, the simplest points to hit when trying to
land a death blow, and the names of the poisons I'd been given in a hidden
compartment in one of my trunks. Nightmoss, a paralytic. Heartsage, to
quickly stop the organs minutes after ingestion. Everleaf, a drug that could
be administered in small doses over a longer period of time and mimic
the slow death of a fatal curse, so all would be distracted with hunting
for a powerful magical being rather than inspecting his food and drink.
And—perhaps the deadliest of all—demon's breath.

It seemed I had a hundred and one ways to kill the prince. All that was left to do was marry him.

Leaning back against the seat, I tried to close my eyes and rest. It would be several days before we even reached the palace, so worrying about details now would be a waste of time. I would have to save those for once I met the prince, confirmed with my own eyes that the palace layout as I'd memorized it was correct, and learned the schedule they expected Princess Briar to keep in the days leading up to the wedding. After that, I could plan how to best accomplish my cursed mission.

"You are more reserved than I expected, from the stories I've heard about you." Junseo's smooth tone startled me from my reverie.

I cast a look at him, trying to sift through his words. How should I react? With annoyance? Disgust? His words weren't formal, but he wasn't being disrespectful either. But what stories had *he,* Captain of the Guard, heard of Princess Briar? And if he somehow already knew things about her, how was I to meet those unknown expectations?

I settled on cold arrogance. Glancing away from him like I couldn't be bothered, I turned back to the window. "You are bolder than I expected, for a lowly bodyguard."

Junseo laughed, but somehow, the sound wasn't cheerful. I had the distinct sense that he disliked me, that he disapproved of me for his prince. My skin prickled. It was bad enough that I had to kill a powerful, immortal fae. Worse still that I had to pass as a fae princess in order to do it. But if I also had to contend with an angry bodyguard who didn't want to see the marriage even happen, how would I succeed?

"In Willowbark, the Captain of the Royal Guard is a revered position. The royal family trusts me with their lives and readily seeks my advice. I am never considered lowly, nor am I received with condescension. I should hope, Your Highness, that even you and your father can see the wisdom in treating those who hold your life in their hands with respect."

I studied him, taking in his confident expression and the casual manner in which he leaned back in his seat. He watched me unabashedly, likely taking in every tic of my jaw and blink of my eyes to read my intentions. The same way I was trying and failing to read his.

Swallowing, I worked to keep my voice level. "Are you threatening me?"

"I would never threaten someone I've been entrusted to keep alive." He shrugged, and a lock of dark hair fell across his brow, adding to his carefree appearance. "I'm simply offering wisdom. Consider it a wedding gift."

Rather than respond, I leaned into Princess Briar's vanity and asked, "What have you heard about me?"

Junseo smirked. "I don't think I should say. Either you're hoping to feed your ego, or you're wanting to fuel your anger at me."

"Are they things your prince has heard about me?"

He crossed his arms. "Considering no members of either of our families have visited one another since my grandfather's generation, it's rather difficult to gather information about you. Whatever I know about you is the extent of Prince Kaede's knowledge."

The carriage bounced as we rolled over something—perhaps a hole in the road or a particularly large stone. I frowned and glanced out at the forest we were entering, thankful for the coolness the shade offered. The closeness of the carriage had begun to grow warm, even with the open windows.

"For the same reason, I know little of your prince as well," I mused. "Maybe you can tell me about him?"

But Junseo scoffed. "Are you hoping for an unfair advantage?"

I quirked an eyebrow. "Advantage? What do you think—"

Just then, one of the horses whinnied and the carriage jolted to a stop. With a muffled gasp, I tumbled out of my seat and into Junseo's lap, my face pressed against his chest. For a moment, I was too mortified to process what had happened, only conscious of the firmness of the muscles I was leaning against and the warmth emanating from his body. My heart thundered in my ears.

Junseo's hands seized my waist, lifting me with ease and setting me down on my feet. He was already standing, though the carriage's low ceiling forced him to hunch forward, his face still uncomfortably close to mine. "A little ungainly for a princess, don't you think?"

My eyes widened as I stared at him, my horror at our closeness suddenly outstripped by my terror of being found out. I could tell my cheeks were flaming. The fae weren't clumsy—a jolting carriage wouldn't shift them off balance so easily with their nimble reflexes—and they certainly weren't modest or shy. Not the ones I had heard about or knew, anyway, and certainly not Princess Briar. I searched for an answer, desperate for some excuse that would be believable.

But Junseo didn't waste any more time teasing me. He pressed a finger to his lips and shoved me gently yet firmly back into my seat, simultaneously drawing a blade from the sheath at his side. "Something is wrong," he whispered. "Stay here."

Before I could even think of a response, he had slipped silently from the carriage, shutting the door behind him.

My blood rushed in my ears as I tried to make myself as small as I could in my seat while peering around the curtain to see out the window. I knew the fae world was deadly, full of creatures that relished bloodshed for the sake of violence or would just as soon feast on one another as trade greetings. I'd been trained to defend myself, though mostly I'd been taught to kill. I knew how to poison a prince, not fight off monsters and magical creatures.

Fingers trembling, I slipped my hand into the hidden pocket of my cloak, palming my dagger's hilt.

Maniacal laughter outside sent shivers down my spine, and then the carriage rocked like it had been struck. Shouts and grunts from bodyguards outside made me unsheathe my dagger and clutch it in front of me as I crouched before the door. Something slammed against it repeatedly.

I caught my breath. *Swing for the throat or eyes.* King Wystan himself had taught me that. *If you can't manage a smaller mark, aim for the torso and strike the heart or lungs.*

The sound of splitting wood assaulted my ears as the door crumpled inward. I ducked to avoid the debris sailing through the air and the swinging axe blade that followed it. When I lifted my head, dagger at the ready, a stocky goblin with a twisting, wart-covered nose glared at me with beady black eyes. When it swung its axe a second time, I rolled, tucking my blade close to my chest. More wood splintered as the floorboards split and shuddered.

For a second, the goblin's blade caught in the wood, giving me the opening I needed to spring out of the carriage. I tumbled past my attacker and onto the dirt road, pebbles biting into my palms. I was on my feet again before the goblin freed its blade and turned to me, swinging again.

Ears ringing, I stepped aside, moving like I had in countless training sessions before when I'd been forced to dodge and parry attacks in case I had to fight against the prince. Blocking out my horror and disgust, I focused on the mechanics of what I had to do. It was kill or be killed. I moved on instinct, shoving the dagger for the goblin's throat. The squelch of flesh and spray of blood jolted me from my practiced motions.

As the goblin's glassy eyes met mine, its axe clattering to the ground, I staggered away from its collapsing body. Nausea coiled up my throat and my stomach heaved as I stumbled to the roadside and was sick.

More goblins were crying out, locked in fights with Junseo's guards, but all I saw was the blood slicking my hands and dagger. It didn't matter that the awful creature had wanted to kill me. I'd just taken a life.

I'd have to take another soon.

Hands shaking, I tried to wipe them clean on the front of my dress.

Something sniffed the air, making my skin crawl. "I bet you'll taste the sweetest," a nasty voice crooned, "when I roast your flesh and pluck out those juicy eyes."

I jolted upright, whirling to find another goblin, this one taller than me as it leered. Its weapon was a wickedly sharp knife, tarnished and brown, like it had seen much blood and never been cleaned. Swallowing bile, I searched for weak points as the goblin advanced. Any hint that it favored one side over the other or had been injured fighting against one of the guards. Nothing.

It was much larger, much stronger than me, and fear was overtaking my rational thoughts.

And then—the blunt edge of a blade struck the goblin in the back of the head. For a second, the creature paused, eyes dazed. Then it pitched forward, collapsing in the dirt mere feet away from me.

Junseo was there, already striding forward as his dark eyes scanned me. "Are you hurt?"

I glanced down at the blood coating my hands and dress and numbly shook my head. "I-I killed him." Though I tried to compose myself, to behave as Princess Briar would expect me to, I couldn't stop the tears stinging my eyes. "You spared this one, and I killed..."

Sheathing his sword, Junseo stepped toward me, his expression surprisingly gentle. He laid a tender hand on my shoulder. "Sometimes, we do not have a choice. When I can, I offer mercy. But these goblins would have killed you without hesitation." His eyes searched my face as if finding something new, something he hadn't expected in me.

Breathless, I stared back at him. I'd never imagined I'd meet a fae who spoke of offering mercy. Who chose to knock a creature unconscious rather than kill. After the violence of Emberglade and King Wystan's cruelty toward his own people, Junseo was so unexpected, I was at a loss.

It was then I realized the commotion had died and we were surrounded by nothing but unconscious or dead goblins and weary guards wiping the sweat from their brows. None of the fae had fallen in the attack thankfully, but Junseo's and my carriage was severely damaged.

Clearing his throat, Junseo stepped back, as if just realizing how close we'd been standing.

"Do goblins pester your roads as much as they do ours?" he asked.

"We have worse," I said darkly. It was true—at least in my human estimation. King Wystan alone was monstrous enough, and though I hadn't ventured far beyond the castle walls, I'd learned that Emberglade was a land in which even its insects tried to kill its inhabitants. It was why the royals had been able to send me with so many poisons that the Willowbark people wouldn't even recognize. Emberglade was a kingdom of poisonous plants and venomous creatures.

Though I could tell Junseo's interest was piqued, he didn't prod for more information. Instead, he hurried to speak with one of the guards, who had a minor injury that he was already wrapping with gauze, and then assisted our driver with unhitching the horses from our ruined carriage. The door and interior weren't all that had been battered, unfortunately. Two of the wheels had been damaged in the fight, perhaps from zealous goblins who'd wanted to ensure their prey couldn't ride away.

I tried and failed to scrub the blood off my hands, only succeeding in staining my dress.

"Here, princess," a female guard said, stepping forward with a waterskin. As I held out my hands, she poured fresh water over them until I washed the blood from my skin. "Was it your first kill?"

I glanced up at her, taking in her kind brown eyes and plaited hair with stubborn curls escaping and framing her freckled face. For a moment, I hesitated, wondering if Princess Briar's deadly reputation had preceded her. But even if rumors had spread, it wasn't as if the true princess would be here to dispel them. And I'd already given away my horror to their captain. There was no point in lying. "My first kill?" I managed. "Yes."

"It's incredible, really, how even slaying a creature that wants to murder and eat you can still inspire guilt," the guard mused. "Goblins are nasty creatures. I'm glad to see that you, however, are kind, unlike them. Only a truly gentle heart would grieve killing one of them." She paused, as if remembering herself, and dipped into a little bow. "Forgive me for the informality, Your Highness. I only wanted to offer comfort."

"No, no." I said hastily. "There is nothing to forgive." I smiled at her, refreshed by her friendly manner. "What is your name?"

"Lavender, Your Highness."

"Does it...get easier?" My stomach churned at the idea of killing becoming less difficult, and yet I also longed for reassurance that I'd find a way to live with myself after slaying the prince.

Lavender frowned. "I suppose when you know you're defending yourself and those you care about, you learn how to stifle the guilt better." She shrugged. "And then there are some fae who are naturally bloodthirsty and live for violence as much as those goblins did. It's rare to find someone like you with a bit of feeling. I'll be honest...I didn't think you would be one of those fae, princess." She dipped her head quickly, as if regretting the words instantly.

But my smile only widened, even if on the inside, I was aching. *You're defending your family. That's why you must kill the prince. That's how you will learn to live with yourself afterward.*

Before I could say anything more, Junseo approached. "I'm afraid I have inconvenient news, Your Highness. Our carriage is too damaged to be operational."

Of course, I'd already noticed that. "I can ride," I said smoothly. "It is no trouble."

Junseo's smile was forced. "Riding isn't an option. You'll be too exposed, and not everyone in the kingdom is thrilled about this marriage alliance.

My task is to do everything within my power to deliver you to the palace alive." He gestured to a covered buggy in the back of the line of carriages, and my heart sank, already anticipating his words. Guards were already unloading some trunks from within, clearing the floor and the buggy's single passenger seat. "We'll be stopping at enough inns along the way that we can dispose of some of our supplies and make room in the buggy."

I wouldn't meet his eyes. "I won't be riding in it alone, will I?"

Junseo shook his head firmly.

I stifled my sigh, resigned. It only took a few minutes for the guards to finish leaving the trunks at the side of the road, which others had already cleared of the goblin corpses. Then, with an exaggerated flourish, Junseo offered me his arm, helping me into the buggy at the rear of the caravan.

As soon as he settled in beside me, my heart jolted uncomfortably. There wasn't enough room on the seat to put any space between us. We were shoulder-to-shoulder, his warm thigh pressed against mine. I tried to tuck myself in, to make myself smaller, but it was impossible.

Junseo glanced at me, clearing his throat. "I apologize for the uncomfortable arrangements." The buggy swayed as the driver urged its single horse forward, and the motion tugged me dangerously closer. For an instant, our faces were far too near. I leaned back, blushing furiously.

"Prince Kaede wouldn't take issue to this?" I ground out, hoping I sounded more annoyed than scandalized.

The bodyguard laughed. "He trusts me implicitly." He cocked his head to the side, surveying me curiously. "Why? Do you think I forced you into this situation so I could woo you for myself?" His dark eyes glittered with mirth.

I crossed my arms. "You mock me."

Junseo leaned his head back against the seat, stretching his long legs as far as they could go in the cramped space. "This may come as a shock to your pride, Your Highness, but you're in no danger of me falling hopelessly in love with you."

I lifted my chin, trying to channel Princess Briar's confidence to cover for my earlier un-fae-like embarrassment. "Well, thank the gods you're spared from falling in love, as you're already hopeless enough that I'm sure it'd be the death of you."

My retort was enough to take the captain by surprise. "Hopeless?"

It was gratifying to see his cool demeanor ruffled for once.

"Yes," I said with a light laugh. "I'm sure you wouldn't have the first idea of how to successfully woo a woman." I ran a hand through my long hair, my fingers brushing against the point of my ear and reminding me that I wore someone else's appearance. "My suitors never left me questioning their intentions. And trust me, I had *many* to pick from."

"And yet your father sold you to Prince Kaede."

"Sold?"

He shrugged. "In exchange for peace rather than gold, yes."

I chewed on my lip, unable to find a suitable response. It was true, after all. Except King Wystan hadn't truly given up his daughter, but me. And not for peace, but for war, for bloodlust, and for his own greedy desire to have the ultimate revenge against his hated enemies.

And in the process, I was selling my conscience for my family's lives.

Before I could sink into another storm of guilty thoughts, Junseo spoke again. "But I *am* sorry that your first introduction to our kingdom was that goblin attack." His gaze dipped to my blood-stained dress. "And that we didn't have time for you to clean up afterward." He paused, but before I could acknowledge his apology, he added, "Though you didn't disclose that you were armed."

"You thought I'd travel to a foreign kingdom unprepared?"

He frowned. "It's something I expected you to share with your bodyguards."

"Because I would trust you alone with my safety?" I raised my eyebrows at him. "I don't know you. I don't know if you truly want to bring me alive to the prince or not. And I will not bet my life on your competence."

"And I don't know that you have truly peaceful motives for traveling to my kingdom," Junseo snapped.

That gave me pause. What if the captain suspected me? My heart slammed against my ribcage as I tried to school my features into nonchalance. "Well, now you know that I am armed for my own protection. As long as you don't threaten my safety, I won't threaten yours."

Junseo's lips twitched. "Very well. Then we're in agreement: no falling in love and no killing one another."

I laughed. "Just so."

CHAPTER SIX

NOW

The water was cool, a welcome refreshment that helped bolster my courage as I watched the dance floor. Most of the other ladies were dancing with the fae nobility while they waited for their turns with Kaede. I, too, had taken a few turns about the room with some of the men, but I'd finally found a chance to slip away and gather myself.

"It doesn't seem right to see such a lovely woman without a partner." The smooth voice broke into my thoughts.

I glanced toward where a man with elegant clothes almost as fine as the prince's himself leaned against the wall nearby, studying me with warmth in his blue eyes. Though there was nothing unkind about his expression, I bristled with wariness all the same. Dipping my head in greeting, I glanced back toward the dancers. Emily Winters was twirling in Prince Kaede's arms, held much more closely than a gentleman in our world would ever dare to dance. But fae balls and feasts were more casual affairs, and they didn't live by the same rules of etiquette. Here, it was not scandalous at all.

Swallowing thickly at the thought of Kaede holding me just as closely soon, I took another sip of my water before replying. "I needed to rest."

"Did I hear you say that your name is Miss Aurelia Sinclair?"

Nodding slowly, he offered a smile and a slight bow. "My name is Florian Brightwing. I'm one of the crown's advisors, and I am honored to make your acquaintance. Would you care to dance?"

Just as I had before, I decided it was best to play along. With a nod of assent, I took Florian's hand and allowed him to lead me out onto the dance floor. The candlelight glistened in his chestnut hair. His smile was charming, his manner polite and kind, but I couldn't trust it.

"Why are you so eager to charm the prince's suitors?" I inquired.

Florian shrugged elegantly as he pulled me in and spun me. The room's colors blended, the sounds of music and laughter all rushing together. "Prince Kaede cannot choose every woman here."

"Ah, so you hope to woo the others and have your pick?" I laughed. "Why a human?"

He laughed with me. "Whyever not? I know you've heard that our kind can be cruel toward yours, but we aren't all that way. Some of us find you lovely, interesting, intelligent... Fine matches. And of course, you already know that your kind help ours have children, so for anyone who wants a family or needs to beget an heir..."

I didn't blush, though once I would have. Talk of how humans were more fertile than fae was commonplace among them, and one of the main reasons human-fae matches occurred. "Is that what you hope for? A family?"

"Perhaps." Florian smiled as we spun into view of Prince Kaede and Emily. For a moment, the prince glanced over his partner's shoulder, and his searing gaze met mine. My mouth dried, and I tried to pretend I wasn't unnerved as I returned my focus to my own partner. "Mostly, I want you to know that I don't view humans the way some of my kind do."

I scanned his expression cautiously, wondering how he may have twisted his words. Or if he might be half-fae or someone who'd made an unholy trade in magic for the ability to lie.

"Whether you believe me or not, I want you to consider me a friend."

"If you are a friend, then can you tell me what is planned for our stay?"

Florian's expression was regretful. "I'm afraid we are all bound by vows not to interfere. King Edwin was quite adamant. Even His Highness can only observe."

Before I could attempt to inquire further, the music came to an end and we were forced apart. As Prince Kaede crossed the floor, I realized it was my turn.

I barely heard Florian's goodbye as my pulse thrummed in my ears. My eyes locked onto Kaede's, who watched me just as intently. *Does he know?* But there was no malice in his eyes.

The musicians began playing a slow song as Kaede paused across from me. I sank into a curtsey.

"Your Highness."

"May I have this dance?" he asked, extending his hand.

I nodded and placed mine in his. A familiar spark ran up my arm at the touch, nearly throwing me off balance. I hadn't expected that after all this time, and I couldn't help but wonder if somehow he'd felt it too. His eyes were inscrutable, giving away nothing.

As he slid his other hand around my waist, I drew a deep breath and gingerly rested my free hand upon his shoulder. My heart ached, and I was keenly aware of the warmth of his body and the strength of his fingers in mine. It brought back memories of another time, another place, another dance.

"Is something troubling you...?" Kaede paused, giving me the opportunity to offer my name.

"Aurelia Sinclair, Your Highness." I paused, considering. "And I was only thinking of how at home, no one ever dances so closely unless they are engaged."

Kaede's lips twitched in the barest ghost of a smile.

It hurt to look at. Once, he'd been charming and lively, always jesting and smiling. He'd been warm and gentle, amiable and attentive. Now he was sullen and unreadable. A stranger.

I'd killed the man he'd once been.

"You are scandalized then?" he asked.

I shook my head. "It is unusual, but I expected unusual." And this wasn't the first time he'd held me close, a fact that left me unnerved for an entirely different reason. It was difficult enough to long for him to pull me close as he once had, but knowing he might suspect I was familiar? That my tone or manner of speech might remind him of the woman he'd known before? That was terrifying.

"And what brought you here?" His rich voice washed over me, that familiar deep rumble that I could feel in my chest. "What do you hope to gain in marrying me?"

This I could answer honestly. "I only came to stay near my sister, Callista. She doesn't believe the stories of how dangerous your world can be, and I wanted to ensure her safety."

"How noble. Unfortunately, I don't believe you." He moved both hands to the small of my back, tugging me against him, close enough that he could lean in to whisper. "Let me tell you a story."

My pulse hiccupped, longing and fear commingling as his breath feathered against my cheek.

"I was betrothed before, to a princess from Emberglade, supposedly to seal an alliance with their kingdom. But they sent an assassin instead of a bride. Though she escaped after striking the fatal blow, my guards captured one of her maids. They gathered information from her—how the princess had actually been a human in disguise. The maid had been bound by an oath not to give the human's name, description, or city of residence. But she did say that my assassin was under thirty years of age, and that her family had recently moved to Riverside."

The world spun, even though Kaede had stopped on the dance floor, his body utterly still. My breath froze in my lungs.

"My father wouldn't give me many options for this contest," Kaede continued, "but he did permit me some. I told him I only wanted participants from Riverside under the age of thirty." He cocked his head, closely studying my expression. "And how interesting that during my dance with your sister, Callista spent much time gushing about the latest fashions and events in her fine *new* home in Riverside."

I tensed. The song ended, and Kaede pulled away, his dark eyes full of something indiscernible. It wasn't warmth, wasn't hate...it was more like a warning. Solemn. Sharp.

Ice ran through my veins, and I was scarcely conscious of making my way to my sister's side, of her demanding why Kaede had stopped dancing and held me on the floor. Of her whining about the preferential attention I'd received with his whispered words.

With every beat of my heart, I was haunted by the knowledge, the same refrain echoing in my head.

Kaede knows who I am.

He knows.

CHAPTER SEVEN
THEN

As the sun dipped toward the west, our buggy slowed and Junseo slipped outside. I shifted to stretch my legs as I listened to the low murmur of voices while the captain consulted with his guards, his deep voice taking on a jesting tone that set his men and women to laughing. When his laughter joined theirs, the rich timbre made my stomach flutter. I scowled at myself, disgusted with how impractical I was being. There was no space for such silly reactions toward the handsome captain, even if he was showing himself to be one of the most charming and kind men I'd ever met, contradicting everything I'd known about the fae.

The door creaked open and Junseo leaned in, his eyes glittering with mirth. Uneasiness squirmed in my stomach along with the butterflies.

"It seems I must be the bearer of bad news once more, Your Highness," he announced. The dimple that flashed briefly at the corner of his mouth told me that he was not sorry.

I settled my lips into a thin line. He was teasing me again.

"And what is this news?" It was easy enough to sound annoyed. Hours in close quarters with this man and his forwardness were giving me a headache. It was difficult to conceal my shy blushes and my shock at how informally he behaved. I was sure at any moment he would accuse me of being a scandalized mortal.

"The goblin attack put us behind schedule. We were meant to stop in Goldleaf tonight, but the town is still at least two hours' journey from here and our horses need to rest. We'll be forced to camp tonight."

My throat constricted. I'd been aching for a room of my own, a place I could retreat and not have to be on my guard, constantly praying my every mannerism and look were befitting a graceful, immortal royal.

Junseo extended a hand to me. "My guards are setting up camp and preparing a meal that I think even you will approve, but in the meantime, perhaps you'd like to stretch your legs?"

I accepted his hand and let him lead me out into the fresh air. The spring evening was growing cool, the breeze carrying a bite to it that reminded me winter hadn't quite released its grasp on the world. As we were still under cover of the forest, the shadows only emphasized the chill, making me repress a shiver and wish Princess Briar had commissioned warmer clothing for me to wear. Emberglade didn't experience the harsher cold weather that we did on this continent.

Junseo's guards were setting up camp off the path along Willow River, which we'd been following for some time—it wound all the way from the ocean toward the palace grounds. The evening light glinted off its swiftly flowing surface as I squinted to try to make out the distant opposite shore. Nearby, the weeping willows the kingdom was known for dipped their leaves into its waters, providing a peaceful shelter.

While the sound of crackling wood and the acrid scent of smoke were welcome signs that someone was starting a fire, I feared I was still in for a cold, uncomfortable night on the hard earth. My headache was unlikely to be alleviated any time soon. I'd be forced to be on my guard, tense and nervous, the whole night through. Would I even be able to relax enough to sleep?

The guards spread out bedrolls and discussed watch rotations as Junseo and I strolled past.

The captain studied my expression with amusement. "Have you ever slept under the stars, princess?"

I chose to ignore him, knowing he only wanted a reaction. "Could I sleep in the buggy or somewhere a bit more...private?"

Stuffing his hands into his pockets, Junseo grinned. "Feeling shy? Does the lady snore in her sleep?"

I gritted my teeth. Would a fae princess be scandalized at the intimate sleeping arrangements, being so close to her guards without privacy? In my world, no one would have questioned my discomfort. "It's cold," I said. "Emberglade doesn't have such chilly weather."

Junseo glanced at the setting sun. "Don't fret, princess. I'll need to keep you close since we're out in the open. You won't be cold." His dimple showed for a moment, though his smile didn't quite reach his eyes.

I swallowed back my horror, thankful he chose that moment to walk away and didn't notice.

"Would you like to warm yourself by the fire, Your Highness?" Lavender's question pulled me from my thoughts.

Nodding in relief, I followed her to the fire, settling on one of the logs the guards had arranged around it. Sage, Daisy, and Ellery joined me, shooting me sharp glances until I cleared my throat and muttered an excuse about needing to freshen up.

"You're not convincing," Daisy snapped as soon as we were deeper in the forest and out of the keen hearing range of the others. "You blush and behave like some foolishly scandalized mortal any time that captain speaks to you." She dug through a satchel she'd lugged with her, retrieving a comb and setting about undoing my hair and brushing it so viciously my scalp stung.

"He is shameless," I muttered. "Even Princess Briar would be offended by his forward behavior. It's not as if he is her equal."

"In their kingdom, he's revered nearly as much as royalty," Sage pointed out as she plucked a vial of my potion from her pocket and laid it in my palm.

I drank the potion swiftly, not wanting any of the effects from last night's dose to wear off before this one could take effect.

"Princess Briar is no stranger to intimacy." Daisy tugged my hair sharply. "Stop acting like you've never been admired."

Ellery gathered a nightgown from my belongings. "He is quite handsome, and you are a princess traveling toward an arranged marriage to a man you've never met. It is likely you'd want to enjoy yourself while you are still free to do so."

That had not been part of my training. "Wouldn't Prince Kaede be offended?"

Daisy laughed. "He's probably making the most of his final days of bachelorhood as well."

Thankfully, Junseo had made it clear he wasn't interested in stealing pleasure from the princess during his time as her escort. I released a shaky breath.

Daisy finished with my hair, and Ellery and Sage stepped forward with my nightgown.

I stared at the flimsy material. "We're outside, not at an inn. I'll freeze in this."

Lifting an eyebrow, Daisy gestured toward my lavender dress, heavy with its embroidery and jewels. "And you're going to sleep in that?"

"Better than catching my death from cold."

Sage rolled her eyes. "Don't be dramatic. A princess would never sleep in her day dress, and you know it."

Sighing, I turned to let Sage unbutton the back and help me out of the heavy monstrosity. When I slipped on the nightdress, I swallowed, instantly feeling too exposed, too vulnerable, and too chilled. It was more elegant than anything I'd slept in back home, with delicate lace and embroidery, but it also hugged every curve and fell just past my knees. My flimsy slippers did little to protect my feet from the roots and pebbles of the forest, but no one had packed me clothing suitable for sleeping in while out of doors.

"Good enough, I suppose," Ellery said while she assessed me from head to toe, as if she thought my illusion would vanish under close scrutiny.

Without another word, I left my maids to walk back to the fire. Though my arms weren't bare, the dress's material was light, making me shiver with every breath of wind that rustled through the trees. I was eager for a bit of warmth, even if it meant facing the captain again.

When I returned, Junseo was seated with several of his guards, chatting animatedly and laughing. One of the men was passing out apples and jerky, while a woman ladled bowls of stew from a pot over the fire. I blinked, surprised at how swiftly they'd prepared the warm meal. Magic must have been involved.

I hoped that didn't mean it would also be full of fae food. Though Kymelle, my Emberglade trainer, had forced me to ingest small portions of their food to build up my tolerance, that didn't mean consuming an entire meal of it would be an easy feat. The worst part would be attempting to act as if I were unaffected.

As I approached the fire, Junseo glanced up. His eyes darted over my ridiculous nightdress, lingering for the briefest instant on the way it hugged my hips. Though I wore Princess Briar's face, my body was still my own. Heat threatened to creep up my neck, but I concentrated on the chill in the air, willing myself not to grow self-conscious.

Seating myself, I smoothed out my nightdress and smiled graciously as Lavender handed me a steaming bowl of stew. I was relieved to find its contents were familiar and delicious, a comforting and hearty meal after a frustrating day.

While I ate in silence, I watched the guards around me. I caught Junseo glancing my way more than once, his lighthearted expression from conversing with his men and women melting away and transforming into something inscrutable.

When I realized I'd been staring longer than would be considered proper, even for a fae princess, I glanced away.

I wondered if he suspected me somehow. Did he think there was something off about me? Had my use of my dagger made him label me a potential threat?

Seated across from me, a man leaned back from his spot perched on a large rock, stretching out his legs. His blue eyes twinkled as he addressed me. "It's nice to meet you, Your Highness. I'm Flint, at your service. I'm sorry your introduction to our land was full of goblins, but I'm sure you'll be pleased later on." The female guards chuckled, like there was a jest I was missing. "Are you eager to meet your betrothed, princess?"

His directness startled me from my thoughts. I set my bowl aside, choosing my words carefully. "Eager is not the word I would choose," I said primly. "Curious, yes. But eager?" I rolled my eyes. "I had countless handsome, influential suitors back home, and now my chance to choose my partner has been taken. An arranged marriage is a duty, nothing more."

A woman seated near Lavender giggled. "You may change your mind when you meet him." She shared a knowing look with Lavender before smirking at Junseo.

I arched an eyebrow in a silent question. Inwardly, eagerness flared to life as I waited and hoped they would share valuable information about their prince.

"It's true," Junseo added, amusement dancing in his eyes. Were they teasing me? Hoping to see me react to their talk of their prince? "He is known for his handsome features and charm. He is quite desired among the women of his court."

Flint and the other guards laughed along with him.

"Ah, so he understands the pain of having every choice available to him...and then none at all." I crossed my arms.

Junseo's gaze swept over me, but this time, I didn't feel embarrassed about the way the nightdress clung to me. Instead, I felt exposed in a different way, as if he somehow saw through the potion's disguise to my human appearance—and even beyond that, into my soul. "He understands his duty to his people."

I swallowed. *As I know mine to my family.*

Finishing the rest of my meal in silence, I set my bowl on the ground and glanced hopefully at the rows of bedrolls the guards had laid out. Junseo caught my eye and stood, nodding to me as a smile twitched at his lips.

Foreboding stirred in my stomach. "Could you show me where I am to sleep?"

"Follow me," he said, turning from the fire and following the riverbank. He pushed past the low-hanging branches of a willow to gesture toward a secluded bedroll, tucked cozily by its thick trunk.

I raised my eyebrows, torn between relief and surprise. "I'm allowed some privacy? It's not too *dangerous*?" I emphasized the last word, thinking of how he'd insisted on sharing the cramped buggy with me as a precaution.

Junseo ran a hand through his hair, mussing it. "Unfortunately, that's not quite true. I'll have to remain nearby. If anything happened to you, I'd be held responsible, and it could start a war between our kingdoms."

My throat tightened, my eyes darting about to reassure myself of something I already knew: there was no second bedroll.

Junseo cleared his throat. "One of my men was careless in packing. We never thought we'd be forced to stop anywhere outside an inn. I'll sleep on the ground."

The fact that he seemed as uncomfortable by our forced proximity as I was brought me a measure of relief. But only a measure.

Swallowing thickly, I turned away so he didn't see the embarrassment and fear on my face. Instead, I pretended to be annoyed—an entitled princess frustrated she couldn't have her way. I sank into the bedroll, which unfortunately was cooler than the evening air due to resting on the chilly ground, and I gritted my teeth to avoid shivering.

Neither Junseo nor I spoke as I closed my eyes, waiting for my body heat to warm the bedroll and praying for sleep to take me. Once I was asleep, he couldn't prod me with questions. And I couldn't fail to act like a convincing fae.

"Goodnight, princess." Amusement tinged Junseo's tone again. Apparently he'd recovered from his earlier discomfort.

Cracking my eyes open, I studied where he lay on the ground, arms behind his head as he peered through the willow's boughs at the stars appearing in the darkening sky. My heart skipped a beat when I realized he'd removed his jacket despite the night's growing chill. In a loose white shirt with its arms rolled up to his elbows, he looked far too casual to be alone with me. *But that is a human thought. Fae do not care about propriety,* I reminded myself. *And your reputation will be tarnished back home anyway if anyone realizes how much time you spent in the fae world—or discovers what you've done here.* Biting back my sigh, I rolled onto my other side to face away from him, only to groan when I settled onto a root.

This time, Junseo didn't hold back his chuckle. It was rich and deep—annoyingly so.

Refusing to respond, I closed my eyes. Somehow, despite the cold, I drifted into uneasy dreams, filled with attacking goblins I slew until blood soaked the ground.

I woke with a stifled groan, blackness overwhelming my vision.

Something pressed against my mouth. Heart slamming against my ribs, I thrashed, finding myself held down by something heavy and solid.

"Hush, princess." It was Junseo's whispered voice, his breath feathering against my ear. "You'll draw unsavory creatures to us if you're not quiet."

Sucking in slow, deep breaths through my nose, I forced my body to still and my mind to calm. Reassured by the way I'd settled, Junseo pulled back enough that I could see his jacket had been blocking my view while he'd hovered over me, pressing his mouth close to my ear. His dark eyes swept over my face as he withdrew his hand. "Nightmares?" he murmured.

The vividness of my dreams was swiftly melting into mortification. Junseo's body was pressed against mine, the hard lines of his muscles too easy to sense even through the bedroll separating us.

"In a sense," I said. "I'm not sure I'll be able to sleep for a while."

"From the fight?" Junseo's expression softened in understanding. "And your kill."

I flicked my gaze away, feeling too exposed under his searching look.

Without another word, the captain shifted off me, taking his body heat. He settled on the earth nearby. "I'll stay awake with you," he said softly.

I forced levity into my voice. "Perhaps I'll die from the torment of being forced to endure your presence."

Junseo chuckled. "Perhaps, but you'll be distracted from thinking about your nightmares."

I sighed.

"There is no shame in being troubled by your first kill." Junseo's voice was surprisingly gentle, without a hint of a jest.

I blinked against the burning sensation in my eyes, wishing I was anywhere but here. If I couldn't cope with slaying a goblin in self-defense, how would I ever assassinate the prince? How would I endure the guilt afterward?

But if I failed, Daisy and the other maids sent with me would report back to King Wystan. There would be no mercy for my family, and it would be as if I had been the one to sign their death warrants. *That* guilt I most certainly would never survive.

After a long moment, I spoke. "I am not used to hearing such words—especially from a captain of the guard." I imagined that if I were the true Princess Briar, I would have said something much harsher, judging Junseo for supposed weakness. She and her father were as vicious and cruel as I'd expected the fae to be.

Junseo's voice turned even softer, as if he were breathing a confession into the night. "Valuing life is not a weakness." He hesitated. "As a guard, one of the things I've learned is that—yes, I may need to stomach violence—but I also need to know when violence is necessary and when mercy is an option. And mercy is not weakness either."

Startled, I turned to him, struggling to study his features in the darkness. Starlight mirrored in his eyes, making them look like a reflection of the night sky—a deep, velvety hue flecked with gleaming specks of silver. His expression was earnest, the charming, jesting man replaced with someone I knew was being utterly sincere. Even if fae could not lie, I knew they could twist the truth, but there was nothing false about Junseo's proclamation. He believed his words, believed in mercy.

Suddenly, my skin felt too flushed, too tight. My breath was trapped in my lungs. I couldn't let myself soften toward this man, even if he surprised me with his gentleness. For all intents and purposes, he was my enemy as surely as Prince Kaede was, and I'd be betraying him as well when I finished my mission.

"How do you manage?" I whispered. "How do you cope with the violence, if it goes against the very nature of your heart?"

Junseo smiled slowly, and I had to avert my eyes from those dimples, from that sharp jaw, and from the tenderness in his expression. My chest ached with an unfamiliar feeling I refused to analyze.

"By knowing that what I do is to protect those I care about."

I huffed out a laugh. "And those you wish you didn't have to be assigned to."

"When you stop pretending to be who you think you're expected to be and show me who you really are...I do not mind it so much."

I drew in a slow, shaky breath. For a moment, raw terror gripped me, before I realized what he was actually saying. The captain had no idea that I *was* pretending to be the princess. He thought I was wearing a mask, behaving like my family and my kingdom wanted me to, rather than being myself.

What would he think if he knew the truth?

"Thank you for comforting me," I said at last, letting my eyes drift closed. I tried to hold his words close—*by knowing that what I do is to protect those I care about.* That was exactly why I was here.

Somehow, I was able to slip back into sleep, this time dreamless.

CHAPTER EIGHT

NOW

Prince Kaede didn't linger long after our dance, as mine had been the last, but his absence did nothing to ease my worry. I tried to feign a carefree attitude as the other women laughed and danced with the nobility, eager to enjoy the festivities.

That was, until Ji ordered the musicians to stop playing so he could make his announcement. We gathered together nervously. Callista remained resentful, refusing my offered hand, still thinking that my close proximity to the prince had been a sign he favored me. My stomach clenched. She had no idea that it was the opposite, a fact that put both of our lives in danger.

"We are thrilled to welcome you to Willow Manor and our competition for Prince Kaede's bride and our future queen!" There was a smattering of applause from the nobles, while we humans waited with breathless anticipation for Ji to expand on his announcement. "In our competition, we will assess your qualities and skills to see if you are fit to rule our land. During the day, you will compete in Prince Kaede's presence so we can see how you interact with both him and his court." Ji gestured to himself and the noblemen and women we'd been sharing our evening with. "Those events will include feasting and dancing, like tonight's festivities, as well as other opportunities to socialize and showcase your graceful attributes. After dark, you will be tested in other ways. Since you arrived in the night, your first test is combined. You already interacted with the prince...and now we will see how you carry yourselves among his court during a celebration."

His tone changed, and I tensed, preparing for the worst.

"It is during these trials that we will search for the qualities we deem most necessary in a future queen. Courage, cleverness, the ability to thrive in our land among our people and our magic..." He waved his hand airily. "I think you gather my meaning."

Nearby, Molly sucked in a breath. "Magic?" she whispered. "Does he mean they are going to test how we handle magic?" The fear in her eyes made it clear that she gave at least a little credence to the stories about fae she'd doubtless grown up with.

"You will also be expected to participate in all of our tests. Trying to leave our competition or avoid a test will draw consequences." Flashing a smile at odds with his warning tone and signaling for the musicians to resume playing, Ji cried, "Now, continue to enjoy our hospitality!"

Fae swept forward onto the dance floor, pairing off or walking toward us to claim a contestant as a partner. Molly lingered at my side as I browsed one of the refreshment tables, wanting a moment away from the chaos to clear my thoughts and analyze Ji's announcement.

"My family made me come to Willowbark," Molly fretted as she trailed me.

I cast her a compassionate look, understanding her pain all too well.

"They insisted it is my only hope for a secure match, and since my father is ill and my cousin is to inherit everything, he and Mother said our time is running out for me to secure my future." She wrung her fingers.

I wanted to encourage her, but everything sounded false in my head.

Just then, riotous shouting interrupted us. I scanned the party, realizing more fae had joined from I-knew-not-where, perhaps invited from the palace itself. Moonlight streamed through the far windows, the late hour seeming to only encourage them as they gulped golden wine and grew louder and more exuberant. Florian was nowhere to be found, having followed Kaede out some time ago. If he had been sincere in his offer of friendship, my only possible ally among these immortals was gone.

"Dance, dance!" a woman with sparkling wings cried, laughing as one of the mortal contestants obeyed her, her feet pounding against the floorboards, her skirt twirling about her ankles.

It was Emily. My stomach soured when I noticed the glazed look in her eyes.

Another contestant—Charlotte—was kissing one of the nobles, which I was certain wasn't something she would have chosen to do of her own volition when she was trying to claim the prince.

A third gulped the fae wine offered her, golden liquid dribbling off her chin.

Harsh laughter surrounded us, and I scanned the room anxiously for Callista. "They're glamouring us," I warned Molly, who watched the unfolding events in horror, her complexion turning ghostly pale.

Laura climbed upon a chair to dance as fae circled her, clapping along to the beat of her stomping feet. Firelight gleamed in her blonde hair as she plucked it from its knot to let it stream freely down her back.

The fae themselves had grown rowdy, some giving themselves to base desires and excess—coupling off to grope each other shamelessly, devouring rich fruits and wines that had been brought out for them to gorge themselves on, or turning violent. Some shoved one another or traded insults, but other altercations grew worse. A few traded blows. A man that appeared to be half-goblin drew a knife.

Before I saw what happened to his intended victim, a contestant fell against a refreshment table, tipping wineglasses that shattered in a shower of multicolored liquid. The slivers of glass cut her arms, leaving drops of blood behind, but instead of crying out, she giggled shrilly.

"It doesn't even hurt!" she said.

A woman with doe ears laughed cruelly. "No? Pick up some more glass and cut yourself."

The contestant obeyed, bending down to retrieve a piece of glass. It bit into her fingertips, staining them red.

"Now take that knife!" the doe-eared woman demanded, her too-sharp teeth flashing.

The lady reached for a dinner knife, pressing it to her palm at the fae's command and watching her own blood drip onto the floor.

I pressed through the dancing couples, scanning the scene for my sister. If I could prepare her, warn her…

She was laughing and dancing among the fae, twirling in a group. Her hair was down, her cheeks rosy from exertion, and her mouth stained with gold. Heart in my throat, I tried to catch her eye, wondering if it was too late for her to be reasoned with.

"Here, eat this." The smooth, lilting tone washed over me like a balm, soothing worries and making all my previous thoughts seem hazy and distant. I turned toward the sound, eyeing a man with rich black hair and searingly bright blue eyes as he extended his hand to me. In his palm lay a perfectly round fruit, its flesh smooth and glistening and a dark shade of indigo but for the veins of silver shimmering along its surface.

Poisonous, my mind screamed, but that warning was quiet compared to the lulling influence of the man's words drawing me to the food he offered.

It looked delicious, like one bite would fill me with joy and peace, making me forget all my fears and pains and regrets. I could lose myself in its decadent taste and the wild beat of the music.

"Good girl. You know it'll taste much better than your mortal food."

He's glamouring you. Icy fingers of dread crept up my spine, combating the effects of his influence. *Fight it.*

I gritted my teeth, considering how to resist. I'd been taught in Ember-glade that, since glamour was all about illusion and control, a human could snap the power a fae had over their thoughts and actions by sharing a secret. Something startling and true, something more powerful than the deceitful thoughts and feelings and visions the fae was weaving.

Of course, my darkest, most devastating secret was one I could not utter here. That would claim my life as surely as the fruit I now accepted, running my fingers along its smooth surface. My mouth watered as I imagined biting into its flesh, a tart yet sweet flavor bursting across my tongue, satisfying all my wants, my hunger, my thirst. I'd never need anything else again.

Callista, Callista. I kept repeating my sister's name to myself, my reason for being here, the reason I had to keep fighting and try to make it back home. I hoped it would help drown out the other thoughts, keeping me from lifting the fruit to my mouth.

Squeezing my eyes shut, I drew it toward my lips, inhaling its sweet aroma. Tantalizing. Inviting. How could something so lovely be deadly? Maybe the stories were wrong...

Callista, Callista, Callista!

Sweat beaded on my brow. I opened my mouth, my thoughts at war. Glamour and my own will vied for dominance, and it seemed almost as if I didn't even have control of my own body anymore.

Inhaling deeply, I squeezed the fruit. "I resent my sister for always getting what she wants and being catered to while I am forced to sacrifice for her." The words came out in a single breath, my cheeks heating with the shame of my confession. It was something I'd hardly dared to let myself admit to myself, let alone say aloud.

Opening my eyes, I tossed the fruit to the floor, listening to it roll away. The man stared at me, his gaze unreadable and his brow furrowed, as if he were confused by what I'd just done to break his glamour.

An indignant huff drew my attention to the side, where Callista herself stood, eyes wide and horrified and glistening with tears. Her hands were fisted at her sides, trembling with rage and hurt. She whirled and tore across the ballroom.

"Callista, wait!" I cried, slipping on spilled wine and colliding with dancing figures as I tried to catch up to her.

Screams rose above the music and laughter, piercing my ears. Glass shattered. I turned to find one of the women whose name I'd already forgotten lying still on the floor, her complexion unnaturally pale, her hand clutching the fruit I'd just discarded. A single bite marred its surface. Her glazed eyes stared at the ceiling.

It had taken her almost instantly.

Across the room, more women screamed as the lady who had been glamoured to cut herself collapsed, laughing in eerie ecstasy as she bled from multiple self-inflicted wounds. Blood glistened in a growing puddle around her.

Callista stopped, gagging and covering her mouth. I grasped her arm, wondering if we would be forced to linger, or if we were free to leave now that we'd both been "tested" with fae glamour in some way.

I turned toward the open doors, only to see Molly already running toward them, her body shuddering with terrified sobs. She nearly tripped on her hem, her slippers skidding through shards of glass, discarded food, spilled wine, and blood. *More* blood.

More and more of the fae's tricks had gone from mischievous or slightly cruel to downright murderous. Contestants were falling, dying. Others were weeping, screaming, or getting sick.

Just before Molly reached the doors, they slammed shut on their own. The manor had closed us in. "Let me out!" she screamed, banging her fists against the wood. "I want to go home!"

A sword sang as it was drawn from its sheath, and one of the guards pulled away from the wall. Without ceremony, he swung his blade and severed Molly's head from her neck in one clean strike. Blood sprayed in a sickening arc, sullying the doors, the floor...

This time, Callista pulled away from me to vomit, her sick splattering across the floor. I choked on my own bile, tears burning my eyes.

Molly hadn't even chosen to be here. She'd been sent to make a future for herself, only to meet a gruesome end.

Someone collided with me, and I whirled, my body ready to flee or defend.

It was only Laura, with Hattie close behind her, both staring at me with blanched faces and tear-stained cheeks.

"I think we were glamoured," Laura whispered. 'But the fae...they were distracted with other women. They forgot us and released us. For now."

Hattie's lip wobbled. "We're trapped here. They'll glamour us again. K-kill us all."

"If we stay out of sight, maybe we can go forgotten until they've had their fill." I seized her arm, urging Callista and Laura to follow.

I led the way to an alcove near one of the fireplaces, pressing myself against the wall and instructing them to do the same.

"Th—this is awful." Hattie's teeth chattered despite our proximity to one of the fireplaces.

Callista was hunched over and motionless, staring as if lost in another world.

"This was a mistake," Laura whispered, wiping at her face and sniffling.

I tried to avoid looking out at the ballroom, its grandness swiftly transforming into a nightmare. It felt like we'd been left to die in a gilded prison.

"Listen to me," I said, instilling confidence into my tone to encourage my companions.

Closing my eyes, I ordered myself to keep my head. Losing myself to panic or hysteria could prove deadly. I tried to think of anything else to block out the sounds and chaos around us.

Somewhere, a clock struck the hour, and everything changed. The floor seemed to drop out from beneath me, startling me so much that I didn't even have time to scream. Nearby, Callista and the twins cried out in terror. And then, the sounds cut off. I opened my eyes just as Callista and I landed with a thud on the four-poster bed in our assigned quarters.

For a moment, we lay there, dazed. Then I stood from the bed, darting to the doorway and peering out into the hall. The door next to ours opened, revealing a pale-faced Hattie.

"Are you both all right?" I asked.

She nodded, glancing around in confusion.

"The test must be over. The manor is magical...maybe when the clock struck the hour, it took us away from there." I drew a deep breath, trying to steady my nerves. "Lock the door and any windows. Try to rest tonight."

Laura peeked over her sister's shoulder. "And then we will be forced to continue competing in these so-called tests for the prince's hand?" She shuddered. "I hoped for adventure—this is like suicide!"

I swallowed thickly and shook my head, at a loss for words. "Just do everything you can to stay safe."

Closing the door, I followed my own advice and bolted it before going to the windows to inspect each and ensure they were all locked.

"So," Callista began, throwing open the wardrobe doors to select a nightgown. She turned her back to me, gesturing vaguely to the laces of her corset. I began tugging on them, helping her out of her frothy white gown. "You resent me." She sniffled.

"Callista, you know I love you. It's only sometimes...sometimes it is difficult that, ever since Mother died, I must always be strong and level-headed. Always the one protecting you."

"And you don't think it's hard for me?" she snapped. As her dress fell to the floor, she turned on me, her eyes shimmering with unshed tears. "I had to grow up without a mother, and then, at your bidding, I sacrificed to keep our way of life acceptable among high society. I endured gossip and being shunned by my own friends when I wore last season's fashions. And now to hear my older sister resents me... As the elder, it is your *responsi-bility* to protect me." Glancing away, she dashed her hand beneath her eyes.

"I know, and I'm sorry," I said hurriedly, stepping forward to take her hands in mine. She refused to meet my gaze. "It's hard sometimes when you don't want to listen to me as I try to protect you."

Callista looked at me, wrinkling her nose. "Because you are so careful, you would prevent me from ever living."

"But in this instance, I was right," I said sternly. "And now is not the time to quarrel. We need to help each other in order to survive this contest and return home. You *know* I'm here to protect you."

Sighing, Callista nodded.

"Let's try to get some rest," I continued.

Unlike Callista's gown, mine didn't include any sort of laces, and I was able to undress myself. The wardrobe contained a whole host of nightgowns, dresses, tunics, and leggings—all in sizes that would suit either Callista or myself. Though the manor didn't seem to like me, if it had feelings about its residents, it at least had provided me with practical garments for whatever was to come.

Meanwhile, Callista settled into bed, falling asleep surprisingly swiftly.

It took me a while to join her. Instead, I went to the washroom to scrub my face, as if the act could wash away the day's events. Every time I closed my eyes, I saw the body of the woman on the floor as she cradled the fruit that had been meant to be my own death. Or Molly's head falling in an arc of blood. Or the coldness in Kaede's eyes as he made it clear he knew who I was.

At last, I removed my boots, tucking the knife I'd stolen beneath my pillow, and crawled into bed.

I wasn't sure it would be possible to sleep with my turbulent thoughts. Had Prince Kaede chosen these challenges? The man I'd once known had been gentle and kind, but the one I'd danced with seemed different.

Sighing, I rolled over, trying to find a more comfortable position. My mind continued to go over Ji's words, trying to guess what the next challenges might be and how Callista and I could survive them.

Though I feared it wouldn't matter if we lived through the contest. Once Kaede had fulfilled his vow not to interfere in the competition, he would be free to exact his revenge on me.

Whatever happens to me, I'll make sure Callista survives to go home.

It was the only promise that I had any hope of possibly being able to keep.

CHAPTER NINE

THEN

I dreamed I was shedding tears, cold and wet and flowing in rivulets down my cheeks. I shivered, reaching up to brush the wetness from my face when something clammy and cold clamped around my throat. Heart throbbing in my temples, I thrashed about, kicking and swinging my legs as my eyes flew open.

Something the same murky green of the Willow's depths, dripping with water and algae, hovered over me, its huge yellow eyes gazing at me hungrily.

Before I could fully process what was happening, Junseo threw himself at the creature, falling to the ground with it in a tangle of arms and limbs. Steel flashed—the glint of a dagger. As he drew his weapon, he continued to fend off the creature's blows with his other hand. Despite its lanky form, it seemed unnaturally strong, nimble, and fast. I sat up, greedily choking down air as I fumbled for my own weapon in the shadows. I'd tucked it beneath some leaves and moss before burrowing into my bedroll, but in the darkness, I couldn't find it.

A splash drew my attention back to the river, where Junseo and the creature were tumbling in the current. Before I could cry out, his guards were racing to the bank, one of them stringing an arrow to a bow and shooting. The arrow sank harmlessly as Junseo and the monster disappeared beneath the surface. I held my breath, searching the water for any sign of them as they wrestled.

Even in the moonlight and the obscure waters, the sudden burst of blood staining the water red was impossible to miss. Several long seconds passed, my pulse matching the ragged rhythm of my frenzied breathing as I rose and stood beside the guards.

Then their captain emerged, shaking water droplets from his hair as he traced a path back to shore, his long, muscled limbs fluid and sure against the swiftly flowing current. When he pulled himself onto the shore, his white shirt clung to him, the moonlight highlighting the toned planes of his chest and abdomen. I sucked in a sharp breath and glanced away, praying no one had noticed my awkwardness.

Junseo's bare feet were before me in mere moments, forcing my gaze up to his face. A lock of sodden black hair fell across his forehead and water droplets clung to his eyelashes. He reached for me. I pulled back instinctively, hurriedly masking my surprise with a scowl. "Are you all right?" he demanded, studying my neck.

I lifted a hand and ran my fingers over my throat, remembering the chilling grip the creature had trapped me in. A wave of dizziness rushed over me, and I teetered on my feet.

Muttering something under his breath, Junseo caught me, his arms warm and comforting despite the fact that his shirt soaked into my nightdress. Lifting me, he carried me toward our shared space beneath the willow. "Patrol the riverbank while I tend to the princess," he ordered his guards with a look over his shoulder. "No one sleeps anymore tonight."

Black spots flecked my vision as the captain gently laid me on my bedroll. I blinked blearily at the tree's swaying leaves, noting the way weakness stole through my limbs.

"That was a water wraith," Junseo murmured, his dark eyes darting over my face, his brow pinched in concern. "They haunt the waters of the Willow, and their touch is poisonous."

My stomach dropped as I absorbed his words. "Poisonous?" I lay my head back. My entire body was heavy. "Then why...why did we sleep along the riverbank?"

Junseo barked a humorless laugh. "Because normally, the water wraiths are only attracted to humans."

Even in my weakening state, my mind snagged on his words, sending alarm shooting through every vein as my heart pounded out an erratic rhythm.

But Junseo went on, seemingly not suspicious of my illusion. "However, your scent would be just as unusual to one, given that you come from across the Bittertide."

My blood chilled even as beads of sweat formed on my brow and the back of my neck. "W-what does the poison do?" I managed to croak.

Junseo laid a surprisingly tender hand against my forehead. "It chills your blood and organs, essentially freezing you from the inside out."

As if in response, a shudder wracked my body and my teeth chattered.

"Don't worry, though;" Junseo went on, "I won't let you die."

If I'd been fully in control of my faculties, I would have made some wry reply about how he didn't have a choice, being that he was duty-bound to deliver me to his prince. Or perhaps I would have questioned how he would prevent me from slowly freezing to death. But I couldn't even form a coherent thought anymore, my mind growing sluggish as my vision grew hazy.

Wordlessly, Junseo cradled me in his arms and helped me back into the bedroll, laying me on my side. This time, he climbed in with me, tucking me against his chest and curling his body around me. I was too overwhelmed by violent chills and growing weakness to have the energy to be embarrassed.

I sank into a listless sleep, half-comforted by Junseo's warm, steady presence and half-tormented by the relentless chill sneaking through my body, slipping through my veins and sinking into my bones. I dreamt of transforming into ice, of watching helplessly as King Wystan and the true Princess Briar murdered my family.

It could have been days or only hours later when I awoke. Sunlight glanced off the river and stung my eyes as I blinked and tried to make sense of where I was and what was happening. After a night of terror and cold, I was cradled in warmth, settled and at peace. I drew a deep breath, relishing the fact that somehow, I was alive.

That was when I realized I was enveloped in a pair of arms, with a muscled chest pressed against my back. It rose and fell to the rhythm of Junseo's steady breaths, reassuring me that he was, at least, still asleep. I wasn't sure I could feign anything but shyness at being found in what human society would consider such a compromising position with a young man.

And what had he been thinking? He'd comforted and protected me, surely, but what would the prince think? Surely there could have been another way to keep me warm and stave off the poison. I'd heard that there were fae who possessed healing magic, after all.

Junseo had claimed he wasn't attempting to woo me, and yet he certainly had no qualms about being in close quarters with me despite the fact that I was betrothed.

Heart in my throat, I cautiously slid my hand toward where Junseo's rested on my waist, trying all the while to ignore the way his splayed fingers sent heat through the thin material of my nightdress. Gently, I started to pry his fingers off me, hoping not to wake him.

His fingers curled around mine, locking my hand in place as my breath caught in my lungs.

"Good morning," he said, amusement lacing his tone. His breath caressed my neck, and I repressed the urge to shudder. The chill that skittered down my spine was entirely different from the ones that had gripped me last night. "Were you annoyed to wake in my arms?"

I swallowed, hoping to project confidence into my tone rather than the uncertainty I felt. Praying no blush suffused my cheeks, I sat up, and this time, he released my hand and didn't resist letting his arm fall away from me. "I was. It hardly felt dignified…as if I were a child who needed comforting in the night." I lifted my chin, thankful that I needn't worry that Junseo would see the lie on my face, since he would never suspect I was capable of doing so.

Junseo chuckled, the rich sound practically vibrating through my entire being. "Well," he said, sitting up beside me so our shoulders touched, "that undignified position saved your life. Our combined body heat kept you warm enough to stave off the wraith's poison."

I slid from the bedroll and stood, smoothing out my nightdress. "Thank you, then," I said primly.

When I dared to meet Junseo's eyes, they were dark and unfathomable, his expression entirely too serious. "I thought we had agreed that pretending did not suit you."

For an awful moment, my heart skipped a beat and my mouth went dry. I couldn't afford to grow attached. "You were the one who said so, Captain. I did not." I let a mask of somberness settle over my face. "I have not forgotten that I am here as part of my responsibility to my people."

"Ah, so you fear you'll develop feelings for me." Smirking, Junseo stretched slowly, languorously, so that the muscles of his arms and abdomen shifted as he did. Realizing I was watching him too closely, I focused my eyes on the surrounding forest, pretending to be searching for the campfire I could smell cooking breakfast.

"If that *were* true, it is hardly a matter to jest about," I insisted. "As you said, I was *sold* to your prince. How can you be so careless?"

That serious look crossed Junseo's face again. Somehow, it made his features even more achingly handsome, and I hated it. I cursed the way I noticed the richness of his eyes, the sharpness of his cheekbones and jawline, and the unexpected gentleness in his demeanor. Most of all, I cursed the way he looked at me...as if, despite yesterday's proclamation that he was in no danger of developing feelings, something integral had shifted between us last night. Between our confessions and our closeness, between waking curled up in his arms and knowing he'd stayed with me through the long, dark hours to keep me alive, there was a growing intimacy there.

A long moment passed before the captain sighed and then spoke. "We shouldn't tarry. There may be more goblins lurking in the forest, ready to avenge the ones we slew yesterday. Besides, if we hurry, we will be able to stay in an inn tonight."

He stood and gathered the bedroll, folding it neatly. It seemed that I was dismissed, that my question would go unanswered. I wondered at his solemnity and what he was thinking.

Without another word, I slipped away to find Daisy and let her clothe me in a new extravagant dress, far too fine to travel in for my taste. She scolded me the entire time for my weakness in crying out and attracting the water wraith to me, nearly revealing my secret and ruining our plans with my close encounter with death. Even if I'd found a point in protesting her endless scorn, I was too weary in body and mind to care, and I endured her words without a sound.

After a hurried breakfast, our party continued onward through the forest, following a well-kept dirt road that wound beside the Willow River. Once again forced to sit close beside Junseo in the buggy, I stared out the window and studied the way the sunlight glinted off the river, internally shuddering as I imagined the water wraiths that lurked beneath its surface. Brytwilde was a strange place, beautiful and enticing and magical, yet deadly and gruesome and cruel. Even after my time training in Emberglade, I still wasn't accustomed to the ways of the fae world.

"Shall we play a game to pass the time?" Junseo pulled my attention from the view out the window as he nudged my shoulder. Withdrawing a deck of cards from his jacket pocket, he raised his eyebrows. "Do you like strategy games? There's one quite popular among us guards right now that I could teach you. But we'll have to lay the cards on our laps in this tight space."

Nodding, I listened as he dealt the cards between us and explained the rules of a game he called "Avenge the King."

"The victor is whoever wins the most out of five rounds. But to make this a little more interesting...at the end of each round, what if the victor can ask the loser whatever question they desire?" He raised his eyebrows. "A game of truth and strategy, if you will."

"All right," I said, gathering up my cards and inspecting them. My one advantage in Brytwilde was that no one expected me to be able to lie, a fact that meant I didn't even need to be a talented liar. I had nothing to lose and everything to gain.

Turning toward Junseo as best as I could on our shared seat, we lost ourselves in the game. I tried to ignore the way our knees and thighs pressed against each other as we lay our cards in our laps and laughed or bemoaned each small victory and loss.

"You're looking at my cards," I teased Junseo in mock-horror, clutching my hand closely to my chest.

He leaned even closer, until our faces were dangerously near. I held my breath, trapped in his gaze, trying not to let myself be affected. "No, no, I think you were peeking at mine." He laughed.

I rolled my eyes, pretending to be offended, and laid down my next card. "I win!" I declared gleefully.

The corner of the captain's mouth twitched. "Beginner's luck." As he gathered up his cards, handing them to me so I could deal for the next round, he asked, "What do you wish to know?"

I'd been calculating what would draw out the most useful information about Prince Kaede, and yet, when I met Junseo's eyes, I longed to ask about *him*. I ached with the desire to know everything about him, from the smallest of preferences like the colors and foods he favored to the bigger things, like his dreams and fears. My mouth dried as the moment stretched between us, the silence becoming fraught with everything I left unsaid.

And then, I turned away, breaking the spell. "The prince." I felt like I was pressing through a fog, everything I'd carefully planned to ask all but forgotten. "Does he...hope the marriage will become a union of love, eventually?" I swallowed. "That is to say, will he want to spend time making my acquaintance?"

Junseo gazed over my shoulder, his eyes distant as he watched the passing scenery. "Yes, he will want to know you."

Wordlessly, I focused on the cards as I dealt them, hoping Junseo didn't see the emotions on my face. Regret. Anxiety. Pain.

It was good that Prince Kaede would want to spend time with me, as it would provide me with plenty of opportunities to strike. But it would also make my mission so much harder.

Trying to force the feelings down, I focused on the game and what new question I could ask, but the captain won the next round.

He leaned back as far as the buggy would allow, stretching his arms, the picture of lazy confidence. "What's your favorite color?"

I clasped a hand over my mouth to stifle an unladylike bark of laughter. "What?"

Junseo dipped his chin toward my dress, an absurd confection that took up far too much space and weighed more than any outfit should with its beadwork and gems. "Surely not whatever shade of green that is. Do you even choose your own wardrobe, or does your father and his court make every decision for you?"

My eyes widened. "Excuse me?" It wasn't difficult to inject indignance into my voice.

"You never would have chosen a dress like that on your own. Or anything you've worn on this trip. It's obvious how uncomfortable you are, even if you try to conceal it." He sat up, his gaze far too piercing. "It's as if you wear a mask, a second skin."

I set my jaw, hating how close to the mark he was. "I wear what is appropriate for a princess of Emberglade." It was a perfectly diplomatic nonanswer.

The captain merely grinned, delight shining in his eyes, as if I'd confessed something. "Your favorite color, princess," he pressed.

"Violet." I closed my eyes and imagined the purple twilight sky at my estate back home, the lavender and hyacinths and violets in the gardens my mother had tended, and the amethysts that had shimmered in her favorite necklace. The one that, after she'd passed, Lavinia had insisted was rightfully hers as the eldest daughter. Slowly, I opened my eyes, finding my vision had gone misty. "It reminds me of my mother."

Junseo's playful grin vanished instantly, solemnity straightening his lips and pain shadowing his gaze. "I'm sorry," he said, startling me.

For a moment, I'd let myself forget who I was supposed to be, and I'd imagined he'd somehow realized what had become of my own mother. *No, he knows Princess Briar lost hers. Because his king murdered her.*

"It wasn't you who slew her." I looked away, not wanting him to see the tears threatening to escape.

"But it was my…" He sighed. "My king."

"It was long ago." A tear slipped down my cheek anyway, and before I could reach up to dash it away, Junseo brushed his thumb over it.

"I'm so sorry to be the cause of your pain, even indirectly," he murmured.

My breath caught in my chest. For a moment, we were frozen, his dark eyes staring into mine, his hand still pressed tenderly to my cheek. He swiped his thumb over my cheekbone in another caress—once, twice.

And then as suddenly as he'd touched me, he pulled back.

Trying to ignore the tension hovering between us, I forced a smile. "Time for the next round?"

But that was when our carriage began to slow, and, looking out the window, I realized we'd left the forest behind and entered a town.

"Greenriver," Junseo announced. "We'll be stopping here for the night. It looks like we'll have to put our game on hold."

Soon enough, we pulled up to the inn, a quaint building of weathered stone overgrown with moss and ivy and surrounded by fragrant flowers and shrubs. Junseo went in to make the arrangements for our stay, but when he returned, opening our buggy door and offering me a crooked smile, butterflies fluttered in my stomach. "I should have informed you sooner that we will need to share a room."

I swallowed thickly. "Surely I'd be safe staying with my maids." Although the thought of being forced to spend the night near any or all of them was stomach-curdling, considering how much they hated me, I worried too much time with the captain would reveal my secret.

Or endanger my silly, traitorous heart.

Junseo shook his head. "Absolutely not. I can take no risks with your life. Last night proved that." His gaze was sharp, as if daring me to contradict him.

"You make it seem as if someone would sneak through the window and murder me in my sleep." I arched a brow at him. "Here, in this little town?"

Silently, the captain offered me his hand, and I took it, trying to ignore the spark of heat that surged up my arm in response to that simple touch as I stepped down from the buggy.

"Not everyone in Willowbark is thrilled with your presence, princess. I would be remiss in my duties if I didn't keep you close."

Though his words, spoken in a rich voice that rumbled deliciously through my chest, made my heart skip a beat, I knew he did not mean them romantically.

And it is foolish to let yourself swoon, I reminded myself firmly. *You just met him, and you're here to assassinate his prince.*

I was a woman of logic, of reason. So why was my heart determined to make me into a fool?

CHAPTER TEN

NOW

Fluttering wings plucked me out of my troubled thoughts. I'd been tossing and turning beside my sleeping sister, trying to puzzle out what terrors the competition might subject us to next. In a single breath, my knife was in my hand and I was out of bed, prepared to fend off an unknown attacker.

But when I blinked, all I found was a bat circling about the ceiling before it stopped, finding a place on the curtain rod to hang. It watched me with its beady eyes.

A chill skated over my skin. How had the bat gotten in if I'd locked the windows? I scanned our quarters, trying to see if anything had changed while I'd been asleep. The fire had burned to embers, leaving the air chilly, but the windows remained securely closed.

Recalling the creature I'd spotted while climbing the stairs to our quarters, I decided the bat must have already been inside when I'd locked us within our rooms.

Returning to bed sounded temptingly warm and cozy, even if I couldn't sleep. My thoughts continued to race, repeating tonight's horrors in an endless loop.

I wondered how many women had survived our first test. I turned back toward the bed, wanting to reassure myself for the thousandth time that night with the sight of my sleeping sister.

Only to find the bed suddenly, inexplicably, empty.

There had been no sounds of her stirring and getting out of bed, and when I scanned the room, she was nowhere to be seen, either.

"Callista?" I called softly.

Only silence answered. My stomach lurched into my throat.

A quick glance at the bedroom door showed me it remained bolted shut.

The bat left its perch and flitted toward the washroom. Fingers locked on my knife, I followed.

Callista was nowhere to be seen. Without a window or any other door, the washroom held no other exit from our quarters. And after the terrors of the feast, I doubted my sister would willingly go anywhere without me.

When I turned back, the doorway no longer faced our room, but a forest. Or rather, a strange space that was part-forest, part-hallway.

Ancient trees with trunks thicker than a man was tall stretched toward shadows, making it impossible to tell if there was a high ceiling or a hidden night sky. Here and there, glimpses of walls decorated with portraits and tapestries peeked out between the foliage. Underneath my feet, roots and moss blanketed the thick carpet. Ensconced candles flickered, offering me tiny pools of light. As far as I could tell, the hall was empty, with not even a posted guard to be seen. Crickets chirped, boughs creaked, and unseen nocturnal creatures stirred in the blackness. A cool breeze wafted toward me, lifting strands of escaped hair from the back of my neck.

"Callista?"

Surely she wouldn't have stepped into this place of her own volition. Not alone.

Had someone taken her?

Or was the manor playing tricks on her? On me? Had it somehow dropped her into a new room in a similar manner to the way it had deposited us into our quarters earlier that night?

I shook my head, scanning the darkness as I stepped forward cautiously, inspecting the scenery for some hint as to where in the manor I might be.

Soft footsteps shattered the quiet, and I whirled, hope firing through my veins.

Only to face Prince Kaede.

The bat that had led me here hung from his collar, blinking beady eyes as if to taunt me before it sprang from its spot and soared through the trees.

Before I could fully register that the prince was *here* and we were alone, he was upon me, wind howling and whipping strands of black hair across his brow as he shoved me to the ground. He swiped the knife easily from my grasp, sending it flying with his air magic until it was lost to the shadows.

Together, we crashed in a heap on the floor, legs tangling, chests heaving. His face was inches from mine.

When they scanned my features, his eyes were sharp. Suspicious. He snaked his fingers around my neck, grasping my throat without applying pressure—a clear threat that he could end my life easily.

My tongue cleaved to the roof of my mouth. Without his court to witness what happened, would he have his revenge here?

"What are you doing here?" The rich depth of his voice was painfully familiar. It would have sent a thrill through me—had done so countless times—if not for the fury lacing each word. Instead, he inspired fear. This wasn't the tender, peace-loving fae I'd once known. This was a stranger.

I'd killed the man I'd loved. Maybe he didn't exist anymore.

Swallowing to alleviate the dryness scratching my throat, I said, "I am looking for my sister."

"So you weren't searching for me, hoping to attack me?"

"What? No. The washroom in my quarters opened to this place. I don't know why the manor brought me here."

He leaned back, finally putting space between us, though he didn't remove his fingers. They rested against my fluttering pulse, unconsciously caressing my skin as if he didn't realize what he was doing. Or maybe he was savoring my fear. I didn't dare move as he glanced toward the trees, his keen eyes seeing things my human ones couldn't make out. "I suppose that explains your sad excuse for a weapon." He cocked his head, and the ghost of a smile flickered across his lips, like an echo of the man he'd once been. "A dinner knife?"

Before I could answer, his lips turned down, likely remembering a different blade, a different room. His eyes went dark, his expression unreadable. "Did you lace it with poison?"

I squeezed my burning eyes closed, haunted by my memories of that day. I tried to find the words to beg for his forgiveness, but before I could speak, his weight lifted off me. I opened my eyes to find him brushing off his clothes.

"Go back to your room," he said firmly. "Don't leave it again."

"My sister—"

"*Go.*"

I didn't know why the low command sent such a sharp bolt of pain through my heart, like it had broken all over again. It wasn't as if I'd expected him to forgive me and rejoice over our second reunion in one night. In fact, I'd expected far worse. Merciful or not, he had every right to demand my execution for what I'd done, for what he suspected I'd returned to do. I turned and ran blindly through the trees, nearly tripping over roots and shrubs in my haste to get away.

When my burning lungs finally forced me to stop, I was thoroughly lost, hair sticking to the back of my sweaty neck. Ahead, a strange door rested within a massive tree trunk. Hoping it would lead to my own quarters, I turned the knob.

The scene before me was surreal. I was within our Greybrooke estate again, except I was watching a moment from my past play out. I saw myself at the writing desk in the corner, poring over the estate's books and scribbling furiously as I calculated where we could make reductions in our expenses to save our home. Meanwhile, Father idly turned the pages of a newspaper while my sisters giggled to one another about an upcoming ball as they adorned their bonnets with fresh ribbons.

"And of course we'll order new gowns," Callista gushed. "I do believe this season's fashion will show off our features to their best advantage."

"I'm afraid that won't be possible. We will have to cut expenses again," I announced, depositing my quill in the inkwell and rubbing my temple wearily.

Lavinia stiffened, looking affronted. "We cannot make an appearance at the Coltons' annual ball in last season's dresses! Have you seen how faded mine has become?"

Callista sniffed. "It would be shameful. We'd be the talk of the town."

I squeezed my eyes shut, trying to force patience into my tone. "We could politely decline the invitation."

Lavinia glared. "And be the talk of the entire *county*? Since you do not care for outings or your reputation, why don't *you* cut back on your own allowance? You can make your excuses and avoid this Season's outings." She lifted her chin proudly.

"I already have," I explained gently, "but some of our other expenses have become rather excessive." My gaze darted to their new bonnets, gloves, embroidered handkerchiefs, and assortment of ribbons on the table. "If we aren't careful, we will have to reduce our staff. Or..." I swallowed. "Sell the estate."

Father set aside his paper, lifting his brows. "Aurelia, this seems rather dramatic."

Lavinia waved an airy hand. "What if we rent the estate out and stay in a small, fashionable townhome in the city?" Eagerness lit her eyes. "Imagine life in Riverside."

My throat tightened. "It would be an indefinite stay, and living in Riverside would hardly help us cut expenses. There would be many more invitations and all the costs of the Season."

"But we would require very few staff."

Sorrow shuddered through me. We'd grown up with Cook, our maids, our footman...they'd watched us since we were children. They'd known our mother before she'd passed.

I swallowed. "This is our home." My voice trembled, though I tried to steady it. "This is where Mother lived."

Lavinia narrowed her eyes. "Really, Aurelia. I didn't think you'd be so sentimental. Mother would want us to be happy. We would prosper in Riverside. And besides, it is only an option. I'm only trying to make the best of a bad situation. We may never have to leave the estate at all."

Father nodded. "If we had to go, we would be among the most genteel."

Callista clasped her hands together. "And we would have far better chances at obtaining good matches."

Lavinia glanced at me slyly. "Which would *also* fulfill our need for money."

I glanced about the room, taking in every familiar sight as a deep sense of melancholy fluttered through me. The responsibility of dismissing the staff would fall to me, as would choosing which items would come with us and which would have to stay.

Now, I walked through the room feeling a similar heaviness to what my past self had endured. Though it had only been an option when I'd made my ill-fated bargain with King Wystan, hoping to save our home, my family had latched onto the idea while I was away. I'd returned to my old estate to find new owners, who had given me a message to find my family at a

Riverside address. It turned out that, once King Wystan had made good on his end of the deal—much to my astonishment—to grant us wealth, they had overspent it all too soon in my absence.

The vision faded, and I was left again in the forest.

Tears clung to my lashes. I'd given up everything...and still lost the home I'd clung to.

When I turned, I faced a different door in another tree. This time, my skin crawled and my breathing quickened. Still, I approached, hoping to find a way out of this accursed hall. The door swung open soundlessly, taking me back to a time I wished I could erase from my memory.

Once again, I was immersed in the past, watching myself live out an event from my time in Emberglade. Hot, sticky air filled my lungs, making every breath feel heavy and turning my skin slick with sweat in mere moments. Despite the unforgiving humidity, my trainer, Kymelle, would not permit a break. Her dark eyes flashed with an inner fire that seemed stoked by endless rage directed at everything and nothing in particular. Today, I was her miserable target.

"Strike again. Harder."

With sweat pouring into my eyes, I slammed my fist into the bag before me. My knuckles were chapped and bruised from days of pounding my fists into it—as well as from sparring with my trainer. Every day, she insisted that an assassin needed to know hand-to-hand combat in order to be graceful and quiet and to strike true, even when attacking a sleeping mark.

"Use your anger."

"I'm not angry," I muttered. "I don't even know this prince."

Kymelle laughed, but the sound was bitter and her expression was hard. "There is always a reason to be angry. Let your rage make you powerful."

I blinked through the sweat dripping into my eyes, thinking how the only ones I was truly angry with were Kymelle and King Wystan. A wicked urge to spin and punch her instead bubbled within me, but my cooler, practical side prevailed. As much as I considered these fae my enemies, striking out against them would only cause me to suffer more.

Instead, I drew a deep breath and tried punching the bag again.

"Why do you want him dead?" It was the most forward question I'd dared to ask in my time here, but now I could not seem to help myself. I wanted to know what drove Kymelle's fury.

She tossed her hair over her shoulder. The sun highlighted her pointed ear as she glared down her nose at me. "He's opposed to all the work King Wystan has done for our people—for our world—and he has been quite vocal about it. He is a threat to our way of life. Meanwhile, Edwin Willowbark's health grows frail. If his son takes the throne upon his death, all of King Wystan's work will be for naught. Especially when he deserves to suffer in his last days by losing his heir. I believe you already know that King Edwin took our queen from us." She sniffed, as if I were beneath her and could never understand. "If Prince Kaede comes to power, he is likely to try to overthrow King Wystan—perhaps even take control of Emberglade. We cannot let that happen."

I frowned, not wanting to consider the politics of the fae world. They were known for their violence, and perhaps violence was their solution to all problems, but from my perspective, it seemed unreasonable and wrong to send someone to murder the prince. Especially for revenge.

I turned and the memory faded, leaving me in the present. A third door awaited me off to the left. Unnerved yet hopeful, I stepped forward and passed through the doorway.

A nightmare awaited me. The scent of blood was heavy in the air within Prince Kaede's quarters. Ahead, my past self was studying the prince's face in horror. Once again, I stared at the betrayal etched across his handsome features and the light leaving his eyes.

Horror gripped me all over again, a nauseating sensation of loss, terror, and guilt. The moment Kaede unleashed his magic upon me, slamming me into the floor, was the moment his anger won over his other emotions.

Stomach churning, I whirled away from the stench of blood and the weight of guilt, racing toward the far end of his room, desperate to get away. Sweat soaked my nightgown and tears blurred my vision.

And then—the scene vanished. I was back in the washroom in Callista's and my quarters. There was no strange door, no fluttering bat—no sign the forest-filled hallway had ever existed at all. Heart pounding, I spun toward the bedroom and found my sister fast asleep in our shared bed.

I wondered if she'd ever left, or if her absence had only been another strange trick of the manor's. Swallowing thickly, I shook my head, wishing I could clear it, wishing I could make sense of the madness. There was nothing logical about this place. Worse still, the fact that it had been taunting me with some of my foul memories meant it knew far too much about me, which meant it could use my fears and weaknesses against me. Maybe even share them with the fae as they conducted their cruel competition.

It took a long time to calm myself and fall asleep.

CHAPTER ELEVEN
THEN

Thankfully, Junseo allowed his guards to escort my maids and me up to our shared room first. I swiftly scanned the space, eagerly noting the adjoining washroom where Daisy was already drawing a hot bath, and frowning at the single bed. Memories of Junseo cradling me in our shared bedroll, of his solid muscle and warmth enveloping me, flitted through my mind until I forced them away. That couldn't happen again. He would simply have to sleep on the floor tonight, and that was that.

"Use this opportunity," Sage said as she plaited my hair to prepare me for bed. "Being alone this often with the captain, who surely knows the prince well, is the perfect chance to learn of Kaede's habits and weaknesses. Learn about your target."

Ellery offered me my vial, which I downed in one gulp. Warmth spread throughout my body. She studied me for a moment, brow scrunched. "I hope your mortal body isn't plagued with weakness tonight from the water wraith's poison. The captain might grow suspicious."

I glanced up warily. After feeling perfectly healthy and warm all day, I had hoped the effects were gone. My skin prickled with unease, but my maids filed out before I could ply them with questions—assuming they knew much more about the creatures that lurked in Willow River.

I sank onto the bed, breathing deeply and relishing this moment of solitude. Slowly, I rose and crossed the room to where the guards had laid out my trunks—all but a couple my maids had insisted be stored in their shared room. Those were the ones with secret compartments that stored my potion and my vials of poison. I sagged with relief, one of my fears regarding being in such close quarters with the captain assuaged.

If only the other problems could be so easily solved.

A knock came at the door.

"You may enter," I called.

"Did your maids inform you I'd ordered dinner to be delivered to our room?" Junseo asked as he stepped inside, his voice soft.

"No," I said slowly. "But I have no objections to that. I find I'm quite tired after...last night." My voice faltered a little at the memory—the fear of death, the weakness and icy cold stealing through my veins, and then the comfort and pleasant heat of Junseo's body against mine.

The mere mention of the night before seemed to send a bolt of heat through the room, lacing the air with tension. Junseo stiffened, his eyes flying to mine as if involuntarily.

His throat worked as he swallowed, as if he was about to say something.

Another knock on the door interrupted us.

"Come in," Junseo said hoarsely, and Lavender entered, bearing a tray heavy with our meals: two heaping plates of braised beef, brown bread, and an assortment of steamed vegetables and sugared fruits. Behind her, Flint carried a pitcher of water and glasses.

Gesturing to a side table, the captain cleared his throat and plopped down unceremoniously in an armchair by the fire, unbuttoning his collar and rolling up his sleeves to his elbows. I hated that I couldn't help drinking in the sight of him, mesmerized by the way the light traced the lines of his throat and gilded his skin, highlighting the toned muscles of his forearms. My stomach lurched when I realized Lavender, who'd deposited her tray on the table, was watching me with a bemused expression.

"It's a lovely evening, is it not?" she asked, the corner of her mouth quirking.

Blinking, I glanced toward the windows and scanned the sky, where heavy clouds threatening rain blanketed any sight of the setting sun. "Um, yes," I stammered.

"That will be all, thank you," Junseo said firmly, his gaze flicking pointedly to Lavender and Flint.

Smiling sheepishly, Lavender nodded and left with Flint, who smirked as he shut the door softly behind them.

Junseo gestured toward the table. "Princesses first."

I rose, collected my plate, and seated myself on one of the low benches at the table, where I had a perfect view out the window at the "lovely evening." My stomach tightened at the sight of vividly-colored fae fruit resting on my plate. If I didn't eat any of it, Junseo would be suspicious, but if I did...

Slicing up my beef, I mulled over my options. Kymelle, King Wystan's trainer, had taught me about the different effects various fae fruit had on human bodies. The ones on my plate would not kill me, but they would make me lose my inhibitions, be more prone to persuasion, and generally find myself untrustworthy with the secrets I carried.

As I ate, Junseo slowly made his way to the table, gathering his food and sitting on the bench across from mine.

"With the delay we had, when do you expect to reach the palace?" I asked, hoping the question would also lead to an opportunity to ask about the prince—but not in a way that generated too much personal information.

Junseo tore a piece off his bread. "We should arrive after one more day of travel, if those gathering clouds don't bring too great of a storm."

I smirked. "The great magic of the spring kingdom cannot stave off a *spring* storm?"

Shifting in his seat, Junseo met my gaze, a challenge in his own eyes. "Ah, I'd say our magic is quite impressive even when we cannot fully control the weather. Sometimes even we are at the mercy of the gods. But what of your powerful magic in Emberglade? Only whispered rumors reach our ears. Talk of mind reading, as well as prophecy and other abilities all but lost to us. Is it true? Are you superior to us?"

I fluttered my lashes like a proud princess. "Do you think I would deny such a claim?"

Junseo leaned forward with an answering smirk to mine. "I have not seen a hint of your magic. Might you provide a demonstration?"

Lifting my chin, I scoffed, trying to act casual, as if I were affronted. It wasn't like I hadn't been instructed on what to do in this scenario. "Why would I need to prove myself to a mere bodyguard? It makes more sense for *me* to see a demonstration from *you*."

His lips twitched, and I hated the way I stared. He noticed, his long, dark lashes dipping as his own gaze fell to my mouth before he caught himself. "That is a good point."

Without taking his eyes off me, he flicked his wrist. Something green and delicate curled through the air and rested in his hand before twisting upward, toward the dim light coming from the window. Junseo lifted his hand to reveal a single violet unfurling its petals in his palm. "This is a mere parlor trick, but I think you can imagine how elemental magic could be useful."

I stared at it, schooling my expression into neutrality while inwardly marveling at its beauty. King Wystan used his telepathic magic for evil, always manipulating and using those around him. Other fae, I knew, wielded their own powers with violent purposes as well. It was refreshing to see something beautiful come from magic. To see something be created rather than destroyed.

I didn't have the energy to fire a quip at him. Instead, I let him see my appreciation. "It is lovely."

Junseo's smile was soft as he plucked the flower from its stem, offering it to me with a flourish. "A gift, princess."

Accepting it, I twirled it between my fingers. "What about a deal?" I suggested, carefully pushing the fruit around on my plate so it was hidden behind my bread and cheese. "Since we didn't have the chance to finish our game earlier... You tell me about your prince, and I will give you a demonstration of my magic."

Junseo swiped at a dark lock of hair, brushing it off his brow. His eyes narrowed. "What do you want to know?" he asked, sitting back in his chair and crossing his arms.

"Anything," I said, waving vaguely. "I'm engaged to a man I know nothing about. Surely you can tell me something. Does he take cream and sugar in his tea? Does he wake early in the morning or prefer to stay up late and enjoy the stars? Does he ride a stallion every day or prefer to indulge in hunting? Is he vain or kind? Does he use his magic to charm ladies the way you do?"

Junseo searched my face for a moment, an unreadable look flickering in his dark eyes. "He takes a splash of cream, no sugar. He prefers to wake early enough to enjoy the sunrise, but most of his responsibilities require that he remain up late, so he has learned to love the stars. He rides well enough, but he generally chooses to walk his grounds in order to gather his thoughts and steal away for a bit of privacy when he can. Most who know him call him weak."

I frowned. "Weak? What do *you* call him?"

He continued to watch me carefully. "You know what I think of mercy, princess. There is no weakness in choosing it."

Something heavy fell between us again, taut with tension. "Would you consider him a friend?" I asked quietly. My voice came out raspy. "You said he trusts you."

Junseo cleared his throat and turned away. "He does. So," he added, forcing brevity into his words, "what about that demonstration? Have I given you sufficient information?"

I considered prying for more, but I wanted to seem like a curious fiancée needing to know whom she was binding herself to, not a stranger demanding odd details regarding the prince's routines. "Very well. Close your eyes."

Blinking in surprise, Junseo chuckled. "Close my eyes?"

"Yes, I won't have you laughing at me and shaking my concentration."

Eyes alight with intrigue, he nodded slowly before complying. I laid the violet down on the table and scooped my fruit into my napkin, folding it carefully on the tray so Junseo would not see it.

"I see a great deal of excitement in your future," I said.

Junseo laughed aloud. "Delightfully vague. Are you not seeing clearly, or purposefully avoiding sharing details?"

Laughing along with him, I squeezed my own eyes shut and sucked in a breath. The image of the violet he'd gifted me danced behind my eyelids. "The future is difficult, since every choice constantly alters it. It is always changing. But I see a woman in violet causing you trouble."

Again, the captain chuckled and interrupted me. "It seems that is already true. You wore violet the first day we met, and you have been trouble ever since."

"Quiet," I hissed. "It's not easy when I cannot focus." I cleared my throat. "I also see great devotion." I laughed, though the sound was forced. "From a large crowd...a gathering. Perhaps you will be recognized for something?"

"I'm always being recognized for my exploits," Junseo murmured in amusement.

When I opened my eyes, I found that he'd obediently kept his closed while his grin stretched wide. "That is all, for now," I said.

He opened his eyes. "It's unfortunate you did not see the water wraith before it attacked."

At first, I feared he was mocking me, questioning my ability, but then I noticed the sincerity in his eyes. There was true regret, as if he wished my fictitious magic could have spared me the pain of last night. "I was a bit distracted." I'd meant it to come out teasingly, as if he'd annoyed me, but that time under the stars with him had been so comforting, so unexpected, that my words came out breathlessly.

Again, tension filled the air, heavy with unspoken words.

Somehow, I dared to whisper the thought that was screaming through my mind. "What would Prince Kaede think if he saw you looking at me like that?"

His voice was husky. "It's not as if your marriage was arranged as a love match. I think I can safely venture to say he would not mind."

"And yet, nothing can happen between us." My brow furrowed. "You said you were in no danger of...having feelings."

My sadness was mirrored in his look. "I was wrong."

Regret made my throat ache. What would it be like to be free of my obligation to spill the prince's blood, to allow myself to grow further acquainted with this tender fae? But that was swiftly followed by another thought: Junseo saw me as a fae princess. Would he be as kind or thoughtful if he knew I was a mortal? "It does not matter what he thinks or feels," I proclaimed at last, "since we are to be married regardless of what we want."

The captain glanced out the window, where the night was swiftly darkening the quaint town. "You should rest, princess. Your body needs time to recover, and even if our travels remain uneventful until we arrive at the palace, they'll still be trying. You can have the bed. I'll be comfortable enough on the floor."

Heart heavy, I clutched the violet and slipped toward the washroom, going about my nightly routine of washing my face and preparing for bed. Thankfully, I'd insisted that I change into a nightgown myself tonight, without the assistance of my maids, so I was able to enjoy a few minutes of solitude. When I'd finished, I all but avoided even looking at Junseo across the room as I stepped toward the bed, burrowing beneath the covers. Though I knew it was hopeless and foolish, I clutched the flower tightly in my fist, wishing the gods could turn back time. I didn't want to slay this unknown prince. I didn't want to betray his kind guard. And I didn't want to injure my own heart in the process, tarnishing any chance of a deeper relationship with Junseo before I could truly get to know him.

It seemed unfathomable to me that merely a day had changed my feelings toward him so completely, and yet, here I was. A single night of baring our hearts to one another and of him saving my life had bound us together in the most unexpected of ways. I longed to know him better, but I knew that would only end in heartbreak. Somehow, I had to build a wall around my heart and stop noticing his gentleness, his thoughtfulness, and his charm. I couldn't let the way he protected and cared for me without expectation of anything in return soften me toward him—I had to remind myself it was merely his responsibility as my escort. Even if cradling me through the night and comforting me after bad dreams was more than necessary. I had to stop letting the deep tenor of his voice send chills along my skin, stop letting the depth of his gaze pierce my soul.

Closing my eyes, I slipped into uneasy sleep, full of goblins, wraiths, and a forbidden fae guard who repeatedly saved my life.

CHAPTER TWELVE
Now

Afternoon light drenched our room, a soothing contrast to the violence of the night before. Callista continued to sleep soundly beside me. Stretching and scanning our quarters, which were devoid of any bats or forests, I even dared to wonder if everything after I'd first drifted off had all been a dream. The feast had been nightmarish enough—believing the manor knew so much about my past and my fears was another layer of terror. How could I plan or reason my way through tests that were designed to target my greatest weaknesses?

Uneasiness crept through my veins as my gaze landed upon a tray resting on the side table, its pot of tea still steaming. Had a fae entered our locked quarters silently and left it while we'd slept? Or was this the work of the manor as well?

Leaving Callista in bed, I crept about the room, checking every corner and possible hiding space, ensuring the door and windows were locked, and tapping points on the walls and shelves and wardrobe to assure myself there weren't any hidden passageways. Finally content that we were as secure as we could be in a magical manor, I studied the contents of the tray. The mugs and teapot were ordinary. I poured myself a cup, lifting it to inhale its steam. A familiar, sickeningly sweet scent invaded my senses, sending horror shooting through my limbs. *Demon's breath*. I deposited the cup onto the saucer, careful not to let a single drop spill.

Catching my breath, I stared at the tray for a moment before rushing both my cup and the pot to the washroom, dumping their contents into the basin and turning on the faucet, letting fresh water run down the drain. Shaking, I wiped loose strands of hair off my brow.

Unlike Prince Kaede, the manor could harm me. Or so I had to assume. Either the tea had been placed as a threat and somber reminder of what I'd done, or it had been a deliberate attempt to kill. Maybe the prince himself had orchestrated it, since an indirect method like poison might have still allowed him to keep his word. Fae were known for their tricky ways and for finding loopholes in their vows—I knew this better than anyone.

My heart twisted. I deserved Kaede's anger—his hatred, even. No apology could assuage the pain I'd put him through, no amount of regret could undo my betrayal. And yet, it broke my heart all the same, especially seeing that he was so unlike the man I'd once known. My betrayal and his death had changed him, darkening his bright, gentle spirit.

Was the Kaede I had known lost forever?

When I squeezed my eyes shut, all I saw were his dark eyes, full of coldness, staring back at me.

The knock at our door came just as I finished tucking the last stray locks of hair into the knot at the nape of Callista's neck. While I'd opted for a tight braid and a practical tunic and pair of leggings, Callista had chosen a flowing dress in a cheerful shade of yellow. I had told her it might prove a challenge to compete in such an outfit, but she'd scowled and waved away my concerns.

"It's comforting to have something lovely after...last night."

Now, I strode to the doorway and hesitated to unlock it before another knock sounded, sharp and impatient, and a female voice spoke. "You are summoned to breakfast immediately. There you will assemble with the remaining competitors and begin the next stage of the challenge."

Swallowing, I unbolted the door and peered at the servant waiting in the hall. Wisteria. Her needle-like teeth flashed as she grinned at me in an entirely unfriendly way.

Callista slipped her trembling hand into mine as we followed Wisteria through the halls. I frowned at the portraits and doors and staircases we passed—nothing was familiar, even after traversing portions of it twice last night. Even the guards looked different, though that wasn't exactly surprising, since I imagined there would have been at least one shift change since last I'd seen them. Before I could question the servant, she paused at the head of a staircase, waiting as a low rumble sounded and every step shifted position until it led in a different direction than before.

Wisteria's moss-green eyes gleamed with satisfaction. "The manor is directing us along the fastest route to the dining hall."

The hum of voices filled the air as we descended the final steps and approached the same dining hall in which we'd partaken in our nightmarish welcome feast.

On the far side of the long table, Ji and the rest of the nobility talked in low voices. In the very center was Prince Kaede himself, clothed in his signature black that perfectly matched his gleaming eyes and dark hair. His chiseled features were set into a stern expression.

As if sensing my inner turmoil, Kaede's eyes locked onto me. I drew a deep breath, keeping my shoulders back and chin raised high. If he couldn't interfere and harm me, that meant Callista was safe as well. There was hope I could get her safely home, even if I doubted I would manage the same fate for myself.

As swiftly as his gaze had met mine, Kaede glanced away, his eyes sweeping over the rest of the contestants, who sat across from the fae.

The sight made my heart sink.

Our numbers had been severely reduced. Only fifteen of us were left.

Slowly approaching the table, my sister and I were greeted by Laura and Hattie, who gestured to the empty chairs beside them. Each of the girls had dark circles beneath their eyes. While Hattie's expression betrayed her fear, Laura tilted her chin up bravely, a defiant spark in her gaze.

Servants filtered into the room, lowering covered trays of food and steaming mugs of tea before us. I sniffed my cup, relieved to find there was no hint of demon's breath this time, only the soothing scents of verbena and lemon.

It felt surreal to be taking breakfast this late in the day, but then again, everything about our circumstances was foreign and uncomfortable.

Ji clapped his hands together, startling the women's gazes away from the prince—for I had not been the only one staring. "Good afternoon, and welcome to the continuation of Willowbark's contest to win the hand of Crown Prince Kaede and become our future queen."

My stomach twisted at his casual tone, as if we were gathered for a lighthearted party full of flirtation and jewels and delicious delicacies, not a fight for our very lives.

"Today we will enjoy some fresh air after we break our fast," Ji continued, "and see how well each of you performs at archery."

Following Ji's lead, we removed the covers on our trays and began to eat the assortment of sugared berries, buttered toast, and eggs set before us. Hattie merely moved her food around her plate, while Laura picked at it half-heartedly. A few seats down, Charlotte looked deathly pale, her perfectly curled hair now hanging in limp strands. She didn't look like she'd had a moment of rest last night, and I wondered what other horrors she'd endured during the feast. What other deaths she had witnessed.

I forced myself to eat despite my lack of appetite. I didn't want our fae company to perceive any rudeness in my behavior, nor did I want to grow weak before facing whatever was to come.

"I think," Ji continued, swallowing his mouthful of pastry, "it is already clear that the first test has been completed, and many of you were found lacking."

I gritted my teeth, refusing to let my anger show. *You murdered them.* Immediately, my conscience pricked at me. *As you murdered the prince.* Could I really act as if I were any better than the fae? My hand trembled as I lifted another bite of egg to my mouth. I scarcely tasted what I was eating. Every motion I made was stiff.

"Willowbark will not accept just any mortal as its queen," Ji said, his voice turning more pompous than usual. "We expect one who possesses certain characteristics and abilities. One who can hold her own in her court, our kingdom, and within our tumultuous world."

Silence reigned, heavy and constricting, as his words sank over us. For a moment, no one, not even the nobility or the prince, ate. Then Ji raised an eyebrow. "Any questions?"

Laura lifted her chin, meeting his gaze squarely. "Will this contest continue until only one of us survives?" she demanded.

I ran my tongue along my teeth, simultaneously admiring her courage while also fearing she'd been too bold and would be punished somehow.

Ji's smile was sharp. "Some of you may survive without becoming queen and return to your homes. But certainly not all of you. Our world is not for the weak or the faint of heart. If you cannot survive it, you do not deserve to rule over it."

Beside me, Callista tried and failed to stifle a whimper. I straightened in my seat, and, hoping to cover for her show of weakness as well as draw attention away from Laura, I voiced a question of my own. "What sorts of character traits do you seek?"

I could feel Kaede's searing gaze again, but I refused to look at him. Surely he knew I held no illusions about becoming his queen.

"Those are for you to discover during the challenges. A queen must have the wisdom to understand what her subjects need from her, after all." His uncanny smile remained in place as he surveyed the table, waiting to see if anyone else had the nerve to speak. "For now, we expect you to socialize with the prince's court, as it will be part of your role as queen, should you be chosen."

As if a spell had been broken, the women met the gazes of the fae across from them and started up conversations, like we were at a party in Riverside enjoying small talk.

The man directly across from me offered a dip of his chin and a bittersweet smile. With golden brown hair pulled into a knot at the nape of his neck and soulful brown eyes, he seemed kind enough. "Good afternoon." His gaze was melancholy as he studied the assembled women. I didn't remember seeing him or Florian during the worst of the feast, after Prince Kaede had slipped away. Did he know what had occurred? Was he sorry for it? "I'm Lord Bentley Russett, though you may call me Bentley."

"Good afternoon," I replied. "I'm Aurelia Sinclair, and this is my younger sister, Callista."

At first, our conversation drifted over unimportant topics like the weather, until at last, I settled on one that I hoped was safe but would also be informative: the manor. "I've never heard of magic such as what it possesses," I confessed.

Bentley shrugged. "No one quite knows how Willow Manor's magic works, or even how it came about. Rumor says that it was built from the wood of enchanted trees, and their power lives on within its walls. Another tells the tale of a hag who lived many generations ago in our kingdom and gave a magical manor as an extravagant gift for the early Willowbarks, claiming that it could discern friends from foes. That story is one reason why most visitors are housed here instead of within the palace."

As breakfast came to an end, Ji announced that we would proceed outside for our test in archery. We followed the fae through the manor's hallway and out a side door that opened onto the palace grounds. A thick maze sat off to the right, while the rest of the gardens boasted finely manicured shrubbery, level paths, bubbling fountains, and a small pool in which fish darted about. Just beyond the garden lay the cherry tree orchard, stretching toward the stables and the glistening palace. The afternoon sun gilded the trees' leaves and blossoms, painting a scene that seemed far too lovely for the location of horrors like the ones that had occurred last night.

Keeping close to my sister, who had engaged Bentley in conversation, I breathed in the fresh air, sweetened by the scents of flower blossoms, dewy grass, and warm earth.

Ahead, Laura, ever bold and confident, approached Prince Kaede and struck up a conversation. Though I couldn't make out their words, her musical laughter, drawing his sunshine smile, thrust a dagger into my heart. I forced my gaze away. *He is not yours. He never was and never will be.*

I reminded myself of the coldness in his eyes, of his hand on my throat.

Bentley heaved a sigh, dragging me from my ruminations. "It is a lovely spring day, the sort that my Rose would have adored. She so loved walking among the cherry trees in springtime and following the Willow River." He shook his head dismally. "*Both poison and balm, the storm and the calm, is love that is lost forever. Though always in pain, still joy will remain, for a heart that is held by its tether.*"

I cast a sidelong glance at him. "Who was Rose?"

"She was my betrothed," Bentley murmured. "A human. I lost her not six months ago to an illness our magic could not cure." He pressed a hand to his heart. "There is a limit to what we can do, especially for mortal bodies."

"That must have been terrible."

"I loved her more than life," Bentley said solemnly, "and now mine feels hollow and meaningless without her in it."

"It's rare to hear of a fae so in love with a human."

Bentley nodded. "I know. Even Kaede himself…" He trailed off, shaking his head. "Well, he and I have been close friends our whole lives, and even he seems hesitant to take a mortal wife, though he's never carried any animosity toward humans." He hesitated. "At least, not before."

All at once, my skin felt too hot and too tight, and yet, I couldn't stop myself from straining to hear every word as we neared an open field beside the orchard where a row of targets awaited us. Bentley slowed his steps, and Callista did too in order to cling to my arm, not wanting to venture far.

Not until the rest of the humans and fae were several yards away did Bentley clear his throat and resume speaking. "Kaede used to be as warm toward humans as I am. He despised how cruelly his father treats them, tricking and glamouring far too many into servitude in the palace. We did what we could to help those glamoured servants—finding loopholes in their vows so they could break the magical hold upon them and flee. Sneaking food and other necessities to them." Bentley's brow furrowed and his gaze grew distant. "But then, after he was murdered…"

I held my breath, the heat in my blood shifting to ice.

"Kaede learned that his killer was not Princess Briar of Emberglade, as was originally thought. She was a human disguised as the princess and sent by King Wystan."

Callista shivered, scrunching her nose in barely concealed disgust. "I don't understand how someone who was dead could be alive now." She stared ahead, squinting against the sunlight to peer at Prince Kaede's distant form. He was still walking alongside Laura, listening intently to whatever she was speaking about. "Is he a ghost?"

Bentley chuckled. "He is as alive as ever, thanks to our good relationship with the Ashwoods and what they can do for immortals who are wrongfully killed. Their magic can bring them back to the land of the living."

I felt ill; the sun was too hot, the air too still, and the sky too bright. I forced myself to count my breaths, the trees, the targets in the distance. Anything to prevent myself from falling into panic.

"Does he know the identity of his killer?" Callista asked.

She had no idea it had been me, but I could see the calculation in her eyes as she studied the other women, perhaps wondering if we'd all been assembled so Kaede could exact justice.

"No," the lord said. "At least, not last we spoke on the matter."

I nodded along, feigning shock and fascination with the story even as bile climbed my throat.

"He's changed since returning from the dead, though." Bentley frowned.

"How so?" I asked, thinking of the rage that lurked within Kaede's gaze. Where once he'd been charming and outgoing, now he was quiet and brooding. Except for now, as he talked and laughed with Laura, showing the same animation that I had missed so dearly this past year. So full of life, laughter, kindness...

"He was a gentle, cheerful soul. Very sociable, too. He and Florian—our other close friend—used to tease me, saying I was the solemn, poetic one. Now? Now he is haunted. He won't tell me exactly, but he says he has witnessed horrors. And he's furious. Not cruel, necessarily, but not as kind as he once was." Bentley set his jaw. "He did not approve of this contest, did not want innocents to be harmed, but his father and the Council insisted, and until Kaede is king, they are the law. He is bound by oath to obey them.

"But he isn't entirely horrified by the prospect of human suffering as he once was. You see, he is fixated on the assassin who escaped. Haunted by the memory of her. He is driven by his desire for revenge."

CHAPTER THIRTEEN
THEN

Shivers overtook my body in the night, making me toss and turn beneath the bedcovers. My limbs were heavy, like my entire body was sinking into the mattress or I was drowning in icy waters. I choked, sitting up in bed as the sound of crashing thunder filled my ears. Darkness surrounded me, and sweat beaded my forehead. I could not tell what was my own panic and weakness and what was the sound of an actual storm outside.

"I'm here," a deep voice murmured as strong arms wrapped around my waist.

I nearly wept with relief from the warmth and comfort enveloping me.

"You're not alone," Junseo went on. "You're going to be all right."

My stomach churned as I turned to face him, my eyes narrowing in the darkness when I tried to make out his features. I mumbled something unintelligible even to my own ears, and I reached out a hand, fumbling past the blankets to grasp the front of his shirt and dig my fingers into the fabric. "What's happening?" I rasped.

His words were gentle, like a hot cup of tea soothing away bone-numbing cold. "It's possible the poison hasn't fully left your body. Nighttime is the worst, for it's when the wraiths are most active."

I frowned, my foggy mind trying to grasp his words. "I don't understand."

"Their poison is connected to their magic. In the day, their victims will experience a reprieve, because the water wraiths rest. But at night, they are active and able to extend the full force of their powers on anyone they've poisoned." He brushed a gentle hand across my brow and tucked a wayward strand of hair behind my ear. "I had hoped your fight was over. Most fae, if they survive the first night, recover rather quickly. But you are unaccustomed to cold, so perhaps you are also more susceptible to the wraith's magic."

Or perhaps it's because I'm human, and I'll never be able to fight it off. Perhaps this will kill me. I shuddered, tears blurring my vision.

"I asked Lavender to fetch you a healer, but in the meantime, I asked her to bring more blankets and some hot tea. Are you strong enough to sit up?"

Nodding dazedly, I let Junseo grasp my arm and assist me in leaning back against the pillows. A soft knock on the door signaled Lavender's arrival. She entered with a bundle of folded blankets tucked under one arm and a tray with a steaming teapot and mug balanced in her hands.

Lavender hastened to prepare me a mug while Junseo took the blankets and began laying them over me, tucking them carefully in at the edges. When Lavender brought me the tea, he approached the hearth, where extra logs rested, and began to build up the fire. Golden and orange light danced across his face and gleamed in his eyes.

"Drink," Lavender urged, her brown eyes full of worry. "Better to burn your tongue and heat your body than to let this chill continue to ravage through you."

I sipped the tea, relishing in the heat that flooded my mouth and then seemed to spread from the inside out, staving off the chill that had been sinking deep into my bones. The comforting flavors of lavender and chamomile danced along my tongue. I drew a deep breath as I cradled the mug and sipped some more, not minding the way my tongue burned when the tea was helping revive me.

"Lavender," Junseo said, voice gentle but firm. "Bring a healer."

"Are you su—"

"Hurry."

At the note of command in Junseo's tone, Lavender didn't hesitate another moment to hurry out the door.

The captain sat on the edge of the bed, studying me. "Any warmer?"

I nodded, still shivering enough that I didn't trust my voice.

He frowned, gaze distant. "I'm sorry I didn't warn you. I'd thought this was over. The healer should be able to help you resist the magic."

My heart thudded dully in my ears as a thought occurred to me: Would a fae gifted in healing magic be able to sense I was human? What if when he or she worked to heal my body, the healer would be able to tell I was a mortal?

A wave of dizziness assaulted me, and I lifted a hand to touch my temple, my other nearly spilling my tea. Junseo reached out to catch the mug, his calloused hand clasping mine where I clutched the handle. For a breathless moment, we both stared at our hands.

Junseo cleared his throat, gently taking the mug. "Forgive me."

Too weak to even feel shy, I leaned back against the pillows and closed my eyes. A moment later, the door opened again and Lavender and a fae man entered. Quietly, Junseo dismissed his guard while the healer approached, his bright eyes swiftly scanning me, as if he could see the poison visibly overtaking my body.

My stomach squirmed with unease. I wasn't sure how healers' magic worked, other than that they had a talent for discerning the wounds that afflicted others and knitting a body back to its natural state.

What if in the process of healing me, he undid my illusion entirely?

I squeezed my eyes shut. I didn't know if I should request that one of my maids be sent for, or if that could even help me now. King Wystan's spies would as soon as kill me as help me if they thought they couldn't prevent my disguise from being discovered.

Junseo hovered near, clasping one of my hands in his as the healer paused at my bedside and lifted his hands over me. My breath caught in my throat, torn between shock that the captain had so casually taken my hand when earlier he'd apologized for brushing it and my fear of the healer.

Then pain ravaged my body, hot and intense, like an inferno searing through my veins and burning away the ice. I bit my lip to keep from crying out even as I writhed on the bed, squeezing Junseo's fingers. Vaguely, in some corner of my mind still capable of conscious thought, I realized why Junseo had taken my hand. Tears streamed down my cheeks.

"I'm sorry, Your Highness," the healer breathed. "I didn't want to waste any time when I heard of your state, and I find it better to let the pain take my patient by surprise so it's over before he or she has time to dread it."

As swiftly as the pain had begun, it vanished, leaving me even more exhausted and weary than before. "It will take time for your body to fully fight off the magical effect of the wraith's poison, but I have expedited the process." The healer's brow crinkled with concern. "Still, you must keep warm. And rest, of course."

My eyelids fluttered. The cold that had flooded my body earlier was still there, but the healer's work had dulled the sharp edge of pain and tempered the chill in my blood. I no longer shivered.

Fighting sleep, I listened to the dull murmur of Junseo's and the healer's voices as they exchanged quiet words. I couldn't make out what they said. Slipping in and out of consciousness, I couldn't recall quite when the healer left or when Junseo slipped into bed beside me, his arms wrapping around me. I sank into his chest, unabashedly relishing the sensation of safety and comfort.

I sank into a brief sleep, waking minutes or hours later to the sound of rain still lashing against the window and the aching absence of Junseo's arms. When I tried and failed to sit up, searching the dancing light and shadows cast by the flickering flames in the hearth, I found Junseo at my bedside, as if he'd just stood to leave.

I reached out, my weak fingers grasping for his wrist. "Please don't go," I rasped. "Stay."

Junseo's throat worked as he swallowed. "Are you sure?"

"Stay with me," I repeated.

He lay back down, tucking my head beneath his and tugging me tightly to him. Immediately I breathed a sigh of relief, letting the sound of his heartbeat and the feel of his fingers tracing a pattern on my arm lull me back into sleep.

I woke entangled with Junseo, the rise and fall of his chest with each breath a soothing rhythm, his heartbeat a reassuring sound. My stomach clenched with a strange mixture of guilt, sadness, and longing. My mind buzzed with confusion. How could someone be this drawn to a man they'd just met? It was illogical.

Frustrated, I sat up quickly, relieved to find my body was stronger and the chill was gone. But would it return again in the night?

"Briar." Junseo's voice was husky from sleep, sending shivers down my spine as he reached for me. Even though he wasn't using my name, he was using the princess's first name, and its intimacy still affected me. "Are you all right?"

I didn't want to meet his eyes, but that would have been rude after all he'd done for me. Besides, I'd been the one to ask him to stay last night. What had I been thinking? Turning, I studied his face, the way the firelight glistened in his dark eyes like golden stars in deep pools of perfect black. His hair was endearingly unkempt, one lock hanging over his eye. "Yes, thank you," I murmured. "I feel much better."

I stood from the bed and trod barefoot toward one of my trunks, gathering clothes to get dressed for the day and slipping into the adjoining washroom.

As I reentered the bedroom, dressed in the simplest dress I could find within Briar's wardrobe—a blue-grey one with intricate floral embroidery along the bodice—I registered the rolling thunder and pattering rain against the window. Last night, in my fight against the wraith's magic, the sounds hadn't fully registered in my mind, and when I'd first awoke this morning, I'd been too embarrassed to pay the storm any heed.

I frowned at the window and then at Junseo, who was gathering up his abandoned blankets by the hearth to drape over the nearby armchair. "Yes," he said, noting my expression. "We'll be delayed again. The roads will be far too muddy for our carriages."

Anxiety clawed up my throat. As much as I dreaded reaching the palace and my mission there, I was beginning to fear spending time with Junseo more. "What if we ride?"

Junseo arched a brow at me. "If I didn't let you travel on horseback before, I certainly won't now that you've already nearly died on me. You'd be far too exposed and difficult to defend galloping through my kingdom."

"Well," I said, straightening. "Then I suppose I'll go downstairs for breakfast."

Junseo cleared his throat. "I've reserved the upper room for our party so we can have a private breakfast. If you want, you can head down the hall to meet with the others and I'll join you shortly."

Nodding, I left the room and swept down the hallway toward an open door on the far end, following the sound of voices.

The Willowbark guards were warm, welcoming me to their table and engaging me in their small talk as we ate a veritable feast of bacon, ham, eggs, toast, fruit, pastries, and cheese. When Junseo joined us, he was his typical charming self, amiable among his guards as if they were old friends and he was no better than them. His humility and care toward each was a delight to see.

Once we finished, we wiled away the day in that room, some guards setting up card games while others lounged, spreading out around the fireplace or near the windows in the large space. I tried to occupy myself within the pages of a book, but the inn didn't have many options aside from tedious historical accounts of endless wars and conflicts among the fae kingdoms of Brytwilde, and I struggled to focus.

Instead, I sighed and tossed the book on an empty chair. I was about to stand and walk about the inn to stretch my legs when Junseo appeared, lifting the book to inspect the cover with a quirk of his lips. He settled into the seat and tipped his head to the side to search my expression. "Not amused by our violent ways?"

"Emberglade is not so different."

Junseo's expression turned gentle. "I know," he said softly. "I suspect you hate it as much as I do. We don't fit in, you and I, do we?"

I met his gaze, swallowing. If only he knew how true that was of me, here in this strange world.

Standing, he offered me his hand. I stared at it blankly. "I have a better idea."

Trepidation and excitement warred within me. "What's that?"

"You'll find out." Junseo's crooked smile told me it was probably something I wouldn't find proper, or reasonable. But I couldn't resist taking his hand.

We made our way out of the room and down the stairs, Junseo carefully sweeping me through the cozy downstairs of the inn, where garlands of flowers framed arched windows and wrapped around the golden candle-light of the lanterns. The fire looked especially inviting, and I had the urge to sink into the vacant armchair beside it to watch the rain and bury myself in a book. A *good* book.

But Junseo led us toward the door, a mischievous smirk playing on his mouth.

"Captain…" I began as he pushed it open to the rain pouring outside. The street was deserted, a mess of puddles and mud.

"I find the spring rain quite refreshing," he told me. "Have you ever let yourself just soak it in and enjoy it?"

"You mean to jump in puddles like a child?" I asked, aghast.

He shrugged. "Jump in puddles, run through the rain, dance…whatever I choose." He turned to me, offering his hand. "Enjoy the moment. Be carefree."

I arched a brow at him. "This is ridiculous." It wasn't proper back home to frolic like a child through the streets, and I imagined even for a fae princess it would be considered unseemly—or at least odd. Surely Princess Briar would find it as impractical as I did.

"Dance with me, princess."

Something loosened in my chest at the low timbre of his voice, somehow both pleading and commanding. My gaze locked with his, and for a moment, I thought I'd drown in their depths. Without another protest, I let my fingers slip around his, let him draw me out into the rain.

Rivulets splattered down my face, soaking my hair and my dress, but it was a warm, fresh rain, bringing the scent of spring. Droplets clung to my lashes as I looked up at Junseo, who pulled me into his arms and began swaying to a song only he could hear. My heart thundered in my chest as I imagined his guards peering out the windows, or someone in town glancing out and seeing us. But I'd already spent nights in Junseo's arms. This was tame in comparison, and yet, with my sopping dress plastered to my frame and my body flush with his, with the music of the rain filling my ears and my face upturned to his laughing one, this somehow felt more intimate.

I couldn't resist Junseo's charm as we swayed beside the inn, my slippers growing wet from the puddles collecting in the street and my hair clinging to my cheeks. Laughter bubbled up in my chest, and I couldn't stop myself from letting it out, joining in with Junseo's deeper chuckle. With a smirk, he twirled me around until my back was to his chest. The steady beating of his heart filled my being, and for a deliciously warm moment, I let his arms encircle me and closed my eyes, memorizing every sensation. He leaned forward, his breath skating along my neck and tickling my ear. "This is the real you, is it not, princess? When you release all the expectations society places upon you, when you allow yourself a moment of joy... This is who you are."

My eyes flew open and I wrenched myself from his grasp. "Captain," I said, my pulse erratic and my cheeks flushed.

He blinked at me, his smile faltering.

"We cannot do this. We can't..." My voice broke.

I wanted this.

I wanted *him*.

What an awful realization it was, crushing my soul and hollowing my chest.

I set my lips in a flat line, raising my chin defiantly. "I am Princess Briar Emberglade, and this is highly impractical. And that is what I am. Practical. Logical. Sensible. I don't know what overcame me...boredom, perhaps...but I am not one to dance about in the rain like a child."

Junseo tilted his head to the side, a droplet of rain sliding down his cheek. "Because you haven't permitted yourself the freedom. Not everything has to be practical to be worthwhile."

I fisted my hands at my sides. "But it does have to be possible and right. For someone who spoke of mercy and kindness, you are being cruel to your prince. To me. This..." I gestured between us and shook my head, my words trailing off. I swallowed. "This cannot be."

But to my surprise, Junseo's expression turned earnest. "What if it could? I am of Willowbark, and I am of good standing with the royal family. Why could our union not be good enough to seal the alliance between our kingdoms? I know the prince would understand."

I gaped at him. "Because... M-my father would never..." I stammered. "I don't think he would accept that."

Junseo ran his hands through his hair, the wet ends growing endearingly tousled. I wanted to reach up and run my own fingers through it, and the impulse startled me. I swallowed and stepped back, as if I could no longer trust myself. Maybe I couldn't. All my practicality was slipping away, my wild emotions tangling with my better judgment.

"We don't know," he said, the look in his eyes turning pleading. "What if he did accept it?"

"And what if he does not?" I forced my voice to turn cold. Anything between us was ill-fated. Junseo thought he was falling for a fae princess. He had no idea I was mortal, an assassin who would murder his friend and then flee to her own world. We could never be for reasons I couldn't begin to explain to him. Soon enough, he would hate me.

Junseo opened his mouth as if to say something else, frustration lining his brow. He reached for my cheek, but I stepped back further, shaking my head and turning toward the inn. "I'm cold," I lied. "I need to change."

Before he could say anything else, I fled inside, nearly slipping on my sodden skirts as I ran up the steps toward our shared room, praying he wouldn't follow any time soon. Wishing for solitude.

But that was a fool's wish. As soon as I swung the door to our room open, my eyes locked on a furious Daisy. She slammed the door shut behind us, locking it, and whirled on me.

"Idiot human," she fumed. "We need to talk."

CHAPTER FOURTEEN

NOW

After last night's test, archery was almost comforting, an easy afternoon pastime as the fae conversed with us. Servants provided light refreshments. It was all surprisingly civilized and welcoming.

But I knew better. The muscles in my neck ached from the tension I carried, waiting for the moment something would go awry. As we each took our turns aiming at our individual targets and comparing our results, I expected Ji to declare that we would next prove our skills by shooting toward our fellow contestants.

Kaede remained mostly by Laura's side, their easy smiles making my chest ache every time I dared glance their way. With her, he seemed like himself again, not the haunted man I'd encountered twice the night before. With her, he was tender, attentive, charming. *Alive.*

It was odd to feel simultaneous relief that the man I loved still existed and envy that he no longer existed for *me.* Around me, he would forevermore be the withdrawn, angry prince stewing on his thoughts of revenge.

Bentley, thankfully, distracted me with encouragement and light conversation. I noticed Florian standing beside Charlotte, though he cast repeated looks our way.

Shooting was fairly easy for me, since I'd been trained in it, but some of the other ladies proved adept, having occupied themselves with archery back home. Others struggled to hit their targets at all. Poor Hattie was among them, a sort of desperation etched in the lines of her brow that made me wonder if she feared repercussions for not performing well.

Laura, however, did so well she even bested me. Her first arrow struck nearer the center of her target, earning her a wide grin. "Well done!" Kaede exclaimed.

And then another of Hattie's arrows missed her mark, sailing so far to the left that it stuck in the branch of one of the cherry trees. White-faced, Hattie lifted her gloved hand to her mouth.

"I'll fetch it, sister!" Laura giggled as she ran from Kaede, dashing toward the cherry tree and starting to climb. Petals fluttered through the air as she moved from branch to branch, stretching toward the arrow. One of her slippered feet slid, and Hattie gasped.

"Don't risk falling!" she cried. "I will fetch another."

Laura shook her head and laughed, her curls bouncing. "I'm fine! I've nearly reached it," she declared.

While Hattie and the other women looked on nervously, the fae nobility watched in eager curiosity, as if even the act of climbing a tree was a test. I frowned, covering my eyes with my hand to block the sun as I sought Laura's target.

My heart leapt into my mouth when I spotted the butterfly fluttering delicately before it perched upon the fletching of Hattie's arrow. Its wings were spotted in a vibrant shade of red I'd never seen in the mortal world—a shade that warned me it was no ordinary butterfly. In this land, everything seemed to be deadly. Cursed.

Prince Kaede noticed Laura's intent at the same instant I did. "Wait!"

Reaching overhead, Laura's fingers brushed the next branch, just beneath the arrow—and the butterfly. It fluttered its wings but did not move, apparently content to let the naïve mortal reach toward its poisonous wings. Laura didn't look, either not realizing Kaede was worried or not hearing him over the gleeful shouts of the other fae.

"Oh, this is awful," Bentley groaned, stepping forward as if to intervene.

But the prince was faster. Kaede tore off his jacket and began climbing the tree, scaling it faster than seemed possible.

Frozen to the spot, I watched Kaede capture Laura's waist before she could stretch toward the butterfly. Her eyes widened, taking in the sight of the handsome prince seizing her, before her lovely mouth opened in another giggle, as if she thought it was all in good fun.

Effortlessly, Kaede hefted her over one shoulder and swung down from branch to branch. As he gently deposited Laura on the ground, he murmured something I couldn't hear. Her gaze turned shocked before melting into something softer, and her eyes swept over his face, snagging for a moment on his lips.

How could I blame her? His chiseled jaw, sharp cheekbones, and deep eyes were mesmerizing in the early morning light, his ebony hair gilded by the sun's rays.

I glanced away, kicking at a pebble.

"Are you all right?" Bentley asked. I could feel his gaze, seeming to bore into my soul as if he could sense a fellow heartbroken soul's grief.

I nodded stiffly. "It seems everything in this kingdom is deadly." My voice wobbled, and I let Bentley think it was out of fear rather than jealousy.

Ji took that moment to step forward and declare Laura the winner. Her cheeks were flushed and her eyes sparkled, the thrill of the competition apparently having taken hold of her. She'd seen that Kaede wasn't like the cruel fae who had tormented and killed last night, and that gave her a reason to keep trying for his hand.

In spite of myself, my heart sank. I *knew* I was in danger, whether I won or lost, and yet my silly emotions couldn't forget the connection I'd once had with Kaede. We'd been ill-fated from the start, illogical and impossible, and yet the wanting remained.

Everyone turned back toward the manor soon afterward.

I was reminded of the fae's endless thirst for excess when we reentered the Great Hall. Once again, the servants had pushed the table and chairs against one wall and musicians were tuning their instruments. Tables were already laden with trays of exquisitely decorated cakes and chocolates and tarts, as well as glasses of glistening wines in shades ranging from gold to navy to blood-red.

Ahead, Kaede turned to Laura, offering his hand and sweeping her into a dance. Other fae paired off, some seeking the hands of the remaining mortals and others dancing with one another. Callista barely concealed her sneer of disgust when one of the fae requested a dance, his tail lashing against his leg.

"She already accepted a dance with me," Bentley said magnanimously, noting my worried expression.

I stepped forward to distract the man's attention from Callista, fearing how he'd retaliate against her scorn. "I will dance with you, if you will accept."

The man winked, seizing my hand and ushering me onto the dance floor. He twirled me closer to his body until his other hand landed on my waist. I clenched my jaw and settled my free hand on his shoulder, hoping I could force him to maintain some distance.

"How thrilling to make your acquaintance," the man murmured, his amber eyes piercing. He seemed to be assessing me, searching for I-knew-not-what. Perhaps he'd been informed that Prince Kaede's killer was among the contestants, and he was trying to find me out. "I am Lord Glen Goldhart. And you are...?"

"Aurelia Sinclair."

His eyes darted over my shoulder. "Is the girl who looks remarkably like you a relation of yours?"

I gave a single nod, my tongue cleaving to the roof of my mouth. Callista was a beautiful woman, and I didn't like the way Glen's eyes were tracking her as she whirled in Bentley's arms.

He smirked and licked his lips. "How deliciously intriguing—that you must compete against her."

My spine went rigid. "It's not as if I must harm her," I snapped.

He quirked a brow. "Is that so?"

Panic lanced through my chest. "What purpose would that serve? Why would Willowbark desire a queen with no loyalty to her own blood? Doubtless she would hold no allegiance toward her kingdom then, either—only herself."

"Ah, you are a wise one," Glen purred. He whirled me in a dizzying circle, making the room spin. "Though there are other qualities aside from loyalty that are important in a queen." He paused. "And a king."

My gaze darted inadvertently toward Kaede.

Glen dipped his head. "He is not like his father. We councilors hope this contest will also hone him into the ruler he needs to become. He's getting closer, but not quite there."

A chill raked down my spine. "How? And how does watching human women die help him toward that goal?"

Glen laughed, but it was not a warm sound. His fingers dug into my waist painfully as he twisted me again. "It hardens him. Reminds him that he is not meant to be soft toward mortals with fleeting, meaningless lives. He is to rule immortals. Even the wife he picks is a tool. You're all instruments toward something—heirs, service, entertainment, pleasure." He flashed his teeth. "I suppose in the case of this contest, you could prove to be all of those things for us."

Bile rose up my throat as we twirled again, the room blurring.

"Though," he said gleefully, watching my expression carefully as if basking in my disgust, "Prince Kaede is closer to the man we wish him to be, now that he's back from the dead. The experience changed him. Unfortunately, it also tainted his magic in a way that is not helpful for our land."

My thoughts buzzed, but before I could ask how his magic was tainted, the song ended and Glen pulled away to offer me a bow, his smile gleeful and cruel. As he strode away, I wondered if he was searching for a new victim to taunt and intimidate or if it was part of another test—to see if we could hold our own as they told us exactly what they thought of us.

When Florian requested the next dance, I released a breath of relief. Though I didn't trust him, he at least had a gentlemanly air.

"You look pale," he said, brow scrunched.

I weighed my options, keeping my tone light when I chose my response. "We didn't experience the warmest of welcomes last night."

"Kaede had been a little...indisposed. He'd requested that Bentley and I accompany him when he retired early. I do apologize that I couldn't enjoy your company longer."

As our steps followed the beat of the music, I mulled over his words and studied his expression. He *seemed* innocent, and yet nothing about his response told me definitively whether he'd known what happened last night in his absence.

"Have you not noticed that our number is much diminished?"

Florian dipped his head. "I assumed some would change their minds and return home once they heard the details about the competition."

I blinked, lowering my voice. "Return home? Surely you know what really happened?"

He frowned, but before we could speak further, the song ended and Ji announced that it was time for us all to retire to our rooms so we could rest before our next test began after sunset.

My head was pounding as Callista and I retired to our rooms. Though I knew resting while we had the chance was vital to surviving this contest, my mind would not quiet when I lay down beside my sister. She swiftly fell into a deep sleep, her rhythmic breathing soothing me. All I could recall was the way Laura had gazed up at Kaede after he'd carried her down the tree, and then the glimpses I'd caught of them dancing together. Of the way his gaze had burned into mine. Of Bentley's words about Kaede's desire for revenge, and Glen's declaration that the prince's magic was tainted.

How much had Kaede changed? And did he care for Laura? The prickle of jealousy growing in my heart made me feel even guiltier than ever. Who was I to envy her after the way I'd betrayed Kaede? I would be fortunate to survive this ordeal and to go on living in the human world, content with knowing Kaede lived.

But my foolish heart ached all the same, longing for a future that could never be, daring to imagine what it would be like if I was once again Kaede's betrothed, but not in disguise. With these wishes in my heart, I fell asleep at last, drifting through memories.

We were only afforded a short nap before servants led us to the great hall once again.

"This time, you will each be alone as you complete this test," Ji explained. He lifted his eyebrows. "You will show us your mettle, how well you could manage during a war. You will move pieces on a board signifying Willowbark's army and enemy soldiers as you play against Willow Manor."

Without further instructions, servants ushered us out of the hall, sweeping us each in different directions. A stoic man with antlers shoved me unceremoniously into a round, windowless room with a large circular table in the center and a fire burning in a hearth opposite me. He slammed the door and I heard the click of a bolt.

For a moment, I gathered my bearings, searching for additional exits, hidden or otherwise. I knew I couldn't escape this test. It was more a habit of my training, paired with my desire to avoid any nasty surprises. What if "playing war" against the manor didn't merely mean moving pieces on a board, but facing off against actual opponents?

I had to anticipate anything and everything. My only weapon was the dinner knife tucked into my boot.

Stepping forward, I surveyed the intricately painted board on the round table. There were armchairs pushed in along its circumference, but I remained standing. Tiny trees and hills and rivers and cities lay before me, making up the fae world of Brytwilde. To the north of Willowbark was the ocean, and beyond that, the illustrations were vaguer, showing representations of the rainforests surrounding the capital of Emberglade and a symbol for the castle and its surrounding city, but little else. Either this board hadn't been updated since the war, or, even after that brief, bloody conflict, Emberglade was still mostly a mystery to the kingdom of Willowbark.

The green and gold pieces clearly represented Willowbark, while the red and black were for Emberglade. My breath caught when one of the Willowbark pieces moved across the board—a tiny wood carving of a ship—and settled in the Bittertide Ocean.

I wasn't going to be representing Willowbark, as I'd expected. The manor was making *me* play as the enemy. That was no coincidence.

It knew who I was, and it was throwing my past in my face.

Grasping the little wooden rake designed to move pieces across the vast board, I settled my own ship replica in the ocean and frowned.

What is the true test? The manor could choose the rules of this war, after all. I could set piece after piece upon the board and watch it be swiped away, any attempts at strategy lost. I ran through Ji's words again, the only instructions we'd received before this test.

You will show us your mettle, how well you could manage during a war.

The round table tilted, as if unseen hands had lifted it, startling me from my thoughts. While the Willowbark ship remained in place, mine slid from the table, landing on the floor with a clatter. I bit my lip as more green and gold ships flooded the Bittertide, pushing toward Emberglade's shores.

I set out horses representing cavalry and carved men symbolizing foot soldiers, scattering them as ambushes in the thick jungle that ran along Emberglade's shoreline, a natural defense against enemies approaching from the water. Willowbark's ships pressed nearer as I set a few lonely ships—Emberglade's number was far smaller than Willowbark's—in the port as a blockade against their advance.

The manor conceded one of its pieces, but as the ship slid from the table, clattering to the floor, a cry startled me. Breath snagging in my throat, I scanned the room again, searching for the unseen person. It had been a woman's cry, full of pain. There was no one. Sweat beaded on my brow.

More of my ships followed. Willowbark was a stronger naval force than Emberglade, and apparently, the manor was ensuring our mock war reflected that.

I moved my pieces into position, forming a semicircle within the jungle to defend the castle further inland.

As a few Willowbark soldiers and horses settled on Emberglade's shores, signifying that their forces had landed, I watched the table rock again, dislodging some of the green and gold pieces.

Thunk. Scream. Thunk. Whimper.

I held my breath, clammy fingers trembling at my sides, as I listened to the pieces fall and the continued noises of women in *pain*. Scared. Suffering.

Some of those voices sounded familiar.

Laura. Callista?

My stomach churned, and I squeezed my eyes shut as the room seemed to spin.

You will show us your mettle.

How well you can manage.

This wasn't a test to determine if we could win a war with no clear rules and too many variables. It was a test to see how cold we could be, how well we could block out the suffering of our fellow humans. How ruthless we would let ourselves be in order to win.

My fingers trembled when I reached for the wooden rake. In one move, I swept all of my pieces from the board. The thuds echoed in my ears as agony spread through my body, pain that spasmed through my muscles and pounded in my head. I couldn't suppress my cry as my back arched and my fists clenched. Sweat soaked my back and my ears rang. Blood pounded and throbbed through my veins, hot as flame. My skin was too tight; my lungs ached.

When I dared to look around, I found that tears swirled in my vision and more drenched my cheeks.

Another spasm of pain dropped me to the floor. I laid my head back, relieved to find the stone tile was cool against my skin, the only reprieve from the endless heat and pain that was devouring me.

But I would not get up. I would not touch another Emberglade piece again. I wouldn't make the other women suffer, going through gods-knew-what each time I won a move.

I closed my eyes and curled into a ball, letting the tears flow, letting the ringing in my ears block out the continued cries from my fellow competitors as others played their own mock wars.

I had survived far worse. I could endure this.

Time lost meaning as I lay there, praying that my sister would be all right. Reciting songs and poetry I'd learned, counting and doing arithmetic in my head. Anything to try to block out the pain and the awfulness of the others' screams.

At last, the agony ended. It happened so abruptly, I gasped. Cautiously, I sat upright, muscles shaking from the exertion. Every inch of me ached.

A creak drew my attention to the door as it swung inward, and Florian rushed to my side. "Ji met with the king and planned most of these tests," he said with a scowl. "They're sadistic."

I wiped the tears from my cheeks. Part of me wanted to focus on his words and what they *didn't* tell me—had he joined them in preparing the tests?—and question him to determine if I could trust him. But right now, that wasn't my main concern.

When I spoke, my voice was raw, each word scraping up my throat like sand. "Is Callista safe?"

"Bentley went to her." Florian offered his hand, and I saw no reason not to at least trust this small gesture of kindness.

"Please take me to her." I imagined her in a room similar to mine, weeping on the floor.

But when we found our way back to the great hall, the other contestants were already gathered. Including my sister. Callista leaned on Bentley's arm, her face pale and drawn.

"Callista!" I stumbled on my way to her, my muscles weak after holding them taut for so long against the onslaughts of pain. Before Florian could grasp my elbow, I caught myself and pressed on. Callista and the other girls appeared as weary and shaken as I felt, but I saw no visible wounds on anyone. Like me, they must have suffered pain without actual injury.

I threw my arms around my sister, nearly knocking her over. She stifled a sob.

Brushing my hand through her hair, I blinked back the urge to weep again, this time in relief. "Are you alright?"

She nodded and leaned into my touch, her body sagging against mine. Despite the tremor lingering in my arms, I found the strength to bear her weight. Unlike me, she hadn't undergone months of training. I could only imagine how much worse off she was.

"Enough theatrics," Ji cut in. "It's time to announce the winner." He waved toward us, and for a confusing moment, I caught his eye and thought he meant *me*. "Callista Sinclair!"

I pulled back, staring in surprise.

"I wanted it to be over," she said, wiping furiously at the fresh tears flowing down her cheeks. "I don't even know how I won...I just kept throwing pieces on the board."

"You're wiser than you give yourself credit for," I murmured.

She mustered a smile and a dip of her head as the court applauded.

I tried to smile and look encouraging for her, but I only felt uneasy.

That night, Laura and Callista, as the victors of the last two rounds in our competition, were both invited to stay after dinner and spend more time with Prince Kaede. Ji dismissed the rest of us, forbidding us to intrude on their time. My stomach tightened as I cast a glance in my sister's direction, but she leaned forward in her chair, eagerly fluttering her lashes while she studied Kaede. It was clear she still hoped to win, still hoped to become a princess of this nightmarish kingdom.

"Be careful," I whispered before I rose from my seat.

Callista arched a brow. "Are you tempted to resent me and my victory?"

My tongue cleaved to the roof of my mouth. Before I could come up with a response to try to soothe her, she'd already turned away to address Kaede.

For a moment, my eyes lingered on him. He appeared much as he did when I'd known him before. His expression was open and warm, a genuine smile dancing across his lips as he interacted with Laura and Callista. I could only hope whatever darkness had affected him was tucked away for the time being, that it was mainly reserved for me.

I filed out with the other contestants, noticing the way Hattie wrung her hands and Charlotte glanced back with a mixture of nervousness and envy wrinkling her brow.

"He seems kind, unlike the others," Charlotte said regretfully. "Will we ever win more time with him?" She turned to Hattie, who sighed and shrugged.

I lingered at the back of the group as they continued down the hallway. Laura's laughter echoed through the great hall and rang in my ears even as the double doors closed behind me.

There were so many other things to concern myself with, and yet the familiar pang of grief and envy stopped me in my tracks. My eyes burned and my limbs were heavy with a sorrow that clung to my bones. I knew better, yet I couldn't resist straining to hear their conversation.

"It truly is a pleasure to make your acquaintance," Kaede was saying warmly.

"I almost didn't come," Laura replied. "My twin sister is my opposite in demeanor, and she fretted so much I wasn't sure I could ever convince her to join. And she is too dear to me to leave behind to...other troubles to face alone." There was a pause. "She tried to encourage me to stay in Riverside, but I refused to be persuaded to do something I didn't want to."

"If only *all* women were of such firm conviction as you." There was a significance in the tone of Kaede's rumbling voice, one that made goose-flesh erupt over my skin.

I had not been firm of conviction. I had let King Wystan persuade me that the only way to save my family was through obeying him.

Before I could hear more of their conversation, I forced my leaden feet toward the staircase. My temples throbbed with a building headache.

I started to climb the steps until Ji's voice rang out from a different room down the hall. He and the other nobles had left Kaede to speak with Callista and Laura alone, but it sounded like he was giving orders to a servant. Like he might have been away from the rest of the nobility.

Gathering my courage, I turned and headed back down the hallway, past the great hall and toward a room opposite it. When I paused in the open entrance, I found Ji alone, seated in an armchair within a study. A freshly burning fire in the nearby hearth and a cup of steaming tea on a side table made it clear he intended to relax alone for the evening. Perhaps the other nobles had already retired.

"Excuse me." I curtsied in the doorway.

Ji's sharp gaze snapped up from the book he'd been perusing. He sniffed. "You. Aurelia, is it? I know you refused to participate in our last test."

"How? Did the manor inform you?"

Ji grinned. "Nothing so magical as that. We had the manor design rooms with spy holes in the ceilings so we could watch the proceedings and choose a winner. Willow Manor can sometimes be temperamental, but we would have found another way to organize the test if it hadn't obeyed." He shrugged. "What I'm curious about is, now that you have so flagrantly defied our contest, how do you plan to beg for my favor? What do you hope to say that will convince me you are a suitable match for our prince?"

"I'm not wanting a favor, sir." I studied his expression, wondering what he knew, what his motivations for hosting this challenge were, and where his greatest loyalties lay: with the king or the crown prince. "I heard that Prince Kaede hopes for justice against the human who murdered him. Is that why humans were chosen as the contestants?"

He leaned back in his chair and laughed, setting his book on the side table as if I were finally worth his full attention. "Ah, you think you were all lured here so he could find the killer and have his vengeance. That maybe we'll keep hosting contests till she's found?"

I barely repressed a wince, praying Kaede wasn't so far gone that he'd willingly call for the suffering and deaths of innocent women.

"No," Ji went on. "The king has been sick for quite a while, and he wants to ensure his line will continue. He wants a future queen that is strong enough to help lead our kingdom but not so strong she'd overpower Kaede."

"But if someone could identify his assassin...would that be enough incentive to call off the competition? Surely part of the reason these tests were planned was for revenge against mortals in general." I forced each word to come out carefully, steadily, trying to clamp down the rise of desperation I felt. "If we found his killer, he could have his revenge. He could choose his own bride, or one of the competitors already in the lead could be declared the victor, and the others could be sent home."

He frowned. "*You* aren't in the lead."

"I don't wish to see more women harmed."

Ji lifted his cup and took a long gulp of tea. I hoped it scalded his tongue. "Well, we have hardly gathered an accurate measure of everyone's virtues yet to declare a winner. And the king has made his wishes clear: the competition will be the deciding factor."

I sucked in a breath. "What about Prince Kaede's wishes?"

With a roll of his eyes, Ji reached for his book again. "He isn't king yet, and he made a vow not to interfere or alter the course of the competition in any way. His wishes don't matter."

CHAPTER FIFTEEN
THEN

"Flirting with the captain is one thing, but your mission is the prince," Daisy snapped. There was ice in her eyes. "You've lost sight of that. Gained feelings. I saw the two of you together. Your frail human heart will give in to his charm, and you'll spoil everything, give away who you are and destroy the mission before we even arrive at the palace." She plucked a note from the pocket of her dress, waving it in front of me. "So I think it's time I remind you of what's at stake."

Daisy shoved the crumpled paper into my hands, leaving me to scour its contents. "A message from the soldiers watching your family," she explained.

We are constantly at the ready for your orders. The women are in and out nearly daily, bringing back bags full of whatever these mortals amuse themselves with purchasing at their shops. Nearly every evening, the entire family departs in their carriage for a social event in their town. But they sleep late each morning, providing an easy opportunity to infiltrate the home and catch them unawares.

My vision swam. They were watching my family and their habits, and all it would take was a single command for them to storm into my home and slay my loved ones. Mouth dry, I struggled to swallow as I held the letter out to Daisy, letting her snatch it back.

"Know that failure on your part will send a swift message to our king and elicit a quick command from him. See that you never forget this."

Knocking on the door made Daisy pause.

"Princess?" Junseo's voice warmed me, almost enough to shut out my panic. "Please unlock the door." He chuckled. "I'm leaving puddles in the hallway. I know you're upset, but... Please let me talk to you."

When I didn't answer, his words turned urgent. "Princess? Are you all right?" He rattled the door knob at my persistent silence.

Clearing my throat, I forced calmness into my tone as I called out to Junseo. "I'm changing. One moment."

Daisy strode to my trunks, yanking out a fresh dress. She didn't attempt to be gentle as she plucked my sodden gown off me and shoved me into the new one, heavy with jewels and frothing lace.

Without another word, Daisy strode to the door and opened it, dipping into a curtsey for the captain and then darting down the hall.

Head spinning, I ran my shaking hands through my damp hair and attempted to look unperturbed as Junseo entered the room.

"Are you all right?" he asked. He was too good at reading me. The tenderness in his eyes made me ache.

I shrugged, refusing to meet his eyes. Letting him assume all my discomfort was due to our dancing earlier.

"I'm going to read," I announced, slipping from the room.

Junseo didn't try to stop me.

Lavender and her friend Pearl found me perusing the limited books the inn contained and had invited me to their shared room with another of the female guards.

"I know from that collection you might not believe it, but we do have some good books in Willowbark too," Pearl had proclaimed, digging through her trunk to pull out a handful of books. "I've already finished with this one, if you want to read it. It's a romance." She winked.

With a smile, I took the book from her, wondering what a fae romance would be like. "Anything is better than dusty history books on war," I said with a laugh.

They welcomed me into their rooms, letting me spend an enjoyable afternoon reading and talking. "The men are kind enough, but sometimes you just need to stay in the company of women."

"Especially when you want to talk about them behind their backs," Violet—the third female guard, who'd joined us later—said with a flutter of her feathery lashes.

"Yes." Lavender cast me a sly look. "Perhaps you have something you'd like to say about your time with the captain?"

"Is it enjoyable sharing a room with him?" Pearl asked coyly.

I bit my lip, trying to keep my cheeks from flooding with heat. "I'm engaged to your prince," I reminded them pointedly. "It doesn't matter what I think of the captain."

Violet shrugged carelessly. "Well, he *is* handsome."

"And you can't say you haven't noticed," Lavender pressed. "I've seen the way you look at him."

"And yet, I cannot marry *him*."

Pearl just snickered, covering her mouth and sharing a look with Violet. "You sound like most of us females who have to be around him at the palace," Pearl added with a laugh.

I shifted uncomfortably and announced that I was growing tired and needed to retire to my rooms.

"Enjoy your rest with the captain," Lavender called with feigned innocence as I bid them goodbye and shut the door.

After a quick detour to see my maids and take my vial of potion, I turned my steps to my shared quarters with Junseo. I knocked on the door, feeling a sliver of panic growing inside me. I wanted far too much. Wanted what I could not have. The idea of having to even look at Junseo again seemed almost unbearable.

"You may enter," the captain called.

He was sitting at the fireside, eating dinner as he perused his own book.

When I stepped inside, shutting the door behind me, he glanced up, a flare of hope in his eyes. He set aside the book, and I noticed that his collar was casually unbuttoned, revealing too much of his neck and upper chest.

I swallowed and glanced away.

"Princess," Junseo murmured. "Forgive me if I made you uncomfortable earlier with my forwardness." He cleared his throat as he searched my expression. "If you're agreeable to it...I would like to be friends."

Hesitantly, I approached his chair as he stood, extending his hand. "Friends?"

"Yes." He offered me a smile. "Astonishingly, I enjoy your company. I'd prefer if we could converse, play card games, and perhaps not be miserably silent and avoidant the remainder of our time together...if that is possible? Could you forgive me and be friends?"

"I can do that," I whispered, accepting his hand. His warm fingers enveloped mine, and instantly, my chest ached with longing. I didn't want to only be friends—knew even that would end in heartbreak for me—but it was all I could offer.

At first, I'd thought taking breakfast downstairs the next morning would be a relief, a chance to be out of my close quarters with the captain. Though he'd slept on the floor again and I'd slept in the bed, I'd yearned for what we could never have. By the time I'd woken, Junseo was long gone, and Lavender and her friends had knocked at my door instead, telling me we would leave today and they would escort me to breakfast.

But as soon as we entered the room, my stomach dropped.

At the far end by the fireplace sat a musician, strumming a guitar.

A human musician.

I tried not to let my eyes linger too long on the curve of his ears or his gaunt face. Clothed in grubby attire, patched and dirty and faded, he sat with a distant, glazed look in his eyes and a half-smile that made me queasy. Worst of all, he appeared young, perhaps only twelve years old.

Swallowing the bile burning the back of my throat, I forced a smile as I seated myself between Lavender and Pearl. A steaming plate of food and a mug of tea already awaited me, though I had no appetite. Across the table, Junseo had a strange expression on his face. His own breakfast appeared untouched.

Some of the other guards were chatting in low voices, but there was an unusually somber mood over the group.

"Good morning, Your Highness," Flint said, his posture too rigid, his smile too wide. "Now that the rain has stopped, I hope you are ready for more travels."

I dipped my head in acknowledgement, unable to force myself to speak.

Abruptly, Junseo picked up his plate, shoved his chair back with a scrape, and stood.

Lavender and Pearl glanced at each other over my head. Flint shifted in his seat, and Violet cleared her throat, staring at her plate. The rest of the table fell silent. I glanced up, the fork I'd been poking my food with still held mid-air, but Junseo's gaze wasn't on me.

He turned, striding across the room toward the musician.

No one spoke. There were only a few other patrons around at this early hour, along with a server, who paused in his work of wiping down a table to watch the captain.

Without meaning to, I found myself holding my breath, the growing tension pressing down on me even though I didn't understand the weight of this moment.

Junseo set the plate down beside the boy. His words, though spoken with the clear charm and cadence of a fae weaving glamour, held no malice. "Stop playing and feel free to eat what you wish from my plate."

Eyes still glazed over, the boy instantly set aside his guitar, resting it against the wall, and stood to grab the plate. He wielded the fork like a shovel, piling heaping mouthfuls onto it and then chewing and swallowing with such violence, my eyes stung. How long had he been surviving on barely enough sustenance?

"Surely the king will discipline you for going against his wishes," came a snappish voice.

Unperturbed, Junseo turned toward the innkeeper as he emerged from one of the back rooms, his complexion blotchy with anger. But when his gaze snapped to the captain, he hesitated, turning white. As if just now realizing whom he had been addressing: the Captain of the Royal Guard.

"Stop," Junseo said coolly, when the innkeeper moved as if to bow. "We appreciate your hospitality toward us, but, after this boy has been fed and given rest, he and any other human servants you have in your inn will be safely returned to their homes. If King Edwin takes offense to this, he can bring his complaints directly to me, his chosen captain of the guard."

The heaviness in the inn was nearly suffocating. A wash of confusion passed over the innkeeper's face, but only for a moment before he dipped his head, humbled and unnerved by the captain's authoritative tone.

As Junseo strode back to the table, solemn and quiet, the inn slowly returned to its conversations. Meanwhile, I blinked and swallowed quickly, overcome with a different sort of emotion. Though I still didn't have an appetite, I forced myself to take a few bites, if only for something to do. I didn't want anyone to catch me staring, overwhelmed by this display of Junseo's compassion. I'd suspected his tender nature expanded beyond fae, but seeing this confirmed? The warmth in my heart and the butterflies in my chest were dangerous, a final warning that I had fallen, irrevocably, for the captain.

After breakfast, as we strolled toward our carriages waiting outside the inn, I inhaled the fresh spring scent of a world washed clean by the rain, wishing I could wash my obligations and guilt away just as easily.

Junseo helped me into a carriage. "Today, I can offer you better traveling conditions," he said with a smile. I was relieved to see we would no longer have to share the cramped buggy. "Flint secured a new carriage to replace our lost one. Even better, I thought with the additional space, you could have one of your maids join us."

My stomach soured. I wanted to request Lavender, Pearl, or Violet instead, but avoiding my own maids would look suspicious, so I nodded and forced a smile. "Thank you."

Sage joined us in the carriage, providing a slight reprieve from my fears of being alone too often with the captain.

At long last, the day drew to a close, the sun sinking in a bloody display to the west, searing my eyelids with the color each time I blinked. Reminding me of the blood I'd soon shed and stain my own hands with. With every clop of the horses' hooves drawing nearer to the palace, my heart thundered a steady rhythm.

Murderer. Murderer. Murderer.

"We will reach the palace tonight, so we aren't stopping," Junseo murmured, his expression indiscernible as he glanced from Sage to me. His eyes flitted briefly to mine before he turned to look out his own window. Though we'd conversed warmly enough today, a change was coming over him as we neared the end of our journey, as if he dreaded it nearly as much as I did.

He had no idea how much more he would despise the very thought of me later.

Somehow, I sank into a fitful doze. I dreamed of creeping down dark corridors full of echoing voices. Open doorways were full of living, writhing shadows that formed skeletal hands groping for me. Raspy words accused me of killing. When I looked down, my dress and hands were dripping with blood, leaving a trail of gore in my wake. Horror made my mouth fill with bile, and I choked on my own scream.

Jolting awake, I found Junseo's face only a breath away, his broad hands clasping my shoulders. "Are you all right?"

I swallowed. My throat ached, like I truly had been screaming.

"Are you cold?" The captain pressed his palm to my forehead, his searing gaze scanning my face.

"No," I whispered. "Only a nightmare."

Junseo frowned, wetting his lips as if he was considering asking more but was holding himself back. After a moment, he pulled away, settling back in his seat across from me.

Sage at least pretended to be a devoted attendee of her princess as she hurried over, but I waved her off. "I'm all right."

Quiet settled over us again, and I turned to my window, finding it was fully dark outside. A thick blanket of clouds provided an ominous setting that shrouded the world in blackness and reminded me of the watching, grasping shadows of my dream.

"We've arrived," Junseo announced, sitting up straighter. He opened the window, just a little, allowing the cool night air to sweep in, offering a refreshing breath after hours of stale air within the carriage.

I blinked and peered deeper into the night, my mortal eyes struggling to discern what the fae could see much more easily. The grounds were stunning, even in the nighttime. Acres of blossoming cherry trees extended as far as I could see in the dimness. As we swept past the glistening river, coursing calmly in the moonlight, I inhaled its scent, wet and earthy and mixing delightfully with the sweetness of the blossoms fluttering on the breeze. Willows dipped their boughs into the water, appearing like graceful ladies reaching out to feel the current.

We rounded a bend in the road and I caught my first glimpse of the palace gardens, perfectly tended with endless rows of flowers in every color imaginable and countless fountains and decorative ponds. Then I saw the palace buildings themselves: extravagant, sprawling structures of carved stone, with stunning towers and pinnacles, arched windows, and filigreed gates opening onto pristine courtyards.

"It's beautiful," I breathed, before I remembered that I was supposed to be a princess myself. But the Emberglade castle had been built for practicality, its square architecture focused on function and protection rather than beauty and warmth. The Willowbark palace was a more inviting space, welcoming others as if longing to host visitors, parties, and feasts.

And yet, I knew that I couldn't let my guard down and become complacent. The fae world was as dangerous as it was beautiful, and I could never forget that, even in the company of one of the kindest men I'd ever met, mortal or immortal.

Without meaning to, I let my eyes stray toward the captain, drinking in the way his face lit up with joy and pride at my pronouncement. It was clear he loved his home.

As we entered the gate, guards saluted and Junseo saluted back. Servants rushed from within the palace to greet us in the courtyard, lining up respectfully to watch our procession. I studied their faces, and my stomach dipped, noting that some of them were humans with vacant expressions and dark circles under their eyes.

Lifting my shoulders, I drew a deep breath and prepared to embrace my looming future.

CHAPTER SIXTEEN
NOW

Another dead end.

I'd lost all sense of time as I'd attempted to find my way back to my rooms. The manor was playing tricks on me, shifting rooms and twisting passages. I'd walk down a familiar hall, counting my steps and making note of the paintings and other décor I recognized, only to find myself suddenly facing a blank wall and forced to turn back. Even the guards I'd passed refused to offer me any help, merely blinking at me when I'd tried to approach one. I hadn't recognized any from my time in Willowbark previously—and even if I had, none would have known me in my human form. As far as servants went, the manor seemed empty.

At last, I caught sight of Callista's and my door, my weary eyes drinking in the carved cherry blossoms and winding river in relief. Silence and darkness greeted me as the door swung silently inward. My stomach sank; I'd half-hoped that Callista had made it back to our quarters during my wandering.

The servants hadn't yet lit a fire, and the room was drafty. I closed the door softly, but the darkness was smothering, and I instantly regretted it. I'd need the candlelight streaming in from the hall to find my way around and strike a match. Turning back, I tried the knob, but the door was locked.

My heart slammed against my ribs.

What was the manor doing now?

Shadows clung to me like a blanket, heavy and restricting. The hair at the back of my neck lifted as I turned toward the room again, scanning the blackness. I was certain I could hear the shadows *breathe*.

Scratch. Scratch. The sound was like claws scraping along wood floorboards. I stifled my breath, trying to be as silent as possible.

My mind raced through different options, going over every creature I'd learned of or faced in the fae world already.

Red eyes appeared in the darkness, boring into mine. I couldn't move, couldn't breathe.

Don't let fear rule you, I chided myself.

I had no weapons, but my eyes were at last beginning to adjust. A sliver of light pierced through the curtains across the room, a glimpse of moonlight.

I blinked and the fireplace came into focus, a poker resting on its hearth.

Scrape.

The thing in the room with me was moving closer, its blood-red eyes growing larger, brighter.

Calling upon every hour of training I'd received, praying my body remembered them a year later, I sprang for the poker. The creature was unnaturally fast, springing toward me in an instant. I barely had time to seize the poker and swing.

As I turned, I met its gaze and caught my first solid glimpse of the creature. It looked more like a fae than I'd first thought, though its eyes were that awful red and fangs protruded from its mouth. Its fingers ended in long, claw-like nails, and its bare feet had similar claws that scraped along the floor when it moved.

Blood dribbled from its chin.

Heart in my throat, I stopped myself right before swinging the poker, my gaze snagging on its eyes. They were unfocused and cloudy, like swirling white clouds covering a red sky.

The creature wasn't looking at me.

I hurled the poker across the room, and just as I'd hoped, it tilted its head and charged toward the noise.

Holding my breath, I crept along the floor as softly as I could, praying its hearing wasn't keen enough to detect the sound of my racing heartbeat.

Could I pick a lock in the dark? I plucked a pin from my hair, silently blessing Wisteria for insisting on styling it for tonight's dinner.

But when I reached the door and once again tested the knob, it was unlocked.

Relief and nerves fluttered like butterflies in my stomach, making me feel ill. Cold sweat snaked down my spine.

I wasn't sure I could trust the door and where it led, now that the manor was allowing me to open it again. But I had no other option to get out of this room, away from the prowling monster.

Casting furtive glances over my shoulder at the creature's shadowy form while it paced the area where the poker had fallen, I pulled at the door. The hall outside was the same one I'd left earlier, bathed in gentle, flickering warmth. Empty. Welcome.

My freedom—or so I hoped. How many more of these creatures stalked the manor?

Was Callista safe?

My thoughts whirled, but I forced myself to quiet them, focusing on my first step: surviving this encounter.

As I cracked the door just enough to slip through, the previously silent hinges let out a creak. My breath snagged in my throat. Was *that* the manor's cruel trick?

Behind me, the monster snarled.

Forsaking all stealth, I flung myself into the hall, slamming the door behind me.

The sounds of its pursuit were right behind me as the door swung wide. Footsteps pounded after mine. The creature's hungry cry—high-pitched and unearthly, unlike any sound I'd ever heard human or fae make—rang off the walls.

Ahead, a door swung open and Verity peered out in alarm. She was barefoot, her hair a tousled curtain down her back, as if she'd been awoken from a restless sleep. "What is happen—"

"Go back!" I shouted. "Lock your door!"

At my commotion, a guard strung an arrow to his bow and shot. He struck true, but the creature didn't even slow, didn't even seem hurt, too caught up in its bloodlust now that it had heard Verity speaking.

She tried and failed to stifle her cry as she reached for her doorknob, but it was too late. Leaping with horrifying speed, the monster snatched

Verity in its hands, long nails piercing into her flesh. Then it dipped its fangs toward her throat and *tore*.

I clamped my hand over my mouth to stifle my scream. I turned toward the first item I could find, a heavy candlestick in a holder on the wall, and wrenched it free. Slamming it against the creature's head with all my strength, I tried to ignore the sight of ripped flesh and blood streaming from Verity's neck. But the creature was undeterred, lost in a feeding frenzy, and swiped at me, drawing a vicious line of scratches along my arm. Reeling back, I scarcely noticed the flash of pain or my blood dripping onto the floor.

Verity was already limp, her eyes glazed and unfocused.

There was nothing left to do for her. Even the guard, who'd been joined by a handful of others, seemed to recognize that. He'd focused his attention instead on releasing more arrows, trying to stop the creature.

I didn't want to wait to see if the guards succeeded. I had to find Callista before she and I met the same fate as Verity. Racing onward, I sought a staircase that would take me to the great hall.

Ahead, the hallway twisted in an unnatural curve, as if the manor was once again bending, playing tricks on me. Moonlight cast long, strange shadows along the walls. Screams behind me made my breath catch—the guards were losing the battle against that strange monster.

And I had no idea where I was. No clue how to find Callista. Nothing here was familiar.

How could I find my way if the way always changed? What strategy was there against madness and magic like this?

Muted footsteps on the carpet alerted me that the creature was pursuing me once more. Throat burning, I clutched the candlestick more tightly. Ahead and to the left, a staircase loomed, leading upward into darkness, but the hallway continued to the right. I flung the candlestick as hard as I could onto the hardwood steps, listening to it clatter.

The creature veered left as I went right. Not wanting to linger in the hall, I approached the first door I found. The knob turned easily, and thankfully, these hinges remained silent.

Every muscle taut, prepared to flee or defend, I crept inside, finding myself in a quiet room, but thankfully, with no sign of another awful creature lurking in its shadows. Cautiously, I shut the door behind me.

Embers burned low in the hearth, leaving the space dim. Moonlight spilled through a gap in the curtains, illuminating the large bed in the center and the form within—the one that I'd awoken with my intrusion.

Prince Kaede.

CHAPTER SEVENTEEN

THEN

A handful of servants escorted my maids and me into the palace. The entrance through the carved double doors was as grand as I'd expected, with glistening starlight tracing patterns on the marble floor as it danced through the panes of the tall arched windows.

"Come with me, Your Highness," said a fae servant. When his mouth opened in a not-so-friendly grin, sharp teeth flashed in the night. He led me swiftly down a fine hallway, where more arched windows lined both walls and offered glimpses of beautiful courtyards and gardens. Windows must have been left open somewhere nearby, allowing a draft of cool air to whisper toward me, fragrant and alluring.

In sharp contrast to the beauty of the grounds and the extravagance of the polished marble floors were the paintings of stern-faced fae and vacant-eyed humans adorning the spaces between each window. A shiver coursed down my spine when I glanced up into the blank gaze of a woman who might have been close to my age when her likeness had been painted. She stood beside a fae with horns protruding from his long chestnut hair and fangs glinting in his mouth. My stomach dipped with foreboding. How many women had been lured into this kingdom either through glamour like this one, unbeknownst to her, or through trickster bargains and deceptive promises? Or like me—forced into a task I did not want to complete because the alternative was unthinkable?

The servant led my maids and me through numerous halls, up winding staircases, and past vast rooms full of humans scrubbing, dusting, and otherwise tending to the palace in the middle of the night. Each glimpse of the mortals performing such drudgery in the hours when the fae could avoid seeing them made my stomach clench with horror and disgust. The humans' clothing was ragged; their figures gaunt. It was a constant reminder that the Willowbark king was as awful as King Wystan. If I failed in my mission, my family wouldn't be the only ones to pay dearly. I could only imagine the sort of retribution that Willowbark would eke out against a would-be assassin.

At last, the servant paused before a white door ornately painted with depictions of a swirling river lined with willows. "Your room, Your Highness." He swept the door open, bowed, and departed before I could even enter.

A handful of maids awaited beside a roaring fire, despite the fact that I was already surrounded by my own. Immediately overwhelmed, I scarcely had time to take in the four-poster bed draped in the finest bed linens, the painted ceiling, the arched windows leading to a balcony overlooking the Willow, or the wardrobe open and already filled to almost overflowing with clothes.

"Your Highness." The foremost maid, with hair as green as the grass outside and eyes a bright shade of pink, dipped into a low curtsey. "We have food awaiting you and will prepare you a bath so you can rest from your journey."

I cleared my throat, lifting my chin and mustering my best commanding tone. "I brought my own maids and won't be needing your services."

The slightest scrunch of her brow was the only indication of the maid's displeasure. "Very well. But if you need anything..."

"Of course. I will send one of my maids to fetch help." I had no desire to deal with any more unknown fae than necessary. It was troublesome enough having to endure the Emberglade trio, knowing they hated me and were spying for their king.

The Willowbark maids filed out the door, allowing my maids and me to enter my new quarters, when a thought struck me. I glanced over my shoulder. "Will I meet the prince tomorrow?"

The green-haired maid's brows rose in surprise. "Were you not informed? It is tradition for Willowbark royalty and their spouses to not see one another until the wedding ceremony is complete." She blinked with feigned innocence. "In the marriage chambers, on the wedding night."

Though I wasn't surprised, my heart lurched at having my fear confirmed. I wouldn't have an opportunity to move against Prince Kaede until we were alone together after our wedding. Certainly, it would be a vulnerable time for him, and easier when we were alone, but it would force me to go through with vows before the gods, ones I would have to break. Light-headed, I plastered a disinterested expression on my face and nodded.

"Sleep well tonight," the maid added before she left. "Queen Ara has requested that you take breakfast with her and Princess Laila in the queen's quarters tomorrow. We will fetch you at the ninth hour, so be ready."

Ellery shut the door behind them.

I wandered to the washroom and soaked in the tub, dreading meeting more fae I'd betray. My maids prattled on about royal etiquette and other needless reminders as they helped me bathe, dressed me in my nightgown, and brushed and plaited my hair for bed.

As I settled into the expansive bed, they unpacked my trunks and filled my wardrobe even further. I drank down my vial of potion in a quick swallow, noting that the stash was dwindling. Now that I was in Willowbark, I was expected to strike soon.

"I trust your journey was pleasant?" Queen Ara's expression held such hope in it that I forced a smile and a nod, not wanting to divulge the stories of the goblin or water wraith attacks. She was the picture of serenity and poise as she sipped her tea, her raven-dark hair falling in a sleek curtain down her back.

At her side, Princess Laila stirred sugar into her tea as she stared out the window at the golden spring day. Her ivory complexion was dusted with a smattering of freckles. While her features and rich dark hair resembled her mother's, her eyes were a more muted shade of soft brown.

The breakfast room in the queen's quarters was intimate and bright, full of windows that offered views of the cherry tree orchard and the expansive gardens. Outside, a small brook ran into a pond full of darting fish. Such tranquility and beauty were a stark contrast to the heavy, staining guilt I carried, and it made everything taste like ash in my mouth as I exchanged pleasantries.

It was clear the princess, Kaede's younger sister, found the whole situation uncomfortable and didn't trust me. Meanwhile, the queen was graceful and kind, watching me as if she dared believe her son and I could one day be a love match. My stomach cramped with every piece of meaningless conversation we exchanged, every polite bite of food, every forced smile and laugh.

I'm here to murder your son and break your heart, I thought bitterly.

"The wedding is to take place tomorrow," Queen Ara continued after asking about the suitability of my quarters, how well I'd slept, and commenting on how lovely the weather would be as I began to settle into my new home. "I thought, given you've had little choice in all this, you would perhaps like to choose from a few different wedding gowns we had prepared for you?"

I blinked in surprise. Princess Briar had mentioned sending my measurements to Willowbark ahead of time, but I hadn't given much thought to it. It mattered little when the wedding was a farce.

Now, I tried to swallow the lump in my throat, hoping my emotional response looked like appreciation for the queen's thoughtfulness rather than regret.

Once we wrapped up our meal, Princess Laila made her excuses.

"She's a shy girl," Queen Ara murmured as she led me toward her adjoining lounge, where an array of dress forms had been wheeled in, each displaying a stunning gown. Since it wasn't customary for fae to wear white for their weddings, the room was full of a rainbow of color. Everything was stunning, in vibrant shades of cherry-blossom-pink, Willowbark green and gold, and blues that matched the hues of the river.

I sucked in a breath, trying not to be overcome as I scanned each dress, forcing myself to run my fingers over the fabric and study each one as if the choice mattered. At last, after murmuring my gratitude, I chose the one I deemed most practical, without a flowing train to slow my steps or a bodice so tight it hindered movement. The fabric felt light and airy, made of a pale purple overlaid with sheer gold tulle.

Queen Ara presented me with a mask that matched the dress. "For the ceremony," she explained, "as it is tradition for neither of you to see one another until afterward."

I stared at the gold and purple mask, one that would cover my entire face but for my eyes. A shimmering ribbon dangled from the back.

In a way, it was a relief to know I wouldn't have to even see much of Prince Kaede during the wedding itself. I could continue to focus on my task rather than think of him as an actual soul with emotions and dreams and fears. Just a mission. Just a way to keep my family alive.

"Thank you so much for your thoughtfulness," I repeated for perhaps the third time, before politely making my excuses and retreating to the solace of my empty rooms.

CHAPTER EIGHTEEN

Now

His dark hair was tousled, edged in silver from the moonlight. Though he'd been startled awake, his eyes were already sharp and alert, taking me in as he threw back the bedcovers.

Despite my fear, embarrassment sent warmth through me when Kaede rose and revealed he was shirtless, his muscled form highlighted by the glow from the window.

"Come to murder me again?" His eyes were dark, his brows drawn.

I struggled to catch my breath, ears still straining to listen for the creature out in the hall.

Before I could say a word, Kaede's hands moved and a gust of wind shoved me—hard. One instant I was standing near the door, and the next I was weightless, stomach in my throat as Kaede's magic sent me soaring through the air and dropped me onto his bed. I lay sprawled on my back, my dress tangled around my legs and my breath trapped somewhere in my lungs as the prince launched forward, pressing his hands into the mattress on either side of my head, his piercing eyes burrowing into mine.

I tried to move and found that I couldn't. Kaede's air magic rested heavily around my wrists, ankles, and even my neck, holding me in place as surely as any chains or rope could have. It felt heavy yet warm, almost as if Kaede himself held me in each of those places, his fingers firm but still gentle.

Wind whispered through the room, rifling through the loose strands of my hair, a chill kiss against my skin that contrasted with the air holding me in place.

I was trapped without Kaede laying a finger on me.

"It *is* you, isn't it?" Kaede's sharp jaw was tight, a muscle jumping in it as his eyes traced my face, as if memorizing every feature. Taking in the true appearance of the woman he'd fallen for and been betrayed by. "Aurelia Sinclair, the assassin who pretended to be Princess Briar Emberglade, who pretended to be merciful and kind. Who seduced me as cleverly as any smooth-talking charmer, all through your quiet gentleness, your seeming innocence." He spat the words, and my cheeks burned with shame, even if gaining his affection had never been my intention. "Who convinced me to lower my defenses and then murdered me."

"I—" I was faint, at a loss for words, full of guilt and fear. Was it better to confess and beg forgiveness that I did not deserve, or to remain silent? "I'm so sorry. King Wystan would have killed my family." My eyes burned with unshed tears.

Kaede closed the difference between us until I was caged between his arms. His breath caressed my cheek. "You could have told me. You could have stopped lying. Why didn't you trust me enough to confide in me, *princess*?" This time, he said the title with a hint of mockery in his tone. "Why didn't you care for me enough to reveal who you truly were? Or was everything pretend—a lie?"

"No," I insisted, my voice cracking. "It wasn't a lie. I—I cared for you. It was just that...my maids were his spies, waiting to send word to King Wystan. Hoping I would fail so they could delight in the face that he'd order my family to be murdered."

"And I would have protected you and your family against them all. Did you honestly doubt that?"

I squeezed my eyes shut, shaking my head. I had no response. "I'd just met you. It was you or my family. How could I risk it? How could I be sure you'd care for me if I'd revealed that I was a human who'd lied to you all along?" *Do you know how I've hated myself?* I thought, but I didn't say it aloud. There was no excuse, no apology that would ever be sufficient for what I'd done.

"And so, you doubted me. You were persuaded by my enemy to let fear win. To let *him* win." When I forced my eyes open, Kaede's gaze was unrelenting. It raked over me, making me feel more vulnerable than I ever had in my life. "*Your* choice made me into this. I'm not the same—I'm a monster. Ever since I returned from the land of the dead, my magic has been all wrong. I've become the prince with the magic that *kills*. The one whose nightmares enter the world and drain the life from innocents. You are the one who started a war that killed my men and women. My friends. My people." His voice shook with emotion. "You are the one I trusted, the one who let yourself be persuaded to act out of fear rather than use the rational mind you pride yourself in."

"Are you to have your revenge now?" I whispered. He was so close, his magic still holding me in place.

Despite his anger, I knew in my bones that the merciful man I'd fallen for was still there somewhere. If it hadn't been, he would have killed me already. His magic could have ripped the air from my lungs, crushed my windpipe, dashed me against the wall, or dropped me from a deadly height.

Kaede's breathing turned ragged. "I can't interfere with the competition, and hurting a competitor would break that vow." His face dipped closer until our foreheads nearly touched. For a wild moment, his eyes dipped to my mouth before snapping back to mine. "Tell me, my lying bride, did you come here to finish the job and kill me for good this time?"

My heart fluttered. "No. This I promise you: I would rather plunge a blade through my own heart than ever hurt you again."

A long moment passed, like the prince was drinking in my words, weighing their sincerity. Whatever he saw in my expression, he didn't question it, but the coldness in his eyes didn't vanish either.

He pulled away abruptly, his magic releasing me as swiftly as it had taken hold of me. I sat up, hurriedly tugging down the hem of my dress.

"What happened to you?" Kaede asked brusquely, his gaze darting to my scratched arm, dripping blood onto his bedclothes.

I shook my head to clear it. "A creature attacked me—and it *killed* Verity. I think it may have killed some of your guards too. Is it part of the next challenge?"

Something passed across his face, there and gone in an instant. "The next challenge has not yet begun." His eyes flicked again toward my arm. "You were attacked by a vampire?"

"Is that what they're called? Creatures with poor sight yet keen hearing, who tear open the flesh and drink the blood of their victims?" My voice shook on the words, the memory of the gruesome way Verity had died filling my mind. "If it's not part of the competition, then why is it here?"

His voice dipped lower, his expression unreadable. "My nightmares. A ruination of my magic. Something that happened when I died and my power connected to healing was polluted. Ever since I wandered the world as a spirit...it is as if I've brought something back with me. Or perhaps it's more accurate to say I continue to bring many somethings. I don't know if they are other restless spirits, summoned by my magic and corrupted by whatever is wrong with me, or if they're something else, such as creatures from the underworld. But they are hungry for more death."

My throat tightened, but before either of us could say another word, Kaede straightened. "I have to stop it."

As he strode for the door, he didn't seem to notice or care what I did, so I trailed him into the hall. Without his nearness or the warmth of his magic caressing my skin, the manor felt cold. Everything was eerily quiet, but I knew better than to think the vampire had miraculously vanished.

As if he knew exactly where the vampire was located—and perhaps he did, considering he'd somehow summoned it or magicked it into being—Kaede walked toward the stairs, following them into shadow. Warily, I crept after him, not wanting to be left behind in this strange manor.

Scratch. The familiar sound on the steps above made my skin crawl. A murky shape stood hunched on a landing, turning at the sound of Kaede's approach. Hateful red eyes glared in our direction.

Then I took my next step, and the stair creaked under my foot. I cringed as the creature tilted its head and then lurched forward.

Kaede threw his arm between the advancing vampire and myself. A gust of wind slammed into it, throwing it into the wall. A twist of Kaede's wrist left it choking, clawing at its own throat.

My mouth dried when I considered that it could have been me in the vampire's place, facing Kaede's wrath. When the creature finally stilled, the prince whirled on me. "You said it attacked others?"

The memory replayed in my mind on an endless cycle, squeezing the air from my lungs. "V-Verity," I choked out. "It killed her. And your guards tried to stop it, but I heard screams and then it was chasing me again, so..." I drew in a shaking breath. "I do not know how many survived."

Cursing under his breath, Kaede shook his head. "I'll have some servants retrieve Verity's body and ensure she's sent home to her family for a proper burial. You must go directly back to my rooms and wait there. I have to check on the guards."

My chest ached, the fresh horror of what had happened washing over me at the same time I experienced a strange sense of relief to hear Kaede's kindness in action once more. He wasn't lost, not as he seemed to believe he was. There was goodness in him yet.

"What about my sister?" I asked, pausing Kaede in his tracks. "She wasn't in our rooms when I returned, so I thought she was still with you." My throat was dry as I imagined her facing the same fate as Verity.

Kaede turned, brow furrowed. "Bentley and Florian joined us at the end, keeping Callista and Laura entertained when I felt the need to retire early. I returned to my room to sleep while they chose to stay up and play a card game." Noting the flash of fear on my face, he added, "She's safe. No other vampires are roaming the manor. I can sense them."

I let my shoulders dropped, the relief washing over me all at once making me conscious of how exhausted I was.

"Hurry. Return to my rooms."

He strode past me, back down the stairs, waving at me to follow. My legs trembled from a combination of the terrors I'd just witnessed and my new anxiety over being in Kaede's presence. He led me back to his quarters, locking the door behind me and leaving me for what felt like endlessly long moments.

I paced the room, listening, worrying. Had Kaede left me here for my safety, or was I his prisoner? *He can't interfere with the challenges. He can't hurt you,* I reassured myself.

As time passed, I became aware of the pain lancing through my arm. I'd forgotten the vampire had clawed me. I examined my torn sleeve and the bloody scratches beneath it. The marks appeared superficial, thankfully, but they still bled enough to leave droplets on Kaede's fine carpet.

Just as I turned my steps toward his adjoining washroom, the lock turned and the door swung inward.

Kaede's expression was grim, his jaw tight, but his eyes immediately dropped to my injured arm and the trail of blood I'd left on his floor.

"You're still bleeding. Follow me." Once again, he bolted the door before moving toward the washroom.

Full of trepidation, I hesitated, almost as afraid of Kaede as I'd been of the vampire. "I thought you could not interfere with the challenges. Wouldn't tending to a competitor be interference?"

"Conjuring a vampire that attacked you would also qualify as interfering. Since that has already happened, I must attempt to set you back on equal footing with the other competitors."

"Did...any of the guards survive?" I asked hesitantly as I trailed him into the washroom.

Kaede's stony silence was answer enough, and I swallowed.

Watching him move about the space, opening cabinets and brushing strands of stubborn hair back from his forehead, I longed to comfort him. Instead, I let my mind wander, trying to distract myself from the tension between us. Earlier, though it had been fraught with anger and pain, it had also burned with countless unspoken desires and feelings. As if he still cared for me on some level despite what I'd done, and still found me beautiful, even though I no longer wore Briar's perfect face. It made me remember the closeness we'd once shared. But that tension was gone now, replaced with a terrible aloofness that chilled me to my core.

So I tried to think of other things—anything but the vampire or Kaede's anger or my guilt. Did Kaede often sleep at Willow Manor? Did he prefer to stay here? Or was he only here for the competition? I wished I could speak to him freely, but I kept my questions to myself.

I ached, but this aloofness was what I deserved, after all. If I were in Kaede's place, would I be able to forgive someone who'd killed me? Someone who had been the catalyst for a war between my kingdom and another, someone who'd altered the way my magic operated—who'd changed who I was?

Silently, Kaede finished gathering supplies, led me back into his room, and then gestured for me to sit on the bed. He handed me a basin of water and a cloth to clean my wounds myself, but he applied a salve, dabbing it on with a cotton pad. Then he lifted a roll of bandages and set to work wrapping my forearm, every brush of his fingers against my skin gentle. They were a sharp contrast to his furrowed brow and the fire in his eyes.

Even as he worked, leaning over me closely, he avoided meeting my gaze. I didn't want to stare at his bare chest, so I averted my eyes to the floor, toeing the carpet with my bare foot as I waited for Kaede to tie off the bandage.

A knock on the door shattered the quiet that cloaked us.

"Your Highness?"

"Yes?" Kaede called gruffly.

The door opened a sliver and a nobleman peeked in, his eyes drinking in the sight of a shirtless Kaede leaning over me like he was witnessing a delicious piece of gossip playing out before his eyes.

"Ah, there she is. We were about to send out hunters for our missing contestant. The next test is about to begin." His gaze pinned me the way a cat's stare would consume a mouse. "I hope you are not growing too fond of taking this one to bed already, considering anything could happen tonight."

A muscle jumped in Kaede's jaw, but he didn't bother contradicting the noble or correcting him for his brashness.

I wasn't sure how I felt about that. In the human world, I would have been mortified at the accusation toward my character, but here, the fae did not care about such things. Being seen alone with a man was hardly worth discussing—unless that man was the crown prince, it seemed. If the nobles thought Kaede favored me, would that help or hinder my own survival? Would they find it within themselves to respect me, or would they hate me?

Kaede glanced down at me, his expression unreadable. "It seems this is where we part ways, princess."

I blinked at him, finding myself once again at a loss for words as I stood, my thoughts whirling in an attempt to decipher his feelings and intentions. There had been no inflection of bitterness or mockery in his tone this time, leaving me confused at his use of the false title. But there had been no warmth in his look either.

I repressed a shiver at the memory of our earlier proximity and the way his air magic had caressed my skin. And then I followed the noble out of Kaede's rooms.

CHAPTER NINETEEN

THEN

Hours of wandering the palace and its grounds, familiarizing myself with its layout, the servants' routes, and the less-trafficked hallways and staircases brought me to the far reaches of the gardens. Guards had trailed me at a respectful distance the entire time, but no one had questioned my desire to explore my new home.

The part of me that made absolutely no sense kept searching the faces of guards for Junseo, as if seeing the captain again would do anything but pain me further. He was likely onto more important tasks, such as watching over the crown prince.

And it was the crown prince who I was hoping to see—or rather, whose location I was hoping to pinpoint. Since I wasn't to meet with him until after the wedding, I had to satisfy myself with observing and listening, trying to pick up scraps of conversation that would help me determine his usual schedule and haunts. A few comments from the queen had made it clear that Prince Kaede was regularly summoned to his father's sickbed for breakfast, and apparently, given a list of tasks to complete for the day in the king's stead. There were daily council meetings held in a lower chamber of the palace that often lasted until luncheon. I wasn't sure where the prince took that meal. And afterward...well, the afterward was what I was trying to uncover. It sounded, from what Junseo had said, that free time was rare for the prince. I was beginning to think he'd left for some other mysterious meeting, or he'd slipped away for a moment of solitude.

The scent of cherry blossoms was heavy in the air as I strolled toward the orchard, admiring the petals caught on the breeze. Today, the weather was warmer than it had been on our journey, full of golden sunshine so rich and shimmering, it felt as if I were bathing in it. For a moment, I paused and closed my eyes, relishing the birdsong and the stillness. I wished, futilely, that I could live in this moment, capture this fleeting instant of peace before everything changed.

A voice cut into my musings. "You'll have to turn back, I'm afraid."

It was Lavender, leaning against a nearby trunk and shaking her head. Nearby, Flint strolled from among some other trees, plucking a flower and twirling it between his fingers. I was surprised by the rush of comfort I felt upon seeing their familiar faces.

They're not your friends, my inner voice admonished.

"I'm sure your prince will be happy to take you for a walk through the orchard after the wedding." Flint's smile was playful, as usual.

Perking up, I scanned the trees.

Flint tossed the flower to the ground with a chuckle and pointed a finger at me. "Ah, no stealing a peek," he scolded playfully.

"So he's here?" I tried to fight the urge to ask, but the words fell from my lips unbidden. "What about the captain?"

Lavender grinned and rolled her eyes, pushing off the tree with her foot. "Oh, the captain is always with the prince. Come along, let's get you out of the orchard before you run into trouble when you've only just arrived. You don't want to make your new family cross with you for ruining their precious royal tradition."

New family. The words made my mouth taste sour with revulsion, but I focused on the information I needed. "Does Prince Kaede walk here often?"

"As often as he can get away," Flint said, joining Lavender in escorting me out from among the trees and back toward the gardens. "That or he's out riding, or practicing with his magic in the open hills between the palace and the city proper. Always afraid he'll hurt someone by accident if he's conjuring a whirlwind or summoning something through the air."

I allowed myself to be escorted back to my rooms, where the rest of the day passed in a haze of planning and agonizing over what I needed to do.

"I wonder who in your family will be first to die, and who will be forced to watch," Daisy mused as she raked a comb through my hair and pulled it back into a severe knot for dinner that evening.

Staring mutely in the mirror, I watched her with forced calm, refusing to rise to her bait. She sneered back at me, clearly annoyed I hadn't dissolved into tears.

Dinner passed similarly to breakfast, for it was another shared meal. This time, I joined not only Queen Ara and Princess Laila, but also members of the council, including Ji, Chief Advisor of Willowbark.

"As part of our marriage alliance, King Edwin had to choose a member of my own court to join his council, and so Ji accompanied me to Willowbark," the queen said as she introduced him. He was a lanky man with a fierce goatee and a sharp grin. Though her expression remained placid, it became clear over the course of our meal that Ji and Queen Ara differed vastly. Clearly, if she'd had the option of selecting who would have accompanied her, it wouldn't have been him.

"We have a few new mortals to join the palace staff, Your Majesty," Ji began at one point during the meal, slicing into meat so rare, it filled his plate with blood. He licked some from his knife.

Queen Ara stiffened visibly, the smile freezing on her face.

"Normally I would not trouble you with such unimportant matters," the advisor continued, "but it seems that your son has been interfering..."

"Please, let us not discuss any troubling matters around Prince Kaede's bride the night before the wedding." Though her tone remained quiet, there was a firmness to it that brooked no dispute.

I forced myself to continue eating as if nothing had upset me, enduring more idle talk until at last it was acceptable to excuse myself for bed, claiming I wanted to rest well before the wedding.

Someone at the table giggled as I walked away. I didn't pause or turn around to see who it was as she raised her voice to make a crass remark about the wedding night.

As I slipped through the palace, breathing deeply and relishing the solitude, I forced all my misgivings away. Tomorrow, for good or ill, it would all end. I had the inklings of a plan, one that I could adapt as needed once I learned what Prince Kaede's expectations following the wedding actually were.

Lost in thought as I was when I neared my quarters, I almost missed who was approaching from the opposite end of the hall until we were only a few feet apart.

"Captain," I breathed, freezing.

Rather than his green and gold uniform, he was dressed in crisp black. He hesitated, his expression earnest, his eyes searching. For a moment, his lips parted, like he wanted to say something. Then he grinned and leaned against the wall, tilting his head to study me. "What are you wearing?"

"My maids thought I should look the part of a princess."

Junseo nearly snorted as his eyes raked over the glistening gown, heavy with lace and beading and intricate embroidery. It was the opposite of anything I felt comfortable in, and he and I both knew it. Still, his gaze lingered on the curve of my hip before flitting back to my face.

Heat rose to my cheeks. "You cannot look at me like that."

For once, Junseo seemed taken aback, pausing and sweeping a hand through his hair. "Right. I..." He cleared his throat.

My heart throbbed in my throat, leaving my chest hollow. I wished I could tell him who I really was, what I had been sent to do.

"Princess," Junseo began, his mouth settled into an uncertain frown, but I cut him off.

"I'm tired and need to return to my quarters," I blurted.

And without letting myself linger another moment, I darted into my room and shut the door. Leaning against it, I squeezed my burning eyes closed.

What a terrible goodbye, after all we'd shared and all I felt for him.

After tomorrow, he would hate me. I already hated myself, for how I'd fled him and for what I was about to do.

It felt a little like I was preparing to cut out a piece of my own soul.

CHAPTER TWENTY

Now

To my surprise, the noble led me all the way to the first floor of the manor and out a side doorway, into the grounds themselves. The air was a soft, warm embrace against my skin, the slightest breeze kissing my face. Above, the sky was blanketed in wispy clouds that half-concealed the moon, elongating the shadows and casting everything in a dim glow that was strangely ethereal and eerie all at once. While the welcoming scents of flowers and fresh grass were heavy in the air, bats chittered and darted through the sky, swooping after unseen insects and reminding me of the one that had intruded upon Callista's and my rooms—or the one, perhaps the same one, I'd seen near Kaede on more than one occasion now.

The night felt like the sort in which clandestine romantic meetings should happen—or in which murderous monsters lurked. I wondered how it could be beautiful and enticing, and chilling and ominous, all at once.

At the edge of this part of the gardens rose a maze, but unlike the manicured hedges on the rest of the grounds, these shrubs looked overgrown and wild. The path was narrow and uneven, and the branches of the bushes growing on either side arched in such a way as to nearly cover it, effectively blocking out most of the sky and its light.

The remaining contestants, along with Callista, waited at its start, murmuring nervously amongst themselves as they watched Ji and a handful of other fae. Most were clothed in their nightclothes and barefoot, while others appeared a little more put together in robes and shoes.

"Welcome," Ji said, his eager, uncanny smile adding to my growing apprehension. "Tonight, the first of you to exit the maze will be the winner of this test. Each of you will score based on the order in which you finish."

Laura frowned. "That seems too simple. A race through a maze? Surely there is some trick or mischief involved."

"I suppose whether there are dangers within the maze will be for you to discover, will it not?" Ji flashed a wide, unkind smile at her.

Then he clapped his hands together, and I pursed my lips. I was growing quite weary of this habit of his, especially as it always seemed to signal his sadistic glee. "I forgot to mention that anyone who does not exit the maze before dawn will...face consequences." His grin widened.

"Very well." Laura was the first to lift her chin and stride toward the maze's entrance, her curls bouncing loosely around her shoulders and her fists clenched at her sides. White-faced, Hattie trailed uneasily after her, loath to enter the maze but also clearly hesitant to be parted from her sister.

There was a breathless moment as those of us left behind watched and waited, listening as the sisters vanished out of sight, following a bend in the path and melting into the shadows. Insects chirred and a breeze rustled through the hedgerows, but there were no other sounds.

Straightening, I sought out Callista among the rest of the gathered women, grasped her hand, and silently urged her toward the entrance. Her fingers trembled in mine as we neared it. "What if we just...leave?" my sister whispered, hesitating just outside the maze. "We could slip away unnoticed. You know this land—you could find transportation for us to get back home."

I tightened my grasp on Callista's hand and shook my head. "Do you think they don't have ways of watching us, even within the maze? The fae will never let us simply leave. As you already know, the consequences would be devastating."

At that moment, Mary did exactly what Callista had been contemplating, though she didn't even attempt to make it a secret. Instead, she bolted from the group, away from the maze and through the gardens, making for the orchard and the rolling hills in the distance. Toward freedom.

Callista and I froze, mesmerized by the sight, Mary's nightdress billowing behind her, her golden hair haloed by the starlight.

Ji rolled his eyes, breaking away from the other fae and sighing as if he were terribly inconvenienced by Mary's desire to escape the terrors that Willowbark was subjecting her to. He lifted his arms and—just as he had so many times before—he clapped his hands together. But this time, the earth shook and split open before Mary. Horror spiked through my veins as a terrible shriek split through the air and she tumbled forward, collapsing into the hole. It shuddered again and closed up over her. Silence descended. Everything looked as it had before, without a sign of the chasm that had opened up in the earth only seconds before.

For a terrible moment, I couldn't breathe. And then, with a sharp look at Callista, my silent *I told you so*, I yanked on her arm, pulling her with me into the maze. Immediately, the shadows consumed us, as if they were living things creeping across our skin, obscuring our vision, and lending weight to the very air, making my every breath feel heavy.

The boughs hanging over our heads seemed too large and leafy to belong to mere hedges. Maybe there were whole trees hidden within the rows. There was a wildness to the space, the air damp and cool and the ground uneven and overgrown with weeds. Next to the beautiful gardens outside the maze, this felt like another world.

In the distance, frogs filled the night with their song, a gentle reminder that there were still lovely things in this world. But here, it seemed as if we were trapped in a waking nightmare. I couldn't stop seeing the vampire tearing into Verity's throat. Couldn't stop seeing Molly's head sliced clean off, or the earth swallow up Mary as she tried to flee.

There was no escape for us. A part of me was beginning to fear that the only survivor would be the one they chose as their winner.

And that meant I had to ensure that Callista won. I had to survive long enough to protect her, to help her make it, and then I'd have to accept my fate. For even if I did survive to the end of the competition—winner or not—I doubted Kaede would ever permit me to go home. He would announce who I was and order me to be punished. He would have his revenge.

My eyes burned. I wanted to wish for impossible things—to not only survive but to win. To convince Kaede that I was worth a second chance, even if sometimes I wasn't sure of that myself. I had betrayed him in the worst of ways, without ever even trying to confide in him, to give him a chance to help me out of my predicament.

I shook the thoughts away, forcing my mind to ground myself in this moment. I drank in the cool night air, heavy with the scent of damp earth and something sickly sweet, like the maze was rotting somewhere on the inside. The hedgerows themselves appeared green and thick, healthy and strong.

Though I knew Laura was within the maze, and surely others had entered by now, I could hear no signs of them. It was as if Callista and I were in here alone, the only sounds our own steps, our own breath.

Worst of all, I couldn't shake the sense that we were being watched.

I glanced over my shoulders repeatedly, searching the shadows, but there was no one around.

As Callista and I approached a spot where the way split into three paths, she shivered and clung to my hand. "Auri, do you hear that?"

"Hear what?" I strained to listen, but I could hear nothing unusual.

Callista sobbed. "Father!" she cried out, dropping my hand and tearing down the path furthest to the left.

"Wait! Callista!" I raced after her, sending stones skittering as I stumbled over the rugged path. Roots sprang up before me, though there didn't appear to be any trees nearby, and the shadows thickened. My toe struck one of them, tripping me, and I lost my balance, slamming into the earth. My forehead struck a rock, and I blinked against my pain and disorientation.

When I lifted my head, there was no sign or sound of my sister. The path lay empty, riddled with rocks and roots—or what I could see of it was. The darkness was like a living thing, its fingers searching, reaching. It devoured the path, choking out any bit of light streaming through the leafy canopy.

Murderer.

The unfamiliar voice whispered so close to my ear that I startled. Pushing to my feet, I whirled around, but I was alone. Unnerved, I searched the shadows to no avail. Drawing the blade from my boot, I hurried down the path, hoping Callista wasn't far ahead and trying to convince myself the dark and my own nerves were playing tricks on me.

But the further I ran, the harder it became to see. The darkness thickened and the path became overgrown. Extended branches reached for me like bony fingers, scratching against my skin and tugging at my hair and clothes. Rocks and roots and other undergrowth sprang up before me, and more than once I collided with a wall of greenery or a wide tree trunk, forcing me to turn and wander deeper into the maze. A maze that was clearly more than a simple path through hedgerows. It felt as if I were lost in a tangled wilderness. When I glanced toward the sky, seeking guidance based on the moon's position and the constellations I could spot, I found only shadows.

Chills raked over my skin. Unseen *things* scuttled through the hedges. I fisted the hilt of my knife until my fingers ached.

"Callista?"

Nothing.

By now, I could have taken a dozen wrong turns, traveling in a completely opposite direction from my sister. Panic threatened to overtake me, warring with my every instinct to puzzle my way out of this new challenge. Surely there was a solution, a way to avoid staggering through this place all night until dawn's light warned me it was too late and I faced whatever awful consequences the fae had for me.

With my sight obscured by the shadows, I focused on my other senses, hoping they could guide me. No new sounds emerged—no footsteps or rustling or anything that would indicate I wasn't alone or that Callista was nearby. But I could smell something different in the air: a dampness that made me think a pond or fountain was somewhere close, hidden in a section of the maze. I concentrated on the scent, winding my way along the increasingly difficult-to-navigate path. The further I went, the narrower it became. Branches scratched my cheeks and hands, stinging as they sliced open my skin.

And then, without warning, I stumbled into an open area. Mud squelched against my boots, and then I slipped, falling to my knees. My hands splashed into cold, still water, sinking to the elbows before I managed to pull myself up. Something cold and slimy brushed against my wrist. My heart lurched and I yanked my arms back, praying that a water wraith didn't lurk in whatever pool I'd stumbled upon.

Wet and trembling with cold, I staggered back and struggled to my feet. I scanned the area, relieved to find my eyes were adjusting to the dimness—or that there was more light in this space. Confusingly, though the light had increased and the boughs overhead had thinned, I couldn't catch a glimpse of the stars. It was as if the clouds had smothered the sky in a heavy blanket.

I frowned, trying to find something that would give me an indication of where I was. I thought, somewhere beneath the scents of water and mud and foliage, I detected a hint of cherry blossom. If I was near the orchard, then I was to the north of the manor. But did the maze end near the manor, or on the exact opposite end of the entrance, which had faced east?

My head whirled, frustration singing through every fiber of my being. How could the fae call this a challenge, a test to discern the character of their future queen, if they gave us no rules or guidelines? This was chaos. *Madness.*

As if they were merely throwing us into danger to sacrifice us, without care of the outcome.

A bloodcurdling scream rang through the maze, chilling me to the bone.

"Callista!" I shouted, to no avail. Where was she?

Another shriek. It didn't sound far ahead. I ran, heart throbbing in my ears, lungs burning, tears muddling my vision.

"Auri." The whimper was so pathetic, so awful, I choked back a sob.

Like a cloud slithering away to uncover the moon and stars, the shadows that had consumed the maze melted into nothing, moonlight flooding the earth. In seconds, I was able to tell based on the sky that I had been venturing northeastward, moving closer to the orchard as I'd suspected.

I took my surroundings in just as quickly. The pool glistened as it reflected the night sky, and the foliage around me appeared edged in silver. I was in what might have once been a courtyard of sorts, but the pool had overflowed onto the dirt, mud overtaking the open space. Across the way, a narrow opening in the hedge wall showed me where the maze continued eastward.

But all these facts faded into the background as my gaze snapped to a bleeding body lying in a heap on the ground.

"Callista?"

CHAPTER TWENTY-ONE

THEN

My gown whispered along the stone pathway through the gardens as I passed the fountain and approached the arch where my groom waited for me. Clothed in black trimmed in Willowbark green and gold with a matching mask, he cut a tall, imposing figure. Even his eyes were inscrutable, for he seemed to be deliberately avoiding my gaze, staring out over the gardens rather than looking toward me.

Almost unconsciously, my eyes swept over the few who'd gathered for the ceremony: the queen and princess, my maids, Ji and the other councilors, and some guards posted about the perimeter of the courtyard. Musicians tucked into spaces throughout the garden played a haunting tune, bittersweet rather than joyful, or perhaps it only sounded that way to my ears.

There was no sign of Captain Junseo, and I didn't know if I was relieved or pained to note that fact.

At last, I paused at the arch, where greenery and boughs of cherry blossoms blocked the evening sun, granting the prince and me a patch of shade.

Turning to face the prince, I found that he towered over me. My mouth dried. Who was this still, silent man I had to kill?

For a moment, I had the mad idea to turn and run. Then I repeated my sisters' names, grounding myself. Leaving wasn't a choice.

"Today, councilors, you bear witness to a much-hoped-for union between the kingdoms of Emberglade and Willowbark," Queen Ara announced.

I couldn't look at her and the hope etched across her face.

I stared at the ground.

If the prince wouldn't look at me, I would avoid his gaze, too.

The queen continued praising the wonders of the marriage that was about to seal the alliance, asking the gods for their blessings upon her son and me and upon the peoples of both kingdoms. Then, as she directed Prince Kaede and me to clasp hands, I forced myself not to startle at the gentleness in his touch. His hands were large, warm, and calloused as they cradled my fingers. Still, I didn't look up, choosing instead to stare at our joined hands.

The heat of my mask made it difficult to breathe. Sweat beaded on my forehead.

"Please make your vows."

This was the part that I'd been carefully instructed on, for fae weddings were not like mortal ones, where we recited traditional vows. Here, we were to come up with our own.

The prince's voice was muffled behind his mask. "Princess Briar of Emberglade, I take you as my bride and princess, to rule my kingdom at my side as my equal. I offer you my loyalty and my devotion. None other will lay claim to my heart, so long as we both live."

My lungs were heavy, the stale air in my mask growing stifling. What a hefty promise from a man whom I'd never even met. Did he truly believe he would fall for Princess Briar? Swallowing the bitter taste in my mouth, I began. "Prince Kaede of Willowbark, I take you as my husband and swear my faithfulness to you." My voice cracked, and I cringed inwardly. I hesitated, thinking of my task. Thinking of a different pair of gentle hands and a forbidden dance in the rain. "Please accept my hand as a demonstration of the peace between our kingdoms, and my vow to uphold the good of both."

Queen Ara closed the ceremony with more words, but I continued to feel disconnected from my body. The time was drawing nearer when I'd be alone with the prince, a time when he'd be most vulnerable. It would be my best chance to strike and then try to flee back to my family.

With each heavy beat of my heart, I shoved the horror further down into my body, letting numbness overtake me. I focused on facts, calculating what my moves would be. I had to keep a clear head.

I could not fail.

As the crowd dispersed to indulge in wine and other delicacies waiting back within the palace, my maids encircled me as my escort back to my rooms. These would be my final moments to collect myself and take my last dose of potion before I entered Prince Kaede's quarters and whatever awaited me there.

"Don't ruin this, or you know what happens," Sage said with a roll of her eyes as she watched me swallow down my final vial of potion. "You're already sweating abominably." She sniffed and lifted a cool cloth to my forehead, trying to wipe away the evidence of my humanity and fear.

"You'll give yourself away before you can strike," Ellery complained. "No *fae* princess would sweat like that. Or look afraid on her wedding night." She crinkled her nose.

I could scarcely concentrate on their talk. Panic had me in its claws, so I focused on the weight of the dagger in my hidden pocket. In my mind, I ran through my escape route, one I'd learned of during my time in Emberglade and ascertained still existed during my explorations yesterday. I closed my eyes and pictured Father, Lavinia, and Callista. Imagined myself finally walking through the doors of my home in Greybrooke. Of collapsing into bed, able to let the weight of my grief and guilt overtake me, but also able to finally feel like my family and I were *safe*. Free.

It was that feeling that held me together, letting me even out my breaths and clear my mind.

When they deemed me relaxed and clean enough, my maids escorted me to the prince's rooms. Daisy tossed one significant glance over her shoulder as they swept away, likely to sneak out of the palace before I struck and condemned us all.

For a moment, I hesitated outside the door with my hand lingering on the knob. I repeated my family's names like a mantra in my head, breathing in, out, in, out. Then, I allowed myself one more moment of hesitation, one brief fantasy of running away. Squeezing my eyes shut, I let it flutter behind my eyelids like a taunting butterfly, lovely and elusive, and then I counted to ten, dispelling the images.

I opened the door.

Everything was surprisingly bright and open, an inviting space lined with shelves overflowing with books, vases of dried flowers, and a thick, cream rug that was possibly more cushioned than my mattress at home. On the far side of the room, the glass doors leading to the balcony were cracked open. They permitted a breeze, heavy with the fragrances of the garden and the sounds of the ongoing wedding celebration.

And in front of those doors, silhouetted in the moonlight, was Prince Kaede, facing away. His view overlooked the gardens, but not the festivities, which were taking place deeper on the grounds. Leaning against the doorframe, he still held his mask loosely at his side, still wore his crisp black wedding outfit.

I approached on light feet, my eyes taking in the rest of the room: the canopied bed to the left, the curtains partially drawn as if to make it less foreboding for our first meeting. A door leading to the halls, another to a walk-in wardrobe, and a third to the adjoining washroom. The low-burning fire in the hearth, casting the bed and the rug spread before it in a warm, golden glow. A side table full of various bottles of wine and other libations, jewel-toned and lovely, along with a half-full wineglass and another, empty and waiting.

"I'm afraid I must beg your forgiveness, princess," came a familiar voice that made shivers ripple up my spine.

I nearly stumbled on my next step as he turned around, discarding the mask on the side table beside the wineglasses.

My stomach tightened; my head grew light. "Captain? Why are you..."

I trailed off, reading the regret and uncertainty in the furrows on Junseo's brow as he stood, not in his Willowbark guard uniform, but the clothes of Prince Kaede, the man I'd just married.

The man I had to kill.

"You..." Mouth dry, I tried to swallow, but my throat was tight, and it seemed the lump that had grown there was trapped.

"I'm sorry that I deceived you, but I wanted to meet you—feared that I was about to be trapped in a marriage with a cruel woman. As prince, I'm required to spend time serving as the captain of the guard, and my other given name is Junseo. Everything I shared with you was the truth, save for..."

"The most important truth that you withheld from me," I whispered, frozen in place, staring at the man whom, in only a few short days, I'd grown so close with, grown to understand so well. The man I'd...

I shook my head. Junseo—Prince Kaede—must have thought I was horrified by his deception, questioning if I knew him at all. But I understood his motivation for what he'd done. I understood, and I hated it, and suddenly all my resolve was shaken for one bone-chilling instant.

Callista. Father. Lavinia. I repeated their names, imagining the horrors that awaited them if I failed in my mission, if I failed them.

Prince Kaede strode toward me, clasping my hands in his warm, calloused ones, cradling them as he studied my face. Desperate. Pleading. "Can you forgive me, Briar?"

The name grated on my ears. He was looking at someone else's face. Using someone else's name.

It was a reminder, sharp and awful.

"I wanted to get to know you, and I couldn't reveal my identity because of my kingdom's tradition and my promise to my mother for my own safety's sake... I had to make my guards vow not to reveal my secret to you, just as I'd been forced to take my own vow. Thankfully, my promises weren't specific enough...they didn't prevent me from venturing out and meeting you as Captain Junseo, and so I went. Because I've been hidden within the palace for so long, there aren't many of my own people who would recognize me, though my guards also ensured I didn't show my face too often while we journeyed." His throat worked. "And it was worth it to have that time with you. Princess, you are unlike anything I expected. You are..." He hesitated, his depthless gaze searing me.

He reached to clasp my face in his hands, cradling it, studying me like he *cherished* me. My eyes burned, and I was sure I was undone. This would be it, the thing that ruined me forever.

"You are kind and gentle and thoughtful," he murmured. "Practical and smart." He laughed. "You give and you give...you are the opposite of everything I was told to expect, everything I feared. You are more than I hoped for—because you are a true friend, a true soulmate."

"Captain..." I caught myself. "Prince Kaede..."

"Please, I have to tell you." Tears glistened in his eyes. "Maybe it is madness. Maybe it is too soon. But I know you felt something too, and I hope, if you can forgive me, it can blossom into what I have known for a while now." For a moment, I thought he'd lean forward and brush his lips against mine, and the idea made my heart lurch, a sickening jolt of panic and pain. But he only leaned closer, letting the words caress my face. "I love you. I'm wholly yours. Not just for an alliance, or politics, but for..." He swallowed. "For a lifetime we could build together. A future. I..." He shook his head. "There are no words to fully describe it, nothing that can do justice to the way my soul is alight in your presence. The way your heart calls to mine."

I blinked, but it was too late. A tear escaped down my cheek, and before Kaede could brush his thumb to wipe it away, I tore myself free of his grasp. I shook my head, muttering something that was nonsensical, even to me.

"I expect nothing from you..." Prince Kaede was saying, his words barely making it past the ringing in my ears.

Father.

I didn't hesitate. Couldn't let another moment go by when this whirlwind of emotions and Kaede's achingly tender, loving gaze were threatening to sway my resolve. I drew the dagger hidden in the inner pocket of my dress, the one my maids had so carefully sewn into it the night before as part of the "final alterations" I'd convinced the queen were necessary.

I didn't meet his gaze, like the coward I was.

Lavinia.

"I'm sorry," I choked out.

Callista.

It was a clean stab to his chest, met with no resistance. He was too shocked to move, to fight.

Kaede released a strangled gasp at the same moment I lifted my chin, and our eyes met.

The moment stretched out, everything happening too swiftly and too slowly all at once.

I wrenched the blade back. It was too late to undo anything. The horror, the finality of it, seized me as blood streamed from the wound, coating my hand in slick, warm gore.

His mouth opened and he reached for me, as if even now, he couldn't believe I'd betrayed him.

Unshed tears stung my eyes. I was past the point of crying any more.

Past the point of feeling anything but a spreading numbness, overtaking my limbs until I wondered if I could run, could escape, or if all my hopeful plans to return to my family were for naught. Maybe it would be better to collapse beside him, to accept my fate.

"B-Briar?" His fingers brushed against a lock of my hair, threading through the strands. He coughed, and blood splattered his chin.

His expression hardened, pain tightening the lines of his face. "An assassin, all along," he huffed with a bitter laugh, collapsing onto the rug, weakness already consuming his body.

My eyes landed on the hand pressed to his chest, blood seeping between his fingers, and snagged on the signet ring he bore—one bearing the Willlowbark crest. One he hadn't worn as just the captain.

His chest heaved. Far too much blood soaked the front of his shirt, the rug under him... He couldn't speak, could scarcely breathe.

I reached for him, and he frowned, lifting his hand. A gust of wind shoved me away, knocking me to the floor so forcefully I lost my breath. Choking for air, I gaped at the ceiling. Kaede couldn't cry out to his guards, but the pain reminded me that I had to flee.

My escape was a frenzied blur of shadows and dancing torchlight as I rushed through the passage adjoining our rooms, twisting through the bowels of the palace. Somewhere along the way, I dropped the dagger, sick with disgust. In my own empty quarters, I scrubbed the blood from my hands and changed into the only nondescript outfit that had come with me from Emberglade: a dark pair of leggings, tunic, and hooded cloak to conceal my face.

Outside in the gardens, the party continued, Kaede's mother and sister and subjects celebrating as he died. Abandoning the heady aromas of wine and florals and food, the thrumming, wild music that pulsed in my bones and through my veins, I crept unnoticed off the palace grounds. No one stopped me when I exited the palace through the servants' gate, for no one had yet discovered Kaede.

Winding a lonely route through the countryside, sweat coated my back and tears wet my cheeks. My lungs burned with every step I took. Under a starry sky, with no one else to witness my pain, I at last allowed sobs to wrack my body, let myself give in to my grief.

Try as they might, the royal healers would be unable to save Prince Kaede from the wound I'd inflicted. I'd coated my blade with demon's breath, an Emberglade poison for which there was no known antidote.

I was a shell of myself, numb of all but a pressing need to find my family and ensure their safety, to reassure myself that King Wystan would keep his word.

There was nothing else left for me.

I'd left my heart in the palace with a dying prince.

CHAPTER TWENTY-TWO

Now

My sister's nightgown was slick with blood, crimson swiftly overtaking the white fabric. Her gaze was glazed over, her expression vacant, pained, and confused. Blood dribbled from her mouth.

"Callista!" My voice cracked and my hand shook as I dropped my blade, leaping forward to cradle my sister. Tears clogged my throat.

"Help!" The word sounded ragged and broken. There was no one to answer, no one to save her.

Callista's form was still in my arms, her last strangled breath leaving her on a sigh.

No! I was supposed to save you.

Horror and guilt screamed through me. I reached for Callista futilely, running fingers stained with her blood through her hair, begging her to stay, to come back. I spoke utter nonsense, trying to bargain with gods who were not listening, and with fae who, if they did hear me, did not care. "Please come back, Callista. Please."

"You'll always fail or lose those you love," someone whispered. I glanced over my shoulder, and though my vision was blurry with tears, I could tell no one was there.

I shuddered, a chill worse than the one that had afflicted me from the water wraith's magic wracking my body. It was soul-deep, wrought of crushing anguish and loss.

Collapsing in the mud beside my sister's body, I sobbed, pleading silently with the gods. Begging. Demanding. Surely this couldn't be how it all ended. I'd fought for my sister. I'd killed Kaede for her. I'd returned to Willowbark for her. She couldn't be dead now.

I can't do this, I thought. *There's no point in fighting now. I can't return home and tell Lavinia and Father that Callista isn't with me because...because...I failed.*

A noise broke through my thoughts. I lifted my head, wiping at my cheeks with the backs of my hands and squinting at the pool, certain I'd heard something disturbing the water. Nothing was there, making me wonder if my grief-addled brain was playing tricks on me. I lowered my gaze back to my sister and my bloodstained hands, hating myself all over again.

This isn't right.

It wasn't the situation, horrific and wrong, but something *off* about it all that pricked at my mind. I tried to dismiss it as my guilt attempting to justify what had happened, but the sense remained. I scanned my sister's form again, taking in her features. Her glazed eyes were open, staring at nothing. Her perfect dark hair lay in thick curls around her, soiled by the mud. I blinked, wondering if my teary eyes were distorting my vision.

No. Her nose wasn't right, just a little too wide. And her lips were slightly too thin. The color of her eyes was a shade too light.

Inhaling deeply despite the stench of blood tainting the air, I forced myself to focus. Just as before, I grounded myself in the present, soaking in the feel of the mud, the scent of the pool, the silver glow of the moonlight. I concentrated on what I believed was real—and then let myself assess what I'd thought was real.

Wild hope unfurled in my chest, growing stronger by the moment. *This isn't Callista.*

Somehow, the fae had glamoured me. Either this was all an illusion, or this was a body belonging to someone or something else, magicked to look like my sister. Whatever it was, Callista could yet be alive, wandering somewhere in this maze. There was still hope.

I rose, seizing my knife and wiping the mud and blood from my hands against my skirts. As soon as I did, the sky shifted again. The moon vanished and the darkness lightened to grey. My pulse raced in my ears. Had the fae also concealed the true sky, tricking me into thinking I had more time than I did?

I hated this. Hated that I couldn't reason myself out of a world that abided by such different rules, ones where magic could distort reality.

Without wasting another moment, I trudged through the mud, determined to make my way around the pond and find my way through the rest of the maze. But as my boots slid along the pond's edge, pushing toward the path on the opposite side, something cold and clammy rose from the water and coiled about my ankle. Nausea and fear were like a punch to my gut as I whirled, hesitating only long enough to see who my attacker was before I swung my knife.

The creature bore no resemblance to a fae, goblin, or other monster I'd encountered in Brytwilde before. It was something different, with the appearance of a man but with green skin, hair like seaweed, and webbed fingers. The creature had eyes that glowed an eerie shade of green in the dark, and its mouth opened like a maw, so large it seemed to consume its entire face. Within, countless rows of sharp teeth protruded in a terrifying circle.

I thrust my blade toward one of its eyes, but the creature was fast and strong, tugging on my ankle and yanking me to the ground. My strike missed. As the breath whooshed from my lungs, I kicked at the creature's face, struggling to dislodge its grasp.

A piercing pang lanced into my leg and I choked on a gasp, feeling blood bloom. With a growl, I pushed all my fear into my motions and lunged toward the creature, hoping to startle it. I nearly collapsed into the pond, but my attacker was unprepared for such an action and loosened its grip. It was just the opening I needed. Wrenching my leg free, I slammed the blade toward the creature's face. This time, the swing struck true, snuffing out one of the glowing eyes as suddenly as if I'd blown out a candle.

Without waiting, I whirled and ran—or did my best attempt at running. Pain throbbed up my leg, each step feeling like a steel splinter was being driven further into my flesh. I stumbled and hobbled, feeling blood drip, likely marking my trail. I nearly fell in the mud again. When I paused to catch my breath and rest my leg for a moment, I heard something slithering and breathing behind me. Glancing over my shoulder, I saw the one-eyed creature crawling after me, its webbed fingers slicing through the mud like it was swimming through water.

Stomach twisting, I pushed myself toward the path, praying that I could make it. Praying Callista was somewhere ahead—not behind—and I would find her before this creature could.

Above, the sky was lighter than ever, the first hint of gold kissing the easternmost clouds.

I stifled a groan. "Callista!" I called out, no longer worried about stealth. The water monster was already following me, swiftly gaining ground.

Sweat beaded on my brow as I lunged for the dirt path, half-trotting and half-hopping to give my wounded leg a rest.

"Callist—"

The water creature leapt, slamming into my back with a gurgle-like growl. Pain speared into my shoulder as it bit down, but I ignored it, clearing my mind to focus on my next move. I rolled so it was crushed to the ground beneath me, swinging my knife with my good arm to strike at its face. If I could blind it, gaining the upper hand would be far easier. As it was, the creature outmaneuvered me in both strength and speed, not to mention I had no idea what type of magic, if any, it possessed.

My strikes eventually connected with something solid, weakening the creature's grasp enough that I was able to launch myself back to my feet. Black blood leaked from the monster's face as it writhed on the ground, its webbed hands covering whatever wound I'd inflicted.

Lightheaded, I stumbled past the creature, desperate to find my sister and reach the end of the maze. Above the hedges, I thought I could make out the first rays of the rising sun, the sight sending a bolt of fear through my chest.

I rounded a bend and nearly tripped in my surprise when I found myself facing the courtiers. When I scanned their group, I found no sign of Callista or the other contestants.

Ji gestured toward the gold touching the eastern horizon. "It looks as if everyone else has failed."

"No." Kaede's deep voice boomed out as he strode from the maze, emerging from a different path to my right, closer to the manor. Wind whipped at my hair and fluttered his jacket loosely behind him as he approached, cradling a dirtied and bloodied form. Laura. Arms wrapped around Kaede's neck, she was conscious, but she lay still and her complexion was pale. Her golden curls spilled over his arm like a curtain, limp with sweat and dirt.

My concern for Laura's condition was alleviated somewhat when I couldn't discern any visible wounds, but, to my dismay, the feeling swiftly shifted to envy. A hollow ache spread through my chest the longer I watched them, his gentle hands cradling her waist and legs, her gaze upon him intent and full of awe.

"Your Highness." Ji forced a bow despite the scowl lining his features. "You are not to interfere."

"You forfeited the rules of this challenge, and therefore my vow has been nullified. You and Father deliberately sent these women into this maze as sacrifices for the uhgmil. That was never part of our agreement. We are to test their strengths as a potential ruler, not use them. For entertainment or anything else."

Ji quieted, clamping his mouth tightly shut and dipping into another bow. He appeared nearly as pale as Laura.

"Fetch healers for these women," Kaede ordered. "Check every one of them. Any still left in the maze will be hunted down. Those already in the manor will be treated for ailments down to the smallest of scratches."

As Kaede swept away, the nobility scurried to obey his wishes, calling for guards to search the maze for other survivors and for healers to be brought out. Swaying on my feet, I stumbled toward the nearest noble, one already racing toward me. Florian. "Please. My sister is in there."

Florian hesitated, a frown creasing his brow. I seized his arm, teetering on my feet. "You're losing blood," he protested. "I need to get you into the manor."

"Not without Callista!" I pleaded. "Please, I lost her and..." The world spun, and I paused to take a breath.

At that moment, a guard emerged from the maze, carrying Callista in her arms.

"Callista!" I cried, trying to turn and run to her.

Instead, inky spots flashed across my vision and I collapsed into darkness.

CHAPTER TWENTY-THREE
Now

Daylight flooded my senses, along with the fresh scents of grass and flowers. Something soft brushed against my hand as a soothing rhythm filled my ears. It took me a moment to recognize the sounds of a flowing river, of a warm breeze rustling through the grass and the trees.

I was lying alongside the Willow River, the sun high in a cloudless blue sky. A rabbit nuzzled against my hand, nose twitching. I tilted my head, considering the little animal before I dared to stroke its soft grey fur. Rather than startle or flee, it closed its eyes, letting me brush my fingers over its velvety ears and nose.

Birds twittered and flitted from branch to branch of a nearby willow whose leaves dipped into the lazily flowing river. Everything was quiet and peaceful, without a hint of the horrors I'd just faced in the nighttime. No vampires, no earth opening to swallow anyone whole. No monsters or wraiths emerging from the glistening water. Only the music of nature broke the stillness.

"I suppose I shouldn't be surprised that it's you."

It was Kaede's voice.

I jerked into a sitting position, searching the area until I found him leaning against the willow's trunk, half-concealed by its low-hanging branches. He peeled himself away from it and stepped forth from the shadows, the sunlight gilding his dark hair and sparkling in his depthless eyes. He was clothed in crisp black, his hair perfectly combed. Hand tucked behind him, he strode toward me with an impenetrable expression.

My pulse throbbed somewhere in my throat, and my mouth dried at the sight of him.

"Where am I?" I glanced about, my mind finally beginning to recall how I'd fainted while trying to get to my sister. "Is Callista all right?" I reached for my own shoulder as I worried about her possible injuries. It smarted, but when I looked, there was no visible wound there or on my leg. Though I was still clothed in the same dress I'd worn into the maze, it was pristine, as if I'd never fallen in the mud or stained my hands with blood—real or imagined.

"In a dream," Kaede said. "And your sister is safe and well." He reached out his hand, and I froze, trying to decipher if he meant to help me up or to use his magic against me. Arching a brow, he offered me a half-smile. "I would never use this part of my magic—my responsibility—against someone. Besides, you cannot sustain lasting injuries in a dream."

Despite his words, when I reached for Kaede's hand, I found it to be as warm and solid as it was in real life. My skin tingled at the contact.

Keeping my hand in his, the prince led me toward Willow River. Dream or not, uneasiness prickled down my spine. "I know your experiences with water have been...unpleasant. But this dream is different."

I frowned as we paused at the bank. "How so?"

Kaede snapped his fingers and the current ceased to flow. He strode forward, wading into the water until it was up to his waist. He gestured for me. "It's not cold, nor full of dangerous water creatures."

My cheeks pinked in spite of myself. I knew he wasn't trying to seduce me, and we'd been in more scandalous situations than this. Still, I couldn't help how self-conscious I was as I set aside my nerves and took a step into the water. My skirts swirled around me as I trod further in, scanning the clear water to find nothing but the glistening sand at its bottom. It wasn't too deep, and it was surprisingly warm, almost as if I were wading into a freshly drawn bath. But while a bath in the real world would have soothed my aching muscles and washed away the filth clinging to my body, here it seemed instead to calm my soul.

"Sit." Kaede waved toward a smooth boulder in the middle of the river.

When I seated myself on it, the river began to course gently around me again, but it ran no higher than bathwater. I closed my eyes, relishing the sense of being in a bath, drinking in the warmth. The peace.

Peace. I couldn't remember the last time I'd experienced it like this. It was freeing. Renewing.

I breathed deeply, no longer even troubled by the aches where I knew, somewhere far from this dreamscape, my wounds remained.

"This is your responsibility?" I murmured. When I opened my eyes, I was unsurprised to find that this time I was in a bath—though, to my relief, still fully clothed—in a washroom unlike any I'd ever seen before. The tub was carved of wood, looking much like an enormous tree stump hollowed out and smoothed. Steam curled from the water, along with the relaxing aromas of vanilla and cherry blossoms. Cherry blossom petals even floated across its surface. Throughout the room, greenery and flowers sprouted everywhere—vines growing along the ceiling, shrubbery decorating the walls, and violets adorning the spaces between the floor tiles. My heart skipped a beat at the sight, recalling the violet he'd once offered me, back when I'd thought he was simply Captain Junseo and he'd thought I was Princess Briar. But had the flowers appeared because of what they meant to *me*, since this was *my* healing dream, or because of what they meant to *him*, because *he* was also in control of it?

Kaede didn't speak, just settled a hand on my shoulder. Something changed, the weight on my heart easing even further, as if he were leaching every ounce of guilt and sorrow and horror from the night away. "Being the heir to the spring kingdom means offering life to mortals and immortals who are in need. By soothing their inner wounds."

I frowned in thought. "Inner wounds?"

"Emotional turmoil. Mental distress. Guilt. Grief."

"By entering others' dreams?"

"I don't get to choose whose dreams I find myself in. This Willowbark magic...we are drawn to whoever needs us." His tone was flat, as if he were forcing the words out.

The smallest sense of discomfort stole over me, one that I refused to let Kaede take from me. Instead, I stood from the bath and—perhaps because it was my dream, or perhaps because Kaede's magic was conjuring whatever I needed to feel most comfortable—I found a warm towel already waiting for me. I wrapped my sodden dress in it and turned away, not wanting to meet Kaede's expression. Knowing that his magic was forcing him to tend to me, that he was only taking my pain out of a sense of obligation, was almost worse than the initial guilt that had drawn him to me.

Tears burned my eyes.

My thoughts distracted me so that I didn't hear Kaede approach. "What did you see in that maze?" A hint of tenderness edged his tone.

"I was shown an illusion that looked like...like my sister." My throat tightened.

There was a pause, heavy with meaning.

"Like she was dead? You thought you'd lost her."

Nodding, I choked on a sob.

As if his tender nature couldn't help himself despite the chasm between us, Kaede reached for me, gently combing his fingers through my hair. The sensation sent pleasant ripples over my scalp and down the back of my neck, loosening the tension in my muscles and steadying my breathing. Without even thinking about it, I tipped my head back, leaning into his touch. Craving it. Craving *him*.

"The uhgmil debilitate their prey by consuming them with vivid hallucinations of their greatest fears before they eat them. Anything that comes within range of their magic can fall under their influence. Sometimes they plague members of our own court who wander too close to the maze they took residence within, and so my father and his court began a habit of sending criminals and enemies into the maze as sacrifices."

I repressed a shudder. Kaede's nimble fingers threaded through my hair, twisting and playing with it, taking away some of the horror of his revelation.

"They don't care if anyone but their winner survives, do they?" I asked.

"Using the competitors as sacrifices was not part of the contest that I agreed to, and why I was able to interfere."

I squeezed my eyes closed. "For Laura."

"She was lost in a hallucination. You pulled yourself free to defend yourself. Your mind found the flaws in the creature's illusion. But the emotional damage lingered enough to bring me here, into your dream." There was bitterness in Kaede's tone, even as he continued to play with my hair.

"Will I remember this, when I wake?" I whispered.

"I don't know. I've never communed with those I've visited afterward before to be able to find out."

"But *you* will remember?"

Kaede's voice dipped lower. He pressed his lips against my ear. "I always remember you, princess."

I shivered involuntarily. Kaede's fingers twisted in my hair, toying with the damp strands, winding them into a braid. "Even when I don't want to," he added.

He gently tugged on my hair, angling my face toward him. "I want to believe that you aren't going to try to kill me." Kaede didn't move away, instead slipping an arm around my waist, holding me to him. His forehead rested against my neck, his breath tickling my skin. "I want to think you've changed."

His closeness made my breath hitch. In my dream, he couldn't harm me, but that could change as soon as I awoke. Because of this, I knew on some level I should have been afraid of him. After all, he was a powerful fae with strong magic who'd come back from the dead with revenge in his heart. And yet I couldn't forget the tender man I'd met. Whatever darkness had consumed him in death, it hadn't swallowed up his heart. Not fully.

"You drive me mad," he muttered. "I don't know if I can believe anything you say—if who you truly are is the woman I knew before or if everything was a carefully crafted ploy. I don't know why your face, your *true* face, torments me in my dreams. You're far more beautiful than Briar could ever hope to be...and that makes you far more dangerous. I don't know what to think. What to trust. What to *want*. I don't know if I want to kiss you or kill you."

With a deep breath, he pried himself away and twisted me to face him, cupping my chin with his free hand so my gaze met his. "But I already made the mistake of trusting you before, sweet torment." His eyes flared with commingling desire and warning as they dipped toward my lips. "And I am not in the mood to be betrayed again."

A breeze rustled through the room, chilly and at odds with the comfort of my dream. Kaede's eyes seemed to blacken further. As he stepped nearer, the wind strengthened, feeling more like grasping fingers preparing to trap me or throw me backward.

"You know," he said, his voice pitching low and sounding husky despite the threat in it, "sometimes, I think the darkness will overtake me completely and make me like the creatures I conjure from my nightmares. That, thanks to you, I brought a piece of death back with me."

Kaede leaned forward, his mouth tilting not toward my own, but toward my neck. I gasped as his teeth scraped against my throat, followed by the warmth of his tongue. My eyelids fluttered closed. What madness had possessed me, that I *wanted* this? He couldn't hurt me here, but what if he acted this way when I was awake too? What if his teeth sank into me the way the vampire's had when it tore open Verity's throat?

Even in a dream, I told myself that logically, I should have kept my distance. All I was doing was hurting myself by letting him touch me. And yet I couldn't move, locked in the fae prince's grasp as his lips, teeth, and tongue worked their way down my neck and along my collarbone. My skin was too hot; my mind and heart screamed at me in a constant battle between what I wanted and what I knew to be true.

It felt as if ages and yet no time at all had passed when Kaede pulled away, his expression indecipherable. For one long, aching moment, we stared into each other's eyes. My lips parted as if to say something, but I knew not what. I was breathless, and all the earlier peace I'd been relishing had melted into an aching longing that could not be satisfied, for he could never be mine.

His fingers slipped away from my chin and settled around my throat, where my pulse beat erratically.

"You cannot hurt me here," I reminded him, even though he didn't squeeze, didn't seem to want to harm me.

"Do you hope to win?" His face was unreadable, studying mine intently.

I licked my lips, and Kaede tracked the movement. "My only hope is to survive and get my sister safely back home. But you could kill me when I wake. I'm at your mercy, as long as I'm in Willowbark."

"You care deeply for your sister."

"I already told you that I made my bargain with King Wystan to protect my family."

"You have a great capacity to love, and so much kindness. At least, for your family. But did you ever care for me? Or was it all part of your need to get close enough to assassinate me?"

"Of course I cared for you—I told you this," I breathed. "If you do not trust the word of a human, trust this: when I first met you, I thought you were only Captain Junseo. I never suspected you were the prince, or that making you fall for me was even a possibility, let alone a way to get me closer to Prince Kaede." My throat ached with unshed tears. "I didn't *want* to fall for you, because I knew what I had to do. I tried to fight against it, and I failed."

Kaede was silent for a long time. I listened to the sound of my own heartbeat in my ears, my own breath rattling through me like an invalid in their sickbed, all because of the effect he had on me.

When he finally moved his hand again, he brushed it against my cheek briefly. His mouth opened like he wanted to say something else—and then he stepped away. "I've done what I must. This dream must end. Wake up, sweet torment."

CHAPTER TWENTY-FOUR

THEN

My first sliver of relief since slaying the prince came when I stumbled back into Greybrooke, leaving the cruel fae world behind. Familiar landmarks welcomed me as I strolled down the street, keeping my head downcast and covered with my hood, not wanting anyone to recognize me and question where I'd been, what I'd done. I didn't know if my family had shared the truth or not, but it was likely I'd be shunned regardless, and though that hardly mattered to me now, I didn't want anyone prying. I especially didn't want to cast my family in poor light.

As long as they were alive and safe.

It'd been like holding my breath for days as I'd traveled here. Though the effects of my potion had long worn off, changing my appearance to my own, I'd still feared for my safety in Willowbark, knowing that being a mortal there was dangerous enough. Even if I no longer wore the face of the prince's killer. When I hadn't been consumed with guilt and grief, I'd been overwhelmed with fear.

King Wystan could have lied. He could have ordered my family to be killed or hurt despite the fact that I'd fulfilled my mission. I had nothing to rely on but his honor, and given the way he'd deceived me once already, I wasn't sure if he had any.

Heart thrumming in my ears, I finally exited the city proper and allowed myself to pick up my pace to a jog. My lungs burned as I followed the twists and hills of the country road, until at last I rounded the last bend and caught sight of our estate.

Nothing seemed out of place. Smoke curled from the chimney, clouding the perfect blue sky. Birds chittered at me from the old oak I'd spent so many hours lying beneath and reading, sometimes alone, sometimes with Mother. Off-key notes from a stable boy singing as he worked with the horses wafted toward me on the spring breeze.

Home. Eyes burning, I sprinted down the road, lifting my skirts and nearly stumbling in a patch of mud as I crossed the lawn and approached the front door. I hardly cared. Father would scold me; Lavinia would frown; Callista might laugh or roll her eyes. But as long as they were safe, and I was *here,* I could manage. I could try to erase the awfulness of the past in my mind, pray that Emberglade would leave us alone and Willowbark would never discover my true identity, and trust that now we could live in peace.

Panting, I paused atop the front steps, swiping at strands of hair that had escaped my knot and stuck to my flushed face. Untying my cloak, I tugged it off my shoulders. For some reason, I lifted my hand hesitantly, choosing to knock rather than simply open the door. I wasn't sure how my family would react to my sudden reappearance, and thought maybe they'd be a little less shocked or alarmed by my state if a servant announced me first.

But when the door creaked inward, an unfamiliar face narrowed his eyes at me. Had Lavinia dismissed Lawrence?

"I'm afraid we haven't met," I began, catching my breath. "I'm Aurelia Sinclair. Could you announce my safe return to my family and ask one of the maids to draw me a bath?"

The man blinked, his nose twitching in silent affront. "Excuse me, ma'am, but this is highly unusual."

"I know I was traveling without an escort, but the circumstances were unusual as well." I cleared my throat. "I'm not sure what Father told you, but I assure you, I wasn't away to cause trouble for my family. I just need to see them..."

The man cut off my rambling. "Sinclair, you said?"

Desperation tightened my chest. "Yes," I said, forcing patience into my tone.

"I'm not sure where the confusion arose, but the Sinclairs no longer live at this residence."

The world lurched and my knees wobbled. "Excuse me...what? What happened to them?"

Eyes widening at my reaction, the servant held up a hand. "They sold this estate to my master and mistress, but if you could wait a moment, I'll provide you with their new address. They'd said someone might call and look for them."

Throat dry, I nodded, unable to speak. As the servant disappeared inside, closing the door, I tried to calm my whirling emotions. *They're alive.* That was the most important thing. But... *They moved?* Had King Wystan followed through on his word of not harming them, but failed to deliver the gold he'd promised?

Or did they spend it already, while I was away and unable to do the bookkeeping and monitor our expenses?

Tears pricked my eyes. Had I killed Kaede and broken my own heart, only for my family to still be in poor circumstances? Were they all right?

After what felt like an eternity, the servant returned, handing me an envelope. "I'd forgotten they left this."

Aurelia Sinclair was scrawled across the front in Lavinia's elaborate hand.

Clearly disturbed by my disheveled appearance, the servant didn't wait around to watch me read, instead bidding me good evening and closing the door. I strolled back toward the familiar oak tree, settling beneath it one last time to open the envelope and read my sister's letter.

Dear Aurelia,

The funds you bargained for were not enough to sustain us for long, and so we made the decision to sell the estate and use the profits to help our situation. Since we could not send word to you in the fae world, we are leaving you this note. We are settling in a smaller but fashionable home in Riverside, where we can continue a genteel lifestyle befitting our station, without fear of the expenses it costs to maintain the estate and a large number of servants.

Yours,

Lavinia

Beneath her signature was an address.

For a long moment, I stared at it, the letters blurring before my eyes. I gave myself time to process and grieve. To stand, press my palm against the tree trunk, and squeeze my eyes shut, remembering times long past.

Then I left Greybrooke behind.

CHAPTER TWENTY-FIVE

Now

Pain lanced through my shoulder and leg, plucking me out of my dream. I stifled a cry, opening my eyes to find a woman with long, wispy eyelashes and violet eyes scrunching her face in concentration as she held my shoulder.

"Hold still; I'm trying to help," she said.

Breathing deeply, I gritted my teeth through the waves of agony that coursed through my wounds. And then, suddenly, the pain melted into warmth as I felt the skin knit back together. Exhaustion swept through me, but it was pleasant and heady, like I'd drank a few gulps of wine.

As my eyelids fluttered, nerves twisted in my stomach. What if Kaede was waiting for me in my dreams? How could I bear to hear him call me his sweet torment again, to feel his lips against my throat, and to know that he could not forgive me? That there was a darkness within him that hadn't been there when I'd first fallen for him.

"I can't sleep," I groaned. Sunlight was filtering brightly through a near-by window of the infirmary I found myself in, signaling it was late in the day.

"There are other contestants recovering today as well," the healer explained, as if she thought I feared for my chances of participating in the day's events to win the prince's hand. "You will not miss any events."

I wanted to ask where Callista was, but a knock on the door interrupted us.

"Is Miss Aurelia Sinclair awake?"

"Briefly," the healer hedged, glancing toward where Florian Brightwing leaned against the door. His smile was too bright as his eyes swept over me.

"She needs rest from the effort her body underwent in recovering from two bite wounds."

Florian arched a brow. "Quite the fight you put up in there," he said conversationally, striding past the healer and waving a dismissive hand at her to send her on her way.

She cast me a hesitant glance before darting from the room. Likely she was more afraid of defying a member of the nobility than insisting he leave me alone so I could sleep.

As Florian pulled up a chair to the bed and settled into it, propping one leg up so that his ankle rested on his other leg, I studied him warily. "I am not sure why my recovery is of particular concern to you," I said.

Florian smirked. "Direct. I like the way your mind works."

"I was of the opinion that logic and facts were not highly valued among the fae. Not in a world of trickery and glamours."

"Ah, but in a world of trickery and glamours where no one can lie and words must be twisted in order to make those tricks, facts are highly valued. One must know the facts to spin them." He winked as if we were sharing a secret, as if we were co-conspirators and I could trust him within an inch.

Pinching my arm to keep myself awake, I sat up against my pillows. "This is all fascinating, but doesn't answer my question. Why are you interested in my well-being? What brings you here?"

"Perhaps I have taken notice of your talents in the competition."

I frowned, moments from last night's horrors flashing through my mind.

"You don't believe me." Florian grinned, amused. "It's true. We had a talented seer who was able to share the events occurring within the maze when you were all within it. The uhgmil taunted all of you with visions of horrors and fears, but you were the only one to see through an illusion and wound one of them. Prince Kaede's guards rescued everyone else." He leaned forward and lowered his voice, as if sharing a secret. "I truly think you have what it takes to win."

In spite of myself, my heart skipped a beat. But winning couldn't end well for me.

"Alas, some of our members made a poor decision in trying to also use you contestants as sacrifices for the uhgmil. Please know that I voted against it. I am not here to relish spectating suffering and death like some of the sadists in this court. I want a queen worthy of our kingdom."

I scanned his face and sifted through his words, trying to discover the trick to his phrasing or some other hint that he wasn't being entirely forthright. But I couldn't find any sign that he wasn't being honest with me. Perhaps Florian Brightwing was one of those rare, kind souls among the fae. More like Kaede. After all, he couldn't lie, only twist words, and he'd spoken very plainly. And hadn't he claimed to be Kaede's friend? Bentley, too, had mentioned that the three of them were close. Perhaps I could let down my guard around him, at least a little.

"And so you came to check on me, even hoping I will win?"

Florian shifted in his seat, appearing almost...uncomfortable. "Well." He cleared his throat. "Since the courtiers tried to sacrifice some of the contestants...the prince's word to them to not interfere is no longer valid. He could do whatever he likes. And I think you and I both know that he's already showing preference for a certain young lady."

My stomach dipped at the reminder. Laura. When I closed my eyes, I could see her in Kaede's arms and the way she'd gazed up at him. The fierce protectiveness in his eyes wasn't something I could easily forget. "You think he will choose her."

And why wouldn't he? Despite the way he'd kissed me in my dream, any hope of truly being with Kaede was no more than fantasy. The part of him that longed for me would never overtake the part of him that had lost all trust in me, that was still convinced, even now, that I was plotting to assassinate him all over again.

If I were in his place, I wouldn't trust myself either.

"You think so too." Florian's expression was surprisingly gentle, his rich brown eyes exuding a warmth that I realized I deeply missed. When was the last time I'd felt understood? Callista and the rest of my family were vain and excessive, viewing me as their sensible caregiver and creating a constant divide among us. To Kaede, I was a traitor. Other than how Kaede had tended to me in my dream—out of his responsibility as crown prince of Willowbark to heal the hurting—when had someone cared for me? "It seems a shame, someone as strong and beautiful as you being overlooked."

Heat stained my cheeks in spite of myself. "Laura has her own qualities," I said diplomatically. How could I resent Kaede for seeing how lovely and brave she was? If he had to choose his future queen, I was glad he had found someone who might make him happy.

Or that was what I told myself.

Florian laid a gentle hand over mine. For a moment, I stared down at where he touched me, uncertain how I felt about the familiar gesture. It was comforting to feel a friendly touch, and yet disconcerting. The last man who'd touched me had been Kaede, even if it was in a dream, and Florian's cool hand was quite different from the heated kisses the prince had pressed to my throat. My breath caught and my blush deepened at the memory of his tongue caressing my skin.

Thinking I'd blushed at his touch, Florian grinned. It wasn't an unkind smile, so I found myself returning it. "Do not despair. I know I am not a prince, but you are not unnoticed. And I'm glad you are recovering, truly. I know you don't trust me, and I can't really blame you given how most fae behave toward humans, but...well, there it is. I hope you come to believe me, and I look forward to getting to know you better in the coming days as you spend time among our court. Whether Prince Kaede sees you or not, I do."

He stood and bowed, a gesture that endeared him to me, just a little, simply because he'd chosen a human custom to make me feel comfortable. It was nice to see something familiar, to feel a bit of home here in this awful manor.

"Rest well, sweet Aurelia."

But as my eyes drifted closed, surrendering to sleep at last, all I heard was the echo of Kaede's words.

Sweet torment.

CHAPTER TWENTY-SIX

NOW

In the late hours of the night, I decided it was time to slip out of the empty infirmary and seek out my shared rooms with Callista. My shoulder and leg no longer hurt, and when I sat up to pull up one leg of the fresh pair of leggings the healer had brought me earlier, I found that my calf was perfectly healed. A similar inspection of my shoulder, when I pulled down the sleeve of my new, untorn tunic, showed nothing but smooth unscarred skin.

I didn't want to wait for the healer to release me before I could go to my sister. For all I knew, the next test was about to begin, with or without me, and I couldn't let my sister endure it alone if there was any chance I could help her.

Or—worse still—Kaede could conjure another vampire from his nightmares to attack the manor's occupants.

But, as usual, Willow Manor proved tricky to navigate. Familiar halls suddenly turned in the wrong direction, and the staircase I climbed to reach the upper levels of the manor shifted while I ascended. Catching myself on the handrail to avoid tumbling down the steps, I ventured upward to find that, instead of leading to the hall that held the entrance to my room, the staircase ended in a single narrow door.

Uneasily, I tried the knob to find that the door was unlocked. I considered trying to turn around and seek my room, but, deep down, I knew the manor would lead me where it wanted me to go, however it had to. The steps could just as easily move again, or the floor could tumble out from beneath me and drop me into a new room. As much as I dreaded seeing where it was taking me, I didn't see any sense in prolonging my wandering by resisting it.

Resigned, I opened the door and stepped into darkness. I was atop a tower under the night sky, starlight bathing the inky darkness in its shimmering beauty. Bats darted overhead, swooping and diving after unseen insects. Frogs chittered somewhere in the gardens below.

And then I saw the form slipping from the shadows, pulling away from the half-wall surrounding the tower. Kaede's chiseled features and deep eyes were as handsome as ever, wisps of his hair moving in the breeze he conjured around him. It swept over me, carrying hints of cherry blossom and spring rain, lifting the hair off the back of my neck and caressing my cheeks and throat. Warmth flooded me, for the touch was surprisingly intimate, as if the air that did Kaede's bidding also let him feel my skin. Like it was his hands and lips on me rather than the breeze.

The sensation was gone almost immediately, though, for a warning pricked at the back of my mind. As familiar as the prince looked, there was something in his expression that was foreign. A bat fluttered around him, briefly hovering by his ear as if sharing its secrets before it darted back into the night. Kaede approached me slowly, his eyes reminding me of the darkness that had haunted them in my dream.

He'd hinted at death not only corrupting his magic, but also changing him. I hadn't wanted to believe it. I'd felt safe with him despite Bentley's declaration that Kaede craved revenge, despite Kaede himself telling me he didn't know if he wanted to kill me. I'd trusted in the tender, merciful man I'd known a year ago.

But that man was dead.

The one before me was a prince of wind and nightmares. He wasn't my heroic captain coming to my rescue, but a vengeful villain eyeing his prey.

I stepped backward, only for the stones beneath me to tilt, knocking me over. My back struck the tower floor, cool and unforgiving.

Slowly, Kaede knelt before me, tilting his head to take in the sight of me sprawled before him.

Like an offering.

Licking my lips, I scanned the tower, searching for a way out. The door that had brought me here now felt like a world away, impossible to access when Kaede blocked my path and could stop me in an instant. I would be better off throwing myself off this tower than trying to run from him.

"Aurelia." When Kaede grasped my throat, his thumb against my fluttering pulse, his hold was surprisingly gentle.

He's still in there. My tender prince. But there was no telling if the darkness would overpower whatever was left of Kaede.

He leaned closer, his breath brushing my ear.

"Is this a dream?" It was a hopeful question, but I didn't believe it. Not this time. The world was too sharp, every sensation too vivid. The cool stone beneath my palms, the heat of Kaede's presence, the scents of spring on the night breeze...they were too real.

"Not this time, princess." There was no gentleness in his tone, only taunting.

I choked on a gasp when I felt cold steel against my neck. Inwardly, I cursed myself. I'd been trained better than that, to notice when a potential attacker was drawing a weapon. But this dark version of Kaede had been so unexpected.

Raw terror gripped me as I stared into his eyes, black and emotionless. The iciness in them chilled me to the core even more than the threat to my life did. It was terrible seeing him this way—the man that had urged me to dance in the rain, who'd comforted me after a nightmare, who'd held me to keep me warm, who'd laughed with his men and women and charmed everyone around him.

"Should I stab you as you stabbed me?" he whispered, lowering the blade toward my chest. "Plunge it through your heart, but in a way that won't kill you instantly. Let the poison on the blade make you suffer instead."

Tears stung my eyes. "I'm so sorry," I choked out. For the past year, I'd been haunted by what he must have endured. The agony. The searing pain shutting down his organs. The utter despair and grief and anger at being deceived by someone he'd grown to care for, someone whose life he'd saved more than once.

"Of course you say that now, when your life is threatened." His tone was guttural.

"No, I've carried the guilt and regret and sorrow with me this whole time," I whispered. "You felt my pain in my dream."

"That was for your sister." Kaede dipped closer to me, his nose brushing along my neck. My heart pounded, and I was sure he could hear it. His teeth scraped against skin, a silent threat.

Frozen, I didn't dare move.

"Let me tell you what happened when you left me," he said. "The poison burned through my veins, smothering me in such agony I was delirious. In and out of consciousness, lost in my tangled emotions and thoughts, wondering why the woman who'd seemed so sincere, so honest and pure, could have betrayed me so viciously."

I closed my eyes against the burn of tears. Regret. Fear. Grief. "Kaede."

"Don't say my name," he snarled, his teeth nipping against my skin. A gasp caught in my lungs. "I'm giving you a reason—more than what you gave me. When I died, I wasn't at peace. I wasn't able to cross into the afterlife—but I wasn't able to find the glade of souls either, the in-between place where ghosts can rest until they're able to move on. I wandered, lost, alone, angry. The only thing that fed me was a need to find you. To know *why*."

My stomach clenched as I imagined his soul, lost and hurt and confused, wandering this world. Unable to find peace.

"It was as if my magic turned against me," Kaede went on. "Instead of peace and healing and life, I knew only torment and anger and death. The nightmares began in death. I watched creatures, ravenous for the blood and strength of the living, materialize from my dreams and attack the innocent. And then, when my faithful guards sought the help of Ashwood to bring me back after my wrongful death...the darkness followed. The contamination continues to plague me, awake and asleep. It makes me crave blood the way those creatures do, makes me want to see them tear out throats. But yours...yours most of all." His teeth pressed against my neck, and a tear slipped down my cheek.

"This isn't you," I whispered. "You can fight it. The guilt will haunt you even more. It already does. Those deaths—"

"Those deaths happened because of you." His voice rumbled his accusation. "If you die, maybe I'll finally be free of this darkness. Maybe this corruption of my magic will be healed."

"And maybe not. Maybe it will make the darkness consume you even more, take away every last bit of the person you truly are." I kept talking as I moved, twisting the wrist that held his dagger and forcing him to drop it while, at the same moment, I leaned into Kaede, slamming my head into his.

Pain pulsed through my forehead, but the movement had been unexpected enough that I achieved my intended result. Kaede pulled back, rubbing at his face as he groped along the tower rooftop for his dagger.

And then, I ran. Not for the door, which I knew would result in a fruitless chase through the manor until Kaede caught me, but toward the edge of the tower. Blood throbbed in my ears and my heart lodged itself somewhere in my throat as I climbed the half-wall.

"Aurelia!" There was anger in his voice, but also a hint of fear.

I prayed I'd assessed the situation correctly, that this calculated move wasn't merely a stroke of madness.

And then I leapt.

CHAPTER TWENTY-SEVEN

Now

"Aurelia!" he roared.

Wind tore at my tunic, whipping it around my body, and stung my eyes, drawing tears. It stifled the cry before it could rise from my lungs, stealing my breath completely. For a moment, it was as if I were suspended in the air, flying among the bats and owls, soaring over the glistening pools and colorful gardens.

And then I was falling, the ground seeming to rise toward me. Trees, shrubbery, plants, the hedge maze...I saw it all drawing closer, each detail becoming sharper and sharper.

If I had judged wrong, I was dead.

Just as my eyes squeezed shut, bracing for the final impact, the whistling air around me changed. It pushed against me, its force cradling me so that instead of plummeting to the earth, it felt more like I was floating. Drifting on the breeze, my pulse slowed as I descended feet-first toward a patch of grass behind the manor. Just ahead, a cluster of people stood in the shadows, gaping at me as I landed, feather-soft. I caught my breath as if I'd been running, relief and uncertainty tangling through me in equal measures. Part of Kaede had feared for me, but the other part—the part that was becoming stronger—had saved me because he wanted to kill me himself.

I resisted the urge to look up and search for him, to see if he was gazing down and assuring himself that I was alive.

Ji emerged from the crowd before me, which, now that I was nearer, I could tell consisted of the court members and the remaining contestants.

Callista was among them, looking healthy and whole, just pale as she stared at me, mouth open.

"Well, I never thought I'd say that I'm grateful the prince can interfere now, but it's good to see you cannot forfeit this next challenge by flinging yourself from the rooftop." He sniffed. "Mortals, so dramatic."

I watched him wordlessly.

"Anyway, you're just in time to start the next stage of our competition." As always, his smile was sharp. I didn't return it. "Previously, we tested your ability to see through glamour and fight through fear. Now, we will assess other qualities, including your wisdom."

"And what are we to accomplish?" Laura demanded, her expression defiant. I wondered what horrors she'd witnessed during her encounter with one of the uhgmil that had caused Kaede to intervene. She seemed fearless, but everyone possessed a weakness.

Ji waved an airy hand. "Oh, it's simple enough. The first one to solve a riddle will win." He gestured to a group of servants I hadn't noticed before, ones who lingered in the gardens' shadows. They stepped forward and distributed sealed envelopes to each contestant. "You may not open these until you're within the great hall, or you forfeit this test."

Laura barely glanced at her envelope, instead crossing her arms and watching Ji skeptically. "In the great hall? Then why did we meet outside?"

"Because the manor is preparing for the test."

A chill raked down my spine at Ji's words. I was sick of the manor's tricks.

Once I received mine, I studied it, feeling the thick paper and flipping it over to inspect the image pressed into the wax. Instead of Willowbark's royal symbol, it was a bat. I frowned, recalling the bat that had fluttered to Kaede's side earlier tonight, before he'd threatened me.

"There will also be an assortment of citizens and guests within the manor, alongside our own number and the servants already occupying it, who will be available to help or hinder you. It is up to each of you to determine whom you can trust."

I crossed the grounds to Callista, quietly taking her hand in mine. She leaned into me, laying her head on my shoulder.

Ji glanced at us. "And no pairing up with each other, or you will both be disqualified."

A lump lodged in my throat. Callista wasn't my competition, and I didn't want to be parted from her again.

But defying the fae's rules would pose dire consequences for us both, so I forced myself to pull away from my sister. She glanced up at me, her expression pale and eyes glassy. Her lip wobbled, but she didn't try to protest. She knew better.

"And begin!" Ji cried, gesturing toward the manor.

I set my jaw and began trudging forward, daring a look up toward the tower from which I'd thrown myself. There was no sign of Kaede. Was he waiting for his moment to attack me again once I was within the manor? Had his nightmares conjured more vampires that were even now seeking new prey? Sweat slithered down my back, and it took a conscious effort to steady my breathing.

"I'm no good at riddles," Hattie fretted to her sister.

"Me neither," Callista muttered, casting a forlorn glance at me.

Florian appeared at my side, tucking his hands into his pockets. "This is the sort of contest *you* will excel in."

I gave him a wry smile. "Once upon a time, I took pride in my sense of judgment, but I have since come to realize I am too easily persuaded into believing the worst in others. Or perhaps too easily persuaded to trust no one at all." My heart twisted as the memory of Kaede's emotionless eyes flashed through my mind. I'd once chosen not to trust him, and now, because of that choice, his growing darkness made him untrustworthy.

Florian shrugged. "Then trust me. I'll make it my mission to help."

I mulled over his words, remembering the way he'd complimented me when he'd visited me in the infirmary just earlier that evening. He'd seemed sincere, but now he could be one of the participants in this test meant to deceive. There were too many ways his words could be twisted. He could have meant he was making it his mission to help one of the other women, or to help his fellow courtiers in their plans to make this contest more challenging, or to help me *lose*.

After King Wystan and his bargain, I knew better than to be tricked by a slip of the tongue or a word that went unsaid.

As we stepped within the manor, the entry hall shifted, the ceiling stretching higher and the flickering candlelight dimming.

Florian smirked. "Ah, Willow Manor, always setting the mood for all of our events."

I wasn't sure what to make of his lighthearted behavior. After all, this challenge was likely to once again devolve into something deadly. I knew better than to expect a simple test to solve riddles. This was no human game.

Ahead, Callista walked arm-in-arm with Bentley in the direction of the great hall. A spark of relief flared in my heart. If there was any other fae I'd consider trusting, it was him, and I was glad he was accompanying Callista.

I started after them when a rumbling sound shattered the quiet and the manor shifted, the hallway suddenly blocked by a wall. Disoriented, I blinked, finding as I turned that Florian and I were in an unfamiliar hallway now, and no one else was nearby.

He chuckled. "This manor loves to play tricks."

Setting a hand to my temple, I breathed through my nose, trying to dispel a dizzy spell along with my mounting frustration. "I thought this test was meant to assess our ability to solve a riddle, not our navigational skills in a manor that's never the same."

Florian's eyes glittered with mirth. "The manor has a mind of its own. Have you heard the rumors that a hag hides somewhere within, long gone mad and entertaining herself by playing tricks?" He shook his head with a smile, as if the idea of a malicious hag toying with us was amusing, not terrifying. "But I'm among those who believe the manor is loyal to the royal family, and that anything it does is not a matter of whimsy or madness, but an effort to protect and serve them." He plucked a hand from his pocket to reach for a painting on the wall, brushing imaginary dust from its frame.

I studied the painting curiously, realizing it was a likeness of Prince Kaede, standing beside the ocean. Under a cloudy spring sky, his eyes were dark and stormy, reminding me of the pain and anger lurking within him now. Had this been painted after he'd died?

"How long have you served the Willowbarks in their court?" I asked softly.

Florian cast me a sidelong glance. "In a way, all my life. I was born at the palace and raised to serve. My father was an advisor before me."

"So you knew the prince..." I swallowed. "Before he died."

"Ah, so you heard the stories."

My chest loosened at Florian's words, relieved to hear that he didn't suspect I was Kaede's killer.

"It's part of the reason the court has been so careful with choosing his bride this time around. They don't want to risk the possibility that we could lose him for good—as much as some members of the court believe he should be more vicious, like his father, they also don't want another conflict with Emberglade. We lost many good men and women, especially our naval battles. And though we managed to force Emberglade to surrender, all because they failed to kill the powerful prince they fear most out of everyone in our kingdom, we also know they haven't given up. King Wystan is greedy." Florian sighed. "But you're not asking that, are you?" There was a shrewdness to his expression. "Perhaps you've heard us speak of Prince Kaede's mercy, but you've noticed a darkness in him. Is that it?"

I nodded slowly.

"It's true. He's different since coming back from the dead. But I can't say I blame him. Wandering about as a spirit after being murdered by your betrothed doesn't sound like a walk in the park." He smiled wryly. "Anyway. Laura seems brave enough to handle him. Maybe that's why he's chosen her."

My stomach twisted at his words, even as I cursed myself for caring. For what good would it do? No matter what, Kaede wanted me dead. I would be fortunate if I could escape with Callista. It was better for Kaede to grow fond of Laura, to let affection for her distract him from his tangled feelings of hatred and desire toward me.

Clearing my mind, I forced myself to focus on the matter at hand. Find the great hall and solve the riddle. Perform well enough in this contest to continue on and protect Callista whenever I was permitted to do so. That was my purpose here. The only time I should have thought of Kaede at all was when I was defending myself from him.

"Do you recognize this part of the manor?" I asked Florian.

He shook his head. "It's always changing. I recognized that painting, but that is all."

I tilted my head, studying it and reflecting upon what Florian had said earlier, about some believing the manor served the royal family. What if the rumor was true, and this painting was some sort of hint?

Touching the frame, I ran my hand along it, only to find that the painting hung loosely on the wall. It slipped, tilting sharply to the right and then, just as abruptly, swinging inward with a portion of the wall, revealing a hidden room.

"Well, I've never seen this before," Florian commented, but I was already stepping inside.

It was a music room, with a windowed alcove where a woman sat strumming a harp, an open space where men and women tuned their instruments, and a corner where a short man who looked to be a cross between a goblin and a dwarf sat polishing and cleaning various instruments laid out upon a cloth-covered table. My skin crawled at the sight, for his goblin-like features brought to mind the ones who'd attacked our party over a year ago, when I'd traveled with Kaede as Princess Briar and I'd known him only as Captain Junseo. When the man saw me, he glanced up with a smile that was all needle-like teeth.

I gave him a wide berth, studying the others in the room. Why had the manor led us here? Florian trailed me as I paused before the woman at the harp. She glanced up, and I recognized her violet eyes: she was the healer who'd tended to me after the maze.

Florian grasped my arm, startling me. "If you're hoping they'll help, I wouldn't trust anyone here."

As if she hadn't heard Florian's warning, the healer smiled demurely and ran her fingers along the harp's strings, plucking a few notes. "Hello, Miss Aurelia Sinclair. How are you feeling?"

I dipped my head in greeting. "Much recovered, thank you. But I'm afraid I don't know your name to properly thank you."

"I'm Azalea of Ashwood. The royal family sent me to tend to Prince Kaede, as an act of generosity and goodwill, and as a show of their loyalty to the alliance the two kingdoms have forged."

"Tend to Prince Kaede? Doesn't he have his own healers?"

Azalea's mouth curved downward, and her fingers paused their thrumming. "None who have seen a condition like his. Ashwood is a little more familiar with fae being brought back from the dead, and though I've never assisted such a soul before, I've studied historical accounts."

"Is it because of the darkness in him? The..." I lowered my voice. "Vampires?"

The healer's eyes widened, surprised I knew. She opened her mouth as if to say more, but we were interrupted by a clock on the wall striking the hour.

"We need to find our way out of here if we want to join the contest in time," Florian said, shifting on his feet uneasily.

"Of course." I glanced back to Azalea, desperately wanting to know if there was a way to stop the progression of the darkness inside Kaede, or if he was doomed. "Are you staying in the manor then?"

She nodded. "For now. We...thought different sleeping arrangements would help Kaede and protect those around him, but it doesn't matter where he is."

I repressed a shudder. "The nightmares keep coming? And—and the monsters?"

"We have guards stationed throughout the manor, especially near his sleeping quarters." She nodded toward a stack of books in the corner. "When I am not taking a break to play and think, I'm reading and studying all I can."

The manor shifted beneath me, as if urging me to move.

"We will run out of time. Aurelia, please." Florian grasped my hand and gently but firmly tugged, drawing me back out the way we'd come.

"I would have liked to speak to Azalea longer— I think the manor wanted—"

"Aurelia, if you don't participate in the contest at all, there could be severe consequences. Don't you understand?" There was a frantic look in Florian's eyes as we stepped back into the hall where Prince Kaede's painting hung, a look that gave me pause.

"You're right." I drew a deep breath. My curiosity had distracted me. As much as I wanted to hope that Kaede would find healing from whatever contaminated his magic, along with his heart, that wasn't my main objective. I couldn't help Kaede, not when he wanted to kill me.

To our left, the hall stretched to a staircase that moved, its steps shifting from leading upward to twisting downward.

"I think we should go that way," I suggested.

Florian's brow pinched. "I'm not sure the manor is helping us."

But I had a feeling—one that I couldn't explain with logic or reasoning. The manor did seem to enjoy playing tricks and throwing me into danger, but that was exactly why I was confident it wouldn't keep me from the next contest for long. I hurried toward the staircase, descending confidently with Florian on my heels. As soon as we reached the last step, I grinned in triumph. "Here we are."

A short distance away, the double doors leading to the dining hall were wide open, warm candlelight spilling from within. Florian and I were the last to enter. Already, the rest of the contestants, nearly all accompanied by various fae servants or nobility, were clustered about the table, opening their envelopes and studying an array of glasses and weapons. The open portion of the room had an odd assemblage of objects, almost like an obstacle course, ranging from targets hanging on one wall to stacked boxes in the middle to ropes hanging from the ceiling.

In the center, Ji stood with other members of the court. To my relief, Kaede was nowhere to be seen.

"Welcome," Ji cried. "As part of this trial, each one of you must sip from the cup that we offer you. Then you have until dawn to solve the riddle. During that time, we will lock the doors. Attempting to leave this room will cause you to forfeit the challenge—something I don't recommend."

My stomach turned as I remembered Molly's fate.

One by one, the women formed a line moving toward Ji, who accepted thimbleful-sized cups from the gathered court members to offer to each contestant. Every woman scowled or cringed as she sipped. Audrey gagged. I bit my inner lip as I stood at the back of the line awaiting my turn.

All too soon, I was the last competitor, and there was nothing left but to step forward. Heart somewhere in my throat, I extended my hand for the cup Ji held out for me.

I wanted to be cautious, to study whatever he'd given me. But forfeiting the contest wasn't an option, and Ji's expression was filled with impatience that I didn't want to push to its limits, so I tipped back the cup and downed its contents in one gulp.

The tang of blood filled my mouth, and bile rose in my throat.

Across the room, Hattie stumbled, teetering on her feet and crying out. She hugged herself as she wailed. All around, other women broke out in a panic, moaning and trembling in pain.

Laura's accusing glare latched onto Ji. "You've poisoned us!"

CHAPTER TWENTY-EIGHT

NOW

Screams rent the air as the contestants began to panic. My eyes flew to Callista, whose gaze was wet with tears. Bentley reached for her, squeezing her hand reassuringly and gesturing to the envelope in her hand. Throat tight, I raced to them, tearing open my own envelope as I went.

I nearly stumbled over my own feet as I ran, hardly noticing that Florian was on my heels.

"Au-Auri," Callista gasped, shaking her head as she scanned her paper. She glanced at Bentley, her eyes frantic. "If this is a test of who we can trust, does that mean every member of the court knows the answer to the riddle? Can you share it?"

His mouth pinched, his expression apologetic. "I'm afraid not. They wouldn't make it quite that simple."

Trembling, Callista lifted a hand to her temple, groaning. "It hurts."

Seizing her hand, I lifted my copy of the riddle with my free one and scanned it repeatedly, analyzing and reanalyzing each word.

I'm as silent as the deepest of tombs,
I'm as gentle as a lover's caress.
I roar with the violence of battle.
I build and destroy, bring life and death.
A taste is all you've been given,
A test to know what you will endure.
With courage and strength, you'll find
Within this room, lies your cure.

Before I'd finished, pain shot through my veins, like fire sweeping through my body. My chest constricted; my vision blurred. I tried to block it out, to clear my mind as I started running through the names and characteristics of every fae poison I'd learned. Nothing seemed to fit the flavor I'd tasted or the symptoms I experienced.

Dropping the riddle, I pulled Callista into an embrace.

"It cannot be poison," I murmured into her ear, hoping she could focus on my words rather than the agony tearing through her. "The prince was furious that they'd sent us all into the maze as possible sacrifices to the uhgmil. He wouldn't permit a test that would poison every one of us and risk that none would survive."

I tried to believe my words. The darkness in Kaede's eyes when he'd approached me earlier, dipping his mouth toward my neck, continued to haunt me. What if the contamination in his magic had changed him so dramatically that he craved all our deaths? He'd confessed to bloodlust, after all.

I repeated the riddle in my head, considering possible answers and how it would relate to whatever we'd been given to drink. *Water,* I thought. *Sometimes silent, sometimes roaring. Life-giving and deadly, both. But if the answer is water, how does that apply?*

It had tasted like blood. *Blood runs silently to our ears through our veins, but roars in our ears. It gives life, but not death unless it is spilled...*

"We can help," Florian announced, cutting into my frenzied thoughts.

"How?" I demanded, pulling away from Callista only enough that I could turn to look at him as I supported her on her unsteady feet. "How can we trust any of you when you stand by and watch us suffer so? When Bentley himself said you cannot give us the answer?"

His jaw worked. "I did not know it would cause pain."

"*It*? What were we given?"

Florian glanced pointedly toward my discarded paper, lying on the polished floor. "The answer is within the riddle. We are not able to say—we were forced to make a vow only allowing us to share certain things."

Across the room, Emily was shrieking at Audrey, gesturing wildly toward the cups on the table. "The cure is in this room! One of those cups—one of those will save us! But there aren't enough."

She seized one of the goblets with both hands, downing its contents in two greedy gulps.

For a long moment, it seemed as if the entire room held its breath. Everyone stared at Emily, waiting to see if her pain would abate. Then she frowned, wiping at her mouth. "It is only water." She groaned as another wave of agony made her muscles spasm and her body contort. She collapsed against the table, sobbing.

"What is happening to her?" Callista spun toward Bentley, tears streaming down her face. A shudder of pain wracked her body, and her face turned white. "Are we next? Did you choose to murder us?"

Shouts from the courtiers and guards across the room drew our attention as glass shattered and a form burst through the window. Though the figure appeared almost like a fae woman, everything was all wrong. Red, cloudy eyes. Sharp fangs and claws. Unnatural speed and grace.

Though the shattered glass must have sliced into her skin, the monster showed no signs of pain. No blood leaked from its skin.

I took a step back, shoving Callista behind me.

"What—what is wrong with her?" Hattie cried out.

A vampire from Kaede's contaminated magic.

And then, all at once, the answer came to me.

What if the tang of blood I'd tasted in the cup was the prince's blood?

"Magic," I muttered. "The answer to the riddle is *magic*, is it not?" I glanced at Florian, whose wide eyes were trained on the vampire. "We drank the prince's blood and the magic that runs in his veins. We've all been dosed with magic."

He gave a wry laugh. "Ah, I knew you'd solve it. We did not poison anyone. Your mortal bodies must be in shock from feeling the magic's power coursing through you."

"We need to get out of here." I clung tightly to Callista's hand. "Tell Ji I've solved the riddle. Make him unlock the doors."

Bentley's throat worked nervously. "Solving the riddle meant you had to follow the riddle's instructions as well. The manor shut us all in, and only it will release us. There's no telling if it will obey us now, even when the test has been...changed."

I scanned the room, searching for guards. "Where are the guards?" I demanded.

"I thought they were needed *outside* to prevent escape more than *inside* the hall for this challenge," Florian muttered dryly.

Fear spiked through my chest. Would the fickle manor even unlock the doors if I did follow the riddle's instructions? I ran through the final words in my head again, remembering it had claimed to be a test of endurance. *With courage and strength, you'll find within this room, lies your cure.* Since we hadn't been poisoned, there wasn't a "cure" for magic. But suddenly experiencing Kaede's magic course through our mortal bodies was causing pain for which we sought a cure. "How does one cure the pain magic brings to a mortal?" I asked, wiping sweat off my brow.

The vampire turned her red eyes toward the fae and mortals on the other side of the room.

Callista opened her own mouth in terror, but I clamped a hand over her lips and shook my head at her, casting pointed looks at both Bentley and Florian.

The vampire bolted with unnatural speed toward the nearest courtier, leaping upon him and tearing into his throat. Blood stained his jacket and sprayed across the floor. Screams rent the air. Someone wretched in a corner, but the vampire was too focused on gulping down the now-limp man's lifeblood to pay any heed to the noisy chaos unfolding throughout the rest of the room.

"Don't let her hear you," I whispered to Callista, and gestured for the nearest window, hoping those were not also locked. "Try the window and help as many others as you can to escape the manor."

Nodding, my sister took Bentley's proffered arm, and he helped lead her away, gesturing toward others to join them.

Satisfied that my sister was protected, I forced myself to ignore the fiery pain still churning through my muscles and strode toward one of the tables near the center, the one upon which countless weapons rested.

Florian seized my arm. "What are you doing?"

I set my jaw. Florian was unaware of my training, so of course my choice to stay behind and fend the vampire off from everyone else who was trapped in the room would seem like madness to him. Even with my training, it was likely madness, for the speed and strength the vampires possessed was even greater than that of the fae I'd sparred with. But I had to try.

"I will not abandon the others," I said firmly, pulling my arm away from him.

"Brave, foolish woman," he muttered under his breath, but he didn't try to stop me, instead joining me in selecting a weapon from the table. While he grasped a sword with an ornate hilt, I gathered a bow and quiver of arrows, hurriedly stringing one and taking aim.

As I set her within my sights, the vampire pulled her head back, blinking red eyes at the ceiling as she wiped the blood from her mouth and dropped the dead man. His pale body struck the floor, wide eyes staring at the ceiling, his mouth frozen in a cry of terror.

My vision blurred as magic flowed within me, pure agony slicing through my veins. Arms trembling, the bow shook in my grasp.

The vampire leapt away, charging for a fae trying to force open the bolted doors. They were all unarmed, trapped between the vampire, who blocked the way to the table of weapons, and the unyielding doors. Fae and mortals pounded on them together, crying out to Kaede, to the manor, to anyone who might hear and be able to free them.

One had the presence of mind to summon her magic, calling upon a flash of light that pained my eyes. Unfortunately, the vampire was all but blind, and that did nothing to halt her progress. Another conjured flames in his hand, aiming them toward the vampire as she slowed her steps, tilting her head to listen to the cacophony of sounds and narrow down her next victim.

As I tracked the creature's movements, I watched as the flames roared through the air and consumed her—and yet didn't. Though her body was enshrouded in dancing fire, she walked on as if unaffected. They licked at her form, charring her dress but never touching her pale skin, never slowing her movements. She sprang at the man wielding fire, snapping his neck and plunging her fangs into his throat.

Stomach churning, I released my arrow. It slammed into the vampire's back, having as little effect on her as the flames had.

Pausing, she lifted her head, chin dripping blood, and sniffed the air, as if seeking the source of the projectile now protruding from her back. Florian grasped my arm, pulling me backward as if we could move quickly enough to avoid the vampire and her speed. If she targeted us, we were doomed. My throat clogged with panic, but I forced myself to think through it. Kaede had been able to slay one of his vampires, probably because they were connected to his magic and the contamination altering it.

And we had all just been dosed with some of his magic. I wondered, vaguely, if whatever darkness lurked within it would alter us in some way as well, or if, as non-magical humans, we would be immune.

However...wasn't absorbing the magic the key to the riddle? To endure the pain the magic put us through as mortals, and then to find a way to embrace and wield it? To prove that the land of Willowbark accepted us, that we were worthy of carrying its most powerful magic?

My head swam. The pain was not abating for me, and I feared it wouldn't until the dose of magic I'd ingested wore off. Kaede hadn't forgiven me, so why would his magic and the land, both extensions of himself, find me worthy?

Laura.

She wasn't among the women trapped near the vampire, nor was her sister. I scanned the room, finding her pushing her twin beneath the table they'd stood nearby before the chaos had begun. Her complexion pale, she scanned the space, seeking out an escape.

As the vampire dashed across the room in the direction my arrow had come from, I abandoned my bow and raced toward Laura. Florian remained silent, though the sideways glances he shot my way as he ran alongside me made it clear he thought I was mad. He, like the others, hadn't yet realized that the vampire was blind, relying on her hearing and sense of smell in a room full of an overwhelming assortment of both.

Curls hanging damp and wild about her face, Laura peered up at me in alarm from her position crouched beside her sister.

"She is blind," I hissed as soon as I reached Laura, kneeling beside her. "But she can hear, so you must be quiet. Prince Kaede's magic can stop her—and we were all dosed with some of it. You have to concentrate on the magic flowing through you and try to wield it. Use it to stop that vampire."

Laura gaped at me, a mixture of confusion and fear shining in her bright eyes. "I— How would I do that? Why *me?*"

I squeezed her arm. "Focus on the magic. Imagine what you want it to do," I begged. "For everyone's sake. You are our hope."

She looked at me in despair. "Why not you? You are so knowledgeable, so confident—"

"He *cares* for you! You are connected to him. His magic will work for you. I know it will."

Laura scrunched her nose in concentration, closing her eyes to block out the horrifying sight that was the vampire, red-eyed and bloody, staggering into the weapons table like a drunk.

My mind flew back to that evening that now felt like a lifetime ago, when Kaede and I shared a room in an inn and knew each other by different names. He'd offered me a violet, showing off his magic in such a charming, endearing manner. He'd been considerate and gentlemanly, kind and attentive... I swallowed. And he'd told me how his magic was connected to his emotions and intentions, like an extension of his will and state of mind.

"Let your determination to defend us guide you," I whispered to Laura. "Think of your need to save your sister. Use your feelings."

Rising from my crouch, I crept backward to give Laura space to work as she crawled from beneath the table and squared her shoulders. Still in her hiding place, Hattie pressed a trembling hand to her mouth. Florian's gaze flicked between Laura and me. I took another step back, breathing deeply and closing my eyes, praying that this would work.

There was a creaking sound and a dizzying, shifting sensation. My stomach rose in my throat as I was jolted, like the entire room had moved.

When I opened my eyes, I was in a new hallway full of flickering candlelight and dancing shadow, facing two new forms. They were grappling together in the darkness, all fists and flashing teeth as they struggled along the length of the hall. One charged while the other backed up until they staggered into a gap of starlight painting the space from a pair of windows.

I didn't recognize the vampire, bloody and snarling, but I knew the disheveled, bleeding figure it was battling.

Kaede ducked as the creature snapped at his throat, landing a punch to its jaw and then grimacing, revealing his own teeth—but they were different.

My stomach churned when I saw that his canines were elongated into fangs that matched those of the vampire.

CHAPTER TWENTY-NINE

Now

I choked on my cry of shock as Kaede peered over the vampire's shoulder and his gaze locked on me. Once again, the manor had brought me to him when he was consumed by the darkness growing within him. Maybe it was loyal to the royal family—maybe it was performing Kaede's will by bringing me to him so he could exact his revenge.

He clamped his teeth down on the creature's neck. My stomach churned as blood flowed, dripping down his chin. The vampire's body spasmed and struggled, but Kaede held fast, his hands like vises as he drank.

"Kaede! She's in danger!"

My voice made him stir, pulling back and letting the vampire's body drop unceremoniously to the floor. My blood pounded in my ears as Kaede's fathomless dark eyes met mine. He licked at the scarlet staining his lips, and I swallowed the bile slithering up my throat.

"Is this a dream?" Kaede's voice was so deep his words rumbled in my chest. He stepped closer, his eyes devouring me in a way that I wished was flattering, but was only terrifying. He was like a predator sizing up his prey. "Or a nightmare, where you've come to torment me again?"

"Laura," I said, my voice firm. I fisted my hands, refusing to back down or flee. I had to bring him back to himself, to remind him of someone he cared for so he could intervene before more people were killed. "She's in danger. You have to save her."

He stopped a foot away, and I gritted my teeth. "Kaede," I repeated. "You must listen to me. Lives are in danger."

The prince moved with grace and speed, so quickly I blinked and he was only a breath away, his hands around my waist and his lips against my ear.

"Indeed, thanks to you." His low tone made gooseflesh rise at the back of my neck and along my arms. "I think this is both a dream and a nightmare," he continued in a whisper, lips tickling my jaw. His nose brushed against my cheek. His mouth caressed my shoulder. My throat.

I swallowed, afraid to move, afraid to breathe. "You care about her, and she could die. You must focus. Go to her before it's too late."

Kaede stiffened, holding himself very still as his mouth lingered near my collarbone, his every breath stirring chills that rippled through my entire body. "Care about her? Laura," he muttered, as if coming to himself.

"Yes, the brave young lady you rescued from the maze. The one who is even now wielding your magic and facing down a monster of your creation to save others. Because she is courageous and kind and determined and sure. Because she trusts the goodness in you and your magic. Go to her." Every word hurt, making my throat burn, but I forced them out.

Kaede pulled away abruptly, scanning me wildly. His pupils were blown wide, and I didn't know if it was from desire or bloodlust. Then he blinked, and clarity spread across his features. He was the prince I'd known and loved again, his brow scrunched in worry—in horror. He glanced over his shoulder at the form behind him, then reached into his mouth, feeling his incisors. Miraculously, they weren't pointed anymore. I blinked, my gaze flicking back and forth between the vampire he'd killed so gruesomely and the prince before me. Other than his tousled hair, he looked like himself again.

"Come," he said, voice stern, and I followed obediently. He waved his hand and, to my shock, we went from walking to flying—though that wasn't quite the right word for it. Instead, it was as if we were walking through the air, our steps never touching the floor and gliding gracefully and swiftly. It felt almost like swimming, or being pushed along a current, as if the air were cradling us in its arms, ushering us gently forward so that our every step took us further than normal ones could. We descended the stairs effortlessly, and in mere moments, we'd wound through hallways and stopped before the bolted double doors of the great hall.

With a flick of his wrist, the manor submitted to his will and the doors swung open wide, permitting the crowd of terrified fae and women an escape. They flooded out like a swollen river, rushing through the hallway to find any refuge they could within the shadowy alcoves or other open rooms, nearly trampling one another in their fear and haste.

That left only Hattie, cowering beneath the table; Florian, who clung to a sword as he searched the corners of the room, likely trying to discover where I'd gone; Bentley, who looked as if he'd just climbed back through the window to help more people to safety; and Laura, pale-faced yet determined as she faced the vampire. A growing wind rippled through her curls, rushing toward the monster. *She's doing it,* I thought.

And then—

The vampire leapt for Laura, who staggered back in fear, the wind dying. She moved just enough for the creature's fangs to miss her neck, tearing into her shoulder instead. Blood sprayed. Hattie screamed.

Kaede landed and shoved at the air, sending it roaring toward the pair of women. It dislodged the vampire, sending her flying across the room, but Laura was caught in the gust. She slammed into the floor, her head cracking with a sickening thud against the gleaming boards.

"Laura!" Hattie shouted, sprinting across the room with her skirts in her hands, nearly tripping over her own feet in her haste. She slid in a growing puddle of blood that encircled her sister, who lay still.

Also safely on the floor again, I joined Hattie. "Wait," I cautioned her as gently as I could as she reached for her twin. I pressed my fingers to Laura's wrist, sighing with relief when I felt a fluttering pulse. "Don't move her just yet. You could injure her further. We need a healer!"

"I'll fetch one," Bentley volunteered, sprinting from the room.

As he vanished, I turned to one of the tables, seizing a dagger and slicing off a piece of the tablecloth. Florian was at my side in an instant, so I turned to him, trusting he would be more reliable in this moment than Hattie, who was dissolving into tears. "Help me wrap her shoulder."

Florian held Laura's arm steady while I worked, applying as much pressure as I could and wrapping tightly in an attempt to staunch the flow of blood.

Across the room, there was a snarl cut short. I didn't lift my eyes from my work, but I knew it meant Kaede had ended the vampire's life—if whatever existence it had led could be called a life at all. His footsteps approached, and as I finished tying off the fabric, I finally dared to glance up.

His jaw was taut, his brow furrowed with concern. For a long moment, he stared at her in silence before his dark eyes flitted to me. "How is she?" he asked, voice gruff.

"Alive, but she has lost a lot of blood, and she appears to have struck her head quite hard." I swallowed thickly. I could not help but feel a measure of responsibility for Laura's condition, since I'd been the one to urge her to wield magic and stop the vampire.

Before anyone could say more, Bentley darted back into the great hall, followed by Azalea, who carried a leather bag slung over one shoulder. She knelt beside Laura, checking her pulse and doing a careful study of her condition and wounds, especially the bleeding gash on her head. "You may move her," she announced at last. "If someone could carry her to the infirmary, I can tend to her injuries and monitor her."

"Will she be all right?" Hattie choked out.

Azalea's mouth was pursed. "My magic can do many wondrous things, but blood loss and injuries to the head are complicated. I cannot replace the blood she's lost, and as for the head wound... It involves more than stitching skin and muscle back together—sometimes the memory is affected. Or worse. Those types of wounds are harder to heal, and more taxing for the patient, as it takes more of their body's energy as my magic works with it. It's...hard to say what will happen to her right now, especially since she's mortal."

Kaede's face was pale as he stooped, lifting Laura effortlessly in his arms. Against my wishes, my stomach tightened at the sight of her tucked against his chest. Even wounded and unconscious, she was beautiful, her golden curls tumbling in a curtain about her face, her delicate features highlighted in the dancing candlelight as Kaede strode toward the hallway. Bentley, Hattie, and Azalea trailed after them, but I hesitated.

Florian lingered near me, noticing my discomfort. "You thought quickly and did well with wrapping her wound," he commended. "Don't blame yourself for what happened. Her recovery will be in no small part thanks to you."

If *she recovers,* I thought darkly.

Florian offered his arm, his mouth twitching in a half-hearted smile, like he wanted to encourage me but wasn't sure how. "May I help you find your sister and then escort you both to your rooms?"

I drew in a shaky breath as I took his arm, finding a measure of comfort in his steady presence as he escorted me out of the room and outside, where we found the escaped fae and contestants huddled nervously in the gardens. I ran to Callista, throwing my arms around her. "It's safe to go inside," I told her.

She sniffled, wiping at her nose.

"This test is over," Ji announced, glancing about nervously. "We will...ah, announce the next round of the competition tomorrow morning."

My mind swirled with questions. The pain from being exposed to Kaede's magic had worn off, making me hope that meant the effects were gone for the other contestants too.

As Florian led Callista and me back to our quarters, I resolved to visit Laura the first chance I had tomorrow. At our door, Florian hesitated, clearing his throat and searching my face. "Tonight could have gone much worse without your quick thinking," he said. He lifted my hand, pressing a gentle kiss to it. "Sleep well tonight, Aurelia."

Bidding him goodnight, I followed Callista into our rooms and locked our door. I leaned against it, closing my eyes.

"Is he courting you?" Callista asked, tilting her head curiously. "When we are all competing for the prince's hand?"

"I...suppose he is."

Callista shrugged, heading for the wardrobe, where she rifled through the clothing to find a nightgown. While she prepared for bed, I went to the washroom, drawing myself a steaming bath to scrub away the day, trying to remove the memory of Kaede's touches. Trying to focus instead on the way Florian's kiss against the back of my hand had felt.

It was nice. He is kind, and he sees your good qualities. I sank back into the water, finger combing through the tangles in my wet hair. *And he isn't trying to kill you.*

What if I let myself consider Florian as a match? Maybe his attentions would soothe the ache in my heart, help me to forget the love I had for Kaede. Help me move on and heal at last.

Maybe.

If I wanted to remain in the fae world, and Kaede chose by some miracle to spare my life, being the wife of an influential member of the court would provide me with protection. More than that, it would provide for anything I could possibly need—maybe even anything my family would need as well. We would never have to worry about money again. From that standpoint, it was a logical match. My family could continue to live in the human world while I sent them funds.

I focused on that, telling myself that was the sort of future I should plan. Not waste time dreaming of something that could never be.

And yet, each time I closed my eyes, it was Kaede's dark eyes, flashing with emotion, that filled my imagination. It was his tousled hair, his sharp cheekbones, and his chiseled jaw that made my heart skip.

It was the memory of his lips that haunted me.

CHAPTER THIRTY

NOW

As we dressed for breakfast the next morning, I noticed how dark the circles under Callista's eyes had grown.

"Were you able to sleep much?" I'd tossed and turned most of the night.

My sister shook her head, shoulders hunched, as I buttoned her into a dress.

"Nightmares?"

"Yes, awful dreams after...after..." She swallowed, her bottom lip wobbling. "I want to go home, Auri."

I squeezed her hand. "I know. Me too. And we will. I promise you."

The weight of that promise settled in my heart. I only hoped I could keep it.

When I swung open the door, Florian was already approaching, his hands tucked in his pockets.

"Oh, good, you're awake." His smile was warm, a welcome sight after the horrors of the night before. "I am here to escort you to breakfast. Ladies shouldn't be wandering about the manor alone."

I cast him a sidelong look. "After last night?"

He pursed his lips, his lighthearted expression melting into solemnity for a moment. "Indeed. I'd like to think that..." He cleared his throat. "Well, that the worst is over."

I accepted his proffered arm while Callista took his other, and we strode together down the hall and toward the staircase. "How can we be sure more vampires won't enter the manor? Or that more are not already prowling about?"

"There are many strange creatures in Willowbark, but vampires? Those are rare. It must have been a fluke—maybe it was drawn by the concentration of magic."

I didn't respond, wondering how many others—if any—were aware of the darkness plaguing Kaede. How many more vampires were lurking within his kingdom because of his nightmares? My mind was split over whether to share the information with Florian—to warn him of the dangers—or to keep it to myself and discuss it with a healer like Azalea first to avoid panic.

As we entered the dining hall, my stomach churned with memories from last night. All signs of the bloodbath had been cleared away, leaving the floor gleaming and spotless.

The gathered courtiers were more somber than usual. A swift scan of the space told me that Bentley and Prince Kaede were both absent. Hattie was poking listlessly at the food on her plate. Her tangled hair and wan face told me she hadn't slept at all last night and that she longed to be at her sister's side. However, she'd probably been forced to join this meal, considering the competition had not yet ended.

"We have a very special challenge, one that we cannot delay until tonight," Ji announced without preamble, before Callista and I had even taken our seats.

With my hand still on his arm, I felt the way Florian stiffened. "We are not...postponing? What did His Highness have to say after last night's incidents?"

Ji's gaze was icy as he assessed the outspoken advisor. "He knows what must be done. Time is of the essence."

A chill rippled over my skin. I studied Florian's profile, but he gazed steadfastly ahead, frowning at the Chief Advisor and the rest of the fae.

"Immediately after breakfast, you are each to meet with Allvar, our esteemed warlock of Willowbark."

"We did not agree to this." Florian cleared his throat, emphasizing his next words. "The *prince* did not agree to this."

Ji sighed loudly, as if he was being a tedious, rebellious child. "We cannot waste time arguing. The king has made his orders clear, and I, for one, refuse to dishonor His Majesty's wishes while he is on his deathbed. We must all remember where our loyalty lies."

Florian arched his brow. "Surely this is a matter in which each contestant could have some assistance? Especially since last night's challenge went awry."

Ji licked his lips, reminding me of a hungry predator. "Allvar will not permit that. They must be one-on-one meetings."

Heaviness settled over the breakfast table, some fae continuing to eat unbothered, probably happy enough to see us humans be sent into further danger, while the remaining women seemed to have lost their appetites.

I swallowed thickly, worrying for Callista. "Is Allvar very dangerous?" I whispered to Florian.

"It is said that he can see into your heart to find your deepest desires and fears, and then he offers you bargains you cannot refuse. Ones that never end well for mortals. He feeds on the youth and strength of the magic-less. It is how he continues to live so long, gaining power in his own magic and life."

I sucked in a heavy breath. "So we are to be your sacrifices again?"

Overhearing my words, Ji looked at me sharply. "No. This is to assess your wisdom and courage."

Florian muttered something that sounded like a curse under his breath.

Shifting in my chair, I met Ji's stare with calm fortitude. "What about Laura? Surely it is unfair to exclude her after she succeeded in wielding Prince Kaede's magic last night. I would imagine if anyone were to be declared a winner of that challenge, it would be her."

"And yet she lies unconscious, perhaps on her deathbed," Ji said callously.

Hattie sniffled.

"And the challenges must continue. A winner must be chosen. I do not care what preferences the prince has shown, or how the previous challenges have gone. We will find a queen, one who is worthy of Willowbark. Prince Kaede knows his responsibility, and he cannot call off this contest for one wounded mortal."

I lifted my chin, considering our options. Given the warlock's reputation, perhaps I could take the brunt of his greed and cruelty. If I could not accompany my sister, I could pray that my meeting would encourage him to be kinder toward Callista and the other women. If nothing else, I would be able to learn more about him and then convey that knowledge with my sister to prepare her.

"Then," I said, "if I may volunteer, I would like to meet with Allvar first."

As I stepped into the room Ji had led me to, I wondered if the manor had altered it to create an aura of mystery, or if Allvar had insisted on such arrangements. The space reminded me of the washroom I'd visited in my dream with Kaede, in which the outdoors had seemed to merge with the indoors. Here, everything was dark and immersed in shadows, with only faint hints of light from flickering candles buried within half-hidden alcoves. The room was long, overrun with vines and trees pushing through the floor.

Ducking beneath a branch, I scanned the room for any sign of the warlock. Instead, a group of twittering birds flitted through the air while a squirrel chirped at me from the branch before flicking its tail and running further into the tree.

"Allvar?" I called hesitantly.

As I pressed deeper into the room, I began to wonder if I was still in the manor or somewhere else entirely. The space seemed to go on endlessly. Soon the floorboards were spotted with dirt and moss and the sound of running water filtered through the air. I drew a deep breath, inhaling the woodsy, earthy scents of a deep, ancient wood.

I paused, wondering which way I should travel next to try to find Allvar, when the floorboards rose beneath me, rippling like water. Heart in my throat, I struggled to keep my balance while the manor lifted me as if carrying me on a wave, pushing me deeper into the room and depositing me before a shallow pool. Here, the lighting was brighter, for a circle of flaming torches dotted the space, their smoke filling the air with a crisp scent. This was also where the sound of running water originated, for a small stream poured down the wall and fell into the pool, stirring foam on its far edge. On my side, the water lay calm and clear, reflecting the flickering orange light. When I peered past it, I found a bed of dirt and pebbles. Tiny fish darted about, nibbling at underwater vegetation.

Left in awe at the way nature had so effortlessly melded with the manor, I didn't hear the approach of uneven footsteps until they paused right behind me.

"Heh," a scratchy male voice said. "You humans are easily impressed." He smacked a cane against the floorboards beside my foot, startling me backward, though I had enough presence of mind to sidestep and avoid a plunge into the pool. "What do you go by?"

I turned to find a hunched elderly man with wild, wispy white hair and a heavily wrinkled face. As unused to seeing age in the fae world as I was, I had to school my features. After all, I knew warlocks were different from the rest of the fae. Their magic followed other rules, draining their own life, strength, and sanity. It was, after all, why they—and their female counterparts—enjoyed meeting and bargaining with magic-less mortals. "Aurelia Sinclair."

The man smirked, his yellow teeth flashing in the dim light. "Did they choose you to be the first sacrifice?" He released a wheezy laugh, swinging his cane about as he turned and hobbled further into the room.

Unnerved, I kept my expression carefully blank. "I volunteered."

He paused, tilting his head to the side and squinting, as if truly seeing me for the first time. "To protect your younger sister, Callista."

My heart skipped a beat. Though Florian had warned me that Allvar could see one's desires and fears, experiencing it was an entirely different matter. It reminded me far too much of how King Wystan had read my mind.

"Come forward, Aurelia. I want to show you something." He tapped his cane upon the ground, like an impatient tutor.

I approached on hesitant feet, wondering what the warlock wanted with me. With any of us. Did he care about Willowbark's future and determining who would be a worthy queen, or did he only want to trick us into making bargains for our greatest wishes?

"What do you hope to gain from this competition?" the warlock croaked as I paused before him. Here, two huge trees crowded out the light from the torches, immersing us in shadow. In the darkness, his bent form and wrinkled face seemed ominous. He emanated power and strength despite his wizened appearance, and his eyes held the wisdom of countless human lives.

"I think you already know."

He smiled. "And yet, I want to hear it from your own lips. Voice your wishes, out loud."

My skin prickled, but I could discern no trick from this request. "I want to ensure my sister survives, so that we can both go home unscathed and live out our lives in peace."

Allvar scoffed, tapping his cane on the ground again. "So noble. So practical. So dutiful." He sniffed. "What do you hope to *gain*?"

I scowled. "I told you what I hope—"

"You told me that you hope things will return to as they were before the start of this competition, so you may go back to your dull mortal life. You told me what is reasonable, not what you *hope*. Tell me what you dream, what impossible thing you long for." He leaned forward, smirking knowingly.

Nerves coiled in my stomach, and my mouth dried. I could not confess that desire, not aloud. Not to him. Not to anyone. I could scarcely acknowledge it to myself. As Allvar had said, it was impossible.

And yet, my mouth opened, words pouring out as if of their own accord. "I want Prince Kaede to forgive me. I want to atone for my past and live without guilt, and I want him to love me again. I want him to...choose *me*." The last words came out in a whisper, breathless and breakable. I closed my eyes, immediately seeing Laura and the tender way in which he'd cradled her while carrying her from the great hall last night.

Allvar grinned, but it was not a kind look. "I know what you must do to atone for your past and have a chance at his forgiveness and love."

This time when he tapped his cane against the ground, light burst forth like a fog around it, swirling and growing in a golden orb. It lifted higher into the air, until it had risen above Allvar's cane and even above our heads, floating as if suspended by unseen strings. Within the orb of light, more colors appeared, coalescing until they formed moving shapes.

And then, as the shapes became recognizable objects and people, sound emerged.

I caught my gasp, for now it appeared as if I were peering through a window into a dim room. Early morning light illuminated Prince Kaede's quarters in the manor. He sat upon the edge of his bed, his hair as messy as the haphazardly tossed sheets behind him. He wore a half-buttoned shirt and trousers, as if he had started to prepare for the day or had never fully undressed before falling asleep the night before. Even here, when Kaede wasn't actually present, my cheeks warmed at the sight of his bare, toned chest. He ran a hand along his jaw, shadowed with stubble, and lifted weary eyes toward the door opposite him as a knock sounded.

"Come in," he called, and Azalea stepped into the room, carrying her bag.

She approached him on swift feet, pausing at his bedside. "Did it happen again last night, Your Highness? Is that why you called for me?"

"Nightmares from which a vampire emerged and murdered someone?" Kaede asked bitterly. "Yes. Staying here in the manor is not the precaution we thought it would be. My creatures can still haunt the palace—not to mention I'm now a danger to the humans here. The vampires don't only attack members of the court. Not now. Now they attack anyone and *everyone*. It doesn't matter where I am or how many guards you've started posting within and without my rooms. And now I'm finding that I conjure them both while awake and asleep. The darkness is taking hold and I am losing control. I am a threat to my own people, and the kingdom must be rid of me—"

She raised a hand to cut him short. "No, Prince Kaede. We've already discussed this. But that is not what I was asking. Did the change happen again? In *you*."

Kaede lowered his head to his hands, his shoulders slumping in defeat. "For a moment, yes. I was the hungry creature growing fangs and claws. I was the one who longed for blood. Am I...turning into one? Will I become even more of a monster than I already am?"

Azalea ran a shaky hand across her brow and cleared her throat. "That's just it. I...well, I was finally able to find a book that mentioned demon's breath, a poison that is crafted in Emberglade. The symptoms match what you suffered. But there's more than that. There was a case in which, by a great miracle of healing magic, a woman survived the poison. However, the book described a change in her and her magic. It became dangerous and unpredictable."

Slowly, Kaede lifted his face to meet Azalea's gaze. "What happened to her?"

The healer shifted uneasily on her feet. "She died, Your Highness. The poison never truly left her. I'm afraid it has never left you, either, despite your death and return to life. You are trapped in a sort of half-life, with contaminated magic and a poison that is slowly but surely killing you all over again."

The light faded, the orb slowly shrinking before vanishing entirely.

I gaped at the space where the scene had played out, my mind whirling with all I'd just learned. "He's...he's dying?" I choked out. "Again? Is this really true? What did you show me?"

"I showed you a moment from the past." Allvar arched an eyebrow. "I need you to know what is at stake."

Nausea clung to my tongue as that old ache of grief seized me all over again. "He...he survived. He cannot die again. There must be a way to stop this."

Allvar's smile widened. "There is. That is why I showed that to you."

He snapped his fingers this time, and another orb of light appeared, floating similarly to the first. This one showed Azalea at a bedside in the manor's infirmary. She sat beside Laura, who remained motionless, her skin leached of color. Nearby, Kaede paced and ran frustrated hands through his hair.

"I wish you'd realized my blood was still contaminated with demon's breath before we dosed all the competitors. Will they die? Have I cursed us all?"

Azalea frowned in thought. "I don't think so. They were given such a small amount, and their mortal bodies would have already shown the effects if so. But it was probably why they suffered so much pain. It wasn't only the shock of your magic coursing through their non-magical bodies."

Kaede cast Laura a worried look. "Could it be making it harder for her to heal? Will she ever wake?"

"She was gravely injured even without being dosed with poison. There's no saying that has had an effect on her recovery at all." Azalea shifted in her seat, sighing. "This is all so unknown. If there were time, I'd travel to Emberglade, see if I could learn more."

"But you told me there is no antidote."

Azalea shook her head sadly. "None recorded that I can find."

"And we haven't the time, anyway." He sighed. "No, it is better that you're here. And better that the poison takes me, if this is what it has done to my magic. I cannot live with myself, knowing I endanger my own people like this. That, when the darkness consumes me, I relish it and truly become a monster who wants to shed their blood. Perhaps the mistake was in my people trying to bring me back to life. They should have let me go, released me to the afterlife."

The scene cut out and the orb melted away before I could hear how Azalea responded.

For a moment, I couldn't think, couldn't breathe. Kaede was dying. Again.

I was killing him all over again.

"Demon's breath has no antidote," I whispered, tears gathering in my vision.

"Not quite true." Allvar's sharp tone cut through the fog in my mind.

"What? Is there a way to save Kaede?"

His lips curled in a cruel smile. "For the right price."

I broke into a cold sweat. *Now that he has me desperate, this is where he lures me into a terrible bargain.* It was all too familiar. "What price?" I managed, my voice coming out hoarse.

"My magic feeds off the magic-less. Promise to grant me your younger sister's youth and beauty, and I will help you."

Rather than allow him to see my horror—though he probably knew it already if he could see my deepest fears—I composed myself and asked, "Help how? Can you heal him?"

"I know a secret, closely held among my kind. One that could be the key to his healing, yes."

"That's not enough for me to make such a bargain. You are not fae, so you can lie."

Allvar shook his head. "I am bound by my magic to speak truth."

"And yet you have given yourself too many loopholes. Your secret could be *any* secret, and merely saying that it could be the key to his healing is not sufficient."

Allvar grunted, squinting his eyes and shifting on his feet. "You are a shrewd one. Very well. My secret involves an antidote, but it is difficult and dangerous to obtain, so knowing this truth is not a guarantee of success."

Shivers coursed over my skin. "I will bargain with you," I said firmly, "but I will not involve my sister. Let this matter be between us only."

My heart thrummed so loudly in my ears, I could scarcely hear Allvar's words.

"Though you are also young and lovely, it is your mind and your heart that give you strength. Vow that I may have them, and I will grant you my secret."

"You may have them, but only after you have given me time to obtain the antidote and deliver it to the prince."

Allvar laughed. "Ah, yes, you will not leave out a single detail. Scrupulous." He reached out a wrinkled hand, and, hesitantly, I shook it.

In a blink, both Allvar and the strange room vanished. Rather than his hand, I held a piece of paper.

And instead of standing inside the manor, I was outside Emberglade's castle.

CHAPTER THIRTY-ONE

THEN

My eyes burned as I cradled my mug of tea, pretending the rising steam could soothe the permanent chill in my bones. But nothing could erase a cold that stemmed from self-inflicted grief, or the ache of guilt that clung to me like a second skin. I was heavy with pain I deserved. It was as if, as surely as I'd plunged that dagger into Kaede's chest, I'd killed myself too.

Whatever this was, it was not living. Every color had dulled while every effort had intensified. I walked through my days trapped in my own haunting thoughts, eating food that tasted of dirt and forcing smiles that tasted of lies. My only purpose was to tend to my family's needs, pretending as if the other lifetime I'd lived in the fae world had never happened, concealing the foul nature of my time and misdeeds there. They didn't care to know and inconvenience themselves with the discomfort of such odious tales, so they didn't pry.

We were all content to ignore my suffering.

But today, a mere month since I'd murdered the man I'd loved, I could not try to bury myself in the mortal world. Today, I sat in a tiny inn at the edge of town, one that was generally avoided by gentlemen and ladies. Dressed in the only remaining fae outfit I had of leggings, a tunic, and a cloak with a heavy hood that, when pulled low, concealed my face, I'd snuck into a shadowy corner of the inn's main room and bided my time. The message had arrived like any of my usual correspondence, taking me by surprise when I'd sliced open the envelope and perused the contents to find a simple note with this location and a time, along with Emberglade's crest stamped at the bottom.

When King Wystan entered the inn, I knew he'd glamoured himself as a human for all but me, because the innkeeper and other guests paid him no heed. He approached my table and settled in the chair across from me, grinning like a devil. His orange eyes were sharp enough to search one's soul. A painful reminder of his magical ability.

I took a sip of my tea, though, to me, it tasted of nothing. It was too hot and burned my tongue, but I scarcely registered the pain.

"Miss Sinclair. Honestly, I never expected to see you again. Alive, that is."

"I know you didn't trouble yourself to enter the human world to exchange pleasantries," I said.

"Indeed not." He tossed a heavy bag jingling of coins onto the table. "This is a matter of business. I consider myself a man of my word, and I promised your family wealth in exchange for you completing your mission successfully. And since that is what you did, and word reached my ear that your greedy family already spent the first portion of your allowance, I've brought more."

Eyes widening at his lack of discretion, I hurried to conceal the bag within my cloak before any of the other guests noticed. "Why not send a servant to deliver this?" I questioned. Surely the king had more important matters to tend to.

His smile was slow and wicked. "I do, but I also came to relish your emotions. They have not disappointed. Since I am not wholly fae, my magic is not sustained by my land's as theirs is. Mine is replenished by feeding off your suffering."

I forced myself to conceal my grimace, even if I knew he could read every disgusted thought and could enjoy my feelings as they bolstered his magic even more. I hated that my grief and misery was strengthening him. I hated *him*.

And that hatred, ironically, probably only strengthened him too.

The waitress bustled over to take King Wystan's order, briefly interrupting our exchange.

My heart sank at the weight of the bag. If only my family hadn't been so foolish and extravagant in my absence. If only we could go in time and undo those mistakes so that they did not have to sell our estate.

Then again, if I was wishing for the impossible, I might as well have wished Prince Kaede back to life.

"There will be a steady supply of coins for you and your family. This is only the beginning. And you have my word that your family will not be troubled or threatened by myself or any of my people. You have my protection."

My tongue felt leaden. "And my identity," I rasped. "My name, my description, my home, my family—all must be concealed to truly protect my father and sisters."

"Yes. As promised, none of that has been or will be revealed."

King Wystan accepted his drink from the waitress, and I paid for mine. As I rose, leaving my half-finished mug, I hesitated. "The war you wanted has begun?"

"Yes," the king said smugly. "Without Prince Kaede, Willowbark will be easy to defeat."

My stomach churned, bile souring my mouth as I considered the awful consequences of Kaede's death. It was unbearable enough to know I'd murdered him, but to consider that I'd also brought misery and death to the kingdom and people he had loved and served? I swallowed, forcing my pain down, down, and clinging to facts.

My family was safe from starvation, humiliation, and harm now. We could continue life as we always had, just in a new city, a new home. My sisters could marry or choose to stay single, such was our wealth. We would never want for anything ever again.

As I exited the inn, I felt King Wystan's eyes searing me, reading my thoughts and relishing my grief.

CHAPTER THIRTY-TWO

NOW

Seeing Emberglade's towers piercing the hazy sunset sky sent a flurry of emotions through me. I could still walk those halls by memory, still recall the darkness that seemed to hover over the space as quiet servants and citizens whose magic wasn't as powerful and oppressive as King Wystan's eked out an existence.

Swallowing, I ducked behind a hedgerow before the guards patrolling the ramparts could spot me, and uncurled the paper Allvar had given me.

To cure your prince, you must craft a potion only shared among the spell-weavers and occasional witch and warlock. The most important ingredient is a drop of blood from the one who orchestrated the victim's death. Unfortunately, you were merely the instrument. You know whose blood you need. Once you've succeeded, I'll bring you back.

My breathing shallowed as I read and reread the note. At last, I forced myself to begin running through my options. Knowing the layout of the castle was helpful, as was my time here, which, if King Wystan's habits remained the same, would aid me in narrowing down his location.

However, none of my training had taught me how to ambush a target that could read minds.

One mistake and I'd be dead before I'd have a hope of undoing all the ways I'd wronged Kaede and his kingdom.

Shoving my fear to the dark recesses of my mind, I approached the castle through a familiar, half-forgotten path through the gardens. I'd traversed this many times during my stay here, taunting myself with the idea of leaving and willing the nightmarish world I felt trapped in to disappear. But always, I'd return to my rooms, shaken to the core with the knowledge that there was no escaping the bargain I was trapped in. If I failed to uphold my end, the consequences were unimaginable.

Sweat beading on my forehead, I paused in a shadowy alcove within the gardens, hidden from the guards by a half-wall covered in climbing ivy. I warmed up my limbs by going through the stretches drilled into me, then plucked the dagger from my boot. It was the one from the table at the great hall, one I'd used to help Laura and then kept, thankful the fae hadn't noticed its absence. Unsheathing the blade, I cut off strips of cloth from the bottom of my tunic. Wrapping my palms, I tucked the dagger securely back in place.

I watched the guard on the outer wall, waiting for his patrol of this area to end. Once she turned the corner, moving out of sight on her way toward the portion surrounding the entry gates, I knew I had sufficient time before anyone would walk that section again. Drawing a deep breath, I began to scale the castle. Outside each window, I paused, peering through the glass to scan the rooms within and check for occupants.

Outside one of the libraries on the third level, the sound of voices drifted toward me through the open windows. I lingered, glancing over the sill just long enough to find two servants dusting and sweeping as they gossiped.

"Surely Prince Kaede doesn't have long now," the male said, sliding a stack of books to the side to thoroughly dust a shelf.

The woman sighed from her spot near the hearth and leaned on her broom. "Who can say? And what will another war bring? Sure, Willow-bark will be weaker with both the king and the prince gone, but will we truly be guaranteed victory? Or will it be another bloody trial where we send our family to fight and suffer while..."

The man cut her off. "Hush, they could hear."

With renewed vigor, I continued my climb, ignoring the shaking beginning in my muscles from the prolonged time I'd been suspended. It had been too long since I'd trained and exerted myself like this. Breathing deeply through my nose to keep quiet, I stopped outside the window leading to the infirmary's storage closet, confirmed it was unoccupied and the door leading to the infirmary was shut, and began working the complicated locks that secured the windows from the outside. One needed a bit of finesse along with the knowledge of the order each gear and mechanism needed to be moved in. It was a system I'd been taught during my time here, for both Kymelle and King Wystan had been too proud and confident in their power to ever imagine I might use this knowledge against them.

Sweat dribbled from my brow as I leaned into the castle wall, supported only by my feet on a narrow ledge and my hand against the windowsill while I worked. My fingers felt clumsy after being wedged into the crevices of the stone wall, and despite the way I'd wrapped them, they were growing damp.

Finally, the lock sprang free, and I was able to push the window upward. I landed in the room, praying I was light enough of foot that a fae in the next room wouldn't have heard. That was one thing I could never fully master—the ability to move so silently and gracefully I was unheard by their keen ears. I'd practiced and practiced, only taking my trainer by surprise a handful of times over the long months.

Moving as swiftly and silently as I could, I approached the cabinets and scanned the shelves, plucking the first empty vial I found. Voices outside the door made my heart rate accelerate, and I returned to the window as fast as I dared. Swinging over the ledge, I slid the window shut, not bothering to waste time on refastening the lock. By the time someone noticed the window wasn't secure, I would either be long gone—or dead.

My final destination forced me toward the opposite side of the castle, so I shimmied along the ledge as far as I could go, ducking beneath windows and constantly scanning for anyone who might spy me from the grounds below. At a corner, I was forced to descend back into the gardens. The next side of the castle faced the wall upon which guards were posted constantly, keeping the gates secure at all hours of the day and night. I would have to act casual, for as a lone figure strolling through the gardens, I wouldn't be suspicious. I forced myself to keep my steps easy, despite my heightened senses and my fear of someone peering outside from a lower level of the castle and catching a good enough look at my face to recognize me. Too many servants and guards would remember the human who'd lived among them for so long, learning their ways.

At last, I turned another corner and slipped out of the posted guards' sight. These walls faced the fields where the horses grazed and King Wystan and his family rode, so the guards didn't stand sentinel here, instead making regular patrols. As before, I waited and watched, sitting on a bench tucked into the shadows to help conceal my face. When a guard completed his paces across this section of the wall and back toward the gates, I rose and stretched once more to limber my arms and legs.

Everything was similar to my last climb, except for my heightened nerves. I couldn't completely block out the fear, not when I knew what was at stake. Not when I was about to face the king who'd doomed me to this cursed life—and, worst of all, doomed Kaede to a cursed death.

As long as his habits hadn't changed since before Kaede's assassination and the subsequent war, he was only a few stories away. When I reached the ledge, my body trembled, and I had to collect myself. With a conscious effort, I worked through everything I needed to do, imagining the room in my mind and the steps I would take. Ever so slowly, the terror subsided enough for my body to relax and my thoughts to clear.

I peered through the window cautiously, finding the form I'd expected lounging in his high-backed chair in the war room. Sweat beading on my brow, I unlocked the window with nimble fingers, praying he wouldn't turn, praying he wouldn't hear. I managed to slide the window up silently, pull the dagger from my boot, and swing within.

I was two steps behind him when he spoke.

"Aurelia. I never expected you to venture here willingly again." He chuckled, low in his throat, before pushing his chair back, rising, and turning all in a few smooth movements. "Who hired you to assassinate me? Or was it another unfortunate bargain?"

The dagger's hilt was slick in my palm, so I tightened my grasp as King Wystan's orange gaze pierced mine.

"Oh." His lips twisted into a smirk as he read my thoughts. "This is even better. You're here to undo the damage done to your prince?" He laughed outright. "Now, now, that would be breaking your word."

I swallowed thickly. "I already killed him as promised. Nothing in our bargain mentioned the prince being brought back to life and needing to die a second time."

King Wystan shrugged. "It doesn't matter. You've failed. I do find it ironic that you've fallen for the man you killed. You are the author of your own heartbreak, and what a deliciously tragic tale it is."

Despair swept through me, and I squeezed my eyes shut, trying to avoid the tears that threatened. Failure was unthinkable. Losing Kaede the first time nearly undid me. Losing him a second time? My own death would be a mercy compared to that. But King Wystan was a sadistic, nasty creature, and now that he knew I was in love with Kaede, he would keep me alive so I could learn of his death and experience the full extent of that loss.

He stepped nearer, bridging the gap between us until I could practically feel the excitement emanating from him. The anticipation of watching me break.

"Perhaps this time I'll glamour you, force you to return to Willowbark so you can watch Prince Kaede's death firsthand, and then force your return here to the dungeons, where you can live out the rest of your short, wretched, mortal days in misery."

My stomach clenched, but I refused to let the power of his words overwhelm me. He was taunting me, wanting to force me into terror and submission. The truth was, he could command me here with his glamour: make me slit my own throat, bow and kiss his feet, or leap to my death from the window. But once I was out of his presence, the hold his glamour had on me would lessen. He was twisting his words, telling me how he could glamour me but not how long the effects of it would actually last.

"It will be a pleasure to watch you fall apart, you foul traitor," he gloated. "To make a bargain with me and then come back to murder me? I will make your suffering so great you will wish your pathetic mortal years were even shorter."

I could feel magic tingling in the air as he silently summoned it, preparing to glamour me, to condemn me to the life he'd been threatening me with.

I let a single tear trickle down my cheek as I squeezed my eyes tightly closed, knowing any second his words could trap me.

CHAPTER THIRTY-THREE

NOW

My body went limp as I collapsed, my head cracking painfully against the floor. But I didn't wince, didn't open my eyes. I floated in darkness as I felt King Wystan's presence hovering over me. His palm struck my cheek in a stinging blow, but I remained still, my breaths shallow and my muscles loose. The dagger I'd clung to was cold beneath my open palm.

Everything relied on King Wystan believing I was truly incapacitated.

Cursing beneath his breath, King Wystan pulled away, his voice growing more distant as his footsteps padded away from me. "Weak mortals, fainting in fear," he sneered. Then he raised his voice. "Guards!"

My heart lurched into my throat as I rose, fingers securely on my dagger hilt once more. I sprang forward on sure feet, abandoning silence for speed.

King Wystan cursed again, but before he could fully turn, my dagger sliced across his arm, a swipe that drenched the blade in his blood. His orange gaze burned hatefully into mine as he spoke, before I could turn and race for the window.

"Stay still," he said, his voice filled with the smooth, hauntingly charming tone of a fae using glamour. I could feel the magic heavy in the air, binding me to the king and his awful commands.

My body twitched and then froze against my will.

But I'd been ready, prepared with the protection he didn't know his trainer, Kymelle, had gifted me.

"I didn't go to Willowbark only for Callista," I breathed, the truth of the confession buzzing through my blood, startling me back into full control of my body. I stumbled backward, fleeing toward the window.

"Stop!" King Wystan shouted, furious.

Footsteps pounded outside the war room and guards burst through the door.

But the power of the truth weakened his continued attempts at glamour.

I swung over the windowsill. "I also went for myself," I panted as I began climbing down the castle wall, forcing the words through my lips so the glamour King Wystan was still trying to fling toward me would fail. "I needed to see Kaede again. Even if he wanted to kill me." My fingers burned, stone biting into skin as I rushed, nearly slipping and falling more than once.

Thankfully, the guards shouting at me through the window weren't armed with bows, but I knew they'd call for reinforcements who would meet me in the castle grounds. My only hope was that Allvar's magic would bring me back as swiftly as it had transferred me here.

Guards were charging through the gardens only moments later. An arrow soared past my ear, ricocheting off the stone. I choked on a gasp of fear. If I went much faster, I risked making a clumsy mistake and falling toward an awful injury or death, but if I wasn't fast enough, I'd be skewered.

"Allvar," I muttered, "now would be the perfect time to sense my success and bring me back to Willowbark."

Another arrow grazed my shoulder, and I couldn't hold in a cry of pain as warm blood trickled down my back. Each motion of my arm sent a bolt of pain through the injury.

"Allvar!" I repeated. "If you do not act soon, I will not live long enough to uphold my end of the bargain."

Whether he'd been watching my progress, heard my words, or simply sensed what I'd accomplished somehow, the world around me vanished as suddenly as it had appeared. In a blink, I was standing on the floor in the Willow manor again, facing Allvar in that strange room. The only signs that I'd been in Emberglade at all were my still-racing pulse, clammy, scraped hands wrapped in tattered pieces of my sliced tunic, my bleeding shoulder, and the vial of blood tucked securely in my boot.

"Very good." Allvar clapped his hands together. "All the other bargains made or discussed in your absence were rather dull. You can feed my magic for years to come." With a yellow grin, he reached out a wrinkled hand, as if he'd snatch my soul right from my body or drain the years of my life with a single touch.

I lurched backward. "No," I said firmly. "Nowhere in our bargain did you state that I must make my sacrifice before you've concocted the antidote. In fact, I stipulated that you must allow me to deliver it to Prince Kaede. I want to be sure he receives it, to know that he has a chance, even if I do not live long enough to see whether it succeeds."

Allvar's gaze narrowed. "You are not in a position to ask for much," he said, "and nowhere did I say I would allow you to *see* him be healed. Delivering it to Willow Manor is sufficient under the terms of our agreement. No one could claim I didn't fulfill my end." He teetered forward, arm extended, but I raised my voice, this time appealing to a different power.

"To withhold the antidote from the prince any longer than necessary when you have the key to crafting it would be a treasonous action. Would it not, Willow Manor?"

The warlock froze, scowling, but around us, the room shifted and shuddered as if in agreement. Without warning, more roots and trees burst through the areas where the floor appeared to be more dirt than wooden boards, encircling Allvar. Vines stretched between the branches, wrapping like ropes about the trunks until Allvar was caged within.

The sense of victory that gripped me was temporary. It was gratifying to know I was right and the manor was loyal to the prince's interests, at least in this matter, but it did not change that soon, I'd have to return to Allvar.

Plucking the vial from my boot, I reached out, hoping to shove it past the ivy growing so thickly I could no longer see the hunched form within. The branches moved like a living thing, twisting around the vial and gently taking it from me before withdrawing back toward the trees and depositing it within Allvar's confined space.

Grunting and muttering under his breath, Allvar began shuffling about, his cane beating against the earth as he moved.

Unable to see what he was doing, I pulled back the collar of my tunic to examine my injured shoulder. The arrowhead had torn through the top of my sleeve enough to graze the skin and cause pain and bleeding, but not enough to bite into muscle. Already, the bleeding was slowing. It would need to be cleaned—or would have been, if I expected to live much longer.

Shaking my head, I replaced my collar and swallowed back my grief. Whatever future I'd imagined had grown dark and dismal anyway, ever since I'd murdered Kaede. Perhaps in death I'd find the peace to move on and into the afterlife.

"Here you are," Allvar snapped, and the ivy surrounding him moved again, a branch extending toward me to deposit the vial into my open palm.

I stared down at the deep red concoction, my heart thudding dully in my ears. Allvar could not lie, but he had given me no guarantee that this would heal Kaede.

Without a word of farewell, I turned and rushed from the room. Whether the manor was helping me or time seemed to move differently now, I wound my way through the trees much faster than I had when I'd entered.

The door swung open to a narrow hallway crowded with the remaining contestants, all gathered together and whispering. Tears clung to Hattie's lashes as she clasped a sniffling Edith's hand. Audrey held her jaw tight, and Charlotte's complexion looked rather ashen. None of the other women looked very pleased either—all except perhaps Callista, who perked up at the sight of me. She pushed off the wall she'd been draped against and ran to throw her arms around me.

I gritted my teeth against the flash of pain when she brushed against my wounded shoulder, but she didn't notice. "Was I gone long?" I whispered.

"What? Oh no," Callista said, pulling away to toss her dark, gleaming hair over her shoulder. "I've been waiting to discuss something with you." She grasped my hand and pulled me away from the others with a furtive glance. "The warlock offered me a deal," she said in a low voice. "Once the contest ends, he can guarantee that I would secure a betrothal to Lord Ainsley back home. I would never want for anything, hold a respected place in society, and run my own estate, far finer than the old, dusty one we shared with Mother and Father."

My stomach twisted at the way she spoke of home. "His bargains come with terrible prices."

"That's just it," Callista said, speaking faster, eagerness and hope written all over her face. "He asked for such a small thing—it would be nothing, really. He said it hardly even hurts. He said he could give that all to me if I could convince you to grant him your beauty to fuel his magic."

Her eyes shone with hope, but I was frozen, my skin going hot, then cold, then numb all over.

It would be nothing, really.

She didn't know what I'd already sacrificed, that I was giving up far more than that to spare her any pain at all. I hadn't second guessed or doubted myself, knowing in my heart I could never see Callista suffer. But she wasn't even sorry to ask me to sacrifice for her.

Like I always had.

The sister who'd always given up everything for her without question. The sister who had bargained for her. Who had faced the dangerous fae world for her. Who had killed the man she loved for her.

Nausea clung to my tongue, and I had to suppress the urge to wretch. It took everything in me to keep the disgust from showing in my expression.

Through the ringing in my ears, I realized Callista was still rambling on. "Will you do it, sister? I know you do not care about your appearance as I do."

"I have to find the prince," I choked out, pushing past her.

"Aurelia, wait!" she cried out tearfully, but I didn't turn around, didn't falter. She hadn't even noticed my bleeding shoulder or the pain in my eyes. Hadn't asked what I might have already given up. Never in her selfish heart had she even considered that maybe I had already given everything for her, and I had nothing left to sacrifice for someone so ungrateful, so self-absorbed. My eyes burned with tears I refused to shed. I'd always known my sisters and father were vain, but this was a fresh betrayal, an aching void in my chest.

I had to push aside those feelings and focus on saving Kaede.

Further down the hall, the fae courtiers were gathered. As soon as his eyes met mine, Florian raced to me, catching my hands in his. "You're hurt. What did Allvar do to you?"

Throat clogged with emotion, I merely shook my head. "Where's Azalea? I need to see her immediately. It's urgent."

For a moment, Florian's eyes clouded with jealousy. Then he seemed to collect himself, clearing his throat. "At Laura's bedside with Prince Kaede,

I believe. They recently moved her out of the infirmary and to the comfort of her own bedroom."

I hated how, even now, envy bit at my heart like a venomous snake, seeping anger and grief and regret through my veins. It was better this way—Laura was a brave, sweet young woman, and Kaede could have a chance at happiness with her when my chances were forever lost. My choice had been made, and my life was forfeit.

"Let me help you to the infirmary," Florian continued. "You're bleeding."

"I can walk well enough alone," I insisted, not wanting to pause to take his arm.

Florian opened his mouth as if to protest, but I hurried onward. His footsteps trailed me, though I didn't slow.

Somewhere behind us, Ji shouted. "We need to announce the winner of this round! Soon, we will prepare for another test. We cannot delay!"

I ignored him, picking up my pace. The floor moved underneath my steps, urging me forward.

But a wave of lightheadedness assailed me, making my vision dance with white spots. I seized the wall, trying to catch my breath.

"Aurelia!" Florian caught me as my knees gave out. His embrace was warm and sure, cradling me closely to his chest.

Embarrassment might have colored my cheeks if I hadn't felt the blood drain from them instead. Desperation clawed up my throat. What if Allvar was draining my life already, demanding his payment before I could deliver the antidote to Kaede?

Florian slipped one hand beneath my legs and the other around my waist, carrying me. "Perhaps you've lost too much blood." He frowned, his eyes dark with concern, and despite my frantic need to rush to Kaede, a brief sense of comfort touched my heart. It was unexpectedly wonderful to have someone care about me again, to want me to be safe and well without any ulterior motive.

My prince wanted me well so he could kill me himself. My sister and the rest of my family wanted me well so I could provide and care for them.

I shook my head. Now was not the time to be overcome with emotion.

Florian, taking it as another refusal for help, sighed and set me down on a nearby window seat. "If you are determined to see Azalea, would you at least spare a moment to rest and let me look at it?"

His gaze was so tender, I couldn't bring myself to open my mouth and find the words to deny him. He settled himself carefully beside me and slowly, gently, pulled back the torn fabric at my shoulder. Cursing under his breath at the sight, he drew back, studying my face sadly.

"What did he do to you, Aurelia?" he murmured, tucking a strand of hair behind my ear. The touch was tender, and I tried to make myself lean into it, but all I felt was comfort. Warm and pleasant, but without the electric excitement that pulsed through me every time Kaede was near.

Still, when Florian leaned in, only a breath away from my face, and his fingers grazed my cheek, I didn't pull away. It was an act of selfishness for a scrap of attention to soothe the aching need in my heart. I hated myself for it, but I couldn't bring myself to resist, not in this moment when I felt so used, so lonely, so desperate. Not when I knew my time was drawing short.

Before I could answer, approaching footsteps made us both turn. Striding down the hall, as if summoned from my thoughts, was the prince, his dark eyes stormy as they locked on mine.

CHAPTER THIRTY-FOUR

NOW

Butterflies danced in my stomach, their fluttering a reminder of both my nerves and my desire—even now, when I knew the darkness consuming Prince Kaede only wanted revenge. He wasn't looking at Florian's and my close proximity with jealousy. Even if I wished he was.

Still, I pulled away hastily, my cheeks burning.

"Your Highness." Florian stood and bowed with a flourish.

There was nothing of Kaede's usual charm and warmth in his expression as he studied us both stonily. My stomach dropped back down, sinking somewhere into my toes. Finding I had recovered enough strength to stand, I rose. "Prince Kaede." I dipped my head in a show of deference that allowed me to avert my gaze. The air seemed to crackle with magic and power, the temperature lowering as a breeze kissed my cheeks. It lifted my hair and brushed along my cheekbone where Florian had just touched me, but I couldn't tell if it was a caress or a threat.

Gathering my courage, I asked, "How is Laura? Is Azalea with her?"

Prince Kaede shifted on his feet. "She is expected to make a full recovery. She's conscious now, so I finally had the opportunity to thank her for her bravery and commend her on her use of my magic."

The warmth in his tone was painful, but I nodded along.

"Azalea remains with her, as she's still weak."

"Thank you." I dipped into a curtsey, thankful my knees didn't feel too wobbly. "I need to speak with her."

"Are you well enough?" Florian asked urgently.

I nodded. "Yes, just a passing moment of weakness... I seem to be quite recovered now." I smiled shyly, thankful for his attentiveness.

As I swept past Kaede in the hall, I felt a hand land on my arm. With a jolt of surprise, I glanced up to meet the prince's unreadable gaze. "What happened?" His voice gave no hint to what he was feeling as his eyes flicked toward my shoulder.

I swallowed against the dryness in my throat, trying to find words. Shaking my head, I pulled away. "It's nothing."

Prince Kaede flashed a mirthless smile, giving me a glimpse of his pointed incisors. My heart lurched. "I've never seen someone's shoulder bleed from nothing before."

I wasn't sure if he was eyeing it with concern or bloodthirst. I imagined him seizing me by the waist and burying his fangs in my throat right there, despite Florian's presence. Perhaps the darkness had consumed him fully. Perhaps he wouldn't be able to resist when he could smell my blood and sense my weakness.

"Still, it is not worth troubling oneself over," I insisted. "Florian was kind enough to help me rest, and I will see a healer soon. Please, go about your business, both of you. Don't concern yourselves with me."

As I hurried down the hallway, neither the prince nor Florian tried to follow. I was alone at last, able to knock at Laura's door undisturbed.

"Yes?" Azalea called.

I opened the door and lingered in the entryway, blinking from the change in lighting. Outside the day was bright, sunshine flooding through the manor's windows. Here, the curtains were drawn and only a single candle burned on Laura's nightstand, immersing the room in a blanket of shadows.

Laura slept soundly, her golden curls strewn across the pillow. Bathed in the buttery candlelight, her delicate features made her look like something from an artist's imagination. Pale yet flawless skin but for the violet circles beneath her eyes. Long lashes against her cheeks. Full lips downturned in the slightest pout, as if, though she lay still, her breathing peaceful, her dreams were troubled.

I was startled to find that Azalea wasn't the only one sitting in a chair at Laura's bedside. Bentley, cradling a book in his lap, peered up at me with a mixture of curiosity and concern. "You're hurt," he said.

I ignored him, not wanting to have that discussion again. There wasn't time. "Please, I must speak with Azalea alone. Could you give us a moment."

Bentley dipped his chin in acquiescence, setting the book on Laura's nightstand and then hesitating, studying her face with a gentleness I hadn't seen in his expression before. Laying a hand over hers where it rested atop her quilt, he murmured something I couldn't hear. Blinking, he dipped forward to press a chaste kiss to her forehead before retreating from the room.

The sound of the door shutting behind him allowed me a sigh of relief. Not that I didn't trust that Bentley had Kaede's best intentions at heart. But I didn't know how much Kaede wanted others to know about his condition, and I didn't want to stir up panic or cause any delays.

"Allvar told me what is happening to the prince," I said heavily.

Azalea stood from her chair and approached me, her expression wary. She glanced toward the door, as if reassuring herself it remained closed. "Have you shared this with anyone else? We don't want fear to spread across the kingdom, don't want them to think both the king and prince are dying without leaving any heirs. Especially when Princess Laila so desperately does not want the throne."

"I did not." My chest was hollow. "Please, tell me again how you came to be Prince Kaede's healer. You are from Ashwood, correct?"

Azalea frowned, likely wondering about my change in subject. But I needed to know if I could trust her, needed her to recount her story so I could attempt to untangle her words to find ways she might weave them deceptively. Though Kaede seemed to trust her, I wanted to feel confident that *I* could. "I serve the Ashwood kingdom. I'm not the royal healer, but I was learning in the palace under him when King Ashwood brought Prince Kaede back from the dead. Because Ashwood and Willowbark have formed an alliance, the royal healer, Kinsey, requested that I use my knowledge in poisons around the world to research Kaede's fate. At first, we thought perhaps we would only need to monitor him and treat him for occasional weakness as he recovered. But as you now know, his condition is not improving."

Her words seemed sincere. Drawing a deep breath, I stepped further into the room. "Allvar crafted a possible antidote."

"I've never heard of an antidote for demon's breath before." Azalea tilted her head to one side, considering me. "You're hurt. Was that part of your bargain?" She came nearer, her eyes scanning my shoulder and then darting toward my cheek. I wondered if it was bruising from where King Wystan had struck me, and was thankful that my hair covered whatever goose egg was developing on the back of my head from my fall. The dull throbbing in my head was as easy to ignore as the pain in my shoulder when all my focus was on saving Kaede.

"In a way," I said evasively, "but I can have another healer tend to me later. We don't have time."

The healer pursed her lips. "Did Allvar give his word that he was gifting you an antidote, or did he say so in a roundabout way?"

The implication that I was a naïve human who could be so easily tricked rankled a little, but I didn't let that show. After all, I once had been. It was a legitimate question.

"He made no guarantee it would work. He said it is a well-kept secret among spellweavers and his kind."

She chewed on her lip. "What if it *worsens* his condition?"

I plucked the vial from my boot and held it out to her. "He's already dying a torturous death," I said, voice breaking. "It could hardly become worse than it already is."

Carefully, Azalea took the vial from me, inspecting it closely. "What did you bargain for this?"

"Nothing that will harm Prince Kaede." The words made my heart crack inside my chest, breaking all over again. He did not care, not anymore. Or at least, not enough to forgive me. I didn't believe that would change once the antidote healed him.

"I'm glad you didn't take it straight to him. Even if I know nothing about this supposed antidote, I can at least observe his reaction." The healer approached Laura's bedside and held the vial near the candlelight as if trying to determine the potion's ingredients. "I need to check Laura's vitals before I leave, and then I'll find the prince."

"He trusts you. Please hurry," I urged. "I know you understand time is short, but the fact that Allvar knew and offered to bargain with me for this... I fear we have very little time left."

Azalea glanced over her shoulder. "He probably read your desires and knew how to best get what he wanted from you." She frowned. "I've heard stories of him. It seems dangerous for the court to test its contestants with him."

"And yet, let us hope it was worth it." I nodded to the potion.

"You must care a great deal for the prince."

I turned away, not wanting her to see my expression. "He is the kindest man I have ever known, and I don't think he or his kingdom deserve such a fate." Shrugging, I departed without another word, praying the antidote would work.

"Aurelia." Florian was striding down the hall toward me. Had he been waiting for me to exit Laura's rooms this whole time? "Did you not have Azalea tend to your wound?"

"She has an urgent matter to deal with. I can go to the infirmary."

"Allow me to escort you there." Florian extended his arm, as charming and gentlemanly as any man courting a woman in the mortal world.

Though the spell of weakness had been short-lived, I wasn't sure it was related to my injuries. Instead, I feared it was a reminder that Allvar was going to drain me of life. Did he even need to be near me? Would he come to collect on his bargain, or would he even need to show his face at all?

But I smiled and accepted Florian's arm, allowing him to lead me to the infirmary and sit with me as a healer fretted over me, laying his hands on my arm until the skin at my shoulder knit back together, the ache in my head vanished, and the smarting bruise developing on my cheek eased. It all felt in vain, like passing comfort, and yet I couldn't bring myself to share with Florian the price I'd paid to the warlock. As I was urged onto a cot in the infirmary, a wave of exhaustion rushed over me from the healing's effects, and I let myself sink into sleep.

CHAPTER THIRTY-FIVE

NOW

Everything was pain, my world a tumult of splotchy colors each time I tried to sit up. I was assaulted with weakness.

"You've had a full day to recover," Ji snapped.

Blearily, I glanced about the infirmary and then up at where Ji hovered over my cot.

"It's time for the final test." His grin was as bone-chilling as ever, though it was difficult for me to even worry with all the other emotions spiraling through my head.

Did my pain mean Allvar was draining me of life? If not, where was he, and when would he come to collect on our bargain? Had Kaede taken the antidote? Had it worked?

"Final test?" It was the only question Ji could answer for me.

"Yes," he snapped impatiently. "The other women are already preparing. You must go to your rooms and have one of the servants help dress you so you look presentable, as citizens have been invited to attend. The land already seems to favor Laura, given her use of Prince Kaede's magic, but we must do a final test to rule out the rest of you before declaring her the winner."

My stomach felt sour. "Surely the prince can announce his preference for her and put an end to all this?"

Ji scowled. "That was not the king's command. We must continue. Don't waste any more time. I'm ready for this business to be over." He spun on his heel and stalked from the room, as if I were inconveniencing him, when *he* was the one tormenting us.

I stared at the ceiling, plagued with the need to know Kaede's fate. Anxiety was a tangible shadow clinging to me and weighing me down as I pulled myself from the cot. The infirmary was deserted, so I left without any fussing from a healer or Florian.

Back in our rooms, Wisteria was swathing Callista in layers of shimmering green. My sister stood before a mirror, lifting her gaze to meet mine as soon as I entered. Her eyes held a silent question, making the back of my throat burn with the memory of her request. I looked down, not able to bear the sight of her one second longer. Her betrayal, her selfishness, hurt far too much, even if I knew, deep down, I shouldn't have been surprised.

Another maid seized my arms, her strange, horizontal pupils eager, as if she enjoyed serving us humans. "Finally. We haven't much time," she muttered.

I felt like a doll, limp and pliable as the maid tugged and primped, pulled and tweaked. She scrubbed my face, clothed me in a light, flowing dress, and combed through the tangles in my hair, leaving the waves to cascade down my back. She brushed a hint of rouge over my lips and a powder along my eyelids before turning me to face another mirror the maids must have brought into our rooms for this occasion.

It was one of the most beautiful dresses I'd ever worn, more stunning for the simplicity of its cut. The fabric was a bold shade of maroon, adorned with countless beads and tiny jewels that glistened in the sunlight. With sleeves that hung off my shoulders in a loose, gauzy material, I would have felt exposed, but the simple scooped neckline was sensible, resting across my collarbones. Though the bodice was fitted, the laces weren't so tight that I couldn't breathe comfortably, and below the waist, light, flowing skirts spilled to the floor. It was surprisingly easy to move in.

I smiled mirthlessly at my reflection, having the morbid thought that I'd been well adorned for my death and transition into the afterlife.

"Aurelia—" my sister began as soon as she saw my maid had finished with me.

A loud rap at our door interrupted us. "Don't keep our audience waiting!" For once, Ji's rude, annoyed tone was a welcome sound.

Escorted by our maids, who continued to primp us with nearly every step, wiping away invisible lint and tugging at our skirts to avoid any wrinkles, Callista and I followed Ji through the endless halls and down the steps to the back exit of the manor. Outside, a warm spring morning greeted us, the sky pure and clean. Everything smelled of fresh rain, the grass still wet. Birds twittered and a gentle breeze heavy with the scents of flowers and greenery kissed our cheeks.

I drew in a deep breath, fighting off the weakness assaulting me.

Ahead, countless fae had gathered throughout an open courtyard in the gardens alongside Willow River, browsing tables strewn with all manner of delicacies, treats, and even wines and liquors despite the early hour. Musicians played a merry tune, and some guests had already coupled off to dance, wings and tails and hair fluttering, feet and hooves stomping.

Nowhere in the crowd did I find Kaede, Florian, or Allvar. I sought out any sympathetic face, but Azalea and Bentley were also absent.

My sour stomach continued to trouble me, anxiety clinging to my every breath. I couldn't tell if it was my fear for the prince or my weakness making my lungs so heavy. All I knew was that my time was running short, and instead of being able to seek out Kaede to see if my sacrifice had been worth it, I would be spending what could be my final hours—maybe even my last moments—as entertainment for vicious fae.

"Gather close!" Ji called as he approached the crowd, gesturing for the remaining contestants—aside from Laura—to gather near.

My eyes snagged on Florian. A breath of relief filled my lungs at the sight of someone welcome and kind, even if there was little he could do to mend anything. As soon as he spotted me, he strode forward, dodging swaying nobles and laughing councilors. "Aurelia, how do you feel?"

I forced a wan smile. "Nervous." It was the truth, though for reasons apart from this next awful test.

He nodded soberly. "I tried to talk them out of this, but I was outvoted. It's a barbaric tradition, if you ask me, and at the very least, it should be something only fae are allowed to participate in. We have a natural affinity for magic, after all, and our immortal bodies can withstand more injuries. Not to mention, we respond better to healing magic." He swallowed. "You only *just* recovered. I tried to convince them that it's clear Prince Kaede and the land have chosen Laura, and to simply end the competition."

His words were frantic. I shook my head, gently pulling away. "Don't trouble yourself, Florian. I knew what I was walking into when I joined this competition."

Ji raised his hands, and the musicians and chatter gradually fell silent. Only the twittering birds and coursing river interrupted the quiet, a heavy contrast to the tension in the air. Callista seized my hand, her palm clammy, and I didn't have it in my heart to withdraw mine. I squeezed her fingers, trying to find comfort in her presence despite the raw wound in my heart.

"Today is a momentous occasion as we finish our competition to choose Crown Prince Kaede Willowbark's bride and the future queen of our kingdom." A smattering of applause and jeering smiles interrupted the quiet. "Obviously, such an important role requires a suitable woman. The land must choose someone worthy of our prince and our magic. So far, one has shown an ability for wielding the prince's power. But the others must be definitively ruled out. And therefore, as is our long-held tradition, we will have our remaining competitors who have not yet manifested magic go through a series of our initiation ceremonies."

Beside me, Callista tried and failed to hold in a whimper. "I don't want to be a princess anymore," she muttered. "I want to go home."

"That's not an option until this contest is finished, Callista, and you know it," I said, as gently as I could. "You saw what they did to those who tried to escape."

"Before," Ji continued, "we dosed the women with some of Prince Kaede's blood so that their mortal bodies could temporarily hold his magic. This time, we will not do so."

Probably because they cannot risk another vampire, I thought.

"These women have already been exposed to his magic, and now it is up to the land to let us know who is worthy," Ji announced. "We will call them forth one by one and determine if they show any signs of magical prowess." As always, his smirk was unnerving as he drew a piece of paper from a bowl a servant held out to him. Unrolling it, he called out: "Caroline Layton!"

Caroline, a petite lady with milky, freckled skin and a shock of strawberry blonde hair, nearly stumbled. Her complexion turned so pale it was nearly translucent, and I feared she might become ill.

"Come, we haven't all day," Ji snapped. As Caroline crept forward, struggling to hold back tears, the advisor turned back to the crowd. Many of the fae were jeering, taunting Caroline and instilling more fear into the poor girl. "I must also add that there is more at stake than the choice of our next queen."

Beside me, Florian stiffened. I cast him a sidelong glance, but his expression revealed nothing.

"Those contestants who survive and also fare favorably but are not deemed the victor will have the option to remain here. We will raise them to positions of prominence in our kingdom, with their choice of fine estates and generous compensation for all they've endured, for they will have proven themselves worthy."

Surprise sparked in my chest. I hadn't thought the fae would be that generous toward those who didn't win the contest. Not that it mattered—even if I hadn't given up my life for Kaede's, my only wish would have been to return home.

But...

Florian's stiff posture. The way he'd been convinced I'd do well in the competition, but that Laura was Kaede's choice.

My mouth soured as realization hit.

"You have been using me," I murmured, voicing my thoughts aloud. "All this time, you courted me because you expected me to do well enough that I would have the option to be honored. You wanted me to fall for you and stay, so we could marry and you would gain further wealth and status alongside me."

"Aurelia," Florian pleaded, turning to me with wide, beseeching eyes. "I care for you. You must believe me, I want—"

Whatever he'd been about to say was lost as Ji raised his fists into the air and shouted. "May the final test begin!"

Fae screamed and cheered and applauded, some chanting in excitement, though they were so loud I couldn't make out the words. Hattie stood somberly before Ji, who waved a fae I'd never seen before forward.

Meanwhile, I stepped away from Florian, my mind and heart reeling. It hardly mattered in the end—I had no future left with anyone at this point. No future left at all. And yet.

And yet.

It *did*.

It hurt, a yawning, all-consuming cavern in my chest. Aside from Kaede, before I'd betrayed him, aside from my mother long ago, before I'd lost her, I couldn't recall a single person who'd truly loved me for me. For everyone else, I was a means to an end. A tool. Someone to serve them and provide and protect them—that was all my remaining family saw me as. A means to gain status and wealth. That was all I was to Florian. And for the warlock, a manner in which to gain more powerful magic.

Even some of the other contestants in this gods-forsaken competition seemed to have begun viewing me as a helper and guide through the horrors of this place.

I was pulled from my painful reverie as the unfamiliar fae—a man with long incisors that reminded me of the pictures I'd seen of elephants and their tusks—curled his hands into fists. Flames burst around his hands, smokeless orbs of furious red and orange that did not burn or hurt him at all. He sneered at Caroline, who choked on a scream, tripping over the hem of her elaborate gown as she tried to retreat. Laughing, he flung the orbs toward her.

Flames burst to life on her clothes—one licking up her skirts while the other singed her sleeve. She screamed and dropped to the grass, beating the flames out of her dress. When she stood, tears tracking down her face, the layers of her dress were charred and smoking, while her sleeve was gone, leaving behind a horrifying burn. The flesh was a terrible mixture of raw red and ash-black, and the odor filling the air made my stomach twist as I fought off the urge to gag.

"Failed!" Ji shouted as the fae laughed and clapped cruelly.

Tears blurred my vision as I tore away from my sister, pulling my hand free and racing to Caroline. "This isn't right!" I cried. "Call a healer!"

I caught Caroline before she crumpled to the ground, unconscious.

Around me, fae cackled. "She'll be fine," a woman said in a gravelly voice, seizing my arm and yanking me away from Caroline with her inhuman strength. Caroline collapsed in a heap.

Two servants dashed to Caroline, lifting her lifeless form and lugging her toward the manor as if she were a barrel of supplies being delivered. Where was Azalea?

"Thank you for volunteering to be next," Ji said, ushering me toward the Willow.

My heart pounded in my ears, another bout of weakness making me stumble and catch my breath as I tried to keep pace with his lengthy steps. Spots sparked before my eyes. I was vaguely aware of Florian shouting something, but the sounds around me dulled in comparison to the sounds of my own heartbeat and the growing ringing in my ears.

One of the courtiers stepped to the edge of the water, grinning wickedly as she lifted her hands. The river began to churn, the current altering until it was a swirling vortex, rushing so rapidly that white foam danced upon the waves and droplets splashed against my dress, soaking the hem.

Without preamble, Ji shoved me into the whirlpool.

Between the relentless current and my heavy skirts, I was sucked down instantly, tossed and thrown in endless darkness. My temple struck something hard and I choked on a gasp, inhaling a gulp of river water. Lungs burning, I flailed my limbs in vain, unable to tell which direction would take me toward the surface. I was utterly disoriented, my head throbbing and my chest aching.

Why fight? The thought was cruel, painful, and yet I knew it rang of truth. I would die soon anyway. My sister would weep, mourning the loss of the one who always gave everything for her. Florian would grieve his hopes of wealth and status. Kaede would, perhaps, still regret that he didn't have an opportunity to sate his desire for revenge.

I let my eyes drift close, for everything was dark anyway, and stopped fighting. Stopped trying to swim. Stopped trying to keep the water out of my lungs.

I embraced the darkness.

CHAPTER THIRTY-SIX

NOW

Dim light suffused my vision, comforting as it dispelled the cold that had sunk into my bones. My pain had vanished, along with the cold and the river's violent current. The noise had abated as well, leaving nothing but the sound of a gentle breeze ruffling my hair and birdsong somewhere close by. I inhaled deeply, breathing in the scents of warm earth and fresh air. Grass tickled the back of my neck, and as I opened my eyes, I became aware of fingers tangled with mine.

Turning, I found Kaede lying on the grass beside me on the river-bank, with no other soul to be seen.

Overhead, early morning painted the sky in shades of pink and gold and violet, a beautiful new beginning. Soft rain clouds hovered overhead, bringing gentle droplets that kissed my cheeks.

"Are we dead?" I whispered. My chest no longer ached; my head was clear.

Kaede's expression was tranquil, his dark eyes drinking me in with a tenderness that nearly broke my heart. This was not the stony-faced man I'd encountered in the hallway only a day before, nor the man who'd wanted to tear out my throat before that. This was the kind prince I'd fallen for, the one who'd seen and known me and loved me for who I was. The one who had encouraged me to embrace all the goodness and joy of life and dance in the rain.

"Unconscious. My magic brought me back to you, to heal your pain." His thumb painted soft circles over mine, and I shivered.

I squeezed my eyes shut. My sister's soul-cutting selfishness. Florian's use of me. My impending death. It all came back to me like a stab to the heart, and I nearly broke down weeping.

Instead, the comfort of this place swept in, Kaede's life magic replacing the pain with peace.

Then, a new wave of worry assaulted me, and I sat up, pulling myself to my feet. Kaede stood with me, his brow furrowed.

"Why are you asleep? Is the poison killing you?" I asked frantically.

Kaede shook his head. "No. Azalea brought me the antidote. When I realized how you had obtained it, through a bargain with Allvar of all things, I raced to meet with him and demanded to know what his price had been. I wanted to run to you, but the antidote affected me much like any healing magic would, tasking my energy and forcing me instead into sleep." He drew an unsteady breath. "I...I owe you my thanks, Aurelia, though I hardly know how to go about it. I've treated you abominably, threatening your life. Carrying this anger and vengefulness in my heart. Perhaps the demon's breath was the catalyst, but it wasn't the only reason my magic had transformed into something so ugly and deadly. I blamed you for the deaths of my people, but that wasn't right."

My eyes burned. "Kaede, what I did was unforgivable. I knew the consequences—not only to you, but also to your people. It was selfish of me."

Kaede reached up, brushing a strand of hair behind my ear. The rain was falling faster now, catching in my eyelashes until I could hardly tell if my eyes were blurring from droplets or tears. "You did it to save your family. You've always given of yourself for those you love, without thought of getting anything in return. Your heart is generous and kind, and what happened...what you did to me...I understand what it cost you. I know why you did it, just as I know that you sacrificed everything for both your sister and me, all to save me." Tears sparkled in his beautiful eyes. "I forgive you."

A tendril of hope unfurled in my chest.

But then he stepped back, a shadow passing over his face. "Florian is more deserving of you, and I don't blame you at all. I've treated you abominably...*threatened* you..." He shook his head brokenly, horror in his eyes. "But even when I thought I hated you, my heart was yours. Even when

I wandered in death, lost and angry, I belonged to you. My soul is tethered to yours eternally, for even death did not break the bond we formed—not for me, at least.

"There was a time when I feared the woman I fell for did not exist, that everything had been a cruel trick, but every moment with you, as your *true* self, has proven to me that you are the one I fell for. The glimpses of your heart that you showed to me when you were disguised as Princess Briar...they shine even brighter now, when you are fully *you*, Aurelia. You are the most enchanting and lovely and pure soul I've ever had the honor of knowing, and I've only ever loved and wanted you. Not Princess Briar, save for when I thought she was you." He laughed, though it sounded nervous. "Not Laura, though I fear I gave that impression to many. Only ever *you*. Please, if I have even the smallest chance of winning back your heart, tell me I do not ache for you in vain."

For a moment, I could scarcely breathe, let alone speak. He forgave me. He *loved* me.

"You've chosen Florian, haven't you?" The pain in Kaede's face was more than I could bear, and I finally managed to speak.

"No, no! Florian is a friend, nothing more. But...Kaede, what I did to you..." My throat ached, and I struggled to speak through the tightness, fighting back the urge to sob. "It broke me. I couldn't let you die again, even if I couldn't stay in the world with you. I couldn't leave you to suffer like you were, and for your people to suffer because of that." A tear slipped free.

Kaede brushed it off my cheek before lifting his other hand, cradling my face so tenderly, I closed my eyes to soak in the moment, to bask in his love.

"I love you. I always have. Not a day has passed that I have not regret what I did with every ounce of my soul."

"Then let us agree never to be parted again," Kaede murmured, pulling me close, "and only to forgive and love one another from now until death tries and fails to separate us."

When he kissed me, I forgot about all my fears, forgot about the rain dampening my hair and skirts, forgot about the pain. He tasted of the spring rain and fresh beginnings, of a love both familiar and new. Moving his hands to my hips, he held me against him, cradling me in his arms as I buried my own hands in his hair and parted my lips for him. He traced them with his tongue, tasting me, revering me, in a way only he had ever done. No one else's love had ever been as pure as his, the only soul who'd ever loved me for me, never wanting anything in return but my own affection.

He groaned, pulling back just enough to whisper against my lips. "You are still my sweetest torment, but you were worth every moment of agony."

Blinking away tears of joy, I pulled him closer and kissed him harder. My prince. My love. My betrothed.

Suddenly, he jerked back with a sharp inhale. "I'm waking up. You must too. I'll find you, Aurelia. It will be all right. Hold on and wait for me."

And then the world was dark again, but no longer silent. Somehow, I could still hear and feel everything. It was full of frantic cries, churning water, and biting cold. My chest and throat ached and burned—and I couldn't breathe. I was drowning, even though my sodden back was on grass. Florian's voice was crying out my name.

"Failed!" Ji shouted gleefully.

Weakness and pain were all I knew. Sounds began to fade. I was slipping away, succumbing to unconsciousness, to death.

Hold on and wait for me.

I tried. I had to. Kaede would find me. He'd chosen me. His magic would tie me to him and to the land. He'd save me...

Something stirred against my face. *A breeze.*

Desperation clawed through me, but also hope, sweet and powerful and intoxicating. Magic burned through my veins, yet this time, it didn't hurt. I reached for the wind as someone pressed against my chest. I coughed up water and opened my eyes, lifting my hand and calling on the wind to whip around me. It tore at my sodden dress and hair, sending droplets of water flying back toward the river.

"Th-that's not...that's not possible," Ji stammered.

He and some of the other fae were pressing in around me, gaping like I was a strange creature on display for them to ogle.

The sweetest sound I'd ever heard broke through the chaos: a deep, rumbling voice full of power and confidence and fire.

"Step away from my bride."

CHAPTER THIRTY-SEVEN

NOW

K aede approached me, his eyes wide with wonder. "Aurelia, the magic has accepted you, proving you've been the rightful winner and my true bride all along."

"She can't be your bride!" someone nearby protested. "Laura Everett won the competition!"

"Yes," Ji insisted. "You agreed to abide by the rules of this contest—"

"Firstly," Kaede interrupted, his tone brooking no argument, "you broke your word by deliberately using these women as sacrifices when the competition was meant to solely be a test of their talents and traits. As you know, that means I am no longer bound by my word to not interfere."

He grinned, reaching for my hand. "And secondly, she is clearly using elemental magic and showing that the land indeed *has* chosen her. Just as I have chosen her as the winner. Aurelia Sinclair has shown the qualities I desire in a wife time and again, and I have no doubt she will be the perfect queen for our kingdom."

A chill rippled through me at his words, each one sounding so sincere, so devoted.

Slowly sitting up, I found Azalea at my other side, her hand brushing my shoulder. I sensed her healing effects immediately, not so overpowering that I grew exhausted but enough to ease the pain in my chest and throat.

"Queen?" Callista shrieked, her hands flying to her mouth. She probably hadn't realized how near to death King Edwin was, or how soon the title of princess would be traded for queen.

It was impossible to tell if her shock was due more to envy or excitement. Surely she was jealous that her sensible older sister, deemed the least lovely of three daughters all my life, had been chosen. But she'd also grown weary of the terrors of Willowbark, and being the sister of a queen would still raise her status and wealth without forcing her to stay in this world. She would be free to go home, while always having an influential sister to call upon when she wanted something.

My head whirled. I wasn't sure if I was dizzy from shock or weakness. Where was Allvar? Was he still drawing strength from me?

I turned to Kaede, but all my fear and doubt melted when I looked at him. Twining my fingers with his, I let him help me stand as if I were the immortal royal fae and he were the lowly human.

"You cannot choose her when the land has chosen another!" Ji spat.

"And not when I have chosen her." Allvar's gleeful voice rang out over the tumult of the crowd, strengthened, it seemed, by magic. He'd appeared as if from the shadows themselves, leaning on his cane amongst the crowd in the courtyard. "Her life is to fuel my magic. The bargain was made and my end was upheld." His yellowed teeth flashed.

"You cannot use her when she possesses magic." Kaede flicked his wrist and air caressed my cheeks, brushing the hair back from my face.

I concentrated on my love for Kaede. His devotion to his people. The solid earth beneath my feet. And then I lifted my hands and gestured as if beckoning to the wind, calling it to me. It picked up, rustling through the grass and rippling through my wet hair.

Allvar's gaze locked on mine. "No," he snarled. "You cannot forfeit. You gave me your word. You liar. You filthy, worthless—"

"She is my bride and your princess," Kaede announced sternly. "Anyone who insults, harms, or threatens her is committing treason."

"The king will have something to say about that," Ji muttered.

Kaede's gaze snapped to him. He lifted an arm, sending Ji flying until he collapsed in a heap in the grass. "This grotesque spectacle is over," he said, turning to the servants in attendance. "Fetch more healers. Tend to these women. Each remaining contestant will be given whatever she needs—a hot bath, food, healing, medicine. They are all my guests, under my protection, and no one is to taunt, threaten, glamour, or intimidate them ever again. When they wish to leave, they are free to go home with escorts to deliver them safely to their families."

The servants hastened to obey while the citizens and nobility in attendance muttered amongst themselves.

"Everyone else is free to leave," Kaede said firmly. "Your entertainment has ended."

As the guests dispersed, along with a seething Allvar, Kaede swept me back toward the manor, using his magic to usher us along faster. The manor seemed to understand his intentions without his having to speak a word, the staircase rippling and rising like a rushing wave to ferry us toward the infirmary.

Healers were already bustling about, tending to Caroline and Laura. My gaze snagged on Hattie and Bentley, who both sat at Laura's bedside, and then Laura herself, who was finally sitting up, alert. Despite her sister's quiet presence, all her attention was consumed by Bentley, who clasped both her hands as he leaned toward her. Their tones were low as they spoke, as if sharing an intimate conversation. My eyes widened. Had his affections already shifted so swiftly from his dear, departed Rose? Had Laura already forgotten about the prince who'd made her blush and giggle?

Nearby, Caroline was asleep, her chest rising and falling peacefully. Her burns had been carefully bandaged already, a fact that gave me small comfort. Between that care and whatever fae magic had been used on her, I hoped she would be pain-free and whole soon.

Noticing my look, Azalea approached, her smile tense but hopeful. "She will be all right when she wakes. How do *you* feel?"

"A little tired," I said with a laugh.

Azalea ordered me to sit on an unoccupied bed so she could tend to me, clasping my hand and closing her eyes in concentration. Kaede pulled up a chair to sit at my side, taking my free hand in his and running his thumb along the back of it. Though the magic that now coursed through my veins was powerful, Allvar had drained me considerably, and I still felt weak. Then, as a gentle warmth rose in my chest and ran through my body, I found myself growing even blearier.

"As usual, my magic will exhaust you and you'll need to sleep," Azalea said, "but you should wake fully restored."

"But she's shivering," Kaede interjected, pressing a kiss to my forehead.

"I'm pretty sure that's from *your* touch," Azalea teased, "but don't fret. There's a private bathing room adjoining the infirmary. We'll draw her a warm bath and get her in some fresh, dry clothes before she sleeps."

Kaede nodded swiftly, squeezing my hand. "Then I'll give you privacy and return shortly." His eyes snagged on mine, so sincere, so intent. I swallowed at the look, nearly overcome by the sweetness I found there, the silent reassurance that he wanted nothing more than to be at my side.

As he left, Callista stumbled into the infirmary and collapsed onto an empty bed, groaning to a male healer about the trauma and upset of the day. I frowned, watching quietly while Azalea left to draw my bath. "I'm shaking...and I ache...and my heart. It's beating too fast." Callista pressed a hand to her chest, fluttering her eyes dramatically.

I chewed on my inner lip.

"There really doesn't appear to be anything physically wrong with you..." the healer explained slowly, brow furrowed as he touched her temple, assessing her with his magic. "Rest in your own quarters may be quieter and help better settle your nerves and eliminate your headache."

Before I could see the outcome of this proclamation, Azalea returned and urged me into the bathing room. Servants scrubbed at my skin and hair as the warmth of the steaming water soaked into my muscles, soothing me. If I hadn't been so weary, my eyes so heavy, I would have asked to wash myself, but as it was, I feared falling asleep in the bath.

When I finally returned to the infirmary, in a fresh pair of leggings and a loose tunic, Azalea led me by the elbow toward my bed.

Callista was already at its side, eyes wide and eager. "I saw you and had to speak with you immediately!"

Apparently, her headache had vanished miraculously while I'd bathed.

"I am so thrilled. You, the future *queen* of Willowbark. We will never want for anything," she crooned. "It's like a dream, Aurelia!"

"Remember, any wealth of mine will belong to Willowbark and cannot be spent frivolously. It's meant for the good of the kingdom," I reminded her sternly.

Her expression darkened. "After what they did to us, they owe us."

That I could not argue. I stifled a yawn and Callista continued to talk, lost in raptures about the future she envisioned for us. For *her*.

Azalea, listening to Callista prattle on about wealth and status without comment, finally intervened. "Aurelia needs to sleep."

Callista huffed as Azalea escorted her out of the infirmary, protesting about how I probably needed company from my sister more. But she didn't fight, and soon enough, I was enveloped in a sleepy quiet. Most of the healers had left, likely to rest, while Azalea settled in a corner, sipping tea and reading a book.

Just as I began drifting off to sleep, I felt a weight settle beside me in the bed.

"Kaede," I murmured sleepily as he lay beside me, draping an arm over my waist and pulling my back against his chest.

"Sweet dreams, Aurelia." He brushed my hair back from my face, and I let my eyes drift closed.

"It's so good to meet you," Queen Ara said, dropping all formality as she approached with her arms wide open, enveloping me in a tight embrace. "*Truly* meet you."

I glanced over my shoulder, raising my eyebrows at Kaede, whose reassuring smile set me at ease. So, he'd told them everything and they'd chosen to accept me anyway.

"You were my favorite," Princess Laila announced. Kaede shot her a look, and she blushed, chastened. "I mean, I didn't approve of the contest, but Father made us watch some—Allvar cast the tests for us to see—and you always cared so much for the other contestants."

"A woman worthy of my son and our kingdom," Queen Ara said proudly, her smile bittersweet. I wondered how much she'd struggled over the years, married to a cruel man yet trying to raise compassionate children. The fact that she'd succeeded so well with both of them spoke volumes about her character.

As the queen urged us to settle into our chairs and make ourselves comfortable, she called for tea. "Now, I hate to go straight to business, but Willowbark is eager for good news. The king is growing quite weak, and so being able to announce an upcoming wedding will be vital to encourage our citizens."

I glanced at Kaede. "But..." My cheeks pinked. "We were already wed."

"While you were using the wrong name," the queen said pointedly. "Besides, if I remember correctly, you both gave vows that extended for the entirety of your lives, and..." She cleared her throat.

Kaede smiled good-naturedly. My stomach twisted, but he grasped my hand. On the settee we shared, already sitting thigh-to-thigh, he drew me even nearer, so that I was practically in his lap. I blushed, but Queen Ara grinned like this was all amusing and made no comment.

"Anyway, whatever private event or vows you wish to share are between you, and I would be happy to attend a more intimate affair at your request, but for the kingdom's sake, we need a public wedding. And soon."

Princess Laila clasped her hands. "We could hold vows in the orchard under the starlight."

I nodded as Kaede's hands encircled my waist and tightened, like he couldn't stop touching me. Though I could hardly blame him. Now that we were reunited, it felt like we'd lost so much time, all wasted when apart.

"Anyway, I can plan the details—I know you two don't want to be troubled." The queen smirked. "Give me two days. I'll arrange everything quickly, I promise, so you may rush away to your honeymoon and enjoy time away from all this chaos."

Again, I blushed, while Kaede's chuckle was so low, it rumbled in my chest.

CHAPTER THIRTY-EIGHT

NOW

"**M**iss Sinclair." It wasn't the voice I wanted to hear, but one I'd expected nonetheless.

Dusk had settled over Willowbark, gilding the flowers in the gardens. The sky's colorful reflection painted the burbling stream in shades of red and orange.

Deeper within the gardens, the pre-wedding feasting and socializing had already begun. Some of the guests had trickled into the orchard, but most were lingering near the food tables, including a few of the contestants who hadn't already gone home—such as Hattie and the mostly-recovered Laura, with a devoted Bentley at her side—and my family. Father and Lavinia had hastened to join Callista and me when they'd received the news of my wedding, overcome with the excitement of our good fortune.

"Not that I am overly fond of fae," Father had grumbled to me, spitting out the last word like it was the name of a disease, "but if he can provide us wealth and good standing in society, I will accept him."

I had merely smiled, holding back my laugh at his proclamation. As if his *acceptance* or refusal of Prince Kaede would have meant anything to me, or persuaded me to change my mind in the least. Nothing would ever convince me away or against Kaede again. No king, bargain, threat, or family displeasure or selfishness would sway my heart.

Now, I listened to him converse with one of the nobility, going on about how he'd always known his daughters' beauty would bring good fortune to our family. Cringing inwardly, I blocked out his words and faced Florian, the one who'd singled me out, finding me lingering alone, away from the crowds. Kaede was lost somewhere in them, mingling with his people as was expected of him, but I'd requested a moment of privacy. He'd been all too happy to oblige, understanding my need for a breath of air away from the stifling new expectations thrust upon me.

I was overjoyed to be Kaede's bride, but learning to be a ruler among cruel, tricky fae would not be an easy task.

"Florian." I dipped my head in greeting, offering him a demure smile.

"I...wanted to apologize." Florian shoved his hands into his pockets. He was finely dressed for the occasion, and something in the firm set of his mouth made me trust he was sincere. Regretful, even. "When I heard that I'd have an opportunity to improve my status and increase both my influence and wealth by marrying one of the competitors..." He sighed. "I was greedy. On one hand, I've longed for change in Willowbark as Kaede has, and thought I saw an opportunity to help be a tool toward that change. But I will confess I was mostly greedy."

This time, my smile widened. Hearing him admit the truth was refreshing after all the vanity for which my own family never tried to make amends.

"And yet..." Florian hesitated, kicking at a pebble along the garden path. "I did truly grow to care about you. You are an exceptional woman, Aurelia Sinclair, and I have no doubt Kaede has made a fine choice. The best choice." He grinned, and if there was a glimmer of sadness in his eyes for a fleeting moment, he was quick at concealing it well. "I can see how much you care for each other. You are meant for one another, and I offer you my congratulations and deepest hopes for the happiest of unions. Together, I know you'll improve our kingdom, and I hope you will accept my faithful service as a member of your court and longtime friend of Kaede."

This time, I laughed aloud. "Of course, Florian. We wouldn't send you away or alter your role here, except perhaps to elevate your rank, if Kaede sees fit. I accept your apology and forgive you. And I do believe you want the best for Kaede and the kingdom." I held out my hand. "And me."

With a laugh of his own, Florian grasped my hand and shook it.

"Wait!" Three of the guards scattered throughout the gardens broke free from their posts, another trailing after, muttering words that sounded like scolding.

I turned to face Lavender, her cheeks rosy and her eyes bright. Though she and her friends, Pearl and Violet, were all in uniform and armed, they looked as eager as party guests. Behind them, Flint shook his head, and I realized whatever scolding he'd been doing had all been playful. His smirk belied his words.

"We are supposed to be on duty," Lavender began, and Flint cleared his throat. She glanced his direction, side-stepping to draw close enough to elbow him. He let out a laugh, and the smile he tossed her way made me wonder if they were a bit closer than friends. "We *are* on duty," she amended. "But we had to wish you well."

"Prince Kaede told us who you are," Pearl said. There was no judgment in her tone, only wide-eyed wonder. Her voice dropped, turning breathy. "That you were the assassin, the one disguised as Princess Briar. And now you have found true love! It's just like one of my romance books."

Violet snorted. "With more death."

"Yes, I'm not sure dying of poison and wandering as a spirit is romantic—"

Lavender cut Flint's comment off with another elbow to his ribs, a little harder this time.

"My apologies, Miss Sinclair," Flint added hastily. "I didn't mean to bring that up again."

"*Anyway*, we wanted you to know you have friends here." Lavender flicked her gaze toward Florian. "Outside of the pompous courtiers the prince is also forced to spend time with."

Florian grinned, taking it all in stride. It was clear he was as used to the guards' antics as Kaede was.

"Are you trying to steal my bride?" Kaede's tone was all playfulness as he strolled toward us, his eyes alight with merriment as they darted from Florian to his guards.

Florian laughed. "Quite the opposite. We were reminding Aurelia that your friends are also her friends, and we wishing you both all the happiness in the world."

"Very good." Kaede turned to me, his eyes devouring. Even though he'd already seen me in my wedding dress—this time in Willowbark green and gold—he couldn't seem to stop drinking in the sight of me. Knowing we had an audience, I flushed at the raw adoration of his gaze, for it felt almost too intimate.

Interrupting the moment, Queen Ara emerged from the crowd, wisps of her dark hair framing her lovely, joyful face. "It's time," she called.

Kaede extended a hand to me, and I took it. He laced his fingers through mine, sending a pulse of warmth up my arm and a shiver down my spine.

Hand-in-hand, Kaede and I walked toward our new beginning.

CHAPTER THIRTY-NINE

LATER

Unable to hold back my laughter, I closed my eyes and held my arms out wide, relishing the way the wind twined around our bodies, as soft as silk. Each step we took was buoyed by Kaede's magic, lifting us so high off the earth that we were among the bats and owls soaring through the night sky. Floating above Willowbark, the air gently pushed us along so that the landscape rushed by in a blur of green.

Kaede took my hand in his, twirling me in his arms.

"It's like dancing among the stars," I declared in amazement.

He grinned, leaning closer to nuzzle my neck. For a moment, I was dizzy with the knowledge that I was motionless, suspended high above the earth in my new husband's arms as he kissed me. The sensation of his fingers tracing patterns down my arms, of his mouth claiming mine, both tender and devouring, was all-consuming. His hands were on my hips, in my hair, and then clasping my face.

Rising up on my toes, I threaded my fingers through his hair, and then, feeling more daring, I trailed them over his biceps, feeling the muscles through the fabric of his jacket.

His tongue traced my bottom lip; his teeth gently nipped at my earlobe. I was breathless, lost in the taste and feel of him. My gasps would have been embarrassing, if anyone had been around to overhear us.

At last, Kaede dipped me backward, as if we truly were dancing, deepening our kiss. When he pulled away, his smile was playful, and my cheeks were flushed.

"As fun as this is," he said, playing with a strand of my hair, twisting it round and round his finger, "I really do have somewhere to take you."

"I thought you just wanted me to experience this," I murmured as he took my hand and we continued walking. I stared upward, searching the stars, picking out constellations. It felt as if I could reach up and touch them, then catch a glittering handful to bring back to earth with me as a keepsake. Like we were both larger than life and infinitely small at the same time.

"Of course," Kaede said, "but we aren't spending our honeymoon in the palace. I have somewhere more special."

A short while later, he leaned close to my ear. "We're getting near. Close your eyes."

As I obeyed, he scooped me into his arms. I bit back my cry of surprise as the air whooshed in my ears and my stomach lifted into my throat. We descended rapidly but smoothly, our speed gradually decreasing until I felt Kaede land gently. He set me down carefully, holding me securely as I adjusted to standing on still earth. Pressing a kiss to my forehead, he whispered, "Open your eyes."

When I did, I clasped my hand over my mouth to cover the unladylike way my jaw gaped. I was standing in a lawn I knew by heart, with familiar gardens bathed in moonlight. The place I'd wandered during my childhood. My favorite haunts with my mother. And beyond that—home.

Tears swam in my eyes, and my shoulders shook with sobs.

"Are you all right?" Kaede asked, his hands tightening on me as if he could protect me from my own emotions.

I laughed through my tears, which tracked down my cheeks. "Oh yes." I sniffled, my sobs devolving into hiccups. "But how did you know? How did you...?"

Kaede ran a hand through my hair, his fingertips caressing my scalp and brushing through the locks in soothing motions. "I had a couple days to do my research. You'd spoken of your mother once...and your memories of her. So I asked your sister about where you'd lived before your recent move, and she shared about your estate and their need to sell it. She said it must have hurt you, to return home after your time away and find strangers living here."

I wiped at my tears, sniffling again.

"She does care for you, in her own way," he went on. "Just not well enough. But, with her help, I arrived at the estate. It might have taken a rather large offer of money and assistance from much of the palace staff—those Mother agreed to spare from the wedding preparations—but the new occupants were moved easily enough. It's all yours now, Aurelia. Not just for our honeymoon, but always."

Another tear escaped, and I found myself at a loss for words.

"Anytime you want to escape the fae world," he continued. "Anytime you need a refuge. This estate is yours."

Dissolving into joyful tears again, I let Kaede take me into his arms, rubbing my back and holding me through the emotions. Months of worries, of guilt, of grief—they melted into a wonderful sense of peace and happiness I'd once not even allowed myself to dream about.

"Thank you," I whispered, finally composing myself and pulling back to study his face.

His eyes memorized this moment, drinking me in. "Of course, princess. You are long overdue this joy." Then his grin turned mischievous as he lifted my hand to his mouth, brushing a kiss against my knuckles. "And I think we are both overdue a real honeymoon."

This time, there was no twinge of guilt, no twist of my stomach at the vague reference to our first wedding night and its awful events. There was nothing but the heat of Kaede's gaze, the anticipation coursing through my blood, and the sweet confidence that I was cherished.

THE END

Thank you for reading *Manor of Wind and Nightmares!* Please consider sharing an honest review on Amazon, Goodreads, or anywhere else you like to post about books.
Keep reading for a short teaser of my next release.

She was prophesied to ruin his family.
He is dedicated to eradicating her people.
But in a cruel twist of fate, the curses that torment them will also bind them together.

A tormented prince with mind magic...
A phoenix shifter whose magic is forbidden...
Curses and prophecies...
Fake betrothal...
Hate to love...

Return to Emberglade in summer 2026

ACKNOWLEDGEMENTS

As always, acknowledgements are not easy to write... They're always surrounded by these last-minute, semi-panicked thoughts: "Oh no! I still haven't written those—how do I ever find the words to share my gratitude?!"

And yet, here I go, trying to do that, because the people in my life deserve to hear about my thankfulness. :)

I am grateful to God and the abilities He's given to me. Every new book is the new "hardest book I've ever written," but this one felt especially challenging. It's the first book I've released since my daughter's birth, and let me tell you, Mom brain is real. It's also the first since having to make a needed career change, which changed my lifestyle completely and left even less energy or time for writing—as if being a toddler mom isn't exhausting enough. This is the first (and I hope only) book I ever had to cancel a preorder for. I've pushed back the release on this one often enough that I've lost count.

And yet, God surrounded me with supportive people. He equipped my brain with creativity despite the occasional "mom" and work-induced brain fog. (Occasional—or frequent...?) He made sure I was born super stubborn, so I don't really know the meaning of quitting.

I need to also give an extra special thank you to Brittany Cox. As a fellow Jane Austen lover, with *Persuasion* being her favorite book of all, she influenced this book in many ways, from helping me create possibly my very best book boyfriend to date (don't tell the others—and please forgive me if someone else is your favorite!), to giving me inspiration for the worldbuilding and plot itself. She listened to my ideas, my woes, my struggles, and helped me work through plot holes and dilemmas, all while pushing me to make sure the original themes of *Persuasion* still shone through.

As always, Sheree Whitelock deserves an extra special thank you as well, for also walking through this wild journey with me. From advice to encouragement to alpha reading edits, you are ready to tear my writing apart (in the best of ways, so it is polished and pretty) and uplift me so I don't give up. Thanks for your positivity, your creativity, and your constant help.

To the two people in my life who encourage me and to whom I owe so much gratitude, even if you never read my books – My husband, who thinks it's wild I have "whole worlds in my head." I love you. Thank you for getting excited about nerdy things with me, even if you only love those things for my sake (like going to bookstores full of books you don't read, but enjoy seeing me read because they make me happy). That's the truest kind of support and love, and I don't think I express often enough how much it means to me.

And Malcolm Carter, my other longtime friend and cheerleader—I know you'll read *this* part of my book! ;D Thank you for reminding me, regularly, that it's an accomplishment to finish or publish *any* book. You've helped me remember the magic in pursuing my dreams.

For my other alpha and beta readers/support team: Beth McMillion, Tricia Ghent, and Lorraine Larson – thank you! Each of you have been with me throughout numerous publishing journeys, and your faithful friendship and enthusiasm mean more than I can describe. I am overjoyed to have you in my corner. Also, special thanks to Beth's son, Eric McMillion, for helping brainstorm creepy competition ideas that helped inspire me as I planned out the tests. And to Beth, for telling me the manor should be sentient. I *loved* writing about a sentient building!

And last but not least, thanks to YOU, my readers, for picking up this book. Whether you've read all of my books or this is your first, I am so grateful for you. I am especially thankful now, when I've seen my audience tested with disappointment by my publishing delays, and instead of frustration, I was met with an outpowering of kind, uplifting messages. Thank you for helping me find the strength to keep going, even when this isn't easy.

ABOUT THE AUTHOR

Rachel L. Schade was born on the first day of summer in a small town in Michigan, only to end up in another small town in Ohio. She attended The Ohio State University to learn how to write obnoxiously long papers, cite people who use big words, and discuss her passion: books. She has a great love for the color blue, sunshine, chocolate, and not folding her laundry. She lives with her husband, daughter, and fur babies, and surrounds herself with books and coffee on a regular basis.

You can find her on Instagram and TikTok: @rachelschadeauthor
www.rachelschadeauthor.com

9 798987 605974